Greig Beck grew up across the ro  Sydney, Australia. His early da sunbaking and reading science ficti went on to study computer science financial software industry and later received an MBA. Today, Greig spends his days writing, but still finds time to surf at his beloved Bondi Beach. He lives in Sydney, with his wife, son, and an enormous black German shepherd.

Also by Greig Beck

The Immortality Curse

Greig Beck

First published by Momentum in 2017
This edition published in 2017 by Momentum
Pan Macmillan Australia Pty Ltd
1 Market Street, Sydney 2000

A CIP record for this book is available at the National Library of Australia

The Immortality Curse

EPUB format: 9781760552251
Print on Demand format: 9781760553722

Cover design by Pat Naoum
Edited by Samantha Sainsbury
Proofread by Laura Cook

Macmillan Digital Australia: www.macmillandigital.com.au

To report a typographical error, please visit www.panmacmillan.com.au/contact-us/

Visit www.panmacmillan.com.au/ to read more about all our books and to buy books
online. You will also find features, author interviews and news of any author events.

Surely God would not have created such a being as man,
with an ability to grasp the infinite, to exist only for a day!
No, no, man was made for immortality.

Abraham Lincoln

Chapter 1

Ragged Falls Park, Muskoka Region, Canada

"Look, Mommy!" At the picnic table the small boy held up one chubby arm, tiny finger extended towards the wall of pine trees.

Lauren followed Jamie's gaze to where a solitary man staggered toward them, his suit looked woolen and heavy, and strangely old-fashioned for someone so young. He paused to sip from a small clay bottle, but found it empty and dropped his arm that now seemed way too heavy. He waved to them and began quickening his pace.

"Oh shit." Lauren got to her feet. "Jamie, come around here." She kept her eyes on the approaching figure.

"Phil...?" She half turned. "Phil...?" Her husband was a federal officer and always knew what to do in these situations.

Phillip Jefferies was a large man with a broad face and an easy smile. He was throwing a sodden tennis ball to Rufus, their overweight Labrador.

On hearing his wife's strained tone, Phil spun and stared. So too did Harry and Beth Freeman, their best friends, with whom they shared the picnic that day. The two families had

1

been friends for years and had driven up together from their home in Vermont for a week's vacation. The park region was open, safe, and they nearly always had it to themselves.

Harry and Beth reached Lauren first, and Beth lifted her phone to record the man's approach.

"He looks sick, or maybe drunk." Harry said. "Or just come from some sort of drunken fancy-dress party – what is that, 1940s chic?"

Phil picked up Jamie, holding the kid on his hip. "Either/or. Best if we don't let him get too close." His hand went to the rear of his belt, Lauren knew he was feeling for his gun, but it was in the glove compartment – her rule when they were out picnicking and one she never regretted.

Phil held up his hand, flat at the man. "Okay buddy, slow it down right there."

The man kept coming, but slowed to a stagger. He didn't seem overly powerful or menacing, but for some reason, Lauren sensed danger and backed up a step.

"Phil, I think he's hurt, but..."

The man stopped and held up a hand. "Please." His voice was little more than a dry croak.

Beth continued to film him, squinting into the small screen. "Hey, there's something on him."

Lauren grimaced; small lumps were beginning to form on the man's face and arms, but moving in waves as the skin rippled and shifted. It looked like there was liquid just beneath the dermal layer of flesh.

He looked at each of them and then groaned. "Please, I don't have much time." He looked quickly over his shoulder and then went to his knees. "Tell her I found it."

"What?" Lauren said.

"The wellspring." He roared in pain then and held his stomach for a moment, before reaching out again. The skin on his hands rippled and slid.

Lauren and Phil backed up, bumping into Beth who jiggled her camera phone.

"Jesus Christ, don't let him touch you." Beth's husband, Harry, tugged on her arm, but she shook him off.

"Leave it, Harry; this is important. Fox will want this for sure." She continued to film.

"Call a paramedic." Lauren whispered. "Phil, get me some water." She went and knelt in front of the man. "Who are you? Are you okay?"

He laughed softly. "I was somebody once." He shook his head. "Now I'm a dead man."

Phil held out a water bottle to her. Lauren took it and offered it to him. "How can we help you?"

He didn't take the water bottle, but instead reached out to grip her wrist.

"Hey!" Phil lunged forward, but Lauren quickly held up her other hand to her husband.

"It's okay, it's okay." She turned back to the man. "What is it?"

"My beautiful Eleanor... tell her..." He reached into his shirt pocket and pulled out a roll of ancient paper and held it out. "Tell her I found it. *Akebu Lan*; I found it."

His voice had become thin and reedy.

Lauren pulled her hands away. "Tell who? Eleanor who?"

Before her eyes the man shriveled. His eyes sunk into their sockets, and the muscles in his arms and shoulders withered to sticks. It was like watching a speeded-up film of something blooming, now working in reverse. His head dropped as if now too heavy to be held up by a scrawny neck.

His sunken cheeks pulled his lips up at the corners. He tried to lift the parchment again but couldn't this time. Lauren took the parchment, and then went to reach out for him.

"*Don't.*" Phil said, turning Jamie slightly away. The man seemed to be winding down like an old clock.

"My angel, my beautiful little angel; I used to call her that." His head came up. "Eleanor van Helling; tell her it's real. I found it." His head dropped again. "And tell her I love her."

Lauren unrolled the paper, running her eyes quickly down the page. "It doesn't even look like writing. Just symbols. I can't read it." She frowned. "But there is a map of sorts, I think."

Beth held the phone over Lauren's head, and tried to focus on the page. "Stay still for a second." But Lauren's hand moved when she snapped it and she only got the top half.

Lauren glanced back at the old man. He remained kneeling before them, exhausted and his oversized head lolling on his shoulder.

"What we need is emergency medical for this guy. He's not going to make it." Phil stared into the old man's face. "Weird; he looks about a hundred now." He turned and moved to get out his phone preparing to call an ambulance.

"Hey." Beth pointed to the forest line. "Look's like he's got friends."

Two men in black suits sprinted towards them. Both looked young, fit, and formidable. One held a carry-all bag. The old man slowly tilted his head to fix one eye on Lauren.

"Run," he croaked.

"About time." Phil waved to the pair as Rufus began a manic barking.

One of the men pointed at the old man. "Everyone stay back."

They slowed as they approached, and the nearest immediately crouched beside the ancient figure. He smiled grimly.

"Hello Clarence; long time no see."

The other remained standing and looked at each of them, his face devoid of expression like he was examining bugs on a windowpane.

"Who is he?" Phil asked.

"He's no one." The first suited man stood. "Did he say anything?" His eyes bored into Phil's.

"Everyone is someone. And this guy has got something seriously wrong with him." Phil handed Jamie to Lauren, his jaw set in a challenge.

The suit ignored him. "Did anyone touch him? Take anything from him?"

Lauren bobbed her head. "Not really, but he asked about a woman: Eleanor van Helling. And he gave me... *um*." She suddenly didn't want to tell these people anything she didn't have to. She folded the scroll in under Jamie's rump. "Did you say his name was Clarence?"

The men just stared. There was silence for several seconds that was only broken by Rufus perhaps sensing the rising tension and raising his level of barking to an aggressive warning level.

"Are you alone?" The first suited man's eyes were unblinking.

"Yes, it's just..." Lauren began. She lowered Jamie to the ground and pushed him behind her.

"No, we're with a larger group. They'll be back in a minute or two." Phil put his hands on his hips. "I think it's time you guys showed me some ID."

"They're alone." The second man said.

Phil's jaw jutted. "Listen, mister, I'm a federal officer, and I am requesting you show identification, *right now*."

Beth lifted her phone. "Smile, assholes."

The man raised a hand to shield his face. "Time to clean."

In a smooth and practiced motion small black guns appeared in each of the men's hands. The first bullet passed through Beth's phone and continued on through her orbital socket into her skull.

Phil went for his gun that wasn't there again.

The second two bullets were for Rufus, the dog's tiny yip of pain the last noise it would make. Then, the killing began in earnest. Bullets thwacked into Harry and Phil and then Lauren felt the mule kick to her chest followed by a sensation like a hot vice tightening around her ribs. Her breathing sounded squashy; her lungs filling with her own blood. There was no pain, and she guessed the bullet had probably severed her spine.

The suited pair didn't hesitate for a second when it came to Jamie's turn. The small boy stood confused and staring down at Phil as they casually shot him in the head. The small body crumpled as though just laying down for a nap.

Lauren felt tears run from only one of her eyes, but couldn't move, speak or even react. She could just watch as the last moments of her existence counted down.

One of the man knelt to open his bag and pull free a long-bladed knife. He leaned forward to look into the old man's face.

"You see, Clarence? See all the trouble you've caused?"

He then set to sawing at the old man's scrawny neck. Even as the blood spurted, the skeletal old man didn't resist, and his face showed no expression. In seconds, the head came fully from the neck, only to be dropped back onto the corpse like a large discarded fruit.

The first man paused, turning slowly. "Clean everything." He looked at his partner. "*Everything.*"

They stared at each other for a moment, before the second man grunted and nodded, and then he and his partner began to drag all the bodies into a pile around Clarence. He grabbed Lauren's arm, and the scroll rolled free. He picked it up to examine it.

"Father was right." His lips set in a line and he shook his head. "Those that take have everything taken from them, *hmm*, Clarence?"

He tucked the scroll into a breast pocket and continued dragging Lauren to the pile, while the other opened the carry-all bag and removed two canisters of liquid. He began to empty one of them over the human pile. It stung one of Lauren's eyes, and immediately everything went blurry.

The men scanned the area slowly, and then looked back to each other. They clasped hands.

"Farewell, Brother Konig."

"Farewell, Brother Montague."

From Lauren's one good eye she saw both men step up onto the pile of bodies and sit down cross-legged. They carefully removed their coats and tore open their shirts. Underneath, their hugely muscled chests had the mark of two keys crossed over each other emblazoned there. But the images were not tattooed; instead the raised red and disfigured flesh told of some method that involved searing heat.

The men then took turns pouring the liquid from the second canister over themselves and began to pray for a few seconds.

"Amen." They finished. They lifted their hands, palms toward each other showing the flesh that was also raised red in the design of the crossed keys.

The fumes were becoming unbearable, and Lauren strained to lift her head, just as she heard the strike of a matchstick. Her world turned a brilliant, agonizing red.

Chapter 2

Mavericks, Pillar Point Harbor, Northern California

Matt Kearns sat on his new surfboard, a 6'8" Hayden Shred-Sled, which Matt regarded as the best on the East Coast. He looked down at the powder-blue deck. It was a thing of beauty with soft rounded rails, a deep single concave through the front, blending into a double vee out through the tail. It almost seemed a sin to ride it.

At 36, Matt was one of the oldest out the back of the island break that day. But with his long hair, youthful features, and smooth, tanned limbs he could have passed for years younger. He was taking some vacation time from his duties as languages professor at Harvard – he needed it. He had been doing a lot of fieldwork that lately had proven dangerous to the point of testing his sanity.

He inhaled the warm salt air as he and his board lifted on the hump of a large swell. Though the break at Mavericks had a fearsome reputation for winter swells that could power up to 80 feet in monster sets, today it was relatively small at around 15–18, with the occasional 20-footer rising out of the warm Pacific like a long, blue hill.

It was early, but already a dozen people fought it out at the break zone, with only three souls, including himself, waiting out the back for the next big one.

"*Set!*"

The yell snapped every head around. Those in at the break area began to paddle furiously to ensure they didn't get caught under the wall of water when it broke. Matt and the other two surfers out back started to stroke hard to get into position. In a set break, the waves usually came in three – with the final one, the third wave, being the biggest, baddest of them all.

Matt led the charge, stroking hard. One of his fellow surfers turned to take the first wave. Rising up over the peak, Matt looked back and down the 20-foot, blue cliff. Wind whipped the spray into his face, and he smiled at the terrified looks of the surfers who paddled and kicked to either get up over the lip or try and burrow through it. Some gave up, and tossed their boards aside and dived deep to hug the sea bottom.

He turned away and dropped into the trough between the waves and saw the massive peak showing behind the second wave, and yet still far out the back.

"All yours."

His remaining surf buddy turned and paddled into the break area to take the second wave.

Matt felt the electric tingle of excitement run from his chest to his toes as he stroked hard. He started to move into position, angling slightly, and then he was being lifted up the face of the third wave. He was picking up speed as the crest started to take him with it, and he looked down on a few scattering surfers, paddling like the devil himself was after them. Wind slammed into his face, and he began to gather speed – *a hellova lot of speed*.

When he was at 45 degrees and beginning to fly, he pushed upright. Even though the wave was glass smooth, the smaller board jumped and bucked against every tiny trough and ripple.

He was flying across the face of the blue mountain, and as the wave deepened and kicked up as it hit shallower water, he found that the speed of the wave was beating his drop down its face. He'd be left at the peak when it started to fold, and that meant a long fall to the bottom. He turned down its face, accelerating, his long hair whipping back behind him, arms outstretched, and knees bent.

A furious wind rushed into his face and Matt gritted his teeth, as the massive wave began to throw its lip over behind him. The sound was a near-deafening roar, like some sort of giant beast venting its anger at the puny human fleeing from its jaws. Matt reached the bottom of the wave and skidded out in front of it – *way out front.*

Shit, he was too flat, and on level water the board immediately decelerated – a rooky mistake. As he slowed, the wave caught up with him, and lifted him up its face. He was stuck as though in mud, and even though he changed angle to try and slide again, the wave had other ideas.

He went up, stuck at the lip for several heart-stopping seconds before it then folded over him. He managed to draw in a single breath, before he and the board parted company. He went over the falls, floating in what felt like zero gravity for a seeming eternity, before about a million gallons of high-force water came down on top of him.

Matt went down, deep, the weight pummeling him and forcing him to the bottom. There was a sharp tug on his ankle, and his leg rope snapped. Matt rolled into a ball, covering his head, and conscious of the rocks he knew were underneath him, and was pummeled in nature's washing machine.

The pressure came in on him from all sides, adding to his disorientation. *Which way is up?* His addled brain asked. One thought stayed with him – *get the hell out of here.* He was in the churn zone, and that meant that the next wave might crash down on him just as he was bursting up for air – he needed to make it to clear water, now!

Matt kept his eyes tightly closed as he felt the fine grit of swirling sand abrading his skin, and didn't need it filling his eyes. He unrolled and started to stroke under the water, once, twice, his shoulder struck the bottom – he was heading the wrong way, and his breath was beginning to feel like a burning vacuum in his chest. He quickly unrolled, jammed his feet down on the hard surface and speared away from it, praying he was heading up, and not vertically away from an underwater outcrop.

It was only a dozen feet to the surface, and Matt breached like a whale, sucking in air, and quickly spinning one way, then the other to quickly get his bearings. Thankfully, he had been washed well in from the churn zone, and saw no new monster sets bearing down on him. That was the good news. The bad news was his board was nowhere to be seen.

Matt inhaled in a deep breath and turned to start his swim. He'd stay in the white water if he could, as off the edge of the reef the water was dark and deep – he knew there'd been shark attacks at Mavericks.

Another surfer was paddling out, pushing something in front of him as he came. Matt waved.

"Sorry dude, thought you had it for a second there." He pushed the front half of Matt's board toward him. "Collateral damage."

"Thanks." Matt grabbed the four-foot section and pulled himself up on the busted new board, half-sinking it. He looked at the surfer and grinned. "Most expensive wave of my life."

The surfer grinned back. "But think of the memories, man." He paddled on.

Think of the memories, Matt repeated as he paddled. He was down here so he could avoid doing just that. The memories that Matt's mind kept packed away weren't the normal type of birthday parties, sunny days, or picnics in the park. Instead were the types that were too rank and horrible to keep front and center.

Matt knew stuff that normal people didn't. He knew there were things that crawled from deep caverns below the earth, lurked in dark impenetrable jungles, or hid in frozen continents at the bottom of the world, waiting to consume flesh and sanity. *Not anymore,* he thought. From now on, he was going to stick to his lecturing work at Harvard, doing some research, tame consulting, and having the odd beer with his students. The money was okay, the work far less deadly.

A half hour later he waded up onto the shore and sat down on the sand facing the water. He watched the huge waves crash down out on the distant break. He could feel the warm sun on his shoulders and neck – he sighed, feeling good, but pissed off.

He stood, lifting the half-board, and quickly looked up and down the shoreline. There was still no sign of the rear half of the $800 board. *Bummer.* He could have at least salvaged the three detachable fins.

He grabbed up his towel and rubbed it a few times over his hair and face. Then slipped his feet into an old pair of deck shoes and picked up a plastic bag containing his keys and phone. There were still a few days of vacation left, and his head hadn't been caved in by the reef, so there was only one thing left for him to do – go shopping for a new board.

Matt quickly checked his messages as he walked – there was only one, and it was from a number he didn't recognize. It was marked urgent. He opened it.

It was regarding obtaining some consulting advice for a multiple homicide case. There was a name and a title – *R. Bromilow, Special Investigator, Federal Bureau of Investigations.*

"Hmm, the Feds, huh?" He pulled in a cheek. Why would they want to speak to him? He was a paleolinguist who specialised in ancient languages. He dropped the phone back into the bag.

"Not my field, buddy." He threw the towel over his shoulder and started up the track. It was a long walk back along the cliff trail and then even more on to the car park.

*

Matt pulled his rented Mustang into the car park of Half Moon Bay Lodge. It was a midnight-blue 2010 V6 convertible and in magnificent condition. The rental was pricey, but it was a holiday treat and this trip he planned to enjoy himself.

As he pressed the button for the roof to lift and cover the cabin, he saw Brittany watching him from the main window. He smiled and waved.

Paying for itself already, he thought.

He left the remnants of the board in the trunk and used his towel to flick the sand from his ankles before heading into the large open foyer. Brittany gave him a blinding, West Coast smile. She leaned elbows on the reception desk top, her crisp uniform straining.

"Hey Mathew, you're back early. How was the surf?"

"Broke my board on a 25-footer." He smiled. "But my spirit is still strong."

She laughed. "Well people have died there, so I'm glad to see you're still in one piece." She turned and pulled a package from one of the pigeonholes behind her.

Someone dropped something off for you at the desk. Didn't see who, but looks kinda important I think." She handed him a large envelope, marked: *urgent*.

"Who even knows I'm here?" He took it from her, turning it around to look at the logo in the right top corner

– it was the circular shield crest of the Federal Bureau of Investigation.

"Thanks." He turned away frowning down at it.

"See you later, Matthew. *Um*, I'm here all day again."

"*Huh?*" He turned and smiled back at her. "Me too – all day and all night. I'll be the lonely guy eating by himself."

"We-*eell*, if you want to go somewhere else…" She blushed as she cast a quick glance over her shoulder. "I could take you somewhere."

He leant forward. "I'd love that."

"Great." Her eyes seemed to darken with promise. "See you later then."

The look gave Matt a sudden tingling in his stomach, and he flashed her a smile before turning to jog up the steps.

The Lodge was only two floors and his suite was at the front overlooking the water. He unlocked the door and pushed it open with an elbow, still staring at the envelope as if trying to draw meaning from the handwritten details on the front. *Nice cursive writing*, he thought.

He tossed the envelope onto the bed and walked out onto the balcony to take in the ocean view. It was still early, only 10 am, and the water sparkled like diamonds on a soft, blue blanket. Further out there was a little haze, which was probably water vapor, kicked up by the huge swells pounding down just around the headland.

He closed his eyes and tilted his head; the sun on his face was a warm kiss and his forehead felt tight from the dried salt. He was here for another few days, and tomorrow's weather promised to be just as good. Matt breathed in, inhaling the warmth. *Life was good*, he thought.

He stripped off and stepped into the shower. His stomach rumbled and he picked up his pace spinning the shower taps. Breakfast was served until 11, and he planned on setting the record for bacon, eggs, and toast consumption.

In no time he was balancing trays of fruit, muesli, eggs, bacon, sausages, and two doorstop-thick slabs of toast, plus juice and coffee, as well as having the envelope and his MacBook tucked under his arm. The smell of the bacon was making his mouth water as he hummed and headed for an empty table in an alcove window.

There were only a few people still having breakfast: an older couple, a family with two amazingly well-behaved children, and a young power couple in the far corner, incongruous in their formal attire at a beach community. The woman turned in his direction and he smiled and nodded, but if she saw him she gave no indication as her implacable expression never changed.

Sitting down he unloaded all his plates and made room for the large envelope and laptop. He jammed a corner of toast in his mouth and tipped the envelope's contents onto the table. Out tumbled a police report, a stack of A4 photographs, and a tiny USB drive.

He shoveled a spoon full of fruit and muesli into his mouth and chewed as he looked at the photographs. He stopped chewing.

The pile of blackened bodies had obviously been out in the open for a while. Faces were charred, skeletal jaws open in silent screams, and some of the limbs lost from the elbows or knees.

"*Jesus Christ.*"

He stared, everything around him vanishing as his mind took him into the crime scene – he could smell the greasy, hot, decomposing flesh; hear the manic buzz of the blowflies; and feel their sticky feet as they tried to land on his face after dancing on the dead. He lifted a rasher of bacon to his mouth and bit off the end – even though he had been ravenous, he couldn't swallow it.

He lifted the next picture. It showed an obscured man dressed in black shielding his face. He disregarded it and went on the next shot. It was of the physical damage – some of the bullet wounds in the center of each forehead – even in the child-sized corpse. That single image made Matt feel more anger than revulsion.

There was a bullet-riddled dog and also a decapitation, with a notification on the picture describing the dead person as: *extreme aged. A grandparent maybe?* he thought. Thankfully, most were killed before the fire, but not all. One young woman had been burned alive.

There was a summary report by a Field Agent R. Bromilow, with another few photographs clipped to it. He quickly read through it – the investigating officers thought that even though all personal valuables were gone, indicating robbery as a motive, the shot placement had been too clean and precise. It was more like an execution.

A hit? Matt grimaced. *Who hits an entire family, including a kid?* He wondered.

The next shots were marked: *forensically retrieved from damaged cell chip.* The first showed a figure approaching the group – a youngish man. He looked to be around 30, but somehow odd. Maybe it was his clothing; the old-style suit of heavy wool was square cut like out of an old movie.

He plugged the drive into his MacBook and opened its directory. There were only a few files in there – one a video – he double clicked and it opened and started.

There came a man's voice and a jerking camera. It was the same guy from the photographs. Matt leaned forward to listen.

The man's voice was strong; he was well spoken and articulate. He said a name several times: *Eleanor van Helling.* He recognized it; she was the New York octogenarian and one of the richest women in North America. *Tell her I found it,* he said. The man's final words were: *tell her I love her.*

His grandmother? Matt stared now, transfixed. The film rolled on, and Matt felt the hairs on his neck rise. The man, the same guy in the old clothing, now seemed to shrink. His hair fell away and his face creased and shriveled. In a few minutes he was little more than a shrunken scarecrow.

"What the hell?" He took another bite of toast.

The man had held out a roll of paper or a scroll, and the next shot was of some of the writing on its yellowed surface. There was also a map, with the bottom half missing. Matt peered closely, taking a sip of coffee. His eyes widened as he recognised the writing. He spluttered, spitting and spilling the tepid liquid over his table.

'No way.' Replacing his cup, Matt paused the film and enlarged the writing, and then laughed softly. "You don't see that every day." He whispered.

Matt noticed the female half of the power couple still staring at him, but now the hint of a small smile rested on her lips. *What, I'm a spectator sport now?* He sighed, dabbed his table with a napkin to mop up the spilled coffee, and turned back to the ancient script.

The scientific part of his mind took over, cataloging, analyzing and organizing the language. The writing on the scroll was Chaldaic, one of the most ancient languages on earth, supposedly the tongue of Noah and Adam and Eve. He knew Chaldaic was an early variant of the Phoenician alphabet, and only contained 22 letters. It was a language used by the first Hebrews and was believed to have been spoken about 4000 to 5000 years ago when they were little more than a wandering sect.

There were only a handful of people who could recognize it, let alone understand it. Chaldaic was a very difficult language to translate due to all the letters being consonants. It was almost like a code. He opened a fresh Word document on his MacBook.

Matt enlarged the image of the scroll and improved the resolution. He wished he had the real thing, as he would have loved to smell its surface. If it was as old as it looked, it should have been written on beaten or brushed animal hide, as paper wasn't even invented until 206 BCE in ancient China.

"Well then, let's just see what you have to say." The more he looked at the image, the more the scroll looked like a rolled-up page that had been ripped from a book, as one side was ragged.

He typed each word or concept as he drew it forth, sometimes deleting one and substituting another that seemed a better fit.

"*Those that – drink from the Ark's fountain*, or maybe, *wellspring, will be absolved from death – for as long as – as long as they drink its life.*" There was a name at the bottom: *Noach* – it was the ancient biblical name for Noah.

Matt allowed a grin to spread across his face. "You gotta be shitting me – the Ark's Wellspring – the Fountain of Youth – and all signed by Noah." He laughed and looked around, expecting to see one of his buddies hiding behind a palm ready to spring out at him.

All was quiet. He turned back to the image. Still, the thing about biblical stories was that they were all intertwined, like the branches of a great tree leading back to a single trunk.

He pushed his laptop back a few inches and folded his arms as his mind worked. In his studies he'd come across quite a few stories of the Ark, its resting place, its strange cargo, and even the mysterious life-giving body of water that remained after the great flood seeped away.

After all, the old boy was supposed to have been the very first to benefit from long life and was said to have lived for 900 years. Noah even had a son when he was 600, so he must have been doing something right. Matt knew that time had a way of magnifying feats and events, but he also knew that there must have been something that generated the longevity tales.

The branches always lead back to a single trunk, Matt thought. He looked again at the images of the guy that had started out looking young, but by the end of the video looked a hundred years older.

Just a few years ago this would have been something that gave him little more than a moment's interest and a small smile. But he had seen things now; things that defied logic and sanity, and he knew that some myths and legends were real. He popped a rasher of crispy bacon into his mouth and chewed slowly. The tale of Noah's wellspring, which became the genesis of many legends for the Fountain of Youth, had haunted imaginations forever.

He lifted his coffee cup and sipped as his mind began to sift through the decades of information stored in his mind. The search for the Ark had been going on for too many centuries to count. Nearly 800 years ago, Marco Polo wrote of a strange mountain where the Ark rested within. Curiously, the reference to *within*, as opposed to *upon*, had intrigued scholars for centuries.

In the 5th century BCE, Herodotus mentioned a wellspring containing a special kind of water in the ancient land of the Macrobians, which gave them exceptional longevity.

And even before that, in stories of Alexander the Great's life, it was said he and his servant crossed a "Land of Darkness" to find a restorative spring. The weird thing was, Alexander was purported to have found it, and after his death, his body was spirited away. Some say he only pretended to die, and in fact was taken to that secret place where he remains to this day.

The early Crusaders searched for both it and the Ark, the Jesuits were asked by the Pope to hunt for it in South America, and even Adolf Hitler dispatched numerous search parties into the deserts of the Middle East when he turned to mysticism at the end of World War II.

Just like with the Ark of the Covenant, or splinters from the cross of Jesus Christ, or even beams of the Ark, sacred relics were all highly prized by true believers, collectors, or even those who would seek to destroy the faith. Some new speck of information, and the race was on all over again.

But this was something new, an ancient language, contemporaneous with the actual time of Noah and his sons, and its reference to the obscure Wellspring of Noah fascinated Matt.

"How's the bacon?" An unfamiliar, confident, feminine voice broke his train of thought. Matt's head jerked up – it was the female half of the power couple. She pulled out a chair and sat down. The young man she was with also invited himself to the last spare chair.

"You mind?" She smiled confidently.

"Sure, as you're already sitting." Matt eased back in his chair, wary.

She stuck out her hand. Her eyes were sharp as she studied him. "I'm Rachel."

"Matt." He took her hand. "Rachel, as in Field Agent Rachel Bromilow."

The smile never wavered. "One and the same." She nodded to her colleague. "Agent Samuel Anderson."

The man nodded. Though youthful, he looked as solid as a rock.

Matt tapped the envelope. "You sent me this, then?"

"No, my superiors did. They thought you could shed some light." She craned her neck to look at his notes on the screen. "And I see you're doing just that."

Matt frowned. "So, this isn't classified? Does the FBI usually send out this sort of information just to anyone?"

"No." She remained relaxed. "But you're not just *anyone*, are you, Professor Matthew Kearns? You've been vouched for as someone who knows how to keep a secret by people high up in the military."

He groaned. "Jack Hammerson, right?"

She shrugged, and looked again at his notes. Her brows lifted. "So, it *is* a language then?"

"Sure is; an ancient one." Matt put a hand on the photographs, fanning them slightly. "I have a million questions."

"And we have a million more. So let's trade." She sat forward. "You first."

He shrugged. "The scroll, where did you, I mean *he*, get it? And where is it now?"

"We don't know." She held his eyes. "The images were taken at Ragged Falls Park, in the Muskoka Region of Canada. A couple of families were holidaying up there. They took these pictures on a personal cell phone." She tilted her head. "Much of the footage was unrecoverable and the physical document is now gone. We only have this image because we think that the killers thought the phone was either damaged beyond usefulness or couldn't find it."

"Obviously a mistake," Matt said. "So, who was this guy and who were the killers?" He tapped the picture of the old man on his knees.

She smiled and leaned her chin on one hand. "My turn." She pointed at the picture of the scroll. "How many people could read, write, or even understand that language – Chaldaic?"

"So, you know what it is?" Matt asked.

"Yes, but that's about it. Even our Hebrew scholars struggled with it." She angled her head. "So, how many?"

"In the USA and Canada?" Matt thought about it. "One, two; more in Israel."

"Looks more Sumerian." Samuel finally spoke.

"You know Sumerian?" Matt's brows went up.

The big man shook his head. "I can recognize cuneiform and have seen examples of Mesopotamian Sumerian."

"Better than most." Matt conceded, reevaluating the young man. "And you're partially right; Chaldaic does use cuneiform. And the age is about the same – the Sumerians were using this type of writing style first developed in 3500 BCE in the city of Uruk."

He turned the screen a little more toward the pair. "But this style might be even older than that. Biblical Hebrew is the archaic form of the Hebrew language, a Canaanite Semitic language spoken by the first Israelites. But this is what's termed Paleo-Hebrew that even predates biblical Hebrew."

Matt looked down again at the old words. "This language was probably first written down nearly 6000 years ago. I can read it, and I could probably write it, but I'd make mistakes, whereas this example on the scroll here is flawless." He pushed the hair back from his forehead. "The strange thing is, the scroll looks like it was written quickly, confidently, and by someone who used this language a lot." He sat back. "And there is no one I know of anywhere that does that – at least not for 5000 years, give or take a century." He grinned. "And definitely not in Canada."

"*Ah.*" She waggled a finger at him. "But do you know how big Canada is, Professor? I'll tell you – just under four million square miles. And only recently, the Geological Survey of Canada estimated that Canada still contained nearly a million square miles of unexplored territory." She rested her hands on the table. "You could hide a city up there if you wanted to."

Matt snorted. "Not with satellite scanning anymore."

She leaned forward. "Thousands of people go missing up there every year, Professor. I wouldn't put all my faith in something that obviously has a lot of blind spots."

Matt lifted his coffee, sipping it, but not enjoying the now lukewarm liquid.

"What did it say... the translation?" Rachel asked, still watching his face.

"It's a myth, a very old and persistent one." Matt looked back at the scroll.

"Go on." Rachel said. "Read it to us."

He sighed. "It's one of the first references to the Fountain of Youth." Matt backed up to the image of the scroll. "Some of the wording is a little difficult, and I'm going to make some guesstimates here and there, okay?"

Both agents sat waiting so he began.

"Those that drink from the Ark's wellspring will be absolved from death for as long as they drink its life."

Matt waited, watching them. Both Rachel and Samuel didn't flinch, and that made Matt think that they knew more than they were letting on. He shrugged. "It's like a hundred other myths and legends. This one just happens to refer to the Wellspring of Noah, better known as the Fountain of Youth." He turned the picture around pointing to some symbols on the scroll. "It even has a real whisper of authenticity to it by the inclusion of the old boy's signature – *Noach* – the ancient biblical name for Noah."

"Never heard that legend before." Samuel said deadpan. "What's Noah doing in the Fountain of Youth business?"

Matt laughed. "It's not a well known association, but one of the stories goes that the receding waters from the great flood were trapped in a pool. You drank from it, you lived forever. Bottom line, you find the Ark, you find the wellspring, and visa versa."

Once again both agents didn't bat an eyelid. Matt scoffed. "C'mon guys, it's *just* a myth."

Rachel studied him. "Eleanor van Helling, do you know who she is, Professor?"

"Sure, she's some rich woman up in New York that's got to be about 100 now, right?"

Rachel smiled. "That about covers it. A rich, old, well-connected woman, whose husband, Clarence van Helling, went looking for the Fountain of Youth around 70 years ago. He never came home."

She opened a flat case she had by her side and withdrew her own folder. In it were several photographs, some black and white. She laid them down in front of Matt. They showed a young man in old-fashioned clothing, looking dashing and confident.

"That's him right there, Clarence van Helling, taken in his New York apartment in 1940." She turned to the next picture. It showed the same young man, in color, and taken more recently. She tapped the picture. "That's him again, taken less than a week ago. His wife has already identified him."

Matt looked from one picture to the other – the guy was identical. "Maybe." The next two pictures were fastened together with a paper clip. He looked at the top one. It showed a cadaverous old man, who was little more than a skeleton with dried skin pulled over protruding bones. He wore the exact same clothing of the young guy, except now it sagged on his sunken frame.

"And we also think that's him. Same guy, Professor." Her eyes bored into him.

Matt pulled the paper clip free of the last picture, and slid it around to the top – it showed a pile of scorched human bones, the head removed.

"Shit."

"That's him again – decapitated – prior to death." She folded her hands.

Matt sat staring down at the table, his mind working. "Why?" he asked softly.

"Why indeed." Rachel sat back. "Why behead Clarence? Why did he seem to be a young man, then aged rapidly? Why kill two entire families? Why destroy the scroll that Clarence was desperate to give them? The scroll that you now tell us refers to the Fountain of Youth. So many strange questions with so few answers, *hmm*, Professor?"

Matt shook his head. "No way."

She went on. "And why do I get the feeling that there's something that someone is determined to keep secret? Something so fantastic that anyone and anything that got in the way had to be totally obliterated."

*

Rachel studied Matt's face as he looked again at the images of Clarence van Helling. His long swept-back hair certainly suited his beach-bum image. But she also saw intelligence behind his eyes, and she knew his reputation as one of the world's leading specialists in ancient languages was well earned.

In addition, the closed military file on the man included reference to missions where he'd helped a branch of the Special Forces that were redacted from the reports. But what was in there was an acknowledgment that the man had seen things that would drive most people insane and survived, if only a little damaged. Bottom line, if you wanted someone to do *weird*, he was your guy.

She leaned her elbows on the table. "Clarence van Helling was 30 when he set off on his adventure, leaving his beautiful, young wife, Eleanor, at home." She shrugged. "It was what you did when you were a young, moneyed gadabout just before we entered the war."

"I guess you had to do something to keep yourself amused before they invented selfies, Facebook and Twitter, right?" Matt gave her a lopsided grin.

"We don't use social media in the FBI." Rachel tilted her chin. "Risk of compromise."

Matt looked mock-serious. "Well, there goes your friend request." His eyes moved between images of young Clarence and old Clarence.

"'*Tell her I found it*', van Helling said. But found what exactly – the Ark, wellspring?" Matt looked up at Rachel, who just shrugged. He stared back at Clarence again. "I've read every biblical text there is, and there is nothing, nowhere, no time, that gives a hint to where the wellspring is. Even the location of the Ark is heavily disputed."

Rachel saw that Matt was becoming hooked. "Apparently a mystery worth killing for, Professor."

"Matt, please."

She nodded. "Rachel."

"Sam," the big man said.

Matt looked down at the image of the bones. "Very interesting."

"His wife spent years looking for him, but his trail went cold, and now..." Rachel motioned to the image. "... here was poor Clarence right back on our doorstep." She looked deep into Matt's eyes. "We need to know how all this happened, and importantly, who killed our citizens – men, women and children – in cold blood."

Matt nodded slowly, but then frowned. "If it's possible proof of eternal life, then what I don't understand is, what triggered its *finality*. Why did he suddenly start aging again?"

"I wondered that myself." Rachel shuffled through some of her own pictures, until she came across another of Clarence approaching at a distance – there was something in his hand. She pulled out a magnifying glass and handed it to Matt. "We enlarged this and cleaned it up; looks like it could be a bottle of sorts. Too small for water; he might have been drinking something."

"*Those that drink from the Ark's wellspring will be absolved from death for as long as they drink its life.*"

Matt turned about, and then leaned his head back and laughed. "The Elixir of Life." He clapped. "I don't believe it; who's putting you up to this? Is it that big oaf, Sam Reid?"

Rachel folded her arms and waited for him to finish.

Matt chortled for a moment more, until her implacable expression obviously told him there was no joke. He sighed and then peered at his coffee cup. "And just for the record, I don't do foreign expeditions anymore."

Samuel shrugged. "That's fine, and that's not why we're here. Clarence's wife, Mrs. van Helling, is an important woman and has lost a man she loved deeply, and, for what it's worth, she has been searching for her husband for nearly three-quarters of a century. She needs closure."

"Closure? From me?" He snorted. "Hey, time heals all wounds, and not sure what I can do after 70-something years."

"Probably nothing." Rachel said. "But apparently she has more information and artifacts, and it has been suggested that an expert such as you might shed some light on their relevance. She knows of you and in fact asked for you by name. Seems she won't show this collection or reveal her information to anyone else."

Matt pulled in a cheek. "In New York, huh?"

Samuel opened his arms wide. "I hope that's not too foreign for you."

Rachel smiled. "And she'll pay all expenses, and a generous consulting fee for your time. There is *no* downside here, Matt. And I suspect on top of all that, it'd be very interesting for someone like yourself." She leaned forward, seeing in his face she had him. "And you are, aren't you, Matthew? *Interested*, I mean?"

"Well, maybe a little. But, I'll need to talk to my faculty at..."

"Harvard, yes, we know. But for your edification, Mrs. van Helling donated $10 million to your university last year.

I think the faculty might just find it in their hearts to cut you some slack if you said you were going to consult with her."

"In an ocean of myth, there is always a drop of truth." Matt looked from Rachel to Samuel, before exhaling slowly. "Down the rabbit hole I go again."

"Good man." Samuel said. "I'm sure Mrs. van Helling will be pleased."

"Matt folded his arms. "What additional material does she have?"

Rachel smiled. "Well, I guess we'll all find out soon enough."

"We?" Matt cocked an eyebrow.

"Sure, how could I resist not finding out as well?" Rachel stood. "So I wrangled an invite on your coattails."

Chapter 3

Vatican City, Apostolic Palace, Borgia Tower subbasement

"They failed." Lucius's words were barely above a murmur, but in the heavy stone room they were clear. He rested his hands on the altar, and stared up at the ancient wooden rood that was made up of a pair of crossed keys.

"Impossible." Drusus got to his feet from his prayers. "Brothers Konig and Montague would not have ascended in the fire unless they had completed their mission. We've never failed in a thousand years."

"Nevertheless, they failed." Lucius crossed himself at the altar and then turned to look at his second-in-command, and the sole occupant of the prayer room. "The FBI recovered a phone and footage of Clarence van Helling."

Drusus bared his teeth for a moment, taking it in. "It matters not. No one will believe what they saw is real. And even if it does get out, we can discredit it."

Lucius shook his head. "It's already out. The FBI have now brought in a language expert." He stared down at the cobbled floor. "Like a small stone dropped into a pond, the ripples begin to flow outward. It only requires one person to believe it, and then…" He let the words trail away and lifted his eyes, holding Drusus' gaze. "We can't let that happen."

Drusus bowed his head. "What do you instruct?"

"Assemble the Borgia. We need to be discreet, but thorough, this time. This entire mess must be cleaned up."

Chapter 4

Matt was picked up at the airport in a long black Chevrolet Suburban and saw that Rachel and Samuel were already seated in the back. For a field agent she was dressed elegantly, and much more expensively attired than Matt was in his chinos and T-shirt with cord sports jacket over the top. Samuel just wore the standard issue dark-blue suit, his arms and chest straining against the material.

"Guess which one of us is *not* from New York?" Matt grinned.

"Well, you are meeting one of the wealthiest women in North America, but I'm sure she'll find you charming." She smiled. "Shabby, but charming."

Driving from the aiport to the city, Matt and the two agents chatted easily, and he couldn't help liking their relaxed manner. He was impressed with Rachel's depth of knowledge about everything from antiquities to old episodes of *Seinfeld*. Even the block-like Samuel displayed a sense of humor and level of banter that had him in stitches.

They entered Manhattan, and Matt never failed to be amazed at the height and size of the buildings. Constructing the pyramids, the Great Wall, Rome's Coliseum and this great city, mankind seemed to want to to touch the sky. *Like the Tower of Babel*, Matt thought, *and that didn't end so well.*

The other thing that struck Matt was the divide between the urban and the wild, or at least semi-wild if you saw Central Park as if it were a forest. Their car was now slugging it out on 59th and travelling beside the park. On one side there were skyscrapers, and on the other a scene of country idyll with old sandstone, huge boughs of emerald green, and rich, thick grass. It made him want to wind down the window and inhale deeply, but he knew he'd probably just get a face full of exhaust.

"Here we are." Rachel said.

They pulled in, then stopped and Matt looked up at the huge edifice looming up beside them.

"Been to the Ritz before?" Samuel asked, smiling.

"*Pfft*, are you kidding?" Matt grinned. "It's like my home away from home."

The Ritz Carlton reminded Matt of the wealth that was packed tightly into just a few city blocks. On the street, the powder-blue runway carpet and brass luggage trolleys stood idle, waiting. On each side of the double doors two affable-looking gentlemen wore long black coats and half top hats.

"Okay, Professor, this is our stop." Rachel pushed on the car door.

"What about Samuel?" Matt thumbed at the big agent.

"Not this time; Agent Anderson and I are working closely together on this one, but today only you and I will be going up to see Mrs. van Helling." Rachel paused in the car with hand on handle. "We're lucky, as she rarely sees anyone these days. Her minder told us that too many people crowd her."

Matt nodded. "Not surprising at her age, I guess."

One of the top-hat men came forward to open the door, and Rachel climbed out. She nodded to him, smiled, and then turned to Matt as he followed her out.

"Well, Matthew, tip the man." She winked and headed up the few steps.

Matt felt around in his pocket. *Shit, how much do you tip?* He wondered. He pulled out some notes, found a ten and held it out.

"Thank you, sir." He touched his hat, and the money disappeared without even a glance. The concierge then held the door open for him, beaming.

Probably, should have given him a five, Matt thought.

Inside, the air-conditioned air smelled of polished wood, fresh flowers and expensive perfume. If opulence was the first impression they were shooting for, it worked on Matt. There were ornate columns, huge urns overflowing with tropical flower arrangements that could have hidden a tiger within their miniature jungles, and circles of leather armchairs like small atolls in an ocean of marble flooring.

"I could grow to like this." Matt said inhaling the scents again.

Rachel avoided the main check-in desk, instead heading straight for an impeccably dressed man almost lost in among the highly polished wood paneling, and standing at a single wooden lectern.

He looked up as they approached, his expression imperious. She smiled confidently.

"Mrs. van Helling's floor; we're expected – the Kearns' party."

He nodded, and lifted a phone to his ear. He whispered a few words, and then replaced the phone, his demeanor little improved. "Very good, Ms. Bromilow, Professor Kearns." He took them to what looked like a single large panel of walnut set in a huge column of concrete, and inserted a key. It was a door that shushed open. Inside was a gleaming white and chrome elevator, with only a few numbers – the penthouse collection.

Matt and Rachel entered and stood at the rear, and Matt noticed there were no buttons to press, but keyholes next to each number. The concierge leaned in and inserted another key into the slot at the very top. It lit up, and he stood back outside the elevator examining them as he waited for the doors to close. Matt could make out a small bulge at his breast pocket and bet he had a gun tucked in there. The door closed smoothly. Matt and Rachel both felt extra weight settle over them as the elevator accelerated.

"Thanks, Lurch." Matt turned and grinned.

Rachel snorted.

"Expensive." Matt looked at the inside of the small elevator. "I can't imagine what all this cost. I bet I could work my entire life and not afford this place."

"You could work a hundred lifetimes and not afford this place." She half-smiled. "And this is only her New York residence."

"Rich and single; sweet." Matt jiggled his eyebrows.

"Rich and ve-*eeery* influential." Rachel looked at Matt from the corner of her eye. "Best behavior, okay?"

"Why?" Matt asked. "She asked for me, remember. Let's hope *she's* on her best behavior."

The elevator slowed and then the doors rolled open.

"Oh boy." Matt had expected a palace complete with ornate gold furniture, crystal chandeliers, and artworks by the masters. But instead they were presented with a room that was gothic dark and smelled of dust.

"Ten bucks says it haunted," he said softly as he panned left. The furniture was large and heavy, the wood of either mahogany or perhaps even ebony. A few fringed lamps glowed orange and though there were paintings on the walls, they were hard to make out as they were lost in shadow. Matt bet they held dour-looking ancestors giving himself and Rachel disapproving glares.

"Professor Kearns." A woman materialized from the gloom and strode toward them.

She looked to be in her fifties, taller than Matt, and quite possibly broader. She had a head of tight iron-gray curls, a strong jaw and pale eyes that didn't blink as she bore down on them. Matt also noticed a pair of powerful-looking hands clasped before her, each with club-like fingers.

"Yes, hello, I'm Matthew Kearns. I'm here, *we're* here, to meet with Mrs. van Helling."

"I know. I'm Greta Sommers, Mrs. van Helling's personal nurse." She smiled tightly.

"Is anyone else here? I mean working up here with Mrs. van Helling?" Rachel asked.

"No one else is allowed on this level." Greta's smile tightened further. "I'm also the cook, cleaner, and primary companion."

"Sounds like a full-time job." Rachel responded, looking away.

"Yes, full-time job." Greta's piercing eyes bored into Rachel for a moment.

"So, you guys like it dark, huh? Is Mrs. van Helling with us now?" Matt looked around and caught Rachel's warning look – *behave*, her expression said.

"She likes her privacy." Greta said. "She also likes some of her rooms more than others, and I've set her up in the viewing room with some refreshments." Her eyes drilled Rachel again, and Matt wondered why she seemed to already harbor some sort of animosity toward her.

"Mrs. van Helling is not well and is restricted in her movements. Also, please talk softly in her presence." She curled one muscular finger and turned. "This way please."

Greta went through an arched doorway, moved along a short passage and came out onto an enormous living room, with one wall fully glassed. The window glazing was tinted, so even with the natural light pouring into the room it was still a soft twilight inside. But it was the view that had Matt catching his breath – Manhattan's Central Park was like a forest laid out before them.

After the visual impressions washed over him, Matt's other senses kicked in, and these brought less pleasant sensations – the smell of medicine, antiseptic, and cloying perfume. There was also the faint hiss of a respirator. He turned his head, seeing a magnificent oval table inlaid with ivory, ebony, and other precious woods in a scrolling pattern that looked to be 300 years old if it was a day. It was set for guests with bone china plates laden with small cakes, geometrically perfect sandwich squares, plus two sterling silver urns, one tall, the other squat – *tea and coffee,* Matt guessed.

On one side of the table, almost camouflaged, there was a wheelchair parked. Its wheels were tucked below the table edge, and a female figure, small and brittle, was seated within.

Rachel strode forward, but Greta headed her off, moving extremely quickly for such as solid woman.

"Ma'am, I'd like to present our guests; Professor Matthew Kearns of Harvard, and Agent Rachel Bromilow of the Federal Bureau of Investigation." Greta turned to Matt. "Mrs. Eleanor van Helling."

The little figure sat facing him with her back to the windows which made her features indistinct, but Matt could feel the tiny eyes on him. For several seconds there nothing but silence and she never moved a muscle.

Matt went to nod, but instead couldn't help delivering a deferential half-bow. "Mrs. van Helling; it's a pleasure to meet you."

He waited, and there was nothing. He began to wonder whether she was awake, and turned to Rachel who stared at the old woman with her brows knitted together.

"You're younger than I expected." The voice was reed-thin and dry with age, but there was sharp authority in every note.

Matt knew it was the voice of someone who got what they wanted and was comfortable with power and wealth.

"Thank you," he tried.

"It wasn't a compliment," she responded.

"Okay." Matt turned to Rachel. "Your turn."

Rachel nodded. "Thank you for inviting us, Mrs. van Helling. On behalf of..."

"I invited Professor Kearns. You invited yourself." The old woman still hadn't moved.

Matt heard Rachel exhale.

He smiled, and bet that the old woman was having the time of her life. "You can call me Matthew or Matt if you like." He half-turned. "And Rach..."

The old woman finally moved, waving a hand to cut him off. "And you can refer to me as Mrs. van Helling. Do you know why you were invited here, Professor?"

"I think so." Matt approached and Greta immediately stepped in front of him. But this time the old woman reached out a bony claw to grip the nurse's forearm and tug her out of the way.

"Sit down. I don't like looking up to people." Her eyes momentarily went to Rachel before sliding back to Matt. "You closest, Professor."

"Thank you." He sat just near her, and Rachel eased into another heavy chair across from them. Greta poured their desired hot drinks, and then stood back at the old woman's shoulder once again like some sort of Amazonian bodyguard. And perhaps that was one of her duties as well, and accounted for her big hands and physique, Matt thought.

Mrs. van Helling reached a bony hand forward and turned over an ornate silver picture frame.

"He used to call me his angel." She studied it for a moment before handing it to Matt. "Do you recognize this young man, Professor?"

Matt looked at the picture. It was an old-style shot that had been colorized, making the cheeks overly pink on a young, fit-looking man with dark eyes and darker hair swept back in a 1940s razor-shave-style haircut.

Matt recognized him as the man that stumbled from the forest in Canada, to be beheaded by unknown assailants.

"I know you do. I can see it in your face, Professor." She snatched the frame back, placing it upright on the table facing her, staring at it sadly for another few seconds. She stroked its surface. "Clarence, Clarence van Helling, my beloved husband."

"Maybe I do," Matt said cautiously.

"That's why we're here," Rachel said. "But the man who appeared in Canada, looking like that… it's just not possible."

"I know that," Mrs. van Helling snapped back. "He disappeared before the Second World War, and today that would make him 115 years old. I've seen the images, and I know you have too. That was him; I know it was." She stared, her eyes penetrating, as if reading every tiny nuance in his expression.

Her eyes moved back to Rachel. "Clarence was a driven man, the sole heir to a fortune, and the greatest love of my life. But he had a mystical side, and sought out things that didn't make sense to us common folk. A myth or legend was an open invitation to him."

She turned her gaze back on Matt. "As it is with you, I understand, Professor."

Rachel straightened in her chair. "Mrs. van Helling, we were led to believe you have some additional evidence or insights you wished to share with us?"

The old woman slowly lifted her gaze to Greta. The tall woman received it as a signal and took hold of the wheelchair and pulled her back from the table.

"This way."

Matt and Rachel followed as Greta and Mrs. van Helling led them back into the depths of huge top-floor apartment, and came to a door that looked like it more belonged in a castle, complete with iron rivets and metal banded fortifications.

"Wow, where's the drawbridge?" Matt asked.

Mrs. van Helling laughed dryly. "A little something Clarence picked up from Castelnau de Guers in France." She leaned to the side in her chair, so she could half turn to them. "He was a collector of the strange and unique, Professor."

"A man after my own heart. I wish I could have met…" Matt clamped his mouth shut.

"I wish you could have met him as well. You would've been kindred spirits." She winked or blinked, Matt couldn't quite tell which, and then smiled for the first time.

Greta went around the chair and unlocked the solid barrier and then pushed it open. It gave a satisfying creak. She took up her position behind the chair and pushed it and the old woman inside.

Matt squinted in the gloomy room. It wasn't completely dark as there were numerous small spotlights hovering over different objects – some were on pedestals, some in frames on the wall, or in glass cases. The room was large and long, but it was hard to tell its exact size, as its far corners were lost in the shadows.

Matt inhaled the ancient scents. The building had only started its life in 1930 when it was the St Moritz, but the artifacts in the room combined to give it a flavor far older, and more akin to something that had absorbed centuries not decades.

He stopped before one of the plinths that held a single object under a dome of glass. He peered in, his eyebrows up.

"Oh, wow."

Rachel stopped beside him, and he lifted a finger to point.

"This can't be real." He stared at the crude weapon. It was a spear tip, made from forged iron, and probably owned by a simple Roman soldier of low rank. Its tip still looked sharp enough to easily pierce flesh. "Impossible," he breathed.

"I assure you everything is real here, Professor." Mrs. van Helling said softly. Greta had wheeled the chair around to face him.

"But, the Spear of Destiny... *really*? Adolf Hitler was supposed to have been the last person to have had this in his possession."

"He did... for a while." Eleanor said.

Rachel frowned. "Looks Roman."

"That's because it is." Matt turned to her. "Have you not heard of the spear owned by the Roman centurion called Longinus?" Rachel looked blank. "If that was just a Roman spear it'd be interesting and worth a few hundred bucks. But this..." He touched the glass. "... this is the *Heilige Lanze* – the Holy Lance. Longinus used it to pierce the side of Jesus Christ. It can have no value because it's a holy relic and *beyond* value. Not to mention supposedly having mystical qualities." He straightened. "Whoever possesses it can rule the world."

"And yet, I'm not ruling the world." Eleanor smirked.

"But you've got to want to." Matt said. "And Hitler nearly did." He stared at the iron weapon. "The last I heard, it was preserved beneath the dome of Saint Peter's Basilica, in Italy. How did you get it?"

"Like I said, Professor, Clarence was a collector, persuasive and very rich. And he never gave up. If he wanted something, or wanted to find something badly enough, he did. Some things he bought legitimately, some he acquired on the black market, and some he sought out himself from the four corners of the world."

Matt leaned in a little closer, and felt something. He raised a hand and pressed his fingertip against the glass. He frowned and turned.

"Yes, it's warm." Eleanor tilted her head. "The steel is always ninety-eight degrees."

"Body temperature." Rachel said softly.

Eleanor nodded and smiled. "No one knows why. It's fascinating isn't it, Matthew?"

Matt stepped back from the glass dome. "Fascinating doesn't begin to describe it." He looked down and along the darkened room. It felt more like a museum than a residence, and he could only guess that it must have occupied one half of the entire penthouse.

"I could spend a week in here." He grabbed Rachel's hand. "Come on."

He was walking quickly now trying to catch up to the wheelchair, and he pointed at different relics as he recognized them.

"Ha! The Shield of Achilles – he used it in his fight with Hector – magnificent."

Matt then pulled up so quickly, he felt Rachel bump into him. He stared at the object under the thickened glass dome in the center of the room. It was the one item that was secured by a cage rising from the floor that covered the glass and plinth.

Eleanor van Helling had Greta push her chair back toward them.

"That's right, Professor, it is what you think it is."

Matt couldn't help his mouth dropping open into a wide smile. "It was said to be the first test that mankind ever failed."

"But the game was rigged, right, Matthew?" The old woman smiled, knowingly.

The item inside was a huge jar, two feet across and made from some sort of unidentifiable stone. The top was sealed with another piece of stone jammed down hard, and there was rope binding it, with red wax completing the job. It looked as old as mankind itself.

"What is it?" Rachel asked.

"That old thing?" Matt grinned. "That's Pandora's box."

"I see." Rachel's brows drew together. "But it's not even a box."

"It's exactly as the Greek poet, Hesiod, described it," Matt breathed, walking around the cage. "Zeus gave it to mankind as a gift. But the gift was that he had sealed away all the ills of the world. He instructed no one to open it."

"Let me guess – Pandora?" Rachel grinned.

"Yes, Pandora. It was an act of revenge on us. According to Hesiod, when Prometheus stole fire from heaven to give to mankind, Zeus wanted his revenge. He knew of Pandora's curiosity, and also knew she'd never be able to avoid opening the box."

"So he *did* set her up to fail?" Rachel said.

"Yes." Matt dropped his arms. "No one said the gods were above treachery."

"Wasn't there something left behind?" Rachel asked.

"Hope." Matt said. He turned to her and grinned. "So let's *hope* it has leaked out a little over the millennia."

"You certainly know your stuff." Rachel checked her watch.

"It's part of my job." Matt heard Greta turning the wheelchair away.

"Please follow. I tire easily, and don't have a lot of time before I need to rest." Mrs. van Helling held up a hand, stopping Greta. "Perhaps you can come back by yourself at a later date, Matthew?"

Matt felt a shot of excitement run through him. "Yes please, and thank you, Mrs. van Helling." He beamed.

"Eleanor," she said, looking up at him briefly.

Matt saw a single picture on a pedestal. It showed a youthful Clarence with a tall and beautiful young woman who looked like an old-time movie star, perhaps a little Greta Garbo in the hair and cheekbones. He walked toward it.

"You?"

"Yes, I was a child bride and more years ago than I want to admit." She pointed and Greta wheeled her closer. "And my dashing Clarence." She sighed. "The years are thieves, Matthew, remember that. And remember to live life and take everything that's available to you when you're young." She smiled up at him. "And we're only young once, *hmm?*"

She held Matt's eyes for a moment then she turned to catch Greta's attention and the woman moved them off toward a dark alcove. "I'm not seeking a day laborer here, young man. All I need is someone to fill an advisory role, with maybe a tiny bit of fieldwork." She smiled. "I know it's something that would be of interest to you."

Greta stopped her at a small dais that had a brushed metal control panel on its surface. She pressed a few of the buttons and the far wall illuminated.

"Clarence's prized possession, and the last he ever sent back to me. It's also the thing that consumed him with the fire of curiosity that he couldn't extinguish."

Matt walked slowly forward. There was a scrap of parchment, the words immediately recognizable – Chaldaic.

He began to translate: "*… those that drink from the Ark's wellspring will be absolved from death for as long as they drink its life.*"

"Like the scroll." He craned his head closer. "But there's more this time." He read.

"*Then the curse of age will not afflict them as long as they remain with him.*" Matt straightened. "*For as long as they remain with him* – what does that mean?" He turned to Eleanor. "Just like the Canadian scroll."

"Or maybe one of the earliest copies." Eleanor was wheeled a little closer. "The provenance of this shard has been carbon dated to 1200 BCE. My Clarence obtained it from a man who called himself Priam. He said he was the last Trojan, and he had been living in a secret place, *a hidden garden*." Her eyes narrowed. "*Priam*, Professor; *Priam of Troy*."

Matt stared for a moment. "*Priam*." Matt repeated. He felt a little light-headed. "King Priam, father of Hector and Paris."

She nodded slowly. "Clarence said that he met the man in Crete. And in my beloved's own words, he grew hideously old right before his eyes." She dabbed at one moist eye. "This is what sent my dear husband off on his final adventure."

Matt rubbed his chin and turned away for a moment to let his mind work. "He said Priam grew hideously old before his eyes." He turned back. "Remember the words of the scroll: *the curse of age will not afflict them as long as they remain with him*. And Priam obviously wasn't with him, whoever that was, anymore. So he began to age." He hiked his shoulders. "And *with him*, where exactly?"

"The Fountain of Youth?" Eleanor's eyes glittered.

Rachel folded her arms. "So, Clarence speaks to a real-life Trojan king, and then took off for somewhere in Canada and then the Middle East in search of Noah's mythical healing waters – the so-called Fountain of Youth?"

"I wouldn't expect you to believe or even understand it with your closed policing mind, Agent Bromilow." Eleanor's eyes went back to Matt. "But *you* do, don't you?"

Rachel's jaw jutted momentarily. "I'm just posing the question – that's my job – and by the way, why Canada?"

Eleanor tilted her head. "There are far more questions than that. But that is a good place to start, my dear. In a note, Clarence said he had come across a clandestine group, or maybe even a person, that seemed charged with the protection of the secret of the wellspring. He thought they could be dangerous." She lurched forward, her eyes blazing. "*It seems he was right.*" Eleanor laid her head back, and Greta reached forward to place one huge palm on her forehead.

The nurse smoothed Eleanor's hair. "We're nearly finished for the day."

"Just a little longer, thank you, Greta." The old woman straightened herself in the chair and seemed to draw on the last of her energy reserves.

"Clarence also thought that this group was operating right here, in America. He knew they were watching him, but couldn't ever spot them. He even employed a private investigator to do some background checking. He produced quite a detailed report."

"I want that report." Rachel said. "What happened to him, the PI, do you remember?

"I do remember; he vanished of course. Either paid off, went into hiding, or more likely murdered. It seems some secrets are determined to stay just that."

"I want that report then." Rachel lowered her brow.

"I just said, both the report and the investigator vanished. It was like the earth opened and swallowed them up." Eleanor then waved Rachel away, and faced Matt.

"And even after this, Clarence still went?" Matt asked.

"Oh yes. '*The son shall show the way,*' he kept saying," Eleanor had a dreamy look in her eyes. "When he brought the scroll home; it was something he believed was a vital clue. It ate at him."

"The son?" Matt frowned. "The son of God; that fits the biblical profile." He paused lost in thought for a moment.

Eleanor closed her eyes; she seemed to be fading. "After that, Clarence became concerned for my safety. He fortified our homes and employed more security. But he still went. The danger just made him more determined. It convinced him that there really was something worth finding." Her eyes snapped open and she turned to Rachel. "Obviously there was."

Rachel tightened her folded arms. "Well, it seems someone is going to a lot of trouble and taking a lot of risks to keep this quiet. Murdering two entire families, just because you wanted to remove all traces of Clarence, is an extreme step. If we hadn't been able to recover the chip from the destroyed phone, there'd be nothing but a robbery-murder to investigate."

"You need to find them," Eleanor said.

"Yes." Matt rubbed at his chin. "I guess at least now you finally know what happened to Clarence. That must give you some sort of closure."

Mrs. van Helling's eyes grew granite hard. "Not by a million miles, Professor Kearns. Clarence was the love of my life, and to find out he had been so close, and to have him trying to get home to me and then have him die so horribly, rips open old wounds and hurts more than you can know." She leaned toward him, making a small fist. "*Find them.*"

Matt sighed. "I think this is where Rachel, *ah*, Agent Bromilow, comes in. Not sure I can help with that."

"There is certainly a job for the authorities to bring these people to justice." She struggled in her chair, and Greta helped her sit upright. "But Matthew, if Clarence was here, right now, he would look you in the eye, *you*, a fellow explorer and seeker of truth, and he would say: find out what happened. And find out *why* it happened."

Matt exhaled. "Eleanor, sometimes the truth is, well, not as truthful or illuminating as we'd like it to be." He turned. "I'm not going back to the Middle East. I'm done there."

"I know you are." She turned and nodded to Greta. The large woman pulled a paper folder from a sleeve in the back of her chair, and handed it to Rachel.

"There is something in Canada. I would think a good place to start might be with the people who tried to conceal the phenomena. They are obviously involved and connected." Her eyes were suddenly ablaze as she leaned toward Rachel. "Find them, and perhaps find more clues to how and why my husband arrived back here, and wanted to come home to me after all the missing years. What was he trying to tell me?"

"That he loved you," Matt said.

"Yes." The old lady's eyes crushed shut, and after a second she nodded. "I still miss him." Eleanor opened watery eyes and tilted her head toward him. "You *must* help me, Matthew. And I will pay you handsomely."

Matt rubbed his chin. Though the idea intrigued him, the thought of embarking on another wild adventure, where there were people willing to shoot children, was not that attractive at any price. He turned and gave the old woman his best apologetic look.

"You see, I'm pretty busy right now. But Rachel here could…"

Eleanor pounded weakly on her armrest. "It's a tangled web of ancient clues and false leads. I don't need another by-the-book investigation, Matthew. I need your analytical mind, and someone who believes in things others would not."

She rose unsteadily to her feet, and Greta rushed to her side. The old woman pushed at the bigger woman, but still used her as a support. She took a few halting steps toward Matt.

She was tiny, no bigger than a child, and looked like she was about to fall. Matt rushed to catch her, and Eleanor van Helling held onto Matt's forearms, her bony fingers surprisingly strong.

"Please help me, Matthew. Help me to find out what happened, so I can rest."

He tried to guide her back to the wheelchair but she clung to him. "Eleanor, I really don't think..."

"If you're worried about the danger, it's too late. They will probably already think you're helping me. You know what that means?" She tilted her head.

"Oh, good grief." Matt's brows drew together.

Her fingers dug in like cat's claws. "Matthew, I need your help, please. Let me finally put my Clarence to rest. Just go to Canada and have a look for me." She turned to Rachel. "The FBI will be with you every step of the way; you'll be safe." She turned back. "And well rewarded, for little more than a few days holiday."

Rachel nodded.

Matt felt himself weakening. Money was always welcome, as even though he was a tenured professor, he was still working his way back up the ranks. Added to that, his insatiable curiosity would mean that if he refused to help, he'd never be able to rest knowing that one of history's most knotted mysteries had been his to untangle.

He steered Mrs. van Helling back to her chair, but she refused to sit or let go. "Okay, okay, I guess I can go with the FBI for a few days." He eased the smiling woman back into her chair.

Eleanor's eyes went from Matt to Rachel. "The last time we heard from the investigator he was at Fort Severn in Canada."

Rachel stared back flatly. "I know it; Fort Severn, located up at Hudson Bay, in Ontario."

"Jesus, that's right up there." Matt grimaced.

"Yep, but at least it's summer now, so it's not snowbound. Nothing but forest for hundreds of miles, and as remote as you can get." Rachel bobbed her head. "If you wanted to hide someone or something, that'd be a good place to start." She turned to the old woman. "Mrs. van Helling, is there anything else you think we need to know?"

She had seated herself again, but looked slumped and shrunken. "If I think of something else, I'll relay it to your *superiors*," she sniffed.

"That will be fine, Mrs. van Helling." Rachel said, and Matt could see her teeth grind behind her cheeks.

Matt bent lower toward her. "We'll report in when we get back." He reached out his hand and laid it over her bony fingers. "Thank you for showing us around. It's been wonderful."

She smiled up at him, her eyes twinkling. "My pleasure, Matthew. It's nice to have a handsome young man in the house again. Perhaps I'll even purchase you a new surfboard – a performance bonus."

"Thank you." Matt wondered how the hell she knew.

"One more thing – your advice on something." She hung onto his hand when he went to withdraw it." She turned to her nurse. "Greta, the scabbard."

The tall woman disappeared into the shadows and came back in moments with a long wooden case. It reminded Matt of a hunting rifle case, complete with brass clips. Greta laid it across Mrs. van Helling's lap. The old woman fumbled with the clips for a moment, before flicking them up, and opening the case. She lifted the contents, and held them out, her eyes on Matt's.

It was a leather sword scabbard, with a few rounded gemstones sewn into it. She handed it to him.

"Can you tell me the value of this – Excalibur's scabbard, I believe."

"Oh my God." Matt felt like getting down on bended knee to accept it. He held out both hands. Matt knew he shouldn't take it, but his hands were acting with a will of their own, grasping it and taking it from her.

"Where's the sword?" Rachel asked.

"Doesn't need a sword; doesn't need anything." He ran his eyes over the tooled leather, and his mind whirled as he remembered the legend. "It was said to have been thrown into a lake by the enchantress Morgana, King Arthur's sister. But then supposedly recovered and spirited away. Lost forever... and now found." He turned to her, his mouth hanging in an open-mouthed grin. "Where...?"

"A monastery in Britain; buried beneath an altar stone, and sealed in a metal box that bore the seal of Arthur Pendragon himself."

Matt squeezed the leather, still feeling its suppleness. He rubbed one of the stones, a sea green emerald the size of his thumbnail. There were also sprays of polished garnet, and some oval rubies. "Priceless."

"Yes." She snorted with contempt. "The jewels have a contemporary value. But what else?"

"You're right; the jewels are not the treasure." He kept his eyes on it. "It is said to have powers all of its own. In Arthurian legend, wounds received by one wearing the scabbard did not bleed at all and were instantly healed." He looked up. "It made the wearer invulnerable."

Eleanor smiled and nodded. "Very good, Matthew. You see, Clarence was obsessed with anything that could restore health... and life."

He cocked his head. "Was that a test?"

"I like to know who and what I'm investing in." She smiled.

He went to hand it back, but she held up a hand flat.

"No, it's yours. A gift." Her eyes became furtive. "Besides, when I die it'll just go to a museum. Better it's owned by someone who can enjoy it."

Matt ran a hand up the scabbard again. "I can't accept it." He held it out to Eleanor, slowly. But his fingertips refused to release it.

Rachel tapped her foot. "Are we about done here?"

Eleanor held up a single hand, pushing it back toward him. "Humor me, Matthew. If it is just a relic, then it'll be a fine addition to your collection. And if it is more, then I'll know that you have something besides your good looks and wits keeping you safe."

Matt grinned, and then nodded. "Well, all right, just for you." He turned to Rachel, holding the scabbard to his breast. "*Now*, we're ready."

Greta handed him the scabbard's case and this time he led off toward the elevator.

"Professor."

Matt turned, smiling, expecting a good luck or farewell from the billionaire.

Eleanor's eyes were gun steady. "The evil that is in the world almost always comes of ignorance." She waited.

"... and good intentions may do as much harm as malevolence if they lack understanding." Matt responded. "Albert Camus."

She nodded, and continued to watch him as the doors silently closed.

*

"What was that about?" Rachel asked.

Matt shrugged. "Not sure, Camus was a French philosopher, and the quote is about the importance of knowledge in defeating the danger of ignorance."

"Sounds like she wants you to be on the front line in that battle." Rachel half-smiled.

"Maybe, but that whole meeting was pretty intense." He turned to her.

Rachel met his eyes. "Sure was, but enough about fossilized billionaires; it certainly seems you made an impression, getting gifts on your first date."

Matt held up the scabbard. "Oh, this old thing?" He tilted his head. "We're just friends, really." He grinned.

"Well, if she was a 100 years younger, I'd say she was flirting with you. Anyway, Romeo, what do you think about her story?" Rachel watched him.

"It's weird, but I've always found that a myth that manages to bulldog its way into today's world usually proves to have a kernel of truth. And whether Noah's wellspring exists or not, what intrigues me is that someone was sure prepared to kill to cover up the evidence that it might."

"And then there's Clarence." Rachel turned back to the doors.

"Yes, intriguing." Matt looked at the scabbard again. It was supposed to keep the wearer safe, and whether it was true or not, Eleanor van Helling had wanted him to have it. He undid his belt, unlooped one side and then slid the scabbard onto the loops. He redid his belt up.

"There, how's it look?"

Rachel shook her head. "Like a kid about to head off to a pirate party, but who lost his sword."

Matt tried to see himself in the silver strips at the corners of the elevator. He turned one way then the other. "You know, Indiana Jones had a whip and a hat. This might be my thing."

The lift glided to a halt, and the doors slid open. The tall urbane guard was there once again, and he nodded to each of them as they passed by. On the way to the door, Matt noticed people watching them, especially one tall, well-dressed man who made no effort to turn away when Matt saw him looking. Perhaps this was the extra security Eleanor talked about, he thought. It now seemed highly appropriate given what the old woman kept up in her penthouse.

At the door, Samuel waved from the back of the car and got out to hold its door open. He caught sight of Matt's scabbard.

"Where did you get *that*?"

Matt shrugged. "People just give me stuff."

Rachel was looking at her phone. "It was a bribe."

"Sure was, and I took it." Matt patted the leather.

"And don't forget the new surfboard she might buy you." Rachel seemed to be scrolling through some data searches. "It's nearly 1200 miles to Fort Severn." She bobbed her head from side to side. "Flying time, not too bad, and this time of year the airport's open. No problem."

"Fort Severn, Canada?" Samuel's brows went up. "All the way up on Hudson Bay; *that* Fort Severn?"

"You got it, buddy." Rachel sighed.

Samuel stood by the SUV door, his eyes still on the scabbard as Matt climbed in. Rachel's phone rang, and she briefly looked at the screen, before turning away.

"Give me a minute."

Samuel climbed in beside Matt and shut the door. The window was open and a warm breeze blew in. Samuel leaned one large elbow out.

"So, what was she like, the witch of the mountain?"

"Eleanor van Helling," Matt turned to him. "Old, but still as sharp as a tack. A little weird, but compared to her nurse, she was a lamb. Hey, did you know about all the antiquities she has up there?"

"No, but I'm guessing a lot if she can afford to give something like *that* away. But then again, she's a huge donor to American education, art galleries, both major political parties, and a number of other charities." He looked out the window and up toward the Ritz penthouse. "If we know what's up there, we might need to check whether it was all obtained legally."

"*Hmm*, so she's using her wealth to buy absolution?" Matt said.

"Using it to buy invisibility, more like. Wealth buys power and influence, and also can cleanse the soul." Samuel raised an eyebrow. "So, what now? Canada?"

"I guess so. We head up to this Fort Severn and see if there really is someone or some cult hiding up there."

"A cult? Does Agent Bromilow think that was who was responsible for the murders?" Sam's brows knitted.

Matt thought about it. "It's a possibility." He adjusted the scabbard at his waist, and then undid his belt to slide it off. He angled himself to allow some light to play on its surface – stones of green, red, fiery opaline, and deep burgundy decorated the leather. With a clean it would be magnificent, but to someone who loved antiquity, its aged skin told a story of something that had travelled through the centuries, being handled by a hundred hands in its life, and at one time, by King Arthur himself.

"You didn't think to get the sword, huh?" Samuel gave him a half smile.

"Nope." Matt turned to look through the rear window at Rachel who was still talking on her phone. She had her back to them. Down the street from her and coming up fast was a tall figure, wearing a fedora hat pulled down and who looked to be jogging, but instead of a track suit he wore a black suit that clung to a powerful frame.

Matt frowned; something about the person seemed out of place. The man reached inside his jacket and pulled out something fist sized. He worked at it, and then increased his speed.

Something's not right, Matt thought.

"Hey?"

The figure accelerated toward their SUV, his hand came up, and Matt caught a hint of something heavy looking and painted a murky green. As the person came abreast of the window, he tossed the item inside, his palm briefly showing, and displaying some sort of tattoo or scar. The thing landed on the seat between Matt and Sam.

Samuel looked down at the baseball-sized object, his eyes widening. "*Fucking grenade!*"

There was yelling – was it his voice or Sam's? Time slowed down, but Matt's mind seemed to work at normal speed. Sam's mouth worked, forming words, his eyes round, and from outside, Matt thought he could see Rachel, head down and sprinting toward the car, but slowly, so slowly.

Frozen with indecision Matt and Samuel sat staring at the lethal object, probably for only a second, but that second made all the difference.

Samuel acted first. Maybe it was his training that kicked in. He snatched up the fist-sized explosive and went to toss it back out of the window, but Rachel appeared there, her face contorted, her teeth bared.

Samuel turned to look at Matt, and at that moment they both knew his decision.

"*Down!*" he yelled and wrapped both arms around the grenade, turning away and hunching over it. Matt just had time to throw himself back to the far side of the vehicle before the grenade detonated.

*

The figure in the black suit accelerated away, but from across the street another man sprinted hard toward them.

Car alarms screamed all around him, and close bystanders were sprawled on the ground, either unconscious or groggy. The SUV itself was peeled open like a giant metallic flower, and he quickly crossed to the still-burning remains and threw himself inside. He frowned at the obliterated mess that was once the FBI agent, and pulled the professor roughly toward him, briefly checking his pulse. He smiled, relieved.

He heard sirens approaching. He needed to hurry now. He ignored the flames and dipped a hand in his pocket and withdrew a small stoppered test-tube that had a clear capsule inside. Within that, there looked to be something like a long coiled glassine hair. It wriggled inside.

Matt groaned and the man dragged his head closer. The young professor was a mess of burned flesh, broken bones and gaping wounds. He'd probably be fully or partially deafened as well. The man gripped Matt's bottom jaw and pulled it down. He up-ended the tube, allowing the capsule to drop into his mouth, and then using two fingers, he jammed it as far down his esophagus as he could reach to get past the tongue, where the swallow reflex would take over.

The man held Matt's chin for a second or two longer.

"Welcome, Brother Matthew." He smiled, and withdrew from the ruined SUV. In another second he too had vanished around the corner.

*

Matt felt he was rising from the bottom of a molasses-thick ocean to hear a high-pitched screaming in his ears. Then the pain came, and every atom of his body howled in furious agony.

Suddenly there was something cutting off his airway and he gagged momentarily. But as quickly as it came it was gone, and in its place an explosion of color.

Matt suddenly experienced the bright flash of a waking dream – there was a long pool of brilliant blue water. It was so inviting, and cool, and promised to bathe his wounds to calm the hot, screaming pain that surrounded him. Then, rising from the water was a woman so intoxicatingly beautiful she could have been a goddess. She smiled at him.

Then came a deep, calming voice: *Welcome, Brother Matthew.*

His pain started to recede. He opened his eyes.

*

Rachel had a hazy memory of being at a cookout and smelling delicious meat roasting. She shook her head to clear it. One second she was talking on the phone, and the next she was slammed up against the front wall of the Ritz Carlton and peppered with shrapnel injuries.

She sat there a moment more as she pulled all her senses together. Someone came to crouch beside her – one of the Ritz concierges. His top hat had been knocked off but she recognized his uniform.

She grabbed his arm and pulled herself to her feet. She identified the smell then – charred flesh.

"Oh, God, no."

The SUV was blown open, and smoke still billowed from inside. There was nothing but a carbonised splatter where the driver had been. In the back it was worse because she could see the damage. There was a single leg, still in a polished black shoe in the foot well, and red, ragged sheets of something that was either suit material or skin spread out over the remains of the flattened back seat.

Rachel gritted her teeth and raced toward the SUV, holding her breath, and looking for Matt.

There was movement. She dived inside.

"Don't move. Help's coming."

She felt liquefied foam rubber from the seats searing her legs and arms. It stuck to her, like toasted marshmallow, but stung like melted pitch. There came another cough, and groan, and then some of the smoking debris was pushed aside.

"I'm stuck." It was Matt's voice.

She pushed in further, ripping away shattered plastics, and other molded materials. There were jagged teeth of armor plating angled every which way, and she carefully avoided these still red-hot daggers.

"Careful. Try not to move," she said as a hand reached toward her. She grabbed onto it, careful not to tug too hard as the arm could have been severely damaged, and only shock was keeping the pain and trauma at bay.

"Easy." She backed up. Matt came with her. She tripped and fell back onto the pavement with Matt on top of her.

He rolled off her and onto his back. Rachel knelt up beside him. His clothing was ripped, burned and smoking, and one of his shoes was missing. His long hair was singed, but looked sticky, and when she examined him she saw that there was a mixture of soot, blood, and gore coating his face.

He coughed and a puff of smoke rose from his throat. Rachel pulled a gobbet of flesh from his cheek and shuddered at the thought that it was most likely a shred of Samuel. There were shards of steel sticking from him, but thankfully, there was no bleeding.

She went to pull a particularly brutal-looking piece from his forehead, but Matt sucked in a deep breath, shivered, and when he exhaled, he coughed, hacking loudly. He spat blood.

"It was a grenade." He held his head. "Did you see the big guy? He threw it in at us." He went to sit up. "I think I recognized…" He groaned and winced.

"Don't move." Rachel tried to push him down, but he swiped her away. She was surprised at how strong he was.

"We need to get after him." Matt got unsteadily to his feet, looking like a shipwreck survivor. His hair was sticking up and matted, and his clothes were little more than smoking rags. One of his arms was red with raw, blistering skin.

She held onto him.

"I said, I'm fine." He pushed her away.

"Well, you don't look fine, mister." She pulled him closer, and the piece of metal fell from his forehead. She frowned. She'd thought it had been embedded in the flesh and skull, but it must have only been stuck on there. The wound seemed insignificant now.

"Samuel?" Matt turned one way then the other. He stuck out an arm, and Rachel grabbed it, supporting him.

"He's gone." She held on tight, and led him to the wall of the Ritz.

Matt wailed and tried to tug away. He put a hand over his eyes and sunk back to the ground, leaning back on the wall.

"He saved me. He took the blast." Matt looked at one of his hands, flexing the fingers. "I'm alive because of him." He stood back up.

"But how?" she looked him over. "You were in an enclosed place with some sort of explosive fragmentation device. You should be dead."

Matt looked about confused. "Huh?" He looked down at his ragged clothing. "You don't think." His hand went down for the scabbard. "The sword's scabbard; could it...?"

The ancient scabbard was torn in half and burned. Even the stones were shattered or missing. He gripped it, and his eyes lifted to Rachel. "I was wearing this."

"Impossible. And for something that's supposed to be invulnerable, that didn't fare so well." She led him back to the wall. "Now goddamn sit down until the ambulance gets here."

"That man, who threw the grenade, I think I've seen him before." Matt turned to the sound of police sirens getting louder and closer. He looked up at her. "You're hurt."

Rachel wiped blood from her eyes that was running down her forehead. It stung like a bitch, and yet Matt was the one in the car, and now he seemed less injured than she was.

"Don't worry about me. Tell me about the guy." She looked into his eyes. "Was it the same people who had murdered the families?"

Matt seemed to think. "Maybe, I don't know. I just can't remember now. I'm sure I've seen... maybe in the foyer of the building, or somewhere else. You think the killers are following us?"

"Unlikely." But Rachel flipped her coat back, exposing her gun. It was in easy reach as she laid a hand on Matt's shoulder and scanned the crowd. "Just stay down."

She looked at the faces of the gathering throng. Sometimes terrorists came back to perform a double tap – a second hit to ensure their target was completely destroyed, or to clean up people who came to help – and that'd be her.

Matt held up his hands, looking at them and making fists. "I feel fine." He ran one hand through his hair. "More than fine." He flicked shards of metal from his hand that had come from his hair.

Rachel gripped his arm. The skin was dry now, and not raw and weeping. "Fine, huh?" She pulled her hands away.

"Yeah." Matt swallowed noisily and smacked his lips. "Odd taste in my mouth, but I'm fine."

*

Hours later, Matt sat in a hotel room. He'd been checked over by a doctor and pronounced fit, but still disorientated. Since then he'd showered and had put on fresh clothes. The ringing in his ears had gone, but the shakes started the moment he sat down on the couch, and he cradled his face in his hands for a moment.

He hadn't really known Samuel all that well, but he seemed like a nice guy, and his last act was one of selfless heroism by wrapping himself around the explosive, just so Matt could live.

He sat back, wiping his eyes. Given the way the car was peeled open, he should also have been dog meat. His eyes went to the destroyed scabbard – it was now junk.

"Was it you?" he asked the burned leather. "If it was, thank you."

His phone rang, making him jump. He didn't want to speak to anyone, so he pulled it from his pocket, intending to switch it off, but saw Rachel's number. He stared for another few seconds and then guessed as she'd just lost a colleague maybe she needed contact more than he did. He answered.

"Hi."

"Matt, how are you?"

"Physically? Okay, I guess. Just feel like crap, you know, about Samuel." He slumped a little lower in the chair and closed his eyes.

"Matt?"

His eyes flicked open a crack. "I'm still here."

"I'm coming over…"

"No, don't…" He groaned as the phone went dead. He contemplated calling her back, but there was already a knock on the door – *of course* – she was just down the hall, he remembered.

He got slowly to his feet, opened the door, and stood to the side. Rachel came straight into the center of the room and stood looking around.

"How are you holding up?" Matt asked, gesturing for the couch as he took a seat.

Rachel shook her head and crossed her arms across her body. "I knew Samuel for a long time." She looked down, her face shadowed. "He was a good agent. A good man."

She was quiet a moment and then cleared her throat. "We're still combing CCTV images in the area, but the guys came out of nowhere." She paced, watching him.

"Guys?" Matt's eyebrows shot up. "I only saw one."

Her eyes narrowed. "Two; the bomb thrower, and another one that jumped into the car afterwards – while it was still on fire. Must have been burned or scared off by the NYPD. Then they both vanished."

"So they had help." Matt said.

"That's what we're thinking."

"Great; the circus comes to town… and just for us." He

closed his eyes again and leaned his head back. He groaned and rubbed his temples. "My head's throbbing like I've got a bad vodka hangover."

"Yeah, a grenade attack will do that to you." Rachel sat down at the opposite end of the couch and hugged a cushion to her chest. "Matt, we need to find out what's going on. If these guys came from Fort Severn, then we need to go there. It's time we got on the front foot."

He looked across at her. "Yeah, well, no offense, but you need more backup. I think you might be a little short on firepower."

Rachel threw the cushion on the floor. "It's a balance, Matt. If I drop into a Canadian town with 50 FBI agents, just how open do you think the locals will be with me? And with that kind of footprint you can't exactly tread softly. Any bad guys will be long gone."

"Well, I'll tell you right now, I'm not a great shot and can't fight. So please don't rely on me." He gave her his best apologetic smile.

She chewed her lip. "The district is patrolled by the Nishnawbe-Aski Police Service, a tribal-based service; they'll be our backup. And don't worry; I can hit a bird's eye at 50 feet. I'll only rely on you for your brain." Her blue eyes twinkled. "And maybe some of your luck." She hunched forward, resting her head on the back of the couch. Matt copied her, their faces only a handspan apart.

"Yeah right, luck," he said. He let his eyes travel from her forehead to her lips; he saw that the attractive features were bleached and drawn.

He sighed. "Rachel, I'm not your guy for this."

She shushed him and leaned across and gently touched the side of his face, stretching the skin near his eyes. Immediately his headache felt better.

"Amazing." She was so close he could smell a soft, slightly

floral scent floating from her skin. She continued to stare into his face. Her hand lingered; her touch warm. "You should buy yourself a lottery ticket, Professor."

"Maybe." He drew in a breath and put his hand on the couch between them. "Rachel, I'm not sure it's a good idea me getting involved in this thing. I think…"

She took her hand from his face and placed it on top of his. "I think we owe it to Samuel, don't you?" she said softly. She looked up into his eyes and held his gaze.

Sultry – the word jumped into his head as he stared into eyes so deep he could have fallen into them. Matt felt his heart beat faster. He nodded. "Yes, we do."

Her phone pinged, breaking the spell. Rachel withdrew her hand and stood up. She strode across the room to examine her phone. Matt swallowed hard and shook his head.

"Get some rest," she said. She headed for the door, grabbed the handle, and turned. "Pick you up early."

"Good, fine, see you then." Matt nodded at the closing door. He looked down at his hand. "And now I've just been guilted into going along." He closed his eyes. His headache was coming back with a vengeance.

Chapter 5

Saudi Arabia, Riyadh, House of Saud

Prince Najif al ibn Saud pulled in another wheezing breath and exhaled, feeling like his throat had narrowed to that of a drinking straw. He had fallen from a horse twice, survived a dozen assassination attempts, walked away from a high-speed car crash, as well as living through two heart attacks, and yet, it was the small pleasure of smoking cigarettes that was hurrying him toward death.

Najif was 72 years old and tenth in line for the Saudi throne, a prince and a direct descendent of Ibn Saud himself, the modern founder of Saudi Arabia. His family numbered over 15,000 members, but the enormous wealth was held by only a few thousand of them, each of them a multi-millionaire or billionaire.

Najif personally had a portfolio of mansions in Paris, New York, London and Berlin, and also a palace in Saudi Arabia, where he now sat, alone in his hunting den. The huge open room was decorated with the skins of lions, tigers and leopards, with dozens of mounted heads of various horned creatures on walls, and in one corner stood his prized possession: a magnificent black rhino trophy, taken decades ago in Mozambique.

The southern wall of the den held a flat-screen television the size of a garage door. It was this that transfixed him. He played again the grainy footage of the man in Canada holding out the roll of paper, and then the image jumped forward to where he had collapsed into decrepit skin and bone. He backed up the film to where the man sipped from the small vessel. He paused it, enlarged it, and then reran it over and over.

Najif stroked a long iron-gray beard until the coughing took him again, forcing him to hold a silk handkerchief to his lips. He knew his life's clock was counting down, and when modern medicine had given up on him, he had at first turned to alternate treatments of vapor inhalations and concoctions of salt bush, kale, and a dozen other revolting herbs and plant extracts. But other than assaulting his taste buds, they proved less than useless.

It was then that he had turned to magic. His researchers had explored every myth and legend of the healing hands, ancient maps, magical cloaks, and potions made from impossible ingredients. But nothing worked, and his research always led him back to the legend of the mysterious hidden wellspring that was a fountain of youth.

He was positive there was something there to be found. And suddenly Mr. Clarence van Helling had turned up. The man was missing for 75 years, and then reappeared looking the same as when he had embarked on his search. It was obvious; the man had taken something or been somewhere that had stopped him from aging.

Prince Najif had enormous wealth but little time or patience now. He also had a ruthless streak that meant he would trample over anyone or anything to get what he wanted. And right now, he wanted to know where Mr. Clarence van Helling had been.

The game was in play. He was aware the Harvard professor had been engaged by the van Helling widow. It was too late to recruit the man himself, but he could certainly keep tabs on his movements.

Najif sucked in a huge and painful breath and levered his bulk forward. There was a panel of buttons set into an ornate table, and he jammed a stubby finger onto one of them. Almost immediately the gilt doors behind him were pushed open and a tall, young man stepped inside.

Najif turned to him. The tall man had black hair swept back and olive skin betraying his Arabic heritage. Although his finer features made him look more European, his coal black eyes were of Saud, and they missed nothing.

The young man bowed. "My prince, is it time?"

Najif smiled at his younger cousin. Khaled ibn Al Sudairi had a weakness for the ladies, but he was probably the most honorable young man he knew. Khaled was distant in his lineage to the Saudi throne, but he was invaluable as a family warrior. He had been trained since youth to be a defender of their faith and family.

Khaled went to one knee beside the stricken prince, and Najif raised himself slightly. He pointed at the television screen.

"They go to Canada; I want to know everything that Professor Kearns does there. Use every informant and source we have."

"The FBI are involved," Khaled said.

"Then use them. We have influence there too. Use whatever pressure you need to bring to bear. Tell the FBI we'll assist in tracking the killers; I don't care who we pay or what we pay, just make sure we know everything that they do."

"Should I go there?" Khaled asked.

"No," Najif said quickly. "It is but one thread in the tapestry of knowledge that is being woven." He laid his hands on his stomach. "What news from Turkey?"

"The expeditions are moving forward, but slowly," Khaled said. "We have lost two of them to the local militias – one is being held for ransom, the other has already been tortured and killed. We also lost our translator."

Najif sighed, the breath sounding like a long, slow whistle. "Down to three." He nodded, "Still acceptable. And where are they now?"

"Approaching the mountain range. But there is a lot of territory, and a lot of possible places to search. Unfortunately, the satellite images are not conclusive. There is confusion now."

Najif nodded. "They need someone who is not distracted by indecision – *you*. Go to Turkey and consolidate the remaining teams. Only you are qualified with your skills of antiquities. They are close, but need some strong leadership now." Najif gripped Khaled's hand. "You must not let anything distract you, and you must hurry."

Khaled straightened. "It shall be so." He bowed and then strode quickly from the room.

Chapter 6

Mount Qardū, Southern Turkey

Khaled ibn Al Sudairi stood looking up at the peak. It rose nearly 7000 feet above a fertile plain that had once been farmland. Hostilities between warring tribes dating back centuries had always made the place one of danger, but now with the rise of the well-financed terror groups, the danger had become intolerable.

Their guides would only deliver them so far and had long since departed. That suited Khaled just fine as for every loyal guide there was another who would sell you to the militias for a song.

"Let's do this." He and his six-strong team had narrowed their search down to this last peak. It was 200 miles south of Ararat, but local stories related how it was also rumored to have been the final resting place of something special – the Ark, he hoped.

He sighed, knowing that most of the tall mountains in the area carried the same legends. After all, the biblical references to the Ark were to the "Mountains of Ararat", and in

Genesis, that was only a general region, not a specific mountain. But Khaled had a feeling about this peak – it was the only one rumored to have had an ancient Christian monastery somewhere on the mountain. One that was supposed to have been destroyed by lightning in the year 776 AD, and any trace of its remains long since disappeared.

Khaled looked up. Why would you build a monastery in a place so remote? Because maybe you had something sacred you wished to protect, he guessed.

The climb to the snow line took all day, and as the sun fell, they arrived at an overhang of stone that was their shelter for the evening. They passed a long, cold, dark night huddled beneath a makeshift tent of nylon sheets secured against the rockface.

On the western slope of the mountain the sun rose slowly. But it lit up the plains behind them to the horizon. Abed Hameel, Khaled's closest friend, lifted his field glasses to his eyes, and he slowly scanned them for movement as the rest of the group packed their belongings and prepared to depart.

A few feet in at the back of their shelter, Hisham rubbed a stubbled face, hard, and Saeeb yawned loudly. "Mountain number five – this is getting boring."

"Boring? Then perhaps you'd like to lead us up?" Khaled said over his shoulder as he hefted his pack onto his back. He went outside and walked a few hundred feet along under the snow line, looking upwards. In the better light, he could see there were several routes they could take. He chose one that had the least snow and ice. His men were ex Special Forces commandos, Airborne Brigade, and had basic climbing experience, but trying to ascend over ice sheets was another skill entirely.

It was almost noon when the last of them crested the final jagged piece of cold stone, and stood on the peak, a misty, flattened cone-like surface the size of 20 football fields. A low cloud had moved in, dropping visibility down to a dozen feet and obscuring the view.

Abed grinned and Khaled slapped his friend on the shoulder as they walked around the peak. His exhalations escaped as small ghosts rushing to mix with the other frozen vapors on the flat mountaintop. He looked slowly around.

"Does anyone see something that resembles an ark?"

Saeeb grinned. "Or even a few pairs of animal skeletons – giraffes, elephants maybe."

Khaled pivoted – *where to start*, he wondered? The peak was not insurmountable and so it had been explored before, probably many times over the centuries. Satellites had mapped the area, and his only hope was to find something conclusive. Something the others had missed.

"Spread out," he called.

His team moved out over the peak. In some areas it was flat, and in others huge sails of stone thrust upwards like icebergs from a foggy ocean. In the more level places there were deep drifts of snow packing down on ice, so anything buried was probably deep.

Each of his team had brought extendable hiking poles, and now had them telescoped to prod and poke at the ground. Rocks were examined in case there were fragments, even minute ones, embedded in their geology. Khaled trusted his team and did the same as them, following a sweep pattern of his quadrant, examining everything in as much detail as he could give it.

They moved slowly and methodically, trying to stay focussed as the hours passed. Abed joined Khaled.

"Nothing." He pointed his pole out over the flat misty mountaintop. "The story goes that around 1300 years ago there used to be a Christian monastery up here – but where is it now?" There's not even a single foundation stone remaining."

Khaled exhaled. "I remember the records – it was supposed to have been 'consumed' by lightning." He turned slowly. "If I was going to build anything up here, it'd be where there is a semblance of evenness in the geology. "There's nothing here now. But after 1300 years, maybe it's been weathered down to sand."

They spent another hour searching the mountaintop, and then more time investigating the slopes on all sides to ensure that there was nothing embedded in the rock further down. Khaled would have been happy with some deep gouges in the stone, or anything to indicate that a ship over 500 feet in size had once rested there.

He checked the time and then called his team in. There were just a few more mountain peaks to check, but as these were quite minor, barely rising 5000 feet and not even snowcapped, he doubted there would be anything there of interest.

His team stood in a semi-circle around him, and when he looked to each of them, they returned a shake of the head or shrug. *Nothing.*

"As I thought."

He looked around at the mist-covered mountaintop. The cloud had dropped completely now, and it was more like a London fog. He could smell the moisture that remained locked up in the cold mist. It was prickly cold against his skin, and its only advantage was that it was like a blanket shielding them from prying eyes.

He sighed. "Well, coffee, and then we go." They could chance a small fire, and it would warm their bellies before the long trek down the slope and then back to the base camp to plan their next mission.

Rizwan and Zahil began to dig into the frozen earth to sink a small pit to place a kerosene burner inside. Saeeb and Yasha then gathered scraped snow into an old jug for melting.

Abed and Khaled walked to one of the peak's edges. Below them the plains and even the sheer slope was lost in fog. It could have been a drop of five feet or a thousand.

Abed leaned one elbow on a spire of rock. "Do you think there was ever an Ark here?" He looked out over the billowing fog. "Or ever an Ark at all?"

"I don't know. Maybe there was, but given it was supposed to have existed over 4500 years ago, then who knows what is fact and fiction now."

"True." Abed opened his thick jacket and pulled out a Saudi flag and shook it out straight. The deep green background with sword and Arabic inscription hung limply in his hands.

"Well, no use being shy about our presence now." He looked up and grinned. "And why not piss our Turkish brothers off even more, *huh*?"

Abed walked to the center of the flat peak, fixed the flag to his hiking pole and used a rock to begin pounding it into the ground. The stake shuddered at first as it tried to penetrate the combination of rock and frozen soil, but then suddenly sunk about three inches and then stuck.

Abed wiggled it, finding it a bit loose, began to pound again. This time the pole never budged so he raised the rock an extra foot, steadied the pole, and then brought it down hard. The pole dropped away, but then with gunshot-like cracking, so did the ground around him.

Abed vanished.

Khaled and his team rushed to where their compatriot had been seconds before. They skidded to a stop and saw where there had been snow and rock, there was now black hole. Khaled threw himself down and peered into the void. There was silence for several seconds, before there came the faint sound of an impact that echoed back up at them.

"Abed!" Khaled waited. "*Brother!*" He and his men moved even closer to the edge when caution held him in his place. "Get back – it may all collapse under us."

The men froze, arms out like tightrope walkers. Their gaze went from the dark hole to each other, and then back to Khaled. They slowly backed up. Only Khaled remained on his belly, peering down.

He slowly reached back for his belt and pulled out a long flashlight, which he angled downwards. There was nothing illuminated, meaning the entire mountaintop might be hollow.

"Abed!" He waited for several seconds. To his relief a moan wafted back up toward him. "He's alive." He yelled over his shoulder and then began to use his light to track the sound to its source. In a few seconds he could just make out the crumpled form of his friend lying among piles of debris some 60 feet down and to the side.

"Can you hear me?"

A single hand was raised. "My leg." Abed groaned again.

Khaled lifted the beam to the edge of the rock he lay on. His side was perched on the top of a cliff wall that gave him support. But closer to his team there was a two-foot skin of rock and ice – exactly like where Abed had punched through. Strangely the stone skin over the void looked quite uniform, almost like bricks.

"Rizwan." Khaled rose up slightly. "Get the spare rope. We'll need to climb down." He pointed. "Over there, tie us off."

Rizwan rushed to a ragged spar of stone and looped his rope around it, tying it securely. He threw the coil of rope to Saeeb who carefully walked it back to Khaled.

Khaled looked to his men. "Hisham, Zahil, Yasha, you three with me. Rizwan and Saeeb, stay on guard, and be ready to haul us out on my word."

As they prepared to drop, a bread loaf-sized piece of stone dislodged and fell into the darkness. Khaled lunged forward to watch it drop. It struck the bottom not six feet from his friend and then bounced heavily away into the gloom. He looked up, jaw set in a hard line. "By all the prophets, *everyone* be careful."

Khaled was first over the lip, and he dropped down quickly to the floor of the cavern. He unhooked himself and stepped away from the drop zone as his next man came down fast. It was dry, and even the sound of the rope *zizzing* through gloved hands echoed in the vast chamber. He lifted his light, scanning the cavern floor.

"Abed?"

"Here." The reply was faint.

Khaled quickly located his man and stepped carefully toward him. While he edged over the tumbled stones, another melon-sized boulder fell from above to impact against the rocks like a small bomb going off.

"*Sharmouta!*" he cursed as he shielded his face from the shrapnel.

Zahil then came down fast, slipping and landing hard. "*Ouch.*" He unhitched himself, shook his head and then held the rope to steady it as Yasha, and then Hisham rappelled down.

Khaled found his friend and crouched beside him. Abed's face was covered in blood from multiple abrasions, and there was a small dent in his forehead. He gripped Khaled's forearm and painfully pulled himself to a near-sitting position.

He groaned in pain. "My leg."

Khaled shone his flashlight along the man's body. One of his feet was lying sideways at an odd angle, the ankle obviously broken. He reached for it, but paused.

"Steel yourself, brother; this is going to hurt."

Abed grinned. "It already hurts." The man gritted his teeth and nodded. "I'm ready."

Khaled pressed on the limb, feeling the bones in the lower leg, foot and then the ankle. It felt unnaturally lose, but thankfully the skin hadn't broken.

Khaled moved back up the man, checking his head, and then shining the light into his eyes. "You might also have a concussion. Also a broken ankle; so no dancing for a while." He patted his friend on the shoulder. The ankle was bad, but the dent in his head was the bigger worry. More than likely, there would be pressure building in his skull and pushing on his brain. He was liable to drop into a coma at any moment.

Yasha and Hisham knelt beside their fallen team member, as Zahil continued to wave his beam slowly around the huge cavern.

"What is this place?"

Khaled rested his elbows on his knees as Yasha helped Abed sip some water.

"Like a bad tooth; the mountain seems to have a cavity, and our friend managed to fall into it."

"Look." Zahil pointed.

Khaled followed his light beam, and then stood, squinting. He turned back to Yasha. "Stay with him."

He stepped across the broken stones, and after another few moments, the rubble disappeared and he found himself standing on smooth, fitted stonework.

"This… is a path." He walked slowly around what he thought was a large misshapen boulder, until he saw what it was from another angle – a massive rough-hewn stone figure, crouching on a table-sized stone plinth. He shone his light up into its face. The thing was ugly, deformed, and was more gargoyle than anything else. He leaned in closer.

Hisham joined him. "Friend of yours?"

"*Ack!*" Khaled jumped, but then chuckled softly. "Not even on a good day."

"Hey, look." Zahil was smiling, holding his light momentarily on himself, before lifting it away to point off into the dark. His beam was just strong enough to light up a small building, all of fitted stone, the remains of a crucifix on its top. "Did you say there used to be a monastery here that was destroyed by lightning?" He grinned.

Khaled shook his head in awe. "A Christian one, built about 1300 years ago – and yes, supposedly destroyed by lightning. Or at least 'consumed' by lightning, as the legend goes."

"Maybe the translation was wrong." Zahil said. "Maybe it didn't mean consumed as in destroyed, but instead meant consumed as in swallowed by lightning. That it somehow fell into this cavern." He turned. "It was swallowed up by this cave."

Khaled lifted his light to the ceiling over a hundred feet above them. "And fell all this way and remained intact? I think not. It's no Ark, but it's something very interesting." Khaled turned and whistled, waving to Yasha. "We need to check this out. Get Hisham, and then help Yasha with Abed."

Whump! Behind them came a ground-shaking thump that reverberated through to the soles of their boots. The men crouched as shrapnel spattered over them.

"Another gift from above," Khaled said as dust and snow rained down through the gap. "We must be quick and then get out. This entire place could collapse on us."

Two of his men bracketed Abed, who hopped sluggishly between them with his head partially lolling on Yasha's shoulder.

"I think his back is damaged as well." Yasha said, easing his grip lower. "Maybe not broken, but he'll be spending some time in traction when we get back."

"I'm fine; just a little dizzy," Abed responded.

Khaled turned toward a pair of huge doors. They'd probably been oak once, but their monstrously thick beams were now rotted through, leaving empty shells and rust marks where iron bands and rivets had once been. Perhaps the freezing air had preserved them for many centuries, but time had still eaten away at their heart.

Khaled pushed at the doors, and one fell inward, thumping to the ground. Inside it was as dark as Hades. The men slowly moved their beams of light over the interior. For a place of worship it seemed strangely empty – not a bench, an altar stone at the front, statue or crucifix anywhere. There was but a single object placed in the center of the room – a stone coffin – a sarcophagus. Its formidable sides seemed to grow from the floor of the building like it was a single piece of stonework. It was as if the church and the casket were one.

"Was the monastery here first or the coffin?" Yasha asked quietly.

"Good question," Khaled breathed. "Who was important enough to have an entire church built around them?"

"And then be hidden in a mountain?" Zahil asked.

Khaled went to his friend, wiping the hair back from his forehead and peering into his face. "Okay, brother?"

Abed nodded and his lips rose a little at the corners. "Tired. Just set me down for a while to catch my breath."

"Good man." Khaled helped him to sit with his back against a stone column. His face was ashen, and when Khaled took his hand away, he saw there was blood on his fingers. They'd need to hurry their explorations.

Zahil moved his flashlight over the room. "This doesn't look like a place of worship, more a crypt. And you're right; this church cannot have fallen in here. It was built down here."

Khaled stared at the sarcophagus. "Maybe it's all a lie. The rocks overhead seemed to have been cut and laid in place like a stone roof. Maybe the lightning story was used as a smoke screen, and the reality was the monastery was always hidden."

"I thought this was supposed to be the final resting place of the Ark." Zahil shrugged. "Final resting place of something."

"Let's get some more light. The old wood will work to make some torches and chase those shadows from the corners. Hurry," Khaled ordered.

The men did as he requested, using some of the wood from the smashed door and wrapping handkerchiefs or strips of fabric around their ends. They used Yasha's cigarette lighter to ignite them and stuck them in nooks and crannies. Only Yasha continued to hold his aloft.

"That's better." Khaled slowly turned to examine the walls. The light showed the carvings in great detail – images of massive waves, islands, or perhaps they were the peaks of mountains rising from great oceans. Pairs of animals of all kinds, and a small group of people standing before a central figure – tall and bearded, with his arms wide.

Yasha shook his head. "Maybe we are closer to our goal than we think."

"Perhaps." Khaled walked to the huge stone coffin. It was roughly nine feet long, four wide and about six high and had a simple stone slab as a lid. He placed his hands on the edge and raised himself up. He still gripped his flashlight in one hand and held it aloft – there was carved writing, but the language was strange for a Christian monastery, and in fact looked a little like Hebrew, but a sort he had never encountered before. He could only make out a few words here and there.

"*Akebu-Lan.*"

He dropped back down, and turned to his team. "I've heard of that before."

"I think it's Arabic," Yasha insisted.

"No, more some sort of root language." He pointed. "This word, it's a name, something like Elysia, Erewhon, Xanadu,

Utopia, they're all names for one place, *the Garden of Eden*. But the oldest name in existence is this one, *Akebu-Lan*. In the kingdom of Bor-Nu." He shook his head. "I can't read the rest, and from what I can, it barely makes sense. We need an expert."

He turned back to the coffin. "Well then, let's see who's home." He waved his team closer. "Everyone on this side, hands on the lid, and on the count of three…"

"Three, two, one and… heave…"

Khaled and his team were all large men and strong, but the stone slab didn't budge.

"Stop."

He walked around the sarcophagus, running a finger along where the lid joined the actual casket. It met so perfectly it could have all been carved from a single piece of stone. He had a sinking feeling that perhaps that's what it was – what he had taken to be a stone cap wasn't a lid at all, but instead the whole thing was a single piece and the join was just a carved line.

He pulled out his short blade and dug it in, working the blade in as far as he could. He held the knife in place and looked around the floor.

"Yasha there, pass me that stone."

His man snatched up the fist-sized rock and handed it to him. Khaled lined up the pommel of his blade and then pounded against it. There was a sharp crack like the breaking of an ice sheet as the blade sunk in about an inch.

"Get back," Khaled said as a white gas escaped from where the lid seal had split. The four men backed away with arms up over their faces.

A low moan lifted from somewhere behind them. Khaled turned, looking toward the door. The sound hadn't come from their wounded man, but instead had seemed to come from outside. It came again, deep, mournful, followed by the sound of cracking, like splitting rock.

"What is that?" Yasha asked softly.

They waited, but there was silence again.

Khaled shook his head. "Just the wind over the mountaintop; forget it." He turned back to the sarcophagus. The mist was still escaping from within it. "Phew." Khaled waved it away as he returned to the sarcophagus. He gripped the blade handle; it was now jammed tight.

"Now, let us see."

The men momentarily froze as from outside the thunderous sound of another huge stone struck the ground, and then another, straight after. Dust rained down on their heads inside the small monastery.

"Time's running out. Again, on three –" Khaled positioned his hands on the hilt of the knife. "Three, two, one, *heave...*"

This time the stone slab slid a few inches. He sucked in a huge breath, tensing his muscles.

"Harder; three, two, one, he-*eeeave...*"

The stone slid and kept sliding. It pivoted and the top half was now over the side of the casket. Khaled wiped his brow and stepped back, and then quickly looked around, finding a tumbled column of stone, which he rolled to the side of the coffin base to use as a step. It was wide enough for he and Zahil to step up.

The pair looked into its interior. At first Khaled could see nothing but an eerie mist that filled the sarcophagus to the brim, but he waved his hand, dissipating it to reveal a single large figure. The man had long white hair and a beard and was dressed in ornate robes of someone held in high esteem. He was so perfectly preserved that the old man could have been sleeping.

"That light, shine it here." Khaled reached in, and felt the cheek, and then neck. The skin was cold and dry, and there was no pulse, *thankfully*, he thought. He continued to feel the cheek.

"Preserved, I think, but not really mummified."

"Creepy if you ask me. He looks like he might wake up." Zahil leaned in a little more. "There's an inscription here." He rubbed at some symbols running around the inside rim of the stone base. "Can you read them?"

Khaled also traced the symbols. "Only this one – *Shmh*."

Yasha frowned up at them. "Is that a word? What does it mean?"

Khaled began to laugh softly. "Not just a word, but a name – *Shmh* – is the very first name for Shem. The first son of Noah."

Yasha grinned. "The son of the Noah?" He waited, perhaps expecting some sort of joke to be revealed.

Khaled leaned in closer to the corpse. "Why not? Only minutes ago we wondered who was important enough to have an entire church built around them. I think we now know."

Beside him, Zahil shone his light further into the casket. "Hey, he's got something in his hands."

"I'm coming up." There was a grunt and then with difficulty, Yasha heaved himself up beside Khaled and Zahil while still holding the burning torch. "What's he got – treasure?"

"Zahil leaned in. "Looks like... a skull. Whose?"

"Adam's," Khaled said. He shone his light on the object that Shem had resting in his hands. It was indeed an age-browned skull, but without the jawbone. The cranium gleamed as if polished.

"In the Biblical stories, the family of Noah were given the bones of Adam to keep safe. When the Ark finally found its resting place, Noah distributed the sacred bones of Adam to each of them. Shem got the skull." He looked along the tall man's remains. "More pieces of the puzzle."

"But not exactly coming together if you ask me," Zahil jibed.

"The skull; lucky guy." Yasha grinned. "He must have really liked it to want to be buried with it."

"A holy relic," Khaled said softly. "But it's not supposed to be here. One of Noah's final commands was for the remains of Adam to be buried in the middle of the earth, where Christ was crucified. That was to be at Karkaphta, or as we know it, Golgotha."

"Why would he disobey his own father?" Yasha asked.

"Who knows, but many of the relics are supposed to have miraculous properties. Remember, Eve was said to have been created from his rib. So maybe the skull also had some sort of power."

"Well, if you can make a woman from one little rib, then I think I'll just rub the skull for luck." Yasha held the torch up and then reached in. His fingers had only rested on the top of the polished skull when there was a ripple of movement.

"*Yish!*" He pulled back. "Did you see...?"

"What is it?" Zahil leaned forward on his elbows.

"Don't touch it!" Khaled stared. It must have been a trick of the dancing light, he thought. But while he watched the face of the corpse, now bathed in the flashlight beams and Yasha's burning torch, began to ripple, and the hair and beard waved like in a soft breeze.

The eyes flicked open.

"By all that is holy, he *is* alive." Zahil jerked backwards but the pupils were jet black in milky orbs. Then what looked like a long hair or thread eased from one of the nostrils. It quested about for a moment, before easing back in.

"What was that?" Yasha held the burning torch closer, the heat and flames only a foot or so from the face. The effect was immediate. The dark pupils in the eyes dissipated and spread away from the center of the eye, like milk poured into a swirling coffee cup.

The cheek twitched, the lips moved, trembling and jumping, and every hair on his head and face took on a life of its own. The corpse of Shem began to swell; first the cheeks ballooned, and then the chest, arms, and stomach, and finally, the old man simply exploded into a mass of squirming thread-like worms.

Zahil was a brave man, but with a yell he jumped backwards from the stone he was standing on.

"Stay there," Khaled yelled to Yasha, whose flame wobbled in his hand as they watched the horrifying sight of the man bursting into separate pieces.

The magnificent clothing sunk in on itself, as there was nothing to hold its shape as everything else in the casket writhed and squirmed as it fled from the heat.

"It's not a man at all," Yasha stammered.

"Maybe it once was." Khaled grimaced. "But now something has infiltrated the body."

Like a wave in a bathtub, the mess in the casket surged up the side toward them. Khaled reached out to snatch the burning torch from Yasha. He jammed it into the writhing horror, and the old clothing caught immediately.

"The prophets preserve me." Khaled ground his teeth. The sound was of a million tiny, screaming mouths, and it grated on every nerve in his body and tore at his sanity. The worms were now boiling like liquid, pitching and frothing as they tried to escape the flames.

The smell of the burning worms was the worst thing Khaled had ever encountered in his life, as the grease from it coated the lining of his nose and mouth. He threw a hand up over his face and stepped back, forgetting his was standing on a rock, and fell to the ground. His flashlight bounced from his hand, but the flames from the open casket revealed the terrifying sight of millions of thread-like worms piling up and then spilling over the rim of the stone coffin.

The abominations were fast. Much faster than he had expected. Once on the ground, many of the glassine threads headed for the darkness or any crack or crevice they could find. But many more simply spread out like an ever-growing pool of viscous liquid.

He scrambled to his feet. "Let's get out of here."

Khaled backed up, wishing he had a flamethrower. He wondered what horrors from hell had possessed this church and corrupted the body of the son of Noah himself. Was he cursed? Was this why the architects of this place had hidden the body away all these millennia?

"Khaled!" Zahil yelled his name, breaking his trance.

He held up a hand and nodded to his men. "We're leaving – help me with Abed, and..." He turned and his words froze in his mouth.

His friend was covered in a moving wave of the worms. They swarmed over him, seeming to investigate every inch of his body, probing, seeking, and exploring. For his part, the man just lay as if asleep and didn't seem to notice.

Outside a stone pounded to the ground, shaking the church. There came another, and then another, almost like a titan's footsteps. Khaled sprinted for one of the other torches they had positioned around the stone room and went to approach Abed's covered body, but Yasha held his arm.

"He's lost. We must go, now."

Khaled felt a surge of anger well up into his chest. "And if it was you? Would you want me to leave you to these abominations?"

Yasha stared for a moment, and then dropped his hand from Khaled's arm. "Sorry, brother."

Khaled swung back to Abed, his arm with the torch outstretched toward the stricken man to ward off the horrifying things. But they were already gone.

Abed coughed, raising one hand to his face. Khaled, Hisham, Yasha, and Zahil raced to him.

"Take it easy." Khaled helped him to sit, while his fellow team members cast worried glances around at the floor and walls.

Abed looked up at him and nodded. He inhaled deeply, and then to their surprise, he grinned.

"How are you feeling?" Khaled saw that where there had been blood on his face and also matting his hair, there was now none. *Did the worms consume it?* he wondered.

Abed got to his feet and held his arms out, looking at each as if checking them. "I feel... fine."

"What?" Zahil face was contorted. "How?"

Abed looked down at his feet and lifted one leg after the other. "I feel fine. My leg is good. It must have just been sprained."

Hisham edged away. "This is wrong."

"That was no sprain." Khaled kept his flashlight on the man's face. "I felt the broken bones myself."

More stones fell, and this time a portion of the roof collapsed inward, as if struck by a meteorite. Zahil looked outside, moving now from foot to foot.

"It's collapsing."

The huge blocks could be heard falling continuously now, and beneath their feet, the vibrations made the stones jump. Khaled knew that with any stone roof architecture, there were key stones, locking stones, and once these were removed, then the entire arching skin over their heads would crumbled in all at once.

"We go, *now.*"

They sprinted down the stone steps, and Khaled paused in confusion – he was sure they had come this way. There was the road, and the table-sized stone plinth, but now it was vacant. He spun one way then the other – where was the giant gargoyle?

The rocks began to fall faster now, so there was no time for wondering about details. The men began to run as if the devil himself were after them. They headed for the column of light and the thread of rope hanging down from above. As they danced over the broken stones, they could just make out the heads of their two team members waving them on from the rim.

"Zahil, you first, and then you help Rizwan and Saeeb pull us all up – fast." Khaled turned to Yasha. "You and Abed next, then Hisham and myself."

Yasha looked nervous, but he bit it down and waited. He helped Zahil tie himself off, and then yelled up to his colleagues who immediately started the jerking tug to lift the man off his feet, and then start to ascend.

Khaled spun looking for Abed. The man had stopped moving and was standing among the debris, a beatific expression on his face. He held out a hand.

"We should stay."

Khaled waved at him. "Get over here and get ready to climb, *immediately.*"

"No." Abed shook his head. "There's nothing to fear. I'm staying... we should *all* stay." He turned back to the monastery. "They need us you know. They've been so lonely, so... hungry." He smiled sadly. "They won't let you leave anyway."

"What?" Khaled frowned back at his colleague. "What are you talking about?" He turned to Hisham. "Bring him here."

From out of the darkness of the cave there came again the moan he had heard when inside the monastery. Its mournful echoes bounced around them, until the sound of falling rocks drowned it out.

"What was that?" Yasha hissed next to him.

Hisham froze on his way to Abed, and Khaled turned slowly. They stood under the column of light from above that diffused outward to form a circle around them of about a few dozen feet, but beyond that, it was as dark as the vacuum of space itself.

"I don't know," Khaled said, turning slowly.

Yasha moved a little closer to the light, and only Hisham and Abed stood a little further back. From the gloom there came the sound of movement, heavy, but fast as if something was circling them.

Khaled pulled his weapon – a Browning semi-automatic pistol, and then laid his flashlight across the wrist of his gun hand. Yasha and Hisham did the same.

Only Abed stood still, his expression almost dream-like. "I told you."

"What is it? What's out there?" Khaled screamed the words, but kept watch on the dark, trying to track the movement with his gun.

Abed smiled. "You'll soon see."

The attack came fast. One second, Hisham was standing at the periphery of the column of light, and the next, something hit him, *took him*, and he vanished with only a single cry of surprise.

Khaled went to charge after him, but Yasha yelled back. "Stay here! You'll be lost in the dark."

As if in response, the remains of their comrade came bouncing back into the light. The man had been torn in half, and his facial features were still screwed up in a mix of agony and horror.

Khaled looked back to the ceiling. "Hurry up!"

Abed giggled and turned to head back to the small building.

"Get back here!" Khaled yelled, trying to keep his own panic in check as the man ignored him. Khaled lifted his face to the hole in the ceiling again just as more boulders dropped from the sky. They landed hard, some shattering into a thousand small, sharp projectiles, and others bouncing heavily like monstrous medicine balls capable of killing instantly.

Zahil was just being pulled up to the rim, and Khaled cupped his hands around his mouth. "Hu-*uuurry*!" The man scrabbled now at the edge, nearly over. Khaled turned to Yasha. "We need to get Abed."

"No." Yasha now had his flashlight pointed at the man disappearing in the darkness. "There's something wrong with him. He's *different*."

Khaled was torn, but glanced up to see Zahil finally disappear over the rim. "Merciful god", he muttered. But then his breath caught as almost directly above them an entire section of the ceiling bent downward, hung momentarily, and then wrenched free. On the way down it separated into multiple deadly missiles, each weighing thousands of pounds.

"Get down!" But he knew there was no shelter where they waited.

It was like being carpet-bombed, as the stones, some the size of a man's head, and some as big as hay bales thudded around them. The sound was near deafening and the vibrations loosened even more blocks overhead. Out to his left there was a huge impact, and he felt something wet splash his cheek and stick there.

He wiped at it as he spun and saw that where Abed had been moments before, now there was just the remains of crushed flesh and clothing.

Khaled has been through commando training himself, had been in death-dealing situations many times as a Saudi warrior and had nerves of steel. But right now he felt his own sanity slipping from naked fear. He tried to run across the rocks to reach his friend, but ever more stones thumped down, and the vicious assault forced him to retreat back under the halo of light, and the only section that didn't have a rock ceiling over the top of them.

He felt the heaviness in his soul at seeing his childhood friend obliterated, but mercifully the boulder hadn't bounced away and after it had crushed him it remained embedded in place and spared them from seeing his face.

A single arm still stuck out, its fingers hooked into claws of agony. And as Khaled wiped his eyes, he was horrified to see the fingers unfurl and then curl. Even though Abed's face and chest was flattened to paste, his limbs refused to give up.

Khaled felt light-headed and turned away. More stones fell – larger and faster now. Eventually the entire ceiling would come down, his men above would tumble in, and then they would all be buried alive.

From the dark, the sound of something huge lumbering around them came again. Whatever it was, it pushed and threw large boulders out of the way and was coming back for them. Khaled remembered the gargoyle – *impossible*, his logical brain thought. But he knew now what it was: some sort of guardian that they had woken by disturbing Shem's eternal sleep.

He raised his eyes. *Hurry*, he prayed.

Dust rained down, and he flashed his beam around the cavern, looking for any other safe haven while they waited. He touched on the small monastery. He was about to pull his beam away when the light glinted back from something on the steps at its front.

At first he thought it was water pouring forth, surging and lapping and constantly changing in the angle of his light beam. Then he saw it for it was – a torrent, but not of liquid, instead of millions of the small thread-like worms that had been inside the body of Shem.

They now surged toward him and Yasha.

More boulders thumped down, making both men cringe with every impact. From above, the rope finally snaked back down. Khaled and Yasha got underneath it, their faces upturned to the light and their salvation.

"We go together," Khaled said.

Yasha nodded, still looking up. He then turned his face to Khaled and grinned, but behind the bravado there was real fear in his eyes.

"Keep looking to the rope, brother," Khaled said, not wanting Yasha to see the horror creeping toward them. He knew the man's sanity was on a knife-edge – as his was.

He turned his flashlight back toward the monastery's steps. The carpet of worms was spreading out, but it was hard to follow now, as it was disappearing into the cracks and fissures between the boulders. He couldn't know whether the things were benign or not, but there was not a chance in hell he was going to let even a single one of them touch his skin.

"Yes!" Yasha clapped his hands once as the rope finally came within reach.

"Lash yourself in, quickly now." Khaled bounded over rocks and joined his man, grabbing the end of the rope, and quickly throwing it around his waist, knotting it, and putting a loop around one wrist.

"Pull up, *now, now, now!*"

They were yanked up a few feet. Khaled snuck a quick look back and saw the worms gathering together, forming a pool below them. They seemed to hurry now, as if sensing their targets were escaping. It was obvious what they wanted – *them*.

More worms poured forth from under the stone that had crushed Abed. *Just like Shem, they were in him*, he thought. Perhaps that was the reason for his friend's strange behavior. He felt gorge rise in his throat and turned his face to the hole in the ceiling.

"Pu-*uuuulll!*"

They rose another few feet. The combined weight of himself and Yasha was challenging the three men hauling them up. The rope tugged and then jumped up another four feet. Khaled worried now that the edge of the rope would be pressing down hard against the jagged stone of the lip.

They hung there for another few seconds. *Come on, faster,* he prayed, and chanced a look back down.

Movement, but not the worms this time – something else, huge and cumbersome, moved into the light. Khaled lifted his gun and fired quickly three times. He knew he hit it, he thought all three times, but the thing shrugged the bullets off like they were nothing but bee stings. Huge yellow eyes fixed on him with such malevolence; he knew that it wanted to grind them into nothingness.

He held his gun up and pointed right between the huge fist-sized yellow orbs. He noticed his hand shook, and he struggled to keep it steady. Below, just where they had been standing a few moments ago, the worms had coagulated into a single, large mass. The hair on Khaled's head and neck rose as the worms climbed up on each other, creating a finger-like extension that stretched up toward them.

"Hurry!"

"What is it?" Yasha looked down and saw the glistening, now wrist-thick limb rising up toward them. "*Gaagh!*" He jerked his legs up beneath him, making the rope swing dangerously.

"Be still, brother, keep looking up, just keep looking up." Khaled tried to keep his voice calm, but felt the fear squeezing his throat. He saw the gargoyle begin to approach and he pointed his gun again, calming his breathing, and aimed at just one of the huge yellow orbs. He squeezed off a single shot and was delighted to see one of the glowing orbs close. The immediate hellish noise that followed confirmed the things could be hurt.

They rose a little higher, and beside him Yasha crushed his eyes shut, and his lips moved in a silent, manic prayer. Khaled stared down as the tendril, now tree-trunk thick at its base but tapering to only finger width at the tip, reached ever higher. In the light thrown down from above, he saw that it shivered slightly as if excited anticipation ran through every living fiber that made up the biological mass. It was within a few feet of his boot now, and he carefully raised his own legs to match Yasha's.

It didn't matter, the tendril rose, and they didn't. *I should cut myself loose, sacrifice myself*, he thought. *So at least one of us can survive.* Khaled's hand went down for his hunting knife, feeling the pommel. He unclipped the hilt strap.

Just then they jerked, firstly back down a few inches, and then they were moving up fast. It was if they were on an express train, and they zoomed up the remaining fifty feet and were at the rim in only seconds more.

The pair rolled free, and the first thing Khaled felt was the bite of snow on his face, and he quickly untied himself. He sat up, and then noticed the second thing – the hole was enormous now, and as they watched another huge chunk sank into the void below. Massive cracks appeared in the surface around it.

Rizwan grabbed at his shoulder. "We need to get out of here."

He jumped to his feet, remembering they were standing on something that was like a giant bad tooth – a rim around a huge crater that had been artificially sealed over with stone.

"Run!"

The five men sprinted for the edge of the mountaintop that had a rock formation like a pair of huge sentinels – it was the closest area that had solid base underneath it.

There came a brittle cracking sound followed by pops then booms as ground began to break apart, and then the entire top of the mountain fell in. The ancient monastery, the statues and stonework, and the hellish worms were buried beneath many million tons of rock and snow. If the mist had cleared, it would have seemed as if the mountain was erupting as huge clouds mushroomed into the air from its cone.

The group fell to the ground, some lying flat and all gasping for breath. After a moment Rizwan started to laugh.

"We're alive."

"Not all of us," Khaled snapped back at his man.

Rizwan held up a hand, and touched his lips and forehead. "Peace be to our brothers, Abed and Hisham. Sorry."

Khaled sighed. "No, I'm sorry, brother." He tried to smile, but still found it hard. "It is our lucky day. It could have been all of us buried."

"Or worse," Yasha said. "This is a place of abominations."

Khaled nodded. "And perhaps that is why it was sealed away all those centuries ago."

Yasha leaned forward. "And God be praised, sealed away for good this time."

Rizwan pulled himself up to sit and rested his forearms on his knees. "But we still have no Ark."

"And no wellspring of youth. *But* now we have a reference to the Garden of Eden." Khaled looked at his friend. "*Akebu-Lan*, in the kingdom of Bor-Nu."

"Do you think that truly is a place?" Rizwan drew in a cheek.

"Maybe there was something like it once. It is all a puzzle, and like I said, we need an expert now." He stood, stretched, and then groaned. "Getting too old for this." Khaled dusted himself off. "And I think it is time I met with our elusive Professor Matthew Kearns."

Chapter 7

Fort Severn, Hudson Bay, Northern Ontario, Canada

Matt stared out the window of the Twin Otter turboprop plane. Though the propellers spun at around 3,000 rpms they were invisible and the sound muffled to a low whine by the reinforced skin of the fuselage.

Normally, the Twin Otter could seat 19 passengers onboard, but today there was only he and Rachel. He still thought they needed more support, especially following the grenade attack, but she had assured him that they could use local manpower, and in the case of indigenous communities, he guessed she was right in that sometimes less was more.

Rachel had organised an initial meeting with the Fort Severn policeman, a Nishnawbe-Aski officer by the name of Oscar Ojibwe. *Just don't expect the red carpet treatment*, she had said.

He felt a sudden squeeze on his knee – *hard*. Looking down he saw her hand moving away.

"Still with me?" she smiled.

"Sure, sure, wouldn't want to be anywhere else," he lied.

"Except surfing?" She raised an eyebrow.

"Well, yeah, there is that." He returned her smile.

She checked her watch, and then leaned toward their window. "We should be coming up on Fort Severn soon."

He looked out; below there was nothing but endless green with the occasional ribbon of water running through it. Even though it was relatively warm weather, the small, salmon-filled streams would be icy cold and their bleak, silver surfaces looked about as inviting as a dip in one of the moons of Mercury. He gripped the armrests, and felt his stomach tingle as the altitude fell away.

"Going down," he said softly.

Fifteen minutes later the plane bumped down onto the packed earth runway, and Matt leaned forward to catch his first glimpse of the far-north Canadian town. There was a single flat building that could have been a scout hall, and a chain link fence, probably to keep the local moose from wandering across the extremely short runway. He couldn't imagine what it must have been like trying to land a plane here in the depths of winter.

The airplane came to the end of the runway and then turned 180 degrees to slowly power back toward the property. It was only then that Matt spotted the solitary figure leaning against the corner of the building.

Rachel began to unbuckle her belt. "That's our ride."

Matt squinted at the blocky figure.

"Chief Constable," she said and flipped her seat belt off. "The Nishnawbe-Aski Police Service has over a hundred Constables who act as the police force up here."

Matt was impressed. "That's sounds a lot given how many people are up here."

"Are you serious?" Rachel scoffed. "Those hundred-odd guys are responsible for a jurisdiction the size of France. They might not get the number of drive-by shootings we see in the big smoke, but they're kept pretty busy."

"And not to mention dealing with the odd FBI agent barging in on them." He raised his chin.

"And her trusty sidekick," she retorted.

Matt cocked an eyebrow. "I'm demoted to sidekick already?"

"Yes, but I did say you were a trusty one." She got to her feet. "C'mon, let's meet Oscar. He'll be our guide, taxi and font of local knowledge about all things local, so be nice."

"You know you said the same thing before I met with Eleanor van Helling, and guess which one of us walked away with a gift?" Matt stood.

Rachel laughed, but then turned to look him in the eye. "Hey, did you bring it?"

"Nah." He shrugged. "The grenade attack destroyed it. It's a piece of junk now. I just hope Eleanor doesn't ever ask for it back."

"You'll certainly lose your teacher's pet status." Rachel gave him a sympathetic smile. She nodded to the pilot as he came back through the plane, unlocked the door, pushed it open and then dropped the steps.

Rachel was the first one down, with Matt following. He inhaled a cool dryness that tickled his nose. There was also a hint of fragrance he couldn't place until he spotted the red dots of wild lingonberries clumped along the edge of the runway.

"Constable Ojibwe." Rachel waved.

The man gave them an almost imperceptible nod, and then pushed off from the edge of the building. As they neared, they saw a battered blue pickup parked just around its corner. Rachel stuck out a hand, and the man grasped it, pressed, and released.

Matt did the same, the skin on the man's palm felt like it was made from old canvas stretched over hardwood. There was real strength in the grip. *Now this is a guy who actually works for a living*, he could hear his father say.

"Howza flight?" His eyes flicked from Matt to Rachel.

The man looked like he sounded – he had broad, strong features, a slight Native American epicanthic fold over each eye, and a well-tanned face. His thick black hair was swept back, and Matt guessed they were about the same age. But then again, who knew, as the guy worked outdoors, he could have really been a weather-beaten 20 year old.

"The flight was good, easy." Rachel swatted at a fly.

"Do you need a place to rest up, grab a coffee, or sumthin?" Ojibwe waited.

"Coffee's always good, probably best if we grab one and talk for a while." Rachel waved away even more of the insects.

There was a whine at Matt's ear, and it was only then that Matt noticed a small cloud gathering around his head. There was a stinging on his neck.

"*Ow.*" He slapped a hand there, but there immediately came another sting on his check. "What the fuck?"

Oscar grunted. "Blackfly. Pretty bad in summer. C'mon." He turned to his pickup. Matt and Rachel followed, lugging their bags. Rachel turned momentarily to the plane and gave a thumbs-up. In the small cockpit window, the pilot touched the brim of his cap, and then the props started up, quickly increasing their rotation in preparation for his return flight.

"Shit." Matt slapped his neck again at another bite as the noise from the plane's propellers drowned out everything else.

The only one of them that seemed untroubled by insects was Oscar. He unlocked the pickup and they quickly clambered in.

"Jesus." Matt rubbed his ears and face. There were a few flies in the cabin that they quickly dispatched. Matt wiped his hands on his pants.

"Why did I have the impression there'd be nothing but pristine water, clear air, and no damned flies? Especially ones that are determined to take big chunks out of you." He lifted a hand still seeing smears of blood on the fingers – *My blood or the fly's?* he wondered.

"You come at a bad time." Oscar shrugged. "Or a good time if you're a blackfly. They're only around for a few weeks, but in that time, all they do is eat and mate. Bit like college kids, *huh,* Professor?"

"Except I'm stuck with the college kids for years not weeks." Matt smiled. Oscar did not share his grin.

The truck smelled like tobacco, old paper, and perspiration. Oscar turned on the wipers to smear away some of the bugs.

"Any tips to avoid them?" Matt asked.

Oscar grunted. "Don't wear perfumes. I know how you city guys like that stuff – but so do the flies." He turned back to the windscreen. "Also wear light-colored clothing, as the flies are usually attracted to moose and bear – both dark animals. Luckily, they're only a problem during the day."

"Got it – avoid dark clothes during the day." Rachel's lip curled down. "Now if only someone had told me that before I left."

"One more thing; it's also mosquito season, and they're worst at night." He grinned, and Matt could see he was obviously enjoying their discomfort.

Matt nudged Rachel. "Is it too late to call the plane back?"

*

The Fort Severn city center was made up of low buildings, none over two stories. It was warm now, but Matt tried to imagine the town in the depths of winter, snowbound, and buried beneath blankets of white. Being housebound for days on end would have driven him insane.

"*Ah,* Officer Ojibwe…"

"Oscar."

"Oscar, thanks... and it's Matt. So, you busy round these parts?"

"Sometimes." Oscar never took his eyes for the road.

Matt waited, but guessed small talk wasn't going to be this guy's forte. Rachel continued to look out her side window. But Matt was determined to open the guy up.

"You must know everyone in the town, *huh*?"

"Pretty much."

"Okay." Matt felt his frustration kick in, but guessed these guys weren't employed to be social guides. "Many strangers come up? I mean other than us."

"Yep. This time of year, we get a whole bunch." He nodded as he drove. "Different time of year, means different people. Around this time we get more fishermen, hunters, trekkers, and a few nature huggers. I try and meet every one of them. Mostly good people."

They pulled into the local council chambers, a long barn-like brick building, with a red-tiled pitched roof. Oscar stopped the car, and shouldered his door open. "Come on in."

They pushed through double glass doors and were greeted by a broad-faced woman at the desk. She chatted with Oscar for a moment, and then smiled at Rachel and Matt, giving them a friendly but close examination as they passed by.

Inside there was more activity than Matt had expected. He spotted half a dozen uniformed men and women bustling about or hunched over desks.

"This way." Oscar took them to an open room, his office, they assumed. There were filing cabinets, a map wall, computer equipment, and cold-weather jackets on pegs.

"Home away from home," Oscar muttered as he headed for a pot of coffee still steaming on the hotplate. He set about assembling three odd-sized mugs into a line. "Hope you're not going to ask for one of those fancy-type coffees." He snorted, and then turned. "Up here it's coffee, black or... black."

"Black is fine," Rachel said evenly.

Matt raised his eyebrows. "Sugar?"

Oscar froze, and then turned. "What'd you call me?"

"I meant... I said..." Matt fumbled.

Oscar slapped his hand on the desk, guffawing. "Little joke. Sure, we got sugar." He turned back to filling the cups as Matt and Rachel exchanged glances.

Rachel nudged Matt and nodded to the knife on Oscar's hip. She raised her eyebrows. "Knew you should have brought the scabbard."

"That might have even fit." He turned to Oscar. "That's some knife."

Oscar's hand went to the hilt, and he pulled it free, holding the huge and gleaming Bowie blade up for Matt to see.

"Hunting knife. Round these parts we all carry knives. Damn bears and all." He winked at Matt.

"Nice one." Matt could not have felt anymore like a city slicker if he tried.

Rachel took her mug of steaming coffee and walked to the map wall. Matt joined her.

"Big territory."

"Yup." Oscar sat and leafed through some papers.

Matt saw there were little red pins in the map out at some remote locations. "Oscar, what're these, small villages or something?"

Oscar looked up. "Nope, just some hunting cabins and supply huts. Pretty rough territory, more so in winter. So we have a few supply places tucked away on mountain slopes and way out. You get lost, hopefully you can make your way to one of those. They're all marked on maps and restocked annually."

Rachel turned to look for a moment, before joining Oscar at his desk. She sat down, rested her forearms on his desktop, and smiled. "We don't want to take up much of your time, Officer Ojibwe."

"Like I said, Oscar." He smiled flatly.

"Officer Ojibwe." Rachel repeated. "Have there been any strangers in and around these parts lately?" She opened a folder and slid forward a picture of the men in dark suits that had slain the family.

He sighed, reached for it and lifted it to his face. He shook his head. "No one wears suits like that up here. This isn't *Noo Yark*."

Rachel never flinched. "Okay, well, are there any remote communities, houses, families, or religious orders that come and go without interacting with the rest of the community?"

Ojibwe examined something in his coffee cup for a second or two, before sipping. "Not really."

"*Not really?*" Rachel's jaw jutted momentarily, and Matt could tell she was moving into interrogation mode. She tapped a finger on the image. "Look again, *think* again, Officer."

He sipped noisily. "This is a waste of time."

Rachel's gaze turned volcanic, but Ojibwe's remained bored. She pulled some more pictures from her folder and sorted through them. She slid one toward him.

"Do you know what that is?"

Ojibwe craned forward, frowned, and then shook his head slowly.

"That is the charred corpse of a five-year-old child. His name was Jamie. There are also four adults and even a dog. They were all shot, and then incinerated by these guys..." she pounded a fist down on the photo of the two men in suits. "... who came out of the Canadian forests, *here*."

Ojibwe started to shake his head and Rachel pushed back her chair, stood up and lunged forward. "Now look and think again, you fucking little backwater asswipe, before I get *my* boss, to yell the eardrums off *your* boss."

Matt froze, cup in hand, just watching the veins bulge in Rachel's neck as she leaned over Ojibwe. Her eyes were so intense he was expecting rays to be emitted from each of her eyeballs, and the Native American officer to be turned to dust.

Ojibwe returned the gaze for a moment or two before his eyes crinkled at the corners. "Okay, okay, settle down, Agent."

He lifted the picture of the men in suits again. "Like I said, no one up here that looks like this." He bit his lip. "But, there are a few families, and individuals out in the sticks that don't come into the village." He snorted softly. "There's even this old priest, who's been up here for as long as anyone can remember, he's…"

"A priest?" Matt sprang forward. "Where?"

Oscar looked over his shoulder at the map, and then got to his feet. He traced a blue line that was the vein of a river running out into an area that was nothing but green. He tapped it.

"About… *here*." He turned.

Matt was still half in his chair. "Tell me about him."

Oscar went and sat back down, allowing Matt to relax back into his seat. Rachel remained standing.

"Not much to tell." Oscar's shoulders hiked a fraction. "I've been the local constable in these parts for 11 years, but never actually met him. Father Xavier Arvod Bernard is a recluse. He's got to be over 90 by now, I think. Arrived before the Second World War to run a small church for the locals."

"And now?" Rachel's eyes were unblinking.

"And now, no one goes up there anymore as far as I know." Oscar toyed with his cup. "And Father Xavier doesn't come down to us neither. Retired I guess, and the old guy has just fallen off the radar."

"How do you know he's even still alive?" Rachel's brow furrowed. "He might have been dead for years."

"He's alive." Oscar nodded. "Pretty sure."

"Pretty sure is not good enough in a multiple murder investigation." Rachel shot back.

Oscar sighed long and slow, and then lifted his phone, hitting a few numbers and turning away to mumble for a second or two. After a moment he swung back and replaced it, and then got to his feet. "Just give me a minute." Oscar left them in his office.

Matt turned to the FBI agent. "What do you think?"

"It's got my attention." Rachel shoved a hand in her pocket. "This case certainly has some religious aspects to it. A remote priest in an area that we know the killers came from and probably went back to? They've got to be holed up somewhere remote."

Matt blew air through compressed lips. "He's probably been dead for decades, and no one has even bothered checking." He looked over his shoulder to the door Oscar just went through. "My money is on some monumental ass covering about to take place any minute now."

The door opened and Oscar returned with a middle-aged woman. "This is Susan Ohnatua, she delivers the mail, as well as runs our computer systems, filing, and cooks a damn fine steak." He grinned at her, and she returned the same. Oscar then faced Rachel. "Susan, please tell them what you just told me."

Oscar sat down and steepled his fingers. Susan looked at Matt first, then Rachel.

"I deliver the mail to Father Xavier once a week."

"I'm Rachel, may I call you Susan?" The woman nodded enthusiastically. "Thank you, Susan. So I understand you've actually seen the Father then?" Rachel coaxed the nervous-looking woman.

Susan thought for a moment, and then finally shook her head. "I think, *no*, actually never. I deliver his mail to a postbox at the edge of town. The next time I put mail in, the previous delivery has been taken."

"Anyone could have taken it." Rachel raised her eyebrows. "Given Father Xavier is 90 or more, perhaps someone is helping him out. Is that fair to say?"

Susan bobbed her head. "Oh yeah, sure."

"I think we need to head out there for a visit." Matt said. He turned. "Oscar, can you show us the way?"

The Chief Constable looked pained.

Rachel stared from under lowered brows. "Would you like to look at the pictures of the murdered family again?"

Oscar's lips turned down momentarily, but he must have seen Rachel stiffen, and he seemed to deflate a little. "Maybe a few of us could take a run out there." He shrugged. "It's only a few hours, and this time of year, the track is passable."

Rachel looked at her watch. It was still only midday. "No time like the present."

*

Rachel and Matt sat up the front with the chief constable, and sharing the back seat of the SUV were officers Manny Tulimak and Gloria Annaya, two police Oscar had rounded up for their expedition. Both were young, friendly, and had a hundred questions about New York for Matt and Rachel as they drove out into the far-north Canadian forest.

Oscar pulled the SUV to the side of the dirt track as it had ended at an impenetrable-looking wall of tangled green.

"From here, on foot."

Matt went to push open the door.

"Wait." Oscar grabbed his arm, and Matt froze. He then opened the map box between the seats and tossed Matt a small, red spray pump. "Strongest we've got."

Matt looked at the small container: DEET – *diethyltoluamide* – one of the strongest insect killers on the market.

"Oh yeah, the blackfly." Matt screwed his eyes shut and pointed it at his face.

"No, no." Oscar scoffed. "Jesus, you want to go blind? Spray it on your hands and apply it like a lotion."

Rachel looked away from the windscreen. "Hurry up. I'll want some of that when you're done."

Matt sprayed some onto his hand and then smeared it on his forehead, cheeks, and neck. It tingled. "This strength is safe, right?"

"Sure, as long as you neither of you want kids." Oscar stared.

Matt chuckled weakly, and then handed the bottle to Rachel. She followed suit lathering up, and Matt nudged her.

"Stop holding your breath, wimp."

"You mean like you did." She gave Matt a wink and a smile and then handed it over her shoulder to Manny and Gloria when she was finished.

They then pushed open the doors and jumped down. Matt inhaled the scents of the wilderness. It was warm, and, down among the green, it was moist and heavy. The blackfly swarmed, but instead of alighting on their skin the pests stayed a few feet back from their heads like tiny satellites orbiting a planet. There was also the deeper *zumm* of insects, not the tiny whine of the irritating parasites, but more the heavy drone of cicadas and crickets.

Manny walked out a few yards, looking at the forest ground. "Nothing new been through here in a while."

"Is this the only way in and out?" Rachel asked.

"No." Gloria said as she zipped up her tan anorak. "But it's the only track. You'd get lost pretty quick if you didn't know the way."

"C'mon." Oscar headed toward a small opening in the brush.

Rachel and Matt burrowed in behind him, followed by the two young police. The green tunnel only ran for about a hundred feet and then opened out into a pine forest with the odd spruce thrown in. Oscar took them around some of the more densely packed areas, but even where they travelled it seemed it was more pushing through branches than following a trail.

Matt felt trickles of perspiration on his chest and back and would have loved to unzip his jacket, but knew he'd be a human pin cushion within moments, so he sighed and put his head down, ducking under another branch.

Sweat dripped from his nose, and on cue the tiny cloud of blackflies drew in a few inches closer as if knowing that his chemical shield would soon be washed away.

"Fuck it." He hoped Oscar brought the repellent, or he'd be as lumpy as a toad by the time he got back.

"This way." Oscar turned at another densely forested area that had an old post hammered into the ground. Maybe one day, long ago, it had held a sign, but now the directions were embedded in the locals' minds and nowhere else.

The officer pushed aside some spindly bushes that hid an opening between tree trunks. Beyond there was a smaller track, darker, that looked to have split logs as planking embedded into the earth. It looked to Matt like a giant ladder that was being slowly consumed by the forest floor.

From somewhere out in the gloom there was the sound of something heavy moving through the denser brush. Matt caught up beside Rachel. "Hey, are you packing?"

"Packing? What are you from Chicago in the forties?" She snorted softly. "Yes, of course." She nodded toward the tree line. "I hear it; probably a bear or moose."

"Yeah, well, one that's keeping level with us." Matt let his eyes travel again over the odd shapes in the dark forested areas. It was so dense in some places it could have hid a Sherman tank. He could have sworn the sound stopped when they did. He turned to Manny who was staring out to where the sound had come from.

"Hey, did that sound like a bear or moose to you?"

He just shrugged but continued to scan the darker depths of the forest.

They walked on in silence for another hour, sipping water as they went, before Oscar slowed and half-turned to look over his shoulder at them.

"Just up ahead." he whispered.

Matt could tell a hunter's stalk when he saw it and immediately tried to do the same, treading carefully and hunching his shoulders. Matt also saw Rachel had lifted one side of her jacket, exposing the butt of a gun on her hip.

Oscar held up a hand, and then stopped. Matt and Rachel came to each of his shoulders and peered through a curtain of green. There was a church, vastly older than Matt had been expecting. Vines scaled its walls and tree roots lumped up upon its foundations as the forest tried to reclaim it. The stones of the ancient church were blackened with age and overgrown with skins of moss and lichen. The style of architecture looked Romanesque with a single pointed spire and heavy ornate carvings on the stonework.

Behind some of the vines, Matt could see that the windows looked to be lead paneled and might have had colored panes in them. It was impossible to tell with nothing behind them but blackness.

"Father Xavier lives in there?" Matt asked.

"Guess so." Oscar shrugged. "That's the only building out here."

"You said you've never seen him; has anyone seen him that you know of?" Rachel kept her eyes on the church.

Oscar seemed to think a moment before turning to Manny and Gloria. Both shook their heads.

"Maybe old Henry who owns the store, but I'd need to check."

"I'm betting he hasn't either," Rachel responded.

Oscar looked back to the old building. "The priest never bothers anyone so no one bothers him."

"Live and let live, *huh*." Matt pulled in a cheek.

Oscar turned. "Up here, if people want to keep to themselves, we respect that."

"Until those people start beheading citizens, shooting entire families, and burning their bodies." Rachel slid her gun free of its holster. "Draw your weapons, officers, and take the left side of the building. Matt, you stay put for now."

Oscar's expression tightened and his jaw clenched. Matt could tell he wanted to bite back, but to his credit, instead he drew a large service revolver. "Gloria, Manny, with me." He began to edge out along the tree line, doing as Rachel suggested.

Matt crouched, watching and waiting, and keeping a lookout for any potential ambushes. Though he wasn't exactly sure what he could do other than yell a warning.

He watched as the group circled the small building, disappeared around its back, and then met again at the front. The door was a solid timber structure, domed with metal hinges and wrought-iron handles. Rachel put her hand to it and then leaned closer to place an ear against it before pulling back and gently pushing.

Surprisingly, the stout-looking door opened without a sound. Someone had to have been tending to it. If it was as old as it looked, the hinges should have screamed like banshees.

Matt squinted; the dark interior gave nothing away and Rachel looked to Oscar momentarily before darting in fast. Oscar followed, his gun up. Manny and Gloria covered the outside, backs to the wall near the door and watching the forest.

Matt swallowed dryly, waiting as minutes ticked by. He looked over his shoulder at the dark forest behind him, which now seemed to be holding its breath and waiting as well. He scanned the wall of tree trunks and bushes. His neck prickled.

There's nothing there, he thought. *Maybe just a moose or a bear... a little bear, just a cub really.*

He turned back slowly and saw Rachel at the door waving him in. "*Yes.*" He jogged down to meet her. She vanished back in before he got there, followed by Manny and Gloria. Matt went straight in and then paused, waiting a few seconds for his eyes to adjust.

Shapes began to materialize from the gloom. He presumed dust, debris, and maybe even cobwebs, to add to the gothic feel the exterior of the church promised. But as the darkness receded he saw that it was clean, sparse, and bigger than he expected purely because there were no pews, or any church furniture other than a small altar before a larger stained glass window at the rear. In each of the walls there were tiny alcoves with statues depicting the Stations of the Cross.

"I've never been in here before." Oscar's voice sounded almost reverent.

"Old, but looks inhabited," Rachel said from his side.

"Both a church and home." Matt replied as he looked around the walls at some of the script. "Italian by the look of the language."

"Jesuits?" Rachel asked. "Haven't they been coming here for centuries?"

"They have," Matt acknowledged. "But the Jesuits' main focus was on South America, and nowhere near this far north. "I've been in old European structures before, and this looks to be easily that old – 1600s easily."

"400 years?" Oscar whistled.

Matt stood staring up at the window. Though much was overgrown, many of the panels were still illuminated from the weak outside sunlight. There were hallowed saints and apostles and magnificent calligraphic words.

"There's writing, but the panel segments look newer than the entire window – as if they were added in later." He peered at the writing. "*Benedisse la casa di Noè.*" He smiled and nodded. "Of course."

"You want to share?" Rachel asked.

Matt stepped closer. "It means: *blessed house of Noah.*"

"Noah?" Rachel looked around. "Then this must be the place." She pointed. "Got a door here." Rachel was behind the altar. She looked back. "Officer, please tell me you have a flashlight."

Oscar held up a small black mag-light. "Never leave home without it."

"Good man." Rachel waved him over. "On three, two, one…" She then pulled open the small door in the back of the altar. It was more like a trapdoor leading to a cellar. The air that escaped was heavy with fungus and damp, and when Oscar shone his light into it, Matt could see there were albino tree roots like white wire springing from the walls.

"Is it too much to expect a light bulb down there?" Matt crouched, looking into the steep hole. It was about as uninviting a place as he could imagine.

"Might be one down lower, but…" Oscar shone his flashlight up and around inside the church. "Do you see any lights up here? More likely to find candles."

Matt stood and leaned over the altar, snatching at the nub of an old candlestick. "This'll help you."

Oscar held up a small cigarette lighter to the wick. It sputtered for a moment and then caught. He handed it back to Matt, and nodded to the pit.

"Me? I don't think so." Matt shook his head and backed away. "I can't go down there." Matt felt light-headed at the thought of going into the dark, enclosed space. He shivered and crossed his arms.

"What's the matter with you?" Rachel asked, reaching out for him. "You're shaking."

"Yeah, I got this thing about going into caves. I've had some bad experiences before." Matt tried to push down memories of ice caves, and things that hid in the dark. "I'll wait here with Oscar."

"We'll go together, okay?" Rachel pulled him closer. "I need you."

He stared down into the dark pit. He felt his breath quicken and his throat constrict. He couldn't do it. But then how could he let Rachel go down by herself?

"It's fine if you really don't want to." She held onto him. "Neither do I."

Their eyes met and they held each other's gaze for a long moment. He drew strength from her and Matt felt his breathing slow and come back under control. He exhaled and straightened. He took Rachel's hand and squeezed it. "I can do it."

Rachel smiled. "I'll be with you. We'll be fine."

With a final squeeze, she released Matt's hand and then took the flashlight from Oscar. "Matt, you follow me. Oscar, you and the officers stay here and cover our asses."

Oscar grunted his assent and then crouched beside the open door. Rachel moved the beam of light around in the hole, before heading down fast. Matt took a deep breath, and then followed her, carefully holding up the candle.

They descended about ten feet below the floor of the church and found themselves in a single square room. Without their lights, it would have been as dark as hell. The walls were of the same stone as the walls of the church, but this was more than just foundation stone, it seemed carefully constructed as a special basement.

Matt wrinkled his nose. It smelled like old earth – *graveyard earth*, he thought morbidly. Matt held up the candle and turned slowly. There was a table with one lonely chair and a single cupboard. Rachel crossed to it and pulled the door open.

"Tools." There were chisels, hammers, and other metal implements. "Looks like Father Xavier was a real handyman. Might have been doing his own repairs to the church."

"Makes sense; can't exactly get a team in and out of here in a hurry." Matt looked up at the ceiling, trying not to imagine it pressing down on him. He swallowed. "And this place has been here for centuries, so if he didn't maintain it, it would have collapsed in on itself a hundred years ago."

He put the candle down on the table and watched Rachel pace around the small room. She turned to Matt and hiked her shoulders. "Gotta be something we missed."

"We did." He pointed at the candle on the table. The flame was bending away from one of the walls. He picked it up and carefully carried it to the solid-looking stonework. He waved it across the rough-hewn surface, and at one of the edges, the flame danced back toward him.

"Something behind here."

Rachel grabbed a long chisel and one of the metal hammers from the cupboard. "Well then, lucky they left me the FBI house keys." She hefted the tools.

"Wait a second." Matt held out the candle to her. "Just hold this for a moment and keep the light on me."

She set the tools down on the table and held the flashlight and candle in each hand. "You got five minutes, and then I'm coming through."

Matt turned back to the wall, and started to press along the edges, of the individual stones. There was no give, no cracks, edges or seams that he could feel. He stood back. "Hold the light up, will you?"

He stood back a step. "*Ha!*" In the corner there was one brick that was slightly lighter in color than its surrounding brothers and sisters – exactly as if it was the only one that was being rubbed by years of touch. He reached up and pushed it. There was a grinding noise and a click, and then the wall panel clanked open an inch.

"Not just a pretty face." Rachel grinned and held up a hand as he went to drag it open. "Hold it." She handed him back his candle, and pulled her revolver again, holding it and the flashlight up and aiming at the hidden door. She stood to the side and then nodded as Matt grabbed the edge of the stone door and eased it open.

*

In the labyrinth of dark rooms the stonework was vastly more ancient that that of the church. In many areas the tunnels appeared to be carved out of the bare rock. The darkness was complete and it was as still and silent as a tomb. Matt felt his heart rate pick up and he took a few steadying breaths. Curiously, there was some basic furniture in some of the rooms.

"I think this is where Father Xavier lived," Matt said.

"No foundation stones; it's just caves down here." Rachel stood in the doorway of one of the rooms, moving her light around inside.

"I think these caves were here long before the church was built," Matt breathed.

"They built the church on top of them?" She turned slowly. "And I think more than just the priest lived here." She turned back to him. "Looks like quite a few people have been coming and going. Do you think Officer Ojibwe knew?"

"*Nah.*" Matt sorted through some papers. "I believe him when he said he'd never been out here." He opened a cupboard and on a shelf inside was a heavy metal box about two feet, by one. "Hello." It wasn't a safe, more a strong box. It was wrapped in a chain and padlock as big as his fist.

"What have you got?" Rachel asked.

"A locked box." He grabbed it and rattled it. "But still strong; let's see if we can find a key." He lifted the box to the ground and then crossed to an old chest of drawers. "Hey, we…" He was just in time to see Rachel swing a large hammer down on the lock – once, twice, and the third time her teeth were bared and the hammer came down from above her shoulder. The chain shattered and fell away.

"I'm guessing that's the way your solve all your problems?" He grinned.

She dropped the hammer. "Why do you think I'm still single?"

"You okay down there?" Oscar's voice carried down the steps and along the dark passageways.

"Yeah, we got this." Rachel yelled back over her shoulder. She turned and nodded toward the box. "After you."

Matt crouched before the strong box. If there was one thing about his work he loved, it was being the first to find some artifact, document, or object from the past. It was a window into another time that had been lost amid the centuries.

He slowly lifted the lid and it creaked satisfyingly. He recognized the smell immediately and loved it – antique, ancient, old ink and paper. It was what someone who dealt in ancient languages lived for. He reached in and lifted one of the documents.

Rachel knelt beside him and dived a hand in. She lifted rolls and folded papers, some wrapped with ribbon and others wax sealed. "Shit, it's all in different languages."

Matt jiggled his eyebrows. "Well then, lucky you brought a linguist." He lifted a sheaf of paper. "Here we are – Father Xavier Arvod Bernard – came here in 1945, following the death of his predecessor, and former ward of this parish, Father Phillip Duran Leurant, who… er… came here in 1869." He read the details, and the lifted another, this one even older. "Father Gerard Francis Bartolone was here before him, presiding over the church for 75 years, and before that..." Matt picked up several more documents, quickly looking at each. "This is weird. Each priest comes for around three quarters of a century, and then dies in the job. No one ever goes home."

"Talk about a job for life," Rachel said.

"But that's just it. I know church rules, and they're supposed to go home before frailty takes them. And did none of them ever get sick? Miraculously, they all managed to hand the baton over on the day of their death." He looked at more of the documents. "The previous priest dies, and then *hallelujah*, we got the new guy already standing at the door."

Rachel took some of the papers from him, looking closely at each. She *hmmd*, and then handed them back. "I'm no expert, but I have worked in document forensics before, and in my opinion, all those signatures look remarkably similar – the cursive loops, curls, and strokes of the letters. Could be fakes." She straightened. "And you know what else is missing?"

Matt looked up at her. "What?"

"If all those priests are dying out here, where are the graves? Where's the crypt or cemetery?"

Matt remembered the thick undergrowth. "Could be lost in the brush; it's pretty dense out there."

"Yeah, maybe you're right." She waved it away. "It's not important. The key thing is to find out where Father Xavier is right now." She pointed. "Keep looking."

Matt dove back in. He sifted through more documents, with more signatures. He lifted several. "Hold that light closer."

Rachel stood over him as he brought the papers close together. Father Xavier Arvod Bernard, Phillip Duran Leurant, Gerard Francis Bartolone, and another for Father Claude Alain Piccard, who took up residence in 1720.

Matt stared – Rachel was right, the signatures did look the same. But where she had suggested they might be fake, his imagination took him in another direction. A hermit-like uninterrupted line of priests, hidden away up here in the remote forest with the same hand writing, same signature – but what if it wasn't a line of *different* priests, but the *same* priest just pretending to die and become someone else to avoid attracting attention. Father Xavier was Laurent, who was Bartolone who was Piccard, and on and on. His mind whirled.

It was impossible, preposterous, but then there was Clarence van Helling who had wandered out of the forest looking not a day over 35 when he was closer to 115. *Madness*, he thought.

"You okay?" Rachel watched him.

"Yeah, yeah, fine." He continued to pull material from the box.

He could feel Rachel's eyes on him, and she reached out to place a hand on his shoulder. "You think of something, you tell me." Her fingers gripped a little tighter for a moment before she released him. "I'm going to take another look around – keep at it."

He nodded, and dug in again, finding Bibles in various languages. In one there was an old black and white photograph of a serious-looking young man in a cassock. There was a large silver crucifix around his neck with some sort of polished stone at its center. He turned it over, but there was no date or name. He flipped it back to study the face. There was something recognizable about the features – strong jawline, thick dark eyebrows overhanging the darkest eyes Matt had ever seen. The gaze was confident to the point of bordering on being imperious. Matt was sure he'd looked into those dark eyes before.

"Is that you, Xavier?" He wiped its surface. "Or maybe it's *all* of you." Matt used his sleeve on his brow, and then stuck the photograph in a side pocket.

"*Matt, get in here.*"

Matt sprang to his feet and rushed into one of the side rooms. It was like a smaller chapel or prayer room, little more than a stone box with an alcove and a statue of Jesus Christ on the cross. There was a single flat stool used for kneeling before it. Matt jumped as he caught sight of something that definitely should not have been there – a pile of clothing and the sharp sticks of bones jumbled in among it. It all looked partially incinerated.

Matt sniffed. "I can still smell carbon – this happened recently." He knelt beside the pile. The skull had rolled to the side but was still scorched. He traced one of the arms to the end. "Left hand is missing."

"Removed?" Rachel also knelt.

Matt shook his head, as he lifted the blackened bones. "Nope, the nub is rounded, so healed. He lost this long ago." He shrugged "Something to go on."

"It's a start." Rachel turned the darkened skull over and then lifted it. She stared into the empty sockets for a moment and flipped it over so she could finger the back. Matt saw there was still a portion of vertebrae dangling from its rear.

She rubbed her thumb and finger together. "This has been severed." She squinted down at the ground, and then moved her light around on the stones. "And what's all this shit?"

Matt lowered his candle, which was now just a nub in his fingers. Near the skull there were tracks in the dust, like where tiny snakes had squirmed away. They ended in dried thread like things.

"Some sort of worm, a carrion eater I assume." Matt pulled back.

"*Yech.*" Rachel dropped the skull on the pile. "They look like they came out of the corpse and tried to make a run for it." Rachel fished in her pocket and retrieved a penknife and an evidence bag that she shook open.

Using the knife, she scraped some of the dried worms into the bag and sealed it.

Matt pulled at the dark cloth. "Could be a priest's tunic – his cassock." There was the tinkle of metal, and Matt lifted more of the burned cloth and found a silver crucifix on a heavy silver chain. The stone set at its center was the deepest red. "Probably a ruby, not theft then. And look…"

He dug out the picture and showed it to her. "The same crucifix."

Her mouth turned down. "Could be but don't assume anything. Might also just be the order they came from."

"Yeah, true." He stood, hanging onto the crucifix. "This is exactly like what happened to Clarence van Helling."

Rachel also got to her feet. "But is *this* Father Xavier, or did Xavier do this?" She stepped back a little from more of the thread-like trails on the ground. "I bet there are no dental records, no DNA and certainly no prints anywhere to identify old boney here. We have no way to really find out who it is."

Matt toed the bones. "Do you know what taphonomy is?"

She gave him a bored look. "No, Matthew, I do *not* know what taphonomy is. Please tell me… if it's relevant."

"It's the study of what happens to bodies over time; especially the bones." He sniffed again. "The soil out here is quite acidic, and there's moisture in the air. Those two things alone should have meant over time the bones should have degraded down to nothing. But the sort of age darkening on the bones of this guy, excluding the incineration marks, only happens over the high hundreds or more like thousands of years."

"But the cut looks recent. Why cut the head off an already dead body?" Rachel queried.

"Or were the…" Matt stopped himself. "*Nah*, that's dumb."

"It probably is, but tell me anyway." She held the light in his face.

"I was going to say, what if the guy was old? I mean far older than we can imagine, and the bones were already like that – *inside him*."

She stared for a moment, and then rolled her eyes. "Yeah, that doesn't really help."

Matt looked back down at the bones. "I've got a feeling we won't be meeting Father Xavier any time soon." He looked up into her face. "Dead end."

Rachel lowered her flashlight. "There's nothing more we can do here. Let's go."

As she left, he noticed she had reholstered her weapon, but had the holster unclipped and ready for fast draw. Matt followed her but paused at the door and looked back into the small crypt-like room. In his work he knew ancient rooms like this had seen magnificent things, secret things, and usually wanted to talk via the clues they left.

Matt let his eyes wander over the tiny cave-like room. Everything in here was brought in and not as old as the room itself. He walked to each object, touching it and running his hands over the edges, looking for hinges, hidden drawers or even levers. He stopped before the statue of Christ on the Cross, and then reached up to let his hands move slowly over its edges. It was on a panel of dark age-pocked wood, and he dug his fingers in beside it – it popped open.

"Bingo."

He carefully eased it wider, immediately smelling an earthy fish-like aroma. It was like a larder inside, but there looked to have been only one thing stored – shelves of small clay bottles, now all smashed. Matt picked up one of the shards – it was an ancient design, no writing or markings at all, but he recognized the clay firing and handle shapes that were predominantly used in the Middle East and North Africa millennia ago.

He sniffed the shard, thinking there might have been some sort of rare home brew stored in them. "*Phew*." He jerked away – it smelled of dank water and rotting fish, but he held onto it. Slowly he looked back at the fragment, and saw the spots of moisture. Matt stared, unable to take his eyes off it. His mouth tingled, then his entire body started to crave the fluid. Before he knew what he was doing he was bringing it to his lips…

"Hurry up," Rachel called from outside.

Shit! He jumped at her voice, and it made him refocus. He tossed the shard back into the closet sized space. He went to close the panel, but paused. He let his eyes run over the tiny room's interior – what was odd was that this hidden area held no food, no gold, weapons, or anything that might have been of value. *Unless it had already been taken*, he wondered. He pushed the door shut and then headed out to join Rachel.

They climbed back out into the main church to find Oscar leaning against one of the walls. "Anything?"

"Bones, some biological traces, and papers which we'll take back to the labs for analysis." Rachel exhaled through compressed lips. "Hey, do you know if there's a cemetery around here? Like where they would bury the old priests?"

Oscar shook his head. "Nope, we got one on the outskirts of town, but no priests there I know of."

Matt walked to the stained glass window again. The outside light had shifted and now illuminated more of the different panels, giving it a 3D effect. From what he could see the workmanship looked exquisite, but some parts were still lost in darkness.

He read again the words he could make out. "*Benedisse la casa di Noè* – Blessed house of Noah." He stared at the huge window. "This is all connected; I'm sure of it."

Rachel joined him. "It's very detailed."

"They were meant to be," Matt said. "The stained glass windows in churches were for more than just decoration. They were designed to tell a story."

"A picture's worth a thousand words?" Rachel asked.

"Exactly. They became hugely popular during the middle ages. You imagine several hundred years ago, when there were no computers, television, or even electric light and you're in a church with a window like this, the filtered light pouring through creating a jewel-like effect – it'd be an almost mystical experience."

"Cartoons for the masses." Rachel half-smiled.

"You're more right than you know. Back then most people couldn't read. But as religion was an important part of daily life, stories were told in the glass. All the way back in the 6th century, Pope Gregory strongly urged artists to paint Biblical scenes on church walls to educate the public. Then in the 11th century, the Synod of Arras transferred the idea to glass. It basically enables illiterate people to learn what books cannot teach them."

Oscar folded his arms. "And what does this one say?"

Matt stepped back a few paces. "It's not typical." He saw there were images of water, an ocean, and great cliffs or a mountain range. Animals of many varieties, as well as thick forests, but there were trees and ferns unlike he had seen in these parts.

"Oscar, those plants, do you recognize them?"

"Nope," he said. "Nothing like that around here – looks more like a jungle to me."

Matt nodded. "You're right, but now imagine this place around the time of the window being created – say four centuries ago."

Oscar pursed his lips. "Nope again, this place has been unchanged for thousands, not hundreds of years."

Matt sighed. "Okay, it was just an idea."

"Maybe it was something the artists just made up." Rachel stepped forward. "Fanciful design and all that."

"No, I don't buy that. These windows take years to create and were damned expensive. And though they are certainly stylized, it is all around some central theme or message. I'm just not seeing it." Matt sighed. "But Oscar's right; it does kinda look more like a jungle. The answer is there somewhere."

"You mean a hidden message?" Oscar grinned. "Be better when the sun gets on it."

"Yeah, it probably would be…" Matt spun, thunderstruck by an idea. "*Hey.*"

Rachel's eyebrows went up. "What?"

"That's it: *the sun.*" Matt said, grinning. "Not the son, as in *son* of God, but the sun, as in sunshine. Remember what Eleanor said Clarence kept repeating?" He bounced on his toes. "He said, "the sun shall show the way"."

Rachel nodded, and Matt turned back to the window. "So, we need the sun."

"Or at least more light," Rachel said.

"There's a message there," Matt said. "But a message only seen and recognized by those needing to see it." He turned to Rachel. "Hey, I don't suppose we can get this window back to a lab?"

Oscar snorted. "No way, mister. You're not digging this out and flying off with it."

Matt turned to Rachel who shrugged. "You'd need to give me some pretty compelling reasons to get an order for that."

"It's not happening," Oscar concluded.

Matt stared back up at the glass. "In that case, I need to get detailed pictures. It's heavily overgrown outside, and I can't make out all the panels. Oscar, can you please go and clear away some of the brush from the exterior?"

Oscar looked hard at him, his lips turned down.

"Please," Matt implored.

Rachel turned to Oscar and shrugged noncommittally. "Humor him."

The officer groaned and headed for the door, muttering as he went. He turned to Manny. "Stop grinning, you can help. Come on."

Manny also groaned and followed.

Gloria waved at her colleague as she watched the pair vanish around the corner.

Rachel came and took Matt's arm. "You know, if there's one thing that small town police guys live for, it's being ordered around by big city folk."

Matt scoffed. "I didn't order him around. And besides as soon as we're done, the sooner we're outta his hair."

In a few moments he saw the outline of some vines being roughly yanked away from the window. More light shone through. He cupped his mouth. "Atta boy, Oscar."

More branches came away, allowing extra light to shine through. Matt stepped back, pulling out his phone. There were now glowing purples, greens, the deepest reds, and sea-blue. The work was magnificent.

"Wow, so beautiful." Gloria said as she stared up at the glass.

"*There*, more writing; what does it say?" Rachel turned to him.

"Not Italian this time, but Chaldaic again – the language of Adam and Eve, and Noah." Matt concentrated. "Weird; it talks of a place – *Akebu-Lan* – it's a very ancient name for the Garden of Eden that far predates the Bible."

Rachel shrugged. "Well, what better place to talk about Adam and Eve than in a church."

"No, no, you don't understand. Talking about it here is fine. But talking about it in Chaldaic doesn't make sense. It's like using code – no one has written or spoken it for thousands of years."

Matt had a thought, remembering the broken bottles downstairs – they were like supplies. "This place, the message designed for a select few, and the stores. It reminded me of what Oscar told us of the supply huts in the wilderness. You came here for directions or supplies."

He pointed up at the window. "But this makes no sense. This panel was designed *not* to be read or even understood by normal people coming in here."

Rachel folded her arms. "I've heard in ancient Greek paintings the artists sometimes inserted hidden jokes and even insults about their wealthy patrons. Is this like that?"

"Well done." Matt grinned at her. "And maybe it's *just* like that." Matt stared up at the magnificent window. "Hiding a coded reference to the Garden of Eden. Why? To keep it secret? And why in this remote place? I don't get it."

Matt looked from Rachel to Gloria.

"Never seen it before." The officer said evenly.

"Few have, I bet." Matt said. "But I know it's all connected somehow." He turned to Rachel. "And the jungle or forests." He tapped his foot. "We know that the climate was warmer and wetter around the time of Noah – remember this was about 2500 to 2750 years BCE – that's nearly 5,000 years ago."

"I remember hearing that even Egypt was very green at the time of the first Pharaohs." She shook her head. "I can't imagine it."

Matt took more photographs of the window. "Yep,' the climate has been changing ever since we had an atmosphere. One day Egypt and the entire Middle East might be green again. We tiny mammalian specks just need to get used to the climate changing one way, and then back the other."

Another huge branch came away from the window, displaying a new section of colored glass panels. Matt took a picture and then lowered the phone camera.

"Ladies and gentlemen, I give you, *the Ark*."

In the corner of the glass there was an unmistakeable boat structure dwarfing the animals and humans surrounding it.

It was a squat-looking craft with no windows and solid ribs running up its sides. Matt concentrated on the dark glass – just away from the Ark, there seemed to be a group of figures kneeling before a pile of stones or very crude statue of something. And close to it, a giant, yellow-eyed figure, pointing.

"What are you trying to tell us?" Matt whispered.

In the opposite corner and along the bottom were hues of green, brown, and blue, all intesected by lines. It seemed more for design and Matt went back to marvelling at the Ark.

Gloria gaped. "I can't believe this has been hidden here the whole time."

Rachel frowned. "The animals are coming off but that doesn't look like any sort of mountaintop to me."

Matt walked slowly forward. "Genesis 8:1–19 – In the seventh month, on the seventeenth day of the month, the Ark rested upon the mountains of Ararat." He turned. "But the thing is, the Bible was not written in one specific year or in a single location. In fact, the first Bible entries were set down around 3000 years ago, with some parts even attributed to Moses and are commonly called the Pentateuch – the five scrolls. But Noah lived long before this. And believe me, as a language historian, I know time has a way of vastly changing stories and history."

Rachel looked up at the window. "So the Ark landing site, may be wrong?" The light moved again across its panels making the image dance and move.

An idea began to form in his mind. He looked from the picture on his phone to the window and then back again. He focussed on the area that he at first thought was just artistic design. "That section in the corner, you know what it reminds me of? The part image on the phone from the murdered families – the lines and contours make me think this might be a map." He grimaced, impatience gnawing at him as Oscar still had some window panels to clear.

Matt pointed. "And are they knights?" Dressed in black tunics, standing before the jungle and swords in hands stood a group of tall men. "Some sort of guard?"

"And what's with the yellow-eyed giant?" Rachel asked.

"Maybe they're pilgrims," Gloria suggested.

"Who knows; hard to make it out clearly. It's still too dark," Rachel observed.

Matt squinted up at the scene. "I don't know, the light is there, but I think it's more that the glass itself is black." He tilted his head. "What do you see?"

She folded her arms. "The boat, an Ark, sitting in water I think, but surrounded by a forest or jungle." She pulled in a cheek and her forehead furrowed. "I can see beams of light, but it seems to be nighttime."

"Could the beams mean a holy light – the radiance of God, maybe?" Matt sighed. "Sometimes you have to try and get inside the head of the author or artist, and try and…"

Two rapid gunshots – loud and close by. Followed by several more.

"*Shit!*" Matt ducked.

"Get down," Gloria yelled as she crouched. "Stay here." She was up and sprinting for the door.

"Wait!" Rachel yelled after her.

Gloria went through the door, flinging it shut behind her. Almost immediately there was gunfire, lots of it. Bullet holes appeared in the door and could be heard striking the sandstone facade of the church.

Then like they had all been dropped into the vacuum of space, there was a moment of total silence.

"Hey…?" Rachel raised her head, just as a long and haunting moan seemed to emanate from all around them.

"What the hell was that?" Matt asked. "It sounded li…"

His words froze in his mouth. The scream was long and sounded excruciatingly painful. It was cut off completely just as something enormously heavy thumped into the side of the church, making dust rain down on them.

The scream came again, this time in agony, and this time from a different throat. But Matt still couldn't tell whether it was torn from a man or woman, such was its inhuman quality.

Rachel spun, teeth bared and already holding her weapon. She held up a hand in front of his face. "You stay here." She turned for the door.

"Not a chance." Matt started to follow, when there was a sound like a trumpet blast.

Time seemed to slow, and Matt somehow knew what was coming next. He leapt at Rachel, grabbing her and covering her with his body as the entire stained glass window exploded inwards, showering the room with millions of razor-sharp projectiles.

He shuddered from the pain and could feel the hot blood running from the back of his head and where his neck was exposed.

Rachel rolled over and knelt, holding her gun out and scanning the area before looking back down at him. She immediately saw the blood running down over his face.

"Jesus, Matt; stay still." She pulled a handkerchief from a pocket and held it to his neck.

Matt also knelt. The pain was exquisite. "Are you okay?" he asked.

"Stay still," Rachel said urgently. "Yeah, me, I'm fine, thanks to you." She gently wiped his face. "I owe you one."

From behind, more of the window frame fell in, and Matt spun back to see something that made his stomach sink.

There was a shape in the now-open frame. It was huge, misshapen and, given that the window was 12 feet up from the ground, gigantic. Yellow softball-sized eyes set in a grotesque head fixed on him. Matt felt his heart begin to smash in his chest.

"We gotta get the hell out of here." Rachel's voice was high as she grabbed him and started to wrench him up.

The thing moaned, long and low, and the sound conjured images of an ancient world that was inhabited by beings that were far older than mankind. Horrifyingly, it then started to come through, tearing out bricks and lifting itself up.

Matt scrambled backwards on his heels and palms.

"Loo... look...!"

Rachel screamed at him. "Out, now!"

The thing had heaved its body up, monstrous shoulders pushed in through the frame. A sudden thought came to him. He screamed the words in the oldest of languages – Chaldaic. He invoked the one name that he could think of, an ancient one, for *God*.

"In the name of *Yhvh*, I command you to stop!"

The figure paused. The yellow orbs remained staring, and a huge maw opened uttering a low moan that spoke of pain and sorrow and an eternity of suffering and servitude. It tilted its head, and seemed to be sniffing – *sniffing Matt*.

"In the name of *Yhvh*, I command you to be gone!"

Matt felt the waves of confusion coming off the thing, as it seemed frozen in indecision – either by what it heard or what it smelled.

Rachel lunged at him, dragging him, and he flipped over. His legs began to move at double speed. Rachel still had him by the shoulder, and together they dove for the doorway, flying through it and rolling onto the grass and dirt outside.

"Shut the door, shut the door." Matt rolled over and did it himself, kicking back hard to slam the heavy wooden slab. He scrambled backwards, keeping his eyes on the closed door.

Rachel was up on her feet, gun up, and pointed at the corner of the building, where Oscar had disappeared.

Matt also leapt to his feet and wiped his head. Glass came free, and he then felt his neck and scalp; they were still wet, but didn't sting anymore. In fact, tracing them with his fingertips, he couldn't feel any cuts either. *Maybe it was the shock more than anything else*, he thought.

"We've got to find the others." Rachel was crouching and scanning the undergrowth. "*Oh shit.*"

Matt followed her gaze. "No, no, no." He ran to the sprawled figure.

Gloria lay on the grass, arms wide and a neat black hole in the center of her forehead. Rachel knelt beside her and placed fingers lightly on the policewoman's neck. It was a useless gesture as even Matt could see from where he stood the spreading pool of thick red soaking into the damp grass beneath her skull.

Rachel looked up over the clearing and her mouth set in a hard line. The small expanse they had crossed to get to the church's front door was now littered with bodies.

Matt briefly marveled at the shooting prowess of the Fort Severn officer, until he took a few steps closer.

They were bodies of men, probably. They wore black clothing, that immediately took Matt back to the figure racing toward his car just before the grenade attack. But any other distinguishing features had been obliterated. It looked like they had either fallen from an airplane or been run over by a steamroller.

"What the hell happened here?" he whispered.

Rachel stood slowly, "Something bad." She held her gun in both hands. "Leave them. Let's find Oscar and Manny."

"Yeah, yeah." Matt backed away. He looked down one last time at Gloria in her tan anorak. Her face was calm, as if she was just sleeping. Whatever had happened out here, she had seemed to have gotten off lightly.

Rachel scuttled to the side corner of the church and slammed her back to the stones, peeking around. She half-turned back to him.

"Get over here."

Matt followed, all his senses keen to any sight, sound or sensation, but there was nothing but silence. Even the insects and few birds they had previously heard now seemed to have given the place a wide berth. He eased up beside her.

Rachel peeked around again, and then turned to him, her face pale and eyes wide.

"What the hell was that thing?"

"I'm not sure." He grimaced.

"This is bullshit." She shook her head as if to clear it. "Must have been a trick of the light."

He pursed his lips. "Sure, that must have been what it was. The same trick of the light thing that killed all those people out front."

Rachel went around the back of the church, and Matt followed close by. Behind the building there were trees right up to the brickwork – spruce, some pine, and a few other rambling bushes covered in dark berries. Oscar and Manny had been doing a fine job of pulling branches away to let the light in, with piles of shrubbery stacked to the side.

But the men were gone, and all Matt could find was Oscar's large knife lying in among the grass.

"Oscar!" He called and the waited. "Manny!" Matt was about to do it again when Rachel grabbed his shoulder and jerked him back, and then put a finger to her lips.

She mouthed *wait here*, and then began to crab-walk along the side of the building for a while, choosing her steps to avoid any noise.

She froze, and then straightened. "*Ah…*"

Matt rushed over. "What is it? Did you find them?"

She grimaced. "I think so." She had her gun in a two-handed grip, pointed down, as she scanned the undergrowth.

Matt looked down at the bodies of the police officers. "Oh god." He remembered seeing a dog hit by a truck once.

The big wheels went over it, all of them – the dog's body was mangled and crushed flat.

"Just like the men out front," Matt breathed.

"Worse," Rachel added scanning the brush.

He frowned – she was right – the two men were somehow intertwined, pulverized together so completely that it was hard to tell where one started and the other ended.

Oscar and Manny were pressed back into the wall and just under the broken window. Their skulls looked like flattened plates, and their torsos were a red mess of conjoined flesh with shreds of uniform material running through it. Pools of blood and other bodily fluids had drained from them into the soil and also stained the old brickwork.

"Oscar's gun." Matt saw that his arm lay out to the side, the revolver was still in his hand, but the barrel bent.

Rachel turned to look at him. "You think that creature did this?"

"You mean that trick of the light we both saw?" He immediately regretted it, as he could see the FBI woman was scared witless. So was he. "Sorry."

"That moan – the noise that thing made. It occurred just as the windows exploded in on us." Rachel crouched beside the body. "You're a scientist; what could it have been?"

"Hey, I'm a paleolinguist, I specialize in old languages so I'm guessing here. It could be some kind of guardian. It might have been guarding Father Xavier." He pointed. "These guys looks like they were run over by an 18-wheeler – several times. You're the cop. You tell me what *you* think happened?"

"Calm the hell down." She looked from the forest line back to the bodies. "And keep a lookout."

Matt nodded jerkily and also scanned the wall of green surrounding them. The trees were too close together and threw too many shadows for him to see any more than ten feet past the brush line. There could have been a herd of elephants hidden behind them for all he knew.

Rachel began to feel the ruined skin of the face and neck of one of the men, Matt couldn't tell which anymore. *A waste of time*, he thought, given the entire head was now like a gruesome pancake. That thought made bile jump to his throat. That, and what she was now doing.

"Please tell me you're not feeling for a pulse again."

"Of course not." She pressed some more. "It takes around 520 pounds of force to crush a human skull. Whatever did this was not done by human hands." She winced, wiping her fingers on the grass. "But there's no real impact abrasions, on either of them, and I can't see any weapon marks. It's like they were…" She brought her fingers together into a tight fist. "… grabbed and mashed together. We need to look around."

"What? The hell we do." Matt looked back at the bodies at their feet. "Rachel, remember when I said we needed backup? Now more than ever." He pointed at Oscar and Manny. "C'mon, be sensible… *look*!"

Her eyes flicked down for a second. "They were police officers and gave their lives for their job, for us. I owe it to them to find out what happened. If we leave now, we may never know."

Rachel stood and wandered around the flattened area. She crouched and put her fingers into some tracks sunk into the soil. "Look." The impressions were big, deep, two toed, and the ends sunk down like it had massive claws. She looked up at him. "Maybe a bear – a big one."

"I'm no hunter, but that was no freaking bear," Matt said softly.

From somewhere out in the tangle of forest there came a low moan, and then a deep thump like a tree was being pushed over or maybe something heavy taking a step.

Rachel got slowly to her feet, her eyes on the tree line. Matt could see doubt forming in her eyes.

"You got everything you need?" Matt scanned the trees.

Rachel continued to stare, her eyes wide. "Three officers down, and we're not sure whether we found Father Xavier or not. We got dead guys scattered all over out front, and we just got attacked by some giant...*thing*." She turned, her eyes burning. "So, all up, no, in fact, we've got fuck all."

"No, we have more information than that." Matt straightened. "We just need to decipher it. The past always leaves us clues, calls to us. We just need to understand what it's saying."

Rachel licked her lips, and refused to turn away from the trees.

"I got a bad feeling, Rachel. Things could get a lot worse; c'mon, let's go home." Matt reached a hand out and grabbed her sleeve.

Large drops of icy rain started to blink down around them. Rachel looked up at the low, iron-gray clouds, as the few drops turned into many.

"Well, that's just perfect." She let him turn her away from the trees, and then followed him.

Chapter 8

Washington airspace

Rachel sat up front with the pilot, having left Matt to himself in the cabin of the noisy aircraft. She knew they were lucky to be leaving at all. At this point in time, the local rangers were still scouring the area for more clues. She and Matt had had to give their depositions in separate rooms to see if they married up – luckily they had, even though it made no sense. And that was after she got Matt to leave out the bit about the thing that had tried to force its way into the church.

It had taken significant pressure from her boss' boss to get them out as the local guys refused to believe they knew nothing about the killing of Oscar, Manny, and Gloria, the destruction of the church, the battered strangers all in black, or the beheaded skeleton in the basement. Rachel snorted softly – why the hell would they believe them? She certainly wouldn't have when they swore they saw and knew nothing. Which as far as she was concerned was basically true.

While they had waited for more back-up, Rachel had examined a few of the black-clad men who had attacked the church. Even though they were crushed beyond use for any mug shot or driver's license ID, or even to make use of dental records anymore, she had seen telltale signs of a professional unit.

Their clothing looked identical to the pictures of the men who had attacked Clarence van Helling. She'd attempted to take fingerprints, but they came up blank – the physical lines, swirls and whorls had all been removed, most probably using acid peel, she bet. When she had ripped the shirt of one open, she had seen an image of crossed keys had been seared into the skin. It was the same on all of them. She had used her phone to take a few pictures.

Rachel exhaled long and slow. She'd already talked to her area chief and now she needed to make one more call – to Eleanor van Helling. Dear Eleanor had been pressuring everyone short of the President of the United States about getting updates. The pushy old woman was determined to get answers, and she was damn well going to make sure she got them from Rachel, or else. When you worked in the FBI, one thing you found out very early on – downward pressure worked. And it was working on Rachel.

She made the connection, and got the weird maid, Greta, on the second ring.

"Field Agent Rachel Bromilow for Mrs. van Helling."

"Yes."

Rachel ground her teeth. "Yes, well, *get her.*" *Personality of a dead-fish*, she thought, as she waited for another few moments. The phone sounded like it was being juggled momentarily.

"Agent Bromilow, Rachel, so nice to hear from you. And so happy to hear you're safe, after all that unpleasantness."

Normally Rachel might have assumed Eleanor was talking about the grenade attack outside of her building, but Rachel could tell Eleanor was somehow already aware of the brutal deaths in the Fort Severn wilderness. She looked at her watch; it had been four hours since they had departed, but only 20 minutes since she had spoken to her superiors. This was one seriously tuned-in woman.

"Thank you, Mrs. van Helling. We're still about three hours out from landing. We'll be heading directly into the office for a formal debrief, and then after that hopefully we can..."

"*No!*"

Rachel recoiled. The old woman's voice came like a slap.

"Do *not* make me wait for all that bureaucratic piffle. Tell me what you've found, *now.*"

Rachel sighed. *What did it matter*, she thought. Her boss would tell her anyway.

"Very well, but this is all very confidential..."

There was a derisive snort over the line.

Rachel continued. "... we can't be sure, but I believe we might have found evidence linking a group who attacked us at the church and the men who killed your husband."

"What evidence?" The old woman's voice took on a sharp edge.

'Well, they were dressed similarly to the men who attacked and killed Clar...your husband."

There was a groan over the line. "That is what the FBI classes as evidence now – similar dress sense?" Eleanor sighed theatrically.

"No, Mrs. van Helling." Rachel's jaw clenched momentarily. "We also think they might have killed the priest who was living there, we found some remains and though there's no positive ID yet, I'm confident it was him."

"Was he like...?"

"Yes, he, *the body*, had been decapitated and then burned up, just like your husband, but..."

"But what?" The voice cut across her.

"We found some anomalies, other specimens, that we've collected. We need to get back to the office and have the labs

analyze what we've found. We don't have much I'm afraid."
Rachel sat back in her seat.

"You certainly don't, Agent Bromilow. And it seems someone is removing all your clues and witnesses faster than you can get to them. One step ahead of you, all the way. This is very disappointing." The old woman sighed impatiently. "Anything else interesting, *hmm?*"

Rachel thought about telling her of the huge apparition that tried to break into the church and probably obliterated the police officers, but knew that would be impossible to explain.

"Nothing else for now," Rachel said quickly.

"Nothing else... *for now?*" Eleanor waited.

Rachel stared out through the window. "We're on it, Mrs. van Helling."

"On it, but you seem to be disappointingly late every time. I think you need help." The voice was steel hard.

"No, we got this." Rachel checked her watch again.

"But I disagree, my dear. In fact, I don't think you've *got it,* at all. This is far too important for bureaucratic protocol, rules, or people's egos to get in the way. Consider it more resources for you. We'll speak again soon, Field Agent."

The line went dead, and Rachel held up the phone, squeezing it for a few seconds, wishing it were the old woman's neck.

The pilot briefly looked across at her, before facing front again.

Chapter 9

FBI Headquarters, 935 Pennsylvania Avenue, NW Washington, D.C.

Matt dozed in the rear seat of the dark sedan, and his mind drifted in a beautiful dream. Once again he saw the long pool of shimmering sapphire-blue water. But this time there was an angel rising from the water. She was naked and long limbed with golden hair swept back over her bronzed shoulders. Her breasts were perked, her eyes were on him, and they were as luminously blue as the water surrounding her.

Her smiled widened, and then widened some more, until her lips pulled so far back she exposed all of her teeth and gums. And still the flesh pulled back further until the skin of her face ripped away, and there was just a screaming skull that dried and flaked and turned to dust.

"*Yaa!*" Matt jolted forward, wide-awake.

He chuckled softly. "Dream." He exhaled, rubbed his face and leaned toward the window. They were nearly at their destination – the massive slate-gray FBI building. It reminded him of something a child would build from their Lego set, with a slab of all their extra Lego bricks on top.

A building with a hat on, he thought, and eased back into the seat.

Beside him, Rachel seemed preoccupied. "Penny for your thoughts?" he asked.

She stared out of her windows for a few moments more, and then inhaled deeply through her nose and let it out slowly. She turned, her face drawn.

"It's nothing." She seemed to slump. "It's all complicated."

"Samuel?" Matt guessed she was still upset about her colleague and being back made her think about him all over again.

She nodded. "Yeah, Samuel, and Oscar, and the dozens of others who fall every goddamn day," she said, her tone melancholy. "And then there's all the other shit that swirls around." She turned back to the window. "And never stops swirling."

"Why don't you quit? Woman like you could get a job anywhere," he said, meaning it.

She snorted. "What, and give up show business?" She pulled in a cheek. "Forget it, I'm just on a downer. I really enjoy the job, more days than not." She looked at him for a few seconds and then lowered her eyes.

"Hey, you don't have to hold it in all the time. I've lost people too; it hurts, and sometimes it keeps on hurting." He put his hand on the seat between them and leaned toward her. "I just want to tell you, there's not many people like you around. You're pretty special."

"Thanks." She laughed softly and reached out to grab his hand. "I know I'm a hard-assed bitch sometimes, but I also wanted to thank you for probably saving my life." She smiled. "There's a lot more to you than I first thought."

"Thanks. And Rachel, if it helps, I don't think you're a bitch *all* the time." He grinned.

She returned the smile. "I'm glad you're here, Matt." She squeezed his hand.

They navigated the building's crash and bomb barriers and passed through multiple checkpoints before pulling into its vast underground car park.

"Now we meet the boss, huh?" Matt asked.

"That's right. First up we meet with Assistant Director Dominic Wybrow, my supervisor. Mrs. van Hellbag is breathing down his neck as well."

"Mrs. Hellbag?" Matt chuckled. "I see you two are getting along famously."

Rachel grinned. "Yeah well, in this job sometimes you gotta laugh to stay sane."

She pushed open her door, and then led him to the secured lift. She typed in a pass code and the doors slid open. Their next stop was the fifth floor, and when the doors whooshed open again, Matt was surprised by the noise and activity. It looked like any other crowded office with the large central room dominated by workspaces, people talking on phones, typing away at computers or chatting in groups. Smaller box-like offices held a single occupant, and toward the end of the large room were the larger senior management suites with names written on doors.

She half-turned to him as she strode down the corridor between cubicles. "Be nice."

"You keep saying that." He winked.

She knocked on one of the doors and a large, bald man looked up. His eyes slid past Rachel to Matt and they seemed to analyse and assess him in a matter of seconds. There was a tiny movement of his head, giving approval to enter.

Rachel pushed the door inwards. "Sir." She then stood aside. "Professor Matthew Kearns."

The man came to his feet. He was big, 6' 4" at least, and had hands like shovels. One shot forward to totally enclose

Matt's hand, but it didn't compress as hard as he expected. Perhaps Wybrow thought that as Matt was an academic, he was used to doing little more than writing on whiteboards and sipping exotic coffee blends with his students.

"Professor Kearns." He sat and motioned to two seats in front of his desk. His club-like fingers meshed in front of him. "Thank you for working with us."

Matt nodded, but didn't want to say it was a pleasure, as frankly, he didn't like the idea of becoming embedded in FBI processes or politics. Suddenly he had the feeling of water rising up to his neck and he swallowed hard. Once he'd written up his report, he would ease himself out of the relationship. He'd been to Canada as he'd promised Eleanor and now he hoped he could wind up his involvement in this bizarre case. He didn't need any more nightmares.

Matt glanced at Rachel, looking at her profile for a moment. He liked her, a lot, but then he shook his head as if to clear it. In his mind a sensible voice whispered: *don't get entangled in this, even if there's a nice girl involved – it just isn't worth it.*

He'd ask a few questions he had, and then say goodbye.

"Any clues on the bombing?"

Wybrow didn't flinch. "None. The bomber was picked up on CCTV coming down the street, tossing the package into your car, and then disappearing around the corner. And I really mean vanishing around the corner, as on one feed the guy was there, and then once he rounds the building, he wasn't." Wybrow shrugged. "Seems this guy knew the layout before the attack."

"I see." Matt frowned. "Hey, haven't you guys got facial recognition software now?"

"Yes, we do." Wybrow replied. "As long as people are on a database somewhere, we can cross check for a visual match. But first we need a clear shot, and our guy didn't give us that.

We've got nothing yet, Professor Kearns." His voice took on an edge. "Don't forget, one of my agents was killed, so be aware that we have no intention of letting this go."

Wybrow breathed in and out for a few moments, his nostrils flaring like a bull about to paw the ground. He turned to Rachel. "We got bodies piling up, and a killer or killers unknown, background unknown, profile unknown, designation or demands unknown, who seem to be one step ahead of us. We still seem to have a lot of work to do, Agent."

Rachel, sitting upright, just nodded.

Wybrow sat back. "And they even followed you to Canada."

"Or were already there," Matt added.

"Maybe." His eyes went to Rachel again. "Agent Bromilow, I've read your preliminary report… not much in it. But you have a few things to follow up on. Is that right?"

"Yes, sir. I've now read the full coronial report on those hitters that turned up to attack us at the church in Fort Severn – no fingerprints, none of them carrying ID, and, as I expected, dental records and facial identification impossible to use as their heads were obliterated. But my gut feeling is that these guys were the same group that attacked Clarence van Helling."

"And I think the bomber was from the same cult," Matt put in.

"It's a cult now?" Wybrow sat back.

Rachel shrugged. "Profile fits; the men all had religious looking iconography seared into their skin – pretty extreme."

"So do a lot of teenagers these days." Wybrow waved it away. "Still, it sort of all ties together if you squint real hard and think of you two as the eye of the cyclone." His eyes narrowed. "Because if it is the same group, then frankly, they seem to dogging you, Agent." His eyes shifted to Matt. "Or maybe you, Professor."

"Terrific." Matt slumped in his chair.

"Professor Kearns needs some lab time to process the glass window images. Also, I have some biological specimens that need to be analyzed," Rachel said.

"About that." Matt held up a hand. "I think I've done all I can, and you probably don't need me anymore. I'm expensive and since we know the language used is Chaldaic, there are several paleolinguists who can be..."

Rachel's head whipped around and she glared at Matt, brows drawn tightly together.

"Don't worry about your fees, they'll all be taken care of for as long as we need you." Wybrow's flat stare pinned Matt for a moment, before sliding back to Rachel. "Labs are ready for you. This is a priority, and I don't need to tell you the political pressure this is drawing, from both our guys and the Canadian government." He turned to Matt. "Harvard has okayed your consulting. I have to tell you that they're very proud of you, Professor."

Matt grimaced as he watched Wybrow press his phone com. "Janine, can you get Agent Moddel up here?" He sat back, smiling benignly at Matt. "Agent Moddel heads up our scientific imaging department. You tell him what you need, and he'll source it, pronto."

"Just a ride home," Matt said, feeling trapped. Rachel threw him a thunderous look and he couldn't meet her eye.

"Anytime you like, Professor." Wybrow leaned forward. "But remember, agents like Samuel Anderson died for you. Let's find out who killed him and bring them to justice. Giving us a few more days is nowhere near the price he paid."

"I just..." Matt felt like an asshole. "Yeah, sure."

Rachel pressed her lips together and looked away.

A slim man peered in through the glass door, before knocking. Wybrow held up a hand, flat, and then turned back to Rachel.

"Move quickly. If we're going to run these guys down, we need to do it while the trail is hot."

"Yes, sir." She got to her feet.

Matt guessed they'd just been dismissed and stood.

"Go with Agent Moddel, tell him what you need. He'll help." Wybrow held out his huge plank of a hand again. "And thank you for choosing to work with us."

"Yeah, no problem." Matt walked to the door, moving stiffly like a jerky robot. He could feel the assistant director's eyes on him the entire way. Outside, it seemed several degrees cooler, and Moddel grinned at him.

"Intense, huh?"

Matt blew air through his pressed lips and then grinned back. "Nah, I deal with the military all the time. This is grade-school stuff."

"Yeah, right." Moddel led him to the elevators. Matt went to say good bye to Rachel but she just nodded cooly and continued down the hallway. Matt paused, watching her go, and then shrugged.

Moddel also watched her shapely form depart. "Forget it; she's way out of your league. C'mon."

Matt sighed and followed the scientist.

Once inside the elevator, Moddel turned to Matt. "I've read some of your papers."

Matt raised his eyebrows, waiting. Moddel simply turned to face the elevator numbers as they rose.

"Well, okay then," Matt said, now wondering whether the guy was a fan or critic.

The lift doors slid open and Moddel strode off, talking as he walked. "You've got some images you want processed?"

"Yes and a sample." Matt said, fishing in his pocket for the plastic bag containing the glass shards.

Moddel held out his hand, took the bag and held it up. "What do you need to know?"

"Composition, spectral analysis, dating, basically everything. And if you have predictive analysis, I'd also like you to reassemble it, and show me what it looked like."

Moddel bobbed. "Maybe, but we'll have no way of knowing what the entire piece looked like. What about the images you mentioned?"

"Ah, they're for my own analysis. I need to try and work out what it says, and what it means. You can use the pictures for reassembly."

"Translation?" Moddel snorted. "We have programs for that now. We've obtained a translation app from Harvard. I can run the language fragment through it and then we'll see what it comes up with."

"Nope, you won't find this language, or its nuance."

"I bet we will. It's top of the line."

"I bet you won't." Matt's lips curled into a smile. "If you got that from Harvard, then it's the language app *I wrote*. Believe me, this language and dialect isn't in there."

Moddel nodded, looking impressed.

"Besides," Matt said. "It's usually never about a straight translation. You need to determine two things – what the writer was saying, and what they were actually meaning. They can vary greatly."

"O-*ookay*." Moddel pushed open a door. "Here we are – welcome to my bat cave."

*

"Here."

Rachel handed Howard "Howie" Bilson, a bureau scientist, the small bottle containing the dried worms.

He held them up, squinting in at the remains. "Tell me about them."

"The geographical location was northeast Canada. I doubt they were indigenous. They were in the basement of a church, and I think they might have exited some human remains… while it was being burned up."

Bilson's eyebrows went up. "An internal parasite?" He turned to his workbench and opened the bottle and emptied the remains into a petri dish. He lifted a large magnifying glass and scrutinised the thread-like things.

"Could be some sort of nematode. Pretty desiccated now."

"Like I said, they were escaping a fire," Rachel said slowly.

"But not charred." Howie slid along his bench to a large microscope, taking the dish with him. He used a pair of long tweezers to remove one of the worms, placing it in another small glass dish. This time he added a few drops of sterile water, and then carefully slid it into the staging area of his scope.

Howie bent over the eyepiece and using one hand began to adjust the focus and changed it up to 50 times magnification. He *hmm-hmmd* and pursed his lips for a few moments before pulling back.

"No discernable mouthparts, and, given its state, I'm not sure what type it is." He took a picture and relayed it to a screen on the wall. There was a dark glistening worm that seemed to have hydrated a little from the sterile water. It was glossy, tapered at both ends with no eyes or external sensory organs at all. Strangely, it seemed a little lighter in color than when it had first entered the sterile water.

The scientist shrugged. "I can get a parasitologist or perhaps an entomologist to look at the specimens to give us an exact identification."

"I need information now," Rachel said. "I don't want to wait weeks while some other nerd – sorry – *specialist* looks them over. Besides, I don't really care about naming it, just finding out what it was doing and why it was there."

"Nerd?" Howie grinned. "I've been called worse. Okay, we can find out an awful lot right here and now. Let's see what these guys were doing in that cadaver. Might give us some more clues."

He selected another of the dried worms and using the tweezers dropped it onto another dish. He then used a scalpel to carefully chop it up. He then added a few drops of water and continued to mash the remains a little more, before scraping the mush into a test tube.

In his chair, Howie rolled along the floor again, making Rachel step back quickly to avoid flattened toes. No wonder they had linoleum floors, she thought. Means these guys never had to get to their feet.

He capped the lid of the small tube and placed it in a centrifuge. He set it to spin and pressed a timer for 20 minutes.

"That'll separate the materials – the serum, proteins, any matrix from the stomach. We'll then be able to use the mass spectrometer to determine what chemical residues are inside. Of course, finding human protein fragments will tell us it was feeding on the body." He spun in his chair toward her and folded his arms. "Why the hurry? These guys aren't going anywhere."

"Priorities – murder investigation." Rachel paced away.

"Hey, I'm busy too, you know. I've got several murder investigations that need evidence analyzed," the scientist retorted.

"My murder was one of our own, plus two entire families." She turned. "If you'd like to speak to Assistant Director Wybrow, let me know." Her jaws tightened and she went to turn away, but froze. She squinted at the screen.

"Hey, and as for these little guys not going anywhere, I think you better have a look at this."

Howie turned in his chair, looking up at the microscope's screen feed. The image of the worm under the scope showed a glassine worm, now fully plumped and whipping back and forth.

"Holy shit – natural rehydration." He scooted over, peering down the eyepiece and adjusted the lens. "Not that uncommon really. There's a sea snake called *Hydrophis platurus*, that can totally dry out, and stay that way for months. Add water, and in an hour or two, it rehydrates and off it goes."

"Well, this took about two minutes." Rachel's lips curled at the revolting image.

"Beautiful." Howie grinned as he peered down the lens. "Maybe I should have expected it. Dehydration is a form of hibernation for creatures at the smaller end of the scale. They convert sugars in their system to something like glass that surrounds their organs to protect them from collapse. You just add water, and…"

"And we're good to go." Rachel said, turning to look at the writhing worm. She stood transfixed as the tiny, thrashing thing continued to inflate. Beside her Howie mumbled, keeping up a steady stream of biology facts and figures mixed with the wonders of the natural world. Time moved on, and she paced, fidgeted, and sighed long and loud.

Behind them the centrifuge timer finally pinged.

Thank god, Rachel thought.

"Now we can see what our little friends have been up to. Or at least what makes them tick." Howie crossed to the centrifuge, lifted the lid, and pulled out the small test tube. He held it up, looking at the bands of different colored matter.

"Excellent separation." He used a pipette to extract each of the solution bands, and piped them onto separate slides that he then slid into a machine that looked like a cross between a photocopier and bar fridge.

"Gertrude." He grinned. "Our mass spectrometer; she's an older model, but still works just fine."

He sat down on a chair and pressed two buttons on the face of the device, causing two trays to slide out, like a CD player awaiting its disc. He carefully placed the slides in each and then nudged the trays closed.

He moved along the control panel to a keyboard and immediately started entering data.

"I'm now telling Gertrude what I'm feeding her today, a-*aaand* what I want back." He lifted a hand, single finger hovering over the enter key. "And *voila*." He hit the key with a flourish and sat back with arms folded. Gertrude seemed to purr.

"How long?" Rachel asked.

Howie smiled for a second or two. The small screen showed graphs of different colors rising and falling in spiked peaks and troughs.

The screen beeped and then displayed a green banner: ANALYSIS COMPLETE.

He pressed PRINT x 2, and immediately two sheets of paper were ejected into a tray. He snatched them up and handed one to Rachel. She glanced at it and sighed.

"Well?"

Howie looked at the information, his lips pursed and he nodded now and then. He stopped and his brows came together.

"Hello... that's weird."

"What's weird?" Rachel looked over his shoulder at his paper, even though she was holding a duplicate in her hands.

"These elements – hydrogen, oxygen, and nitrogen – basic chemicals, but their proportion are way too familiar." He spun in his chair so fast Rachel had to leap out of his way. Howie then grabbed up a computer tablet and started to type furiously, opening multiple pages in a flurry. He snorted as he read the results.

"Yep, knew it, amino acids." He showed her the results, but the chains and connectors meant nothing to her.

"Amino acids?" She leaned over him. "So?"

"Human."

"But you expected that – you already said if you found human protein fragments, that'd just confirm the parasite might have been ingesting the body."

"Yeah, I did." He grinned. "But think about what I said – I was talking about protein fragments. And that's not what we've got here. What we've got here is... so much more." He whizzed back over to the mass spectrometer. "I think, no, *I know*, we've got indicators for hormones." Howie practically bounced in his chair. "It's basically 75 per cent hormone – 75 per cent freaking *human* hormone."

She grimaced. "*Huh*, so you're telling me they were feeding on this guy's hormones?"

"No, no, no." He looked exasperated. "For them to be at this concentration in the parasite, these things weren't *taking* them from the host, but were so loaded they were excreting them *back* into the host's system." He started to type again. "But which one?"

"It's a specific one?" she asked, leaning over his shoulder.

"I think so." He hummed as he typed. "Let's see if we can isolate it." He clapped once. "Yes – FGF21 – good ol' Fibroblast Growth Factor 21."

Howie continued to nod and read figures, and Rachel's impatience swelled. "Well, what the hell is that?"

"Oh, it's what we call a growth and repair hormone. The thymus gland produces it and it's very prevalent in our bodies... but only when we're young. We stop producing it as we age." He turned. "It's actually *why* we age, as some specialists say it protects the immune system against the ravages of age by giving us super defenses against disease and cell destruction, and it also super charges our repair system." He straightened. "You know what? I think this thing might not be a parasite at all, maybe more a symbiote."

He rubbed at his chin. "Or perhaps it was just a super-efficient parasite – just taking what it needed to keep itself and its host alive." His brows knitted. "If you had this much FGF21 in your system you could live for... " His eyes flicked up at her. "This guy that the worms came from, how old was he? What did he look like?"

"What did he look like?" She snorted sourly. "The remains of a fucking bonfire."

*

"From Fort Severn way up in Canada, you say, Professor?" The science agent, David Moddel, *hmmd*, as he looked from the glass fragments up at the image. "And from within an old Christian church?"

"Yep," Matt replied. "From that stained glass window." He nodded up at the conglomerate image assembled from all the pictures he had taken from his phone camera that was now projected up on the wall.

Moddel looked again at the enlarged image. "Magnificent."

"It was – right before it was shattered into a million pieces." Matt sighed.

"A damned crime." Moddel cursed softly. "This glass sample." He looked skeptical. "Matt, do you know how long stained glass has been around?"

Matt nodded. "Yeah, I know, a long time."

"Colored glass was produced by both the early Egyptians and the Romans." He grinned. "So yeah, a damn, damn, damn long time."

"And these pieces?" Matt nodded toward the fragments of glass on the bench top.

Moddel leaned over the shards, smiling down on them for a moment before picking up a metal probe, and moving them around, fitting them back together.

"You know, I wish we had all the shards, no matter how tiny, we could have put this back together like a giant jigsaw." He looked form the fragments to the screen again, using it as a guide to push another piece into place.

"Yeah, well, we were kinda rushed there at the end. We've got to work with what we've got. So, how old?" Matt pressed.

"It's around 1500 years old." He looked up. "Makes it one of the earliest specimens of the craft in existence – now you know why I would have liked more of it." Modell's brow creased. "So, why would someone place a stained glass window that is absolutely priceless, way out in the sticks?"

"Good question." Matt stared at the fragments, his mind working – *why was it there?* A *very* good question. But the real burner for him was why, after all those centuries, was it destroyed just as they got there?

Moddel joined some pieces together, into what looked like a single large yellow orb. Matt recognised it immediately; one eye of the thing that tried to come into the church, and totally destroyed the window – he saw it – it had *meant* to destroy it.

Matt felt a tingle of fear race up his spine and he began pacing. "And why would they black some of the panels out? Even back then they knew about the night sky, and other stained glass windows have images of the moon and stars. They wouldn't have it pure black. It doesn't make sense."

"Not a very clear picture you took." Moddel folded his arms and looked up at the image. "But it was beautiful." He sighed. "And someone robbed future generations of its magnificence."

"Because someone didn't want us to see it." Matt stared.

Moddel looked from the image to Matt. "The medieval windows usually contained a message, and this one was very detailed." He looked back to the full window.

"There was writing, in many languages. But there was one that was the most ancient form of Hebrew in existence called Chaldaic. Supposedly the language actually spoken by Noah and his sons. The thing is, no one speaks this language, no one writes it, and no one has for thousands of years."

"What did it say?" Moddel straightened.

"It referred to a place, the Mother of Mankind – *Akebu-Lan* – it's an old name for the Garden of Eden."

The scientist shrugged. "Intriguing, but still not exactly earth-shattering. Or window shattering." He jiggled his eyebrows.

"Maybe." Matt tilted his head. "Hey, can you rotate that image? Roll 90 degrees right."

"Sure." Moddel fiddled with the projection controls and the image rolled on the screen.

Matt folded his arms and walked closer to the image. He tilted his head. The shades of green, brown and blue, with the line running through them started to make sense. The line seemed to be following a countour. "You know what this looks like to me? A map." He pointed. "The blue is water, I can see a coastline, and that could be a trail of sorts."

"Yeah, you're right, it could be a map." Moddel studied it a little more. "But there are no names or points of reference. Could be anywhere."

"Could be, but it isn't." Matt started for the door. "Can you send this to Assistant Director Wybrow?" He waved. "And thanks buddy, that was very helpful."

*

Matt and Rachel met back in Wybrow's office. She was still acting cold toward him, but seemed to warm up as they began to try to make sense of what they had learned. To Matt's pleasant surprise, Wybrow was very good at drawing out the details and asking questions that acted as springboards to answers, or even better questions.

"So, you've got a piece of a map that might correspond to somewhere in the world – that's a pretty big playing field." Wybrow shrugged. "But if the window is 1500 years old, then the map has got to be about the same vintage. Maps then weren't the same as today, were they?"

"No, that's right," Matt agreed. "Some European countries were fairly well mapped, but not all. Same as the Far East, but as for the far-flung countries, many weren't even discovered back then. They were still in the great unknown areas, the ones with dragons drawn on them."

"Then they'll be no help," Rachel said. "If only it had a single point of reference – anything."

"It already does." Wybrow's mouth curved into a smile. "The ocean."

Matt began to grin. "He's right, you know. Though the mapping of interiors was pretty superficial at best, the seafarers were mapping coastlines for centuries longer than that. And the coastlines nearly always had a point of reference. Their shape alone can be recognizable."

"What's the closest coastline to Mount Ararat?" Rachel asked. "Might as well start with somewhere that was the last known place for Noah."

"Good as any place to start; let's side by side it," Matt said. "Bring up a map of Ararat, and see if we can identity anything that matches close by. The nearest large-scale body of water is 150 miles to the Caspian Sea in Azerbaijan. Then about 150 miles to the Black Sea, but still in Turkey."

Rachel took control of the computer and split the screen. She brought up the Turkish landmass and began to drill down. She sat back. "And about 600 miles to the Mediterranean."

Matt let his eyes flick from one to the other. "I can't see any coastal similarities." He leaned forward and cupped his chin for a moment. "Hey." He clicked his fingers. "Try for any maps from 1500 years ago – anything you can find."

Wybrow pulled in a cheek. "Reaching a bit now aren't you, Professor? From 1500 years ago? How many of those are lying around?"

"Alexander the Great made plenty of maps, and he was last around in 323 BCE. Also there's Claudius Ptolemy's 150 AD regional map. Plus, the Roman Empire ruled that entire part of the world a few hundred years before that and they were diligent mapmakers. Sure, there'll be plenty of gaps, but we might find useful examples that correspond to the shoreline we're interested in."

Wybrow nodded. "Over to you."

Matt squeezed in next to Rachel. "Let me." He started to type, accessing several libraries he knew that had antiquarian maps online. He looked at the candidates and rejected them over and over.

"Bummer." He sat back. "No dice; the older they are, the rarer they are." He shrugged. "And the rarer they are, the more valuable and less likely they are to be shared online. All I'm getting is references, but no images."

Wybrow's mouth twitched in readiness. Matt held a hand up flat to him.

"I know, don't say it." He sat back in his chair. "The high-value maps are either in the hands of private dealers or locked in government vaults." Matt had good contacts, but anything sold on the black market was unrecorded and probably gone for good. Added to that, even the recorded stuff, if held by overprotective governments, was off-limits to anyone anytime.

He used both hands to push his hair back off his face. "This is where we need to tap into someone's network, someone who has access to all the private map dealers – people not on the formal radar. Someone who is known to have their own collection, wealth, status and credibility – the only criteria that matters for these guys."

He spun in his seat, grinning. "And who do we know like that?"

"Please don't say Eleanor van Helling." Rachel sighed.

Matt pointed at her chest. "Bingo."

"You think she can help?" Wybrow's brow creased.

"I have a list of exclusive antiquarian libraries in Europe that we can try. But they wouldn't even sniff at me, or the American FBI for that matter. But they might open the doors for Mrs. van Helling. And I'm sure she knows a few other private map dealers, who don't exactly advertise what they have in their collections." Matt shrugged. "Yeah, I think she can open doors for us."

"For you," Rachel added, her lip curled.

"For *us*." Wybrow stared hard at Rachel.

She looked pained. "Assistant Director, I really don't think…"

"But I do think, Agent Bromilow." Wybrow clasped large fingers on his desk. "The professor is a subject-matter expert. But *you* are our agency expert – both skills are vital here." He looked at her from under lowered brows. "That's final."

"Yes, sir." Her gaze was flat.

"Anything else?" Wybrow asked.

"Yes, sir." Rachel slid the lab results to him. "These were the things that we found next to the body from the church basement, that may or may not have been Father Xavier."

Wybrow turned the folder around and flipped it open. His brows came together as he read. "Says here, they're still alive?"

"Yes, sir – worms – seems they were in hibernation, just waiting for rehydration."

"That's weird." Wybrow's nose wrinkled and he turned another page. "And pretty damned revolting."

"Agent Bilson thinks they might be some sort of nematode." Rachel seemed to enjoy Wybrow's disgust. "The worms probably exited his body after death. They seemed to be excreting a particular human hormone – FGF21 – responsible for bolstering the human system to fight aging."

"Anti-aging worms?" Matt grinned. "The cosmetic industry will go wild."

"The cosmetic industry, the military, politicians, just about anyone would go wild for it. But first they'd have to know about it." Wybrow looked up at her, his eyes narrowed. "Clarence van Helling?"

"Exactly what I was thinking, sir," She responded. "That's why they burned him up – to destroy everything."

"So where did they come from?" Wybrow opened his hands, his fingers spread over the notes. "I doubt they're from around here."

"They're not. Agent Bilson has never seen anything like them. They've never been documented before, anywhere," Rachel said.

Wybrow turned in his seat to stare out through the window. "You're right; an obvious attempt to destroy evidence and leave us nothing to go on."

Matt and Rachel waited, and Wybrow put a hand up to rub his jaw, the rough surface making a chaffing sound. He turned back. "This case is getting more confusing the more we know." Wybrow's jaws worked behind his cheeks for a moment, and he turned Rachel. "Time for some answers, Agent Bromilow."

She nodded. "I agree, sir. We have a few leads we can run down."

Matt looked again at the split screen showing the map fragment. "Someone went to a lot of trouble to place that map there, but then also to obscure it so it was hidden from anyone other than those who knew what they were looking for. After all, finding a 1500-year-old stained glass window in Canada is like uncovering a Roman sword in the hands of a Neanderthal skeleton."

Wybrow stared and Matt leaned forward. "That map was showing the way to somewhere important." He nodded at the map fragment. "Whatever it is that lies at the end of that map's trail, will give us the answers we seek." He turned back to Wybrow. "But to find its destination, we first need to find where to start."

"Eleanor van Helling, here we come." Rachel sat back.

Chapter 10

Central Park South, New York, New York

"Why not?" Matt raised his chin.

Rachel rolled her eyes. "Matt, c'mon, really? You can't possibly believe that map is going to lead you to Noah's Ark, or the mysterious Fountain of Youth, or even some sort of mystical Garden of Eden, do you? It's all make-believe."

He glanced at her, incredulous. "You did see that thing that tried to break into the church, right?"

"I don't know what I saw, *now*." She looked away. "Things like that can't exist."

"Maybe they do, but we just aren't supposed to see them." He turned to face her. "I have a theory about it. There's these immortal creatures, angels, that had fallen to earth."

"Fallen angels?" she rolled her eyes.

"Exactly, they're called Nephilim; their name actually *means* fallen from God's light." He bobbed his head. "It also means the violent ones. The thing was, the Nephilim were said to be banished to Earth to act as sentinels and servants, violently, if necessary. They would perform these tasks until the world ends, or until they managed to return to God's light through their good deeds and actions."

She turned to him. "Sentinels or servants to who?"

He held up both hands. "That, I don't know. But just keep an open mind, okay? It wasn't that long ago that the city of Troy was just thought to be a fable. And rumors of pyramids in America were laughed at." He raised an eyebrow. "Hell, we even discovered a real life lost world atop a plateau in Venezuela." He shrugged. "All I'm saying is, I've seen things that would stretch a normal person's imagination or sanity. I've found that myths and legends always have a grain of truth."

"Well, I want it on record as saying I think you're well off beam on this one." She sighed.

He scoffed. "Well, what do *you* think is happening?"

Rachel sighed. "I don't know; that we're all going insane, maybe."

He chuckled. "Yeah, probably. But the important thing is that someone sure *thinks* there's something at the end of that map. Something important enough to kill for."

She groaned as they pulled up in front of the Ritz Carlton. "Do I really need to go upstairs? Your old girlfriend is hard work."

Matt grinned and nudged her. "Just remember what your boss said – this is a team effort, or something like that." This time it was him that reached across to squeeze her leg. "After all, you wouldn't leave me alone with just Franken-Greta *and* my snippy old girlfriend, would you?"

"Just snippy, *huh*?" Rachel scoffed.

The car stopped, and this time another FBI support vehicle pulled in about 50 yards behind them. There'd be no bombers getting close this time – or so Matt hoped.

Matt was first out. He held the door for Rachel and looked up at the towering edifice. "I've got a good feeling about this."

Rachel looked up as well. "You do know she's probably pulling the strings... on all of us? I bet even the Assistant Director is dancing to her tune."

"*Meh*, so what? As long as we're all pulling in the same direction." He shut the car door. "My curiosity is piqued now. If this woman can help us, and keep the authorities all onside, then who are we to argue?"

Once again Matt and Rachel found themselves travelling up in the immaculate elevator. This time as the doors opened the enormous Greta was waiting for them. She stepped aside to reveal a beaming Eleanor van Helling.

The old woman clasped her hands together. "You have some news." Her eyes sparkled.

Matt crossed to her and went to gently shake her hand, but she pulled him closer for an air-kiss on his cheek. He miscalculated and his lips touched her flesh – it was powdery dry, and smelled of way too much perfume.

She pulled back a little. "Careful you don't lick *all* my makeup off, Matthew."

Matt felt his fact go hot. "Sorry." He stepped back and rubbed the powder off his cheek and lips.

Eleanor waved a hand behind her, and Greta maneuvered her chair around into the living room. There was a table set for tea and coffee, with cakes and small sandwiches already waiting. It was set for four, but only two chairs were pulled out for Matt and Rachel, and another vacant spot on one side for the wheelchair.

They both sat, and Matt immediately began to pile sandwiches and cake onto a plate. Greta tucked Eleanor into the space. She smiled, showing a row of neat, little brown teeth.

"So, tell me everything, and leave nothing out."

Rachel and Matt glanced at each other, but Rachel offered her hand to Matt. "Over to you, Prof."

"Okay." He put down half a sandwich. "We found something in Canada."

Eleanor's eyes slid to him. "Clues to the people who killed my Clarence, I hope?"

"I think so, and it's certainly looking like there's a big connection between events now." Matt then told her about the death of Officer Oscar Ojibwe and his deputies, finding the old church and also the dead priest in the basement. He rushed over the beheading and burning of the body, and completely left out the detail of the worms that had seemed to come from inside him. As he spoke he shifted his eyes to Rachel who nodded, so he guessed he wasn't betraying any FBI classified information.

He cleared his throat. "In the footage retrieved from Clarence's, *uh*, death, we saw the appearance of the two men who were dressed in black. They were never identified from their remains." Matt sat forward. "I'm also pretty sure now it was one of their group that threw the grenade into our car." He glanced briefly at Rachel again, and saw her eyes narrow slightly as she listened.

He continued. "And then again, all the way up at Fort Severn, they were waiting for us. They would have killed us, if not for…" Matt stopped himself, not wanting to even try to describe the ogreish being they had seen to the old woman.

"If not for what, Matthew?" Eleanor tilted her head.

"We think it might be some sort of cult or secret order." Rachel added. "They either killed Father Xavier, or got there too late to protect him." She shrugged. "Maybe they thought we killed him."

"Maybe they were also trying to find the secret of the wellspring, *hmm*?" The red tip of Eleanor's tongue peeped out to lick her lips. She craned forward.

"Well, there's no way to test that theory now; they're all dead." Rachel raised an eyebrow. "I checked one of the bodies, and they had scarred themselves with a weird cross. It must be some sort of ancient religious order." She pulled her phone out and scrolled to a picture showing a flattened chest with the seared cross. She handed it to Matt.

"There could have been one on their foreheads as well, but it was too hard to make out due to the… trauma."

"Interesting." Eleanor's eyes narrowed. "What sort of order would be prepared to kill so ruthlessly?" She eased her tiny frame back into her chair. "There are many ancient orders still in existence. Clarence used to deal with some of them in his pursuit of his strange and unique artifacts all around the globe."

"Freemasons?" Rachel asked. "Aren't they religious?"

"Nah. They have their own belief system, but it's not really a religion." Matt stared at the image of the cross and rubbed his stubbled chin. "And I think they're far older than the Freemasons. And besides, these guys were like professional soldiers – warriors." He tapped the phone. "I've seen something like this before."

"The Knights Templar." Eleanor smiled. "They date back to 1129, and even though they were disbanded by the Pope in 1312, they are thought to still exist. And fighting was all they did."

"That'd make sense," Rachel said. "And it would tie in with the crucifix scars on their chests."

Matt stared at the picture on Rachel's phone. "This is not a crucifix. The cross symbol has been around for thousands of years, and it was first used to signify a crossroad between life and death."

"And between life and death is eternal existence." Eleanor's eyes blazed.

Matt shrugged. "In the group of wise Magi who visited baby Jesus, it was said that one of them had a tunic baring the cross symbol – that was well before the crucifix was associated with Christ."

Matt looked down at the image. "It's hard to make out, because the flesh is so severely damaged, but I think it's a pair of keys crossed over each other."

Eleanor sighed. "I wish Clarence was here; he would know what it all meant."

"Thanks for the vote of confidence." Matt snorted, and then tapped the small screen. "I know this; there is, or *was*, an ancient order who had a similar crest – two crossed keys, one representing the power to bind us here on earth, and the other to unlock heaven."

"Keys? That probably means it can't be that old then," Rachel said.

Matt looked up at her. "Are you kidding? Keys and locks are older than you think. The first locks appeared in ancient Babylon, over six thousand years ago."

"Okay, that's old." She sat back. "So, who then?"

"The Vatican," Matt said.

*

"The Vatican?" Rachel looked heavenward. "I thought you said it wasn't a crucifix."

"Or more precisely, the Borgias," Matt confirmed. "A very powerful Italian family from around the 15th century – they were well connected, ruthless, and even produced two Popes, which is why the Vatican still has the crossed keys as its crest. The Borgias were thought to have been involved in several assassinations, and also had a private army that was blindly loyal to them."

Matt shrugged. "Their problem was they became too powerful and a threat to the government. They were attacked from all sides and eventually simply vanished from history. Many historians believe they were forced underground where they still exist somewhere and in some form today."

"That's it, Matthew?" Eleanor's lip curled. "It's true that the Borgias were the Rockefellers of their day and ten times as dangerous. But they came and went in a hundred years."

"I know." Matt sat staring at the image for several moments letting his mind work. "But they were just one face of something that was far older." He held up a finger. "Hear me out here; the Borgias were the last large and powerful group to bear the crossed keys. But you can trace it all the way back to an ancient warrior race called the Bruttians." He opened his hands. "Like the Borgian soldiers, they were aggressive, loyal, and fiercely independent, and fought against the Romans, defeating them many times."

Matt rubbed his chin. "The biggest historical anomaly was when they joined forces with Hannibal."

"Hannibal? Elephants-crossing-the-Alps Hannibal?" Rachel's eyebrows went up.

"The one and only." Matt nodded to her. "When Hannibal invaded Italy, they rose up in support of him. Many couldn't understand why, but some theorized that it was only because they wanted to help Hannibal when he was warring with the Romans in defense of Carthage. When Hannibal returned to Africa, the Bruttians went with him. Together, they kept Rome out of Africa for a hundred years."

Matt shrugged. "And just like the Borgias, after a time Bruttian customs and language just disappeared – it was like they thrived for a while, did the task required of them, and then vanished back to where they came."

"Or wherever they're hiding now." Eleanor's eyes narrowed. "Pieces of a puzzle."

"There's more." Matt then described the magnificent stained glass window, and he recounted its age, and the clues hidden within the geography and the absence of any landmarks.

"And that's where we hit a snag," he said glumly. "Without knowing the place to start on the map, we have no way of finding where we need to go. Bottom line: we need to get access to some old maps – some *very* old maps."

"Old maps." Eleanor's eyes lit up. "My dear, I can walk you into the Library of Congress Geography and Map Reading Room today."

"Not good enough," Matt responded. "The maps we're interested in usually inhabit museum libraries and private collections. I just don't have the contacts, and even the FBI has little chance of muscling their way in to get a peek at them, let alone being allowed to examine them."

"And you think I can?" Eleanor smiled, one pencil-lined eyebrow raised.

Matt smiled back. "No, I *know* someone as persuasive and charming as you can." He tilted his head and widened his smile. Beside him Rachel looked away.

"Your investigations are proceeding." Eleanor folded her bird-like hands in her lap. "But I think it may end up taking you offshore now. Perhaps even to somewhere on the other side of the world." Her eyes gleamed. "Perhaps the maps you seek are there." Her mouth turned down slightly. "But just like Clarence found out, our influence does not extend much beyond our borders. That world, even today, is an exotic, dangerous and very mysterious place."

The old woman's eyes widened as she sat straighter in her wheelchair. "But where my influence ends, someone else's begins."

Matt leaned toward her. "You've got something to share with us, haven't you, Eleanor?"

She reached out one bony hand to place it over Matt's. "Never underestimate the power of influence, my dear boy." She turned to look up at Greta, who soundlessly left the room. She returned seconds later escorting a man. Rachel immediately shot to her feet.

He was tall, swarthy, and had eyes as dark as coal that moved from Matt to Rachel, and then to Eleanor. He came and stood at the edge of the table and bowed slightly. Eleanor waved him to sit down.

Now Matt understood why there was another setting at the table. The man's lips just hinted at a smile, and Matt saw that he was not intimidated by Eleanor, and certainly not by himself or Rachel.

Eleanor held out a hand to him. "Professor Matthew Kearns, Agent Rachel Bromilow…" she looked up at Rachel who was still on her feet. "Oh, do sit down, young lady. You look foolish standing there like a clothes rack." She turned back to Matt. "I present, Mr. Khaled ibn Al Sudairi."

Khaled grinned, showing strong white teeth, and reached a hand out to Matt. "A pleasure and an honor, Professor Kearns. I have heard much about you and your work."

"From Eleanor?" The man's name was familiar but he couldn't place from where.

Khaled shrugged. "Yes, and also from the academic grapevines, as well as other places. Your work deciphering the Necronomicon was…" he raised a single dark eyebrow, "… out of this world."

"Also, top secret, so I'm guessing you heard that one from one of those "other" places you mentioned." Matt's smile faded.

He nodded subtly, and then turned to Rachel. "And Agent Bromilow, also nice to meet you." He held out his hand.

She gripped it and held on. "You wouldn't happen to be Khaled ibn Al Sudairi, nephew of Prince Najif al ibn Saud, of the House of Saud, would you?"

"One and the same; tenth nephew," he replied smoothly.

"The House of Saud?" Matt straightened in his chair. It was no wonder the guy wasn't overawed by Eleanor van Helling; he probably could have bought her a hundred times over. The Saud family was worth billions, many, many billions.

"Holy cow." Matt stuck out his hand again.

Khaled laughed and gripped it hard. "So, you have a map, I hear?" He released Matt's hand and then poured himself a small cup of thick, dark coffee. He sipped and waited.

"*Ahh, um…*" Matt bobbed his head, and looked to Rachel. "Well…"

"That's classified." Rachel's gaze was direct and professional, as she seemed to slip back into FBI mode.

Khaled looked at her apologetically. "I already overheard everything." He sipped again. "I suggest we join forces. Share what we have found."

"And what have *you* found?" Rachel folded her arms.

"Would you like to know where I've just come from?" Khaled didn't wait for her to even bother guessing. "Turkey, where we scaled six mountains looking for the relics of Noah, following some credible information we received. We had found nothing and were due to leave until we scaled an obscure peak called Mount Qardū in the south."

He sipped his coffee, his eyes on Rachel. "It was there we found something quite… startling."

Matt leaned forward, feeling like the air had been sucked out of the room, as he waited for the man to go on. But Khaled sipped again, in no hurry.

"Well?" Rachel demanded.

He replaced his cup on the tiny saucer. "An old monastery, hidden and buried under a massive, constructed ceiling within the mountain peak."

"No way." Matt edged forward another inch.

Khaled nodded. "Inside there was a perfectly preserved body. But there was more – horrors – I lost some good men."

"Horrors?" Matt asked softly.

Khaled waited for a second or two, his lips curling at the corners. "Your turn."

Matt felt Khaled's gaze slicing right through him. "*Um, okay, well…*"

"Hang on there, Matt." Rachel reached out and laid a hand on his arm. "I'll need to clear this."

"Consider it cleared." Eleanor's chin jutted toward Rachel momentarily. "As Assistant Director Wybrow has already told you, it is in your interest to collaborate, as your own investigations are now at a dead-end!" Eleanor paused as Rachel's cheeks reddened. Eleanor turned to Matt. "Proceed, Matthew."

Rachel's lips compressed into a thin line. Matt could tell she was fighting to keep a few hostile sentences behind her lips. He didn't want to land Rachel in any trouble, or for that matter, piss her off, but he knew the old woman was right. He looked toward Rachel.

"It's okay, we need to give to get, right?"

Rachel's nod was barely perceptible but it was enough.

"I guess you heard about the killings, the dead priest and the map hidden within the stained glass window?"

Khaled nodded and waited.

"Then just like you, there's more." Matt decided how to begin. "We also found some weird biological remains."

"Biological remains?" Khaled's brows came together. "Go on."

"Worms, like parasitic nematodes, possibly that had come from the body of the priest that was burned up and beheaded," Matt said. "And, according to our analysis, they might have been responsible for cell life extension and regeneration. Maybe playing a symbiotic role within the body." He half-shrugged.

"Interesting." Khaled's jaw tightened. "In the old monastery, we encountered a similar thing – worms, and they too erupted from the cadaver – millions upon millions of them. They also infected one of our men. He died."

Rachel gripped the edge of the table. "Describe them."

"Thread-like, clear and shining like tiny streaks of glass," Khaled said. "They were filling the preserved body to the point that when they exited, the entire body, collapsed to nothing."

Eleanor's mouth turned down in disgust. "Revolting." She shut her eyes and shuddered.

Rachel's brows were knitted. "We could find no obvious way the worms benefitted from their host, other than being housed within them. We thought it was some sort of symbiotic relationship, and we did find that they excreted a human hormone – FGF21 – the one responsible for health and longevity."

"Longevity?" Khaled's smile returned. "Then that would be why the sarcophagus identified the body as being that of Shem, the son of Noah."

"Shem?" Matt's eyes were wide. "And you said he was identified, how; was there pictoglyphs, writing?" Matt was stunned and sat staring at the man for several seconds.

"Yes, there was writing, but I couldn't decipher much of it. It was a little like Hebrew, but the inscriptions, the sarcophagus design and its symbolism were lost to me. But I believe the monetary was built just for him. It was a crypt, but even though the historical legends stated the building was destroyed, it was actually hidden by the construction of the roof."

"Did you bring back any proof?" Rachel asked. "I mean, the son of Noah. That's a big call, and frankly, one that is hard to swallow."

"What?" Khaled looked confused.

"I mean anything, a lock of hair, a scrap of clothing, a tiny piece of rock with this strange writing on it." Her eyes narrowed.

Khaled shook his head. "No, we were a little... pressed for time as we departed."

"A cave-in?" Matt asked.

"That and something else, worse." Khaled's vision seemed to turn inward. "Like I said, I lost good men."

Matt leaned forward on his elbows. "What did you see? What was it?"

"There was..." Khaled paled slightly. "There was something in there, the cave, alive. Huge, it attacked us."

Matt felt his own heart begin to race. "Something big, yellow eyes like saucers, fast, strong."

Khaled lunged forward. "You've seen it too?"

"I've seen something. I think it was a Nephilim, a sentinel." Matt said.

Rachel shook her head. "One of Matt's fallen angels."

"They're biblical guardians," Matt added.

Khaled exhaled. "Guarding Shem's body. Yes, it makes sense."

The silence stretched for a few seconds, before Rachel tilted her head. "And I take it, you saw the Ark as well?

"I never said anything about the Ark." Khaled lifted his chin. "In fact, I don't think the Ark ever made it to the Ararat or any of the surrounding mountains. That was a story that gained currency when the Bible was written, thousands of years after the actual event."

"I knew it." Matt wiped some crumbs from his mouth.

"And I believe sometimes, some things are not meant to be discovered." Khaled tilted his head toward Matt. "I put it to you, Professor Kearns, that the Ark is not, and never was, on Mount Ararat. Instead what lay there was the remains of one of Noah's sons, still looking like he could sit up and talk."

"Then why didn't he?" Matt looked at Rachel. "If these... worm things are so good at longevity, why wasn't he still alive? After all, the Bible mentions that Noah was fathering children at the age of 500 and lived to be over 900."

"Maybe they do somehow consume their host eventually," Khaled said. "Maybe after so long, Shem had just given up." He sat back.

"I don't know; the FBI scientist suggested they could possibly be a super-efficient parasite," Rachel said. "Maybe they don't even know they are benefitting us and are just keeping us up and running as a mobile house and food source – the longer we're alive, the longer they have a meals on wheels."

"*Yech*." Matt grimaced.

"Yes, both fascinating and revolting. But the mystery is why haven't we known about these creatures before?" Khaled asked.

"I bet someone does. And that someone isn't too keen for anyone else to find out – remember the beheaded and burned bodies, and the murdered families." Matt looked back to Rachel. "And I'm betting they'll do anything to protect their secrets."

"Well then." Khaled slapped the table. "Then we need to know their secrets. Once we find the answers, then they have nothing to protect anymore."

"And that brings us to our problem." Matt put a few more sandwiches on his plate. "We now believe we have a map, or at least a fragment of one. But no points of reference – it could be anywhere in the Middle East, and that's an area you don't exactly go about doing too many exploratories."

Khaled snorted. "I wouldn't exactly recommend doing too many meanderings in some of your cities after dark either, Professor." Khaled grinned. "We're close now. You see, clues are like stepping-stones; our next one is probably right before us. We just need to find it."

Rachel sat back. "Golly, why didn't we think of that?"

"Jesus, Rachel." Matt scowled at her, and turned to Khaled. "Go on; what are you thinking?"

"If what we seek is in the past – then that's where we must look. Firstly, let's think about our problem logically, and not just biblically." Khaled lifted a glass of water, and looked into it. "Let's begin with the flood."

"Logically, huh?" Matt rubbed his face. "Okay, did it ever really occur?"

Khaled smiled. "Do you really think that a flood submerged the entire world around 5000 to 4500 years ago?"

"No, I don't. That period coincided with one of the last interglacial epochs, but computer extrapolations have shown that even if all of the world's ice melted today, it still wouldn't submerge the planetary landmass." Matt sat back. "So no, I don't believe there was ever a worldwide deluge."

"But there probably was something, yes?" Khaled's dark eyes gleamed. "The story's genesis."

"I like your thinking." Matt grinned. "There *was* a flood, an unprecedented one, but maybe it was more localized."

"Yes, this is what I think." Khaled's grin widened. "And I also think I know where that might have been."

Matt nudged a stony-faced Rachel. "That's it, I'm hooked."

Khaled sat forward. "Unexpectedly finding Shem's body made me wonder what we really knew about the great man himself. What was real, what was fable and what was nothing more than historical distortion. So I did some research." He turned to Rachel. "What do you know about Noah, Agent Bromilow? I mean really know?"

She shook her head slowly. "Matt's told me a little. But really, just the Sunday School stuff – the guy lived somewhere in the Middle East, was some sort of farmer, built the Ark, animals two by two, and final resting place was Mount Ararat." She gave him a lopsided grin.

Eleanor had Greta wheel her chair closer to them. The Saudi man nodded to her, and then turned back to Rachel.

"Even in that summary, there is so much wrong. You see, Noah was never a poor man, and further, many people immediately place all biblical references in the Middle East, which is not the case for Noah."

"Africa." Matt pointed, gun-like. "I mean, the Bible says that Abraham's ancestors came out of Africa. Noah is one of those ancestors, right?"

"Exactly. Between 5000 and 4500 years ago it was the time of the great ancient kingdoms. Noah was a descendant of a Proto-Saharan ruler and these kings of the wetlands controlled the major water systems of Lake Chad, the Nile, the Tigris and Euphrates. The interconnected waterways were their highways and trade routes. In other words, Noah would have been extremely wealthy, familiar with boats and likely had a large fleet."

Rachel scoffed. "So he was already a boat builder? And I suppose he also had herds of animals hanging around."

"It's history that is speaking now, Agent. Let us listen to it." He waited a few seconds until she sighed and nodded, before he went on. "In answer to your question, the Proto-Saharan rulers such as Noah kept menageries with male and female specimens for breeding purposes. There are your animals."

"Shit," Rachel muttered.

"I think Africa is a good place to start, but where?" Matt asked. "All I know is it's somewhere referred to as *Bor-Nu*, the Land of Noah."

"And I believe that's Lake Chad." Khaled sat back.

"Lake Chad? *In* Chad?" Rachel's jaw dropped. "Jesus, could you pick a more inhospitable country?"

"Stop being a little princess." Eleanor snorted in derision. "I know that area and toured there in the sixties. Lake Chad is shallow and only about 500 square miles. It's little more than a marsh in some areas."

"That's right, today it is. But hear me out." Khaled grinned. "Remember what I said – let history guide us. Travel back 5000 years, and what do we now see?"

"Africa was much wetter, greener," Matt said eagerly.

"Exactly. Africa was a paradise and yes, much wetter than today due to the African geological rifts that generated watersheds and rain shadow troughs over the continent. Your own American satellite photographs reveal striations in the geology that tell us that Lake Chad was more than just a huge body of water then, but instead it was a magnificent inland sea. At its peak, it was the largest of four Saharan paleolakes and would have covered an area of nearly 400,000 square miles." He leaned forward. "That's larger than the Caspian Sea is today."

"And the land in that area is very flat." Matt nodded. "Perfect for flooding."

"Even thousands of years later, during the time of Noah, the lake still had a surface area greater than that of your Lake Superior and with a depth of around 600 feet. And remember, Noah controlled the waterways of the entire Lake Chad Basin."

"He would have been like a king," Matt whispered. "And if there was a surge in rainfall and significant flooding, the inland sea would have become an ocean again – turned back into its prehistoric version of itself – it would have seemed big enough to flood the world, or their at least *their* world."

"Yes, Professor Kearns, yes indeed." Khaled eased back into his seat. "There's a reason no one has ever found Noah, his great Ark, or his wellspring of life; it's because we have all been looking in the wrong place."

*

Khaled looked at the faces of the trio. As he expected, the FBI Agent's expression held suspicion. Professor Kearns' was open, interested, and bursting with curiosity, just as he'd hoped from a field-working academic. But the older woman was harder to read. Her eyes were half-lidded, and sometimes when he thought she had dozed off, he realised she had only closed her eyes to slits and was watching them all closely.

"Sounds like you're well on top of all this, so why do you need us?" Rachel waved away a sandwich Matt held out to her.

Khaled shrugged. "My expertise is more that of an enthusiastic amateur, whereas Professor Kearns is at the top of expert level. When we were down in the monastery, I saw ancient writing on the sarcophagus lid and sides. I could read next to none of it. I expect that there will be more clues and we cannot afford to miss or misunderstand a single one." He held his arms wide. "I'm smart enough to know when I need help and humble enough to ask for it." He shared his most charming smile. "I need your help."

Rachel raised an eyebrow, unmoved by his charm. "So you need our help. But what do you get out of it? Why are you pursuing this... *myth*?"

Khaled sighed, deciding to lay more of his cards before them. "The prince is not a well man. He has tried everything, but his body continues to fail him. If this wellspring of life exists, and it has the restorative and healing powers it is supposed to..." He shrugged. "... then please do not blame an old man for wanting to live a little longer."

Eleanor van Helling's eyes had shifted to Matt and seemed to glow with excitement. "And now, we are back where we started; still needing a goddamn map."

"Like Khaled said, we need to let history guide us." Matt hiked his shoulders. "We need a world map: old, but with high detail. They're very rare, but I do have one in mind."

"Go on." Khaled raised his chin.

"It's Roman, the Peutinger Map, or *Tabula Peutingeriana*. It's one of the earliest roadmaps of what was called the *cursus publicus* – the road network of the Roman Empire."

"I'm no expert, but the Romans weren't even around at the time of Noah," Rachel said.

"The Peutinger Map; I know it, well." Khaled chuckled. "It is kept at the Austrian National Library in Vienna. The original map upon which it is based probably dates to the 4th or 5th century and was itself based on a map prepared by Agrippa during the reign of the emperor Augustus."

"The very one." Matt nodded enthusiastically. "We need to examine it and try and line it up with the fragment of map from the Fort Severn window."

"Good." Eleanor smacked her lips. "I think I might be able to get you in there. I have contacts."

"Yes." Matt clapped his hands together.

"That version is worthless." Khaled's gaze was direct.

"What?" Matt's eyes widened. "It covers most of Europe, much of the Middle East, and even down to North Africa."

"Yes, it does, but just the tip of Africa, which was a Roman province established after they finally defeated the mighty Carthage nation in the Third Punic War."

Rachel tilted her head back. "Close but no cigar; what's the next option?"

"No, we're on the right track." Khaled stabbed a finger onto the table. "Over the millennia, the Peutinger Map has been copied and changed hands many times. In fact, the map presently held in the museum is a 13th-century copy and covers Europe, North Africa, the Middle East, Persia and India. But when the original was purchased by Prince Eugene of Savoy in the early 1700s for a significant sum, there was another bidder, who offered just as much."

Khaled lifted his small coffee cup and sipped, and then carefully replaced it on its saucer. There was breathless silence, and he knew he had them. "The anonymous seller found out something interesting about both the potential buyers – Prince Eugene had never seen the map, and so had no idea what it really contained or what he was potentially buying. And the other buyer was only interested in certain portions." He smiled.

Matt tilted his head back to laugh out loud. "Of course – he made *both* sales. *He split it up.*"

"*Yes.*" Khaled slapped the table. "This crafty seller decided to maximize his profit, and so he removed a portion and sold it separately."

"The greater Africa portion." Matt grinned. "That contained the Chad Lake basin."

Khaled nodded.

"And I'm betting you know where it is," Rachel added. "And I'm also betting you've known about it all along." She scoffed. "Why were we even playing this game?"

Khaled lowered his eyes, but the corners of his mouth turned up. "Yes, forgive me. I hoped the information might be of assistance. Now I know it will."

"I've never heard of this African portion." Eleanor's tiny brown teeth were clamped. "And where is it now?"

"The current owner might be persuaded to allow us to take a peek." Khaled watched their faces. Matt was perched on the edge of his seat, but Rachel looked wary.

"Who and where?" she asked.

Khaled sat back, his palms up. "My home."

"Saudi Arabia?" Rachel's nose wrinkled.

"Of course. My uncle is also a collector of antiquities and bought the *Afrik Fragmenta Tabulæ Antiquæ* on the black market decades ago. I've seen it and believe it might bring us closer to what we seek."

"Ship it here under my protection," Eleanor said softly.

Khaled pulled in a cheek. "I'm afraid his goodwill would not extend to that type of risk."

Matt folded his arms. "I'm not up for a trip to the Middle East." Agent Bromilow glared at him. "Not exactly a place where—"

"Ah yes, I'd heard; your recent time in Syria." Khaled scrutinized Matt. "I know that has colored your perception of our region. But Professor, I assure you, where we will be heading is an oasis of calm, modernity and luxury."

Matt didn't look convinced, so Khaled pressed him harder. "You have my word that you will be protected by a small army and never have to set foot outside the city." Khaled held his hands out, palms up. "It'll be little more than a lavish holiday."

Rachel glared at him. "In a place where women aren't even allowed to drive cars."

Khaled spun at her. "And you had over 13,000 gun-related murders last year, Agent Bromilow, we had 28." He shared his most sympathetic smile. "We are slowly moving our population to being more tolerant of sexual equality, but we must be patient and pragmatic with our people. All I ask is you be tolerant of our faults and patient as well?"

She sighed. "Will I need to cover my head?"

"It might be wise." He gave her a half-smile, but Rachel's nostrils flared in return.

Matt sat back, and his vision seemed to have turned inward. Khaled could see he was struggling with the decision. He reached out to grip his wrist and was surprised to find the professor trembling.

"Professor, a few days, and you get to see the oldest map fragment in the world. Saudi royalty will protect you, and, I might add, you will be safer there than you would be here. I know about the attack downstairs."

"*Arrgh.*" Matt threw his head back and grimaced as though in pain. Khaled noticed the FBI woman blanch.

"*Okay, okay...*" Matt said finally. "And damn my professional curiosity."

"Excellent." Khaled clapped once.

"I can be ready," Eleanor said.

"*You'll* be ready?" Matt squinted at the old woman.

Khaled held his arms wide. "You see, Agent Bromilow, Professor, it seems the older generation are made of sterner stuff, both physically and mentally, than we fragile persons today."

Greta returned and laid a hand on Eleanor's shoulder. Matt noticed that the fingers were long and strong and gently rubbed her blouse. Eleanor looked up and nodded. "And Greta will be accompanying me, of course."

"Greta?" Matt straightened in his seat.

Eleanor looked at Matt from under lowered brows. "My Greta has been with me since she was a little girl. I rescued her from an East German orphanage in the sixties, and, in a way, she is like my daughter." She looked up at the hulking woman. "And so much more." Her eyes narrowed. "Greta is coming."

"When?" Matt asked the Saudi.

"Tomorrow morning, first thing," Khaled said. "I'll have a private jet waiting for us at Teterboro."

"Private jet." Matt looked at Rachel and raised his eyebrows. "Nice."

"What sort of jet?" Greta asked. "Mrs. van Helling has special needs." Her eyes on Khaled were like pale lasers.

Khaled smiled. "A Gulfstream G-550; it has four living areas and seating for eighteen people. Also full medical facilities and ramps for your chair, Mrs. van Helling."

"The G-550 will be just fine." Matt grinned.

"Then we're done – 6 am, we'll be on the runway." Khaled stood up and bowed to Eleanor van Helling, and then to Rachel. He shook Matt's hand, and then lent in close to his ear and spoke softly in Arabic.

"Trust no one."

*

"What did he say?" Rachel asked as soon as they were in the back of their car.

Matt saw the creases between her eyes deepen as she waited for his answer. Khaled couldn't possibly have meant her, and more likely referred to the people who were tossing grenades into their windows, or maybe even Eleanor, or that frightful female bodyguard of hers.

And yet, he didn't say be careful, he said *trust no one* – there was a difference. Matt shrugged it off. "Nothing important; he just wanted to know if we needed extra security – the bomb blast and all."

Rachel studied him for a moment, before settling back into her seat. "You have all the protection you need... *me*."

"Yeah, I can't thank you enough," Matt said sarcastically. "I mean, if it wasn't for you, I'd be frittering my life away on some sandy beach right now. My biggest worry would be sunburn." Matt sighed, looking away. "You know, I shouldn't even be involved in this anymore." He turned back to her. "I think I should sit this one out, so..."

Rachel looked like she'd been slapped. "Seriously, Matt?" she said, raising her voice. "We *both* nearly died, *you* saved my life, and it's not over yet. Now you want to kick us, me, into the long grass?"

Matt was silent a moment, not knowing what to say. "Okay," he said quietly. "It's just..." He trailed off.

"Why do you keep trying to leave?" she asked, her blue eyes pinning him.

Matt looked away first. He rubbed his hand across his face. "I want to help, Rachel, I do. But some of the things I've been through… They never leave you, you know?"

Rachel put her hand to his cheek and turned him back to face her. "When I went to you after the bomb went off, I thought you were dead. *Dead*." He stared into her face. Her blue eyes seemed to pulse. "And then when you saved me at the church…" She bit her lip. "I'm not as tough as you think. I can't do this without you."

"Forget I said what I did." Matt put his hand on hers. "I'm not going anywhere."

*

She pulled him into her room, left the lights off and grabbed his shirtfront, dragging him toward the living room chair, and then pushed him back into it.

Matt smiled in the dark.

She kicked off her shoes, and rose up, her hands on the armrests of the chair and leaning forward. He smelled her perfume and was intoxicated by it. Rachel kept coming and her lips just brushed his ear. Matt felt the tiniest flick of her tongue on his lobe. Her voice was just a whispered breath in his ear.

Rachel moved her face to his and ran the tip of her tongue along his lips, top and bottom. It was the most sensual thing he'd felt in a long while. He reached up to encircle the back of her head and pulled her closer. She came fully onto his lap and their mouths locked. His tongue now fought with hers in their mouths, and she tasted like cinnamon and soda.

She pulled open his shirt as she moved back and forth on his lap for a moment before it became an urgent race to pull clothing free and fling it to the side.

*

Matt crept from Rachel's hotel room around 4 am. He was tired, and now sore, but in a good way. He smiled; for all her brusque toughness, she had her heart in the right place. He couldn't help it; he liked her, *a lot*.

He had plenty of time now to shower and shave, grab his stuff and meet Rachel and the car downstairs at 5.15. He wasn't sure exactly what he needed to bring, but Khaled had told him not to worry so much, as he had to only ask for something and it would be obtained within the hour for him.

He threw a few items of clothing, a shaver and toothbrush into his case, and then went to stuff the folder containing his pictures of the Fort Severn stained glass window in on top. He couldn't resist one last look, and dragged out the main image – to the untrained eye it was a few contours, different colors, a few dots and squiggly lines. But he knew there was a small piece of coastline, and the geography was distinctive enough that it could be recognized if they just found the broader context. And most importantly, he *knew* those squiggly lines had to be a trail.

I know you're in there, he thought, and then jammed it all into his case.

Matt sucked in a breath and then let it out slowly. The longevity, the worms, the people in the shadows, the giant thing looming in through the window; it all gave him a knotted feeling in his gut. He'd been here before, and it never turned out well.

He sat on the edge of his bed and stared off into the dark corners of his room. Matt shuddered, feeling his nerves run away on him at the thought of going back to the Middle East. He knew he was damaged goods and even getting involved in something that was turning out to have an element of the mysterious, not to mention deadly-dangerous, was insanity.

Then, as if dropping from the sky the mysterious Khaled arrived to help them advance their investigation. Good fortune, or by design? *Trust no one,* he had said. *Not even you?* Matt wondered. He sighed. *I should never have let Rachel and Samuel sit down. I should have stayed surfing that weekend,* he thought. He flipped the lid of his case closed.

"Damn; I'm a hostage to my own curiosity." He stood and gave a mirthless laugh to the empty room. "Or stupidity."

It was 5.10 am when he exited the revolving doors to find Rachel already waiting by the car. She looked fresh, alert and professional as always, and not at all like someone who had been vigorously shagging only a few hours ago.

"Sleep well?" she asked, and opened the car door.

"No, but had some great dreams." He jumped in and slid across.

Rachel took a last look up and down the street, and then ducked in behind him, slamming the door. "That was no dream." She smiled at him and Matt grinned back. Rachel cleared her throat and smoothed a hair behind her ear. Matt had the impression she was putting her professional game face back on.

"What do you think about Khaled? Seems too good to be true, him turning up just when we needed him." He watched her nose wrinkle.

"I don't trust him." She turned to the window. "Or, for that matter, Eleanor or Greta." She turned, one corner of her mouth quirking up. "Still not 100 per cent sure about you yet either."

He remembered Khaled's whispered warning – *this was turning out to be one fine working relationship,* he thought.

"We've got to work as a team." He shrugged. "No choice."

"We're not a team, Matt." Rachel stared into his face. "We're just a group all riding on the same train – when we get to our destination, and then we'll see who gets off where."

Chapter 11

Eleanor and Greta met them at the airport, and Matt watched with amazement as the big woman lifted Eleanor like a child and carried her up the stairs. He was going to offer to help, but he had the feeling Greta could have carried him as well if he'd asked.

The flight was long, 15 hours, and after crossing the Atlantic and then refueling at Heathrow, London, they were back in the air without disembarking. Matt hadn't felt claustrophobic at all. The entire cabin was theirs and the seats were in a pod-type arrangement, facing each other and with small coffee table before them.

He and Rachel were left to themselves as for most of the flight Eleanor dozed and Greta read a book, not even interested in looking in their direction. Khaled was up in the pilot's cabin, doing some of the flying. *The life of the rich*, Matt thought and sighed with envy.

The G-550 jet climbed higher as they crossed Israel and Jordan before entering Saudi Arabia. Looking down from a cloudless sky, Matt saw that the land was much greener than he expected.

The cabin door opened, Khaled smiled widely and came and joined them on one of the vacant chairs.

"Everything all right?"

"Everything's great." Matt pointed to the window. "So much green."

Khaled looked out past him. "Yes, the al Khanafah, a natural wildlife sanctuary. It's several hundred miles wide. But it'll be behind us soon, and then we enter the deserts."

"How much further to go?" Rachel asked.

"Another few hundred miles; maybe an hour. We'll pass over the cities of Buryadah and then az Zulfi, and then on to Riyadh." He grinned as he stood. "You'll love it." He looked down the cabin to Eleanor and Greta but seeing the old lady asleep, he nodded and left them for the front of the plane again.

Matt turned to the window. As Khaled had told them, the green was now behind them as they entered the deserts, and now there was nothing but yellows and browns, ancient and parched, for mile upon mile. Matt put a hand on the glass window; even in the scrubbed and chilled atmosphere of the luxurious jet, he could almost feel the dry heat emanating from the landscape.

In another half hour, rising up in the distance like an Atlantian city from an ocean of sand hills was the Saudi Arabian capital, Riyadh.

It was large, but not sprawling, and home to nearly six million people. The city reminded Matt of crystals that had been grown in a petri dish, lifting higher and higher as you approached its center. There, thrusting upwards like a large sea creature breaching the water's surface to snatch something from the air was the Kingdom Centre Skyscraper that rose up 41 stories. The sun glinted off its polished windows like the million faceted faces of a jewel.

Khaled rejoined them. "Coming up on Riyadh International Airport."

Rachel turned her head. "I would have thought being a member of the royal family you'd have your own airport."

He shrugged. "The king and many of the princes have their own airports. But their security would not let us come anywhere near them. If we tried without authorisation, well…" He grinned. "They have Israeli design surface to air missiles – they never miss."

Khaled peered down at the main airport that looked like a band of interlocking silver scales. "But we do get our own runway." He got to his feet. "Buckle up; I'm going to take her in."

He looked down the cabin at the sleeping Eleanor. She had a photograph of Clarence held tight to her chest. "Maybe we should wake her soon, yes? Or *you* should." Khaled grinned and gave them a small salute before heading back to the cockpit.

The plane glided in, and its wheels touched the tarmac with a feather-light kiss. Khaled obviously knew what he was doing.

The brakes engaged and woke Eleanor van Helling, and like a magician, Greta produced a small glass of orange juice with a bent straw and held it to the woman's lips.

Matt wondered how long the old woman had left in her, as she seemed little more than a bundle of sticks swaddled in Prada and Chanel. He turned to place his face closer to the window edge to see forward along the tarmac, and spotted that they were being directed toward a smaller shell-shaped building, and half a dozen cars were driving out to meet them.

"Here comes the welcoming committee," he said to the glass.

Khaled brought the plane in to a gentle stop and handed over the post-flight check down work to the pilot. He came through the cabin to unlock the door and pushed it open, lowering the steps. A single man in a suit bounded up, bowed slightly to Khaled and the pair spoke rapidly in Arabic. Khaled turned. "Customs and Immigration."

The man efficiently checked their passports, entered the information into a tablet, stamped their paperwork, and then bowed again to Khaled before vanishing back down the steps.

"You see." Matt grinned. "That's the way to do it; no queues, and they come to us."

Rachel peered out the window at the man scurrying away. "He'd probably be beaten if he insulted a Saudi royal."

"What about an American FBI agent?" Matt watched as their bags were taken toward a line of waiting diamond-black, tank-like Mercedes SUVs. Each with two bulky men in dark sunglasses standing by their side – bodyguards or small army – *just how safe is it?* he wondered.

Khaled waved to them from the door.

"Let's go." Matt got to his feet, followed by Rachel. He first went to help Greta with Eleanor, but the tall woman waved him away like he was an annoying bug.

It was midday, and the first thing Matt noticed was the difference in the atmosphere as he passed from the synthetic cool air of the jet, to the hot dryness of the Saudi sunshine. He winced as it actually stung his exposed skin. He cursed his lack of foresight for not packing a baseball cap, and he'd put it top of his list for things to order.

He inhaled the smells – even though they were at the edge of an international airport, he smelled spices, heating sand and rock, and something sweet, that he later found out was fermenting dates from the lines of palms outside. Matt had been in many deserts in his life, dozens, and they all smelled the same, especially the ones that had been dry for thousands of years. But the main difference here was that the other smell that floated in the air was intangible but obvious to the eye instead of olfactory nerves. It was of the filthy lucre – money. The car parks and streets were full of Mercedes, BMW, Porsche, Lamborghini, Ferrari, Aston Martin and too many Rolls-Royce to count.

"This way, quickly." Khaled hurried them to the cars. The huge men opened the doors, and then immediately looked left and right, turning their heads slowly to take in their surroundings. Matt could see in the back of one of the SUVs there was a rocket launcher, RPG, out of its case and ready. *These guys played for keeps*, he thought, and didn't know whether all the defenses made him feel safer or more nervous. *More nervous*, he decided and swallowed with a dry throat.

Khaled escorted Eleanor and Greta to one of the huge cars and spoke to them for a moment before their door was shut. Matt, Rachel and Khaled then went into the other, with the last SUV seeming to be just for the RPG and their luggage. Matt could also see more people jammed inside and guessed his thoughts on this being a small army ready to spring at any threat was pretty accurate.

Rachel also noticed. "Threat level pretty high here, *huh*?"

"Unfortunately, always," Khaled said as a matter of fact. "For every 10,000 people that love the rulers and their family, there will always be that one that hates us. And modern weapon technology means that one man could bring down an entire aircraft." He turned to her. "Let alone a few people standing out in the open on a tarmac."

Khaled smiled. "We'll be fine, as long as we follow the instructions of our security teams."

Rachel turned to Matt. "Remember how he said you'd be safe here?"

Matt groaned as the door was shut, heavily, and the security guards also entered their vehicles. He wondered at the extra paneling, and he tapped the glass.

"Bulletproof?"

Khaled in the front seat turned and smiled. "Yes, and an external layer of aluminum oxynitride – much lighter and tougher than traditional polymers. Can stop .50 caliber armor-piercing rounds." He turned to Rachel. "Courtesy of the US military."

"We get your oil, and you can have our tech." She smiled tightly. "Good deal."

In another few moments they were outside the airport and speeding down the wide, perfectly smooth road. The cars seemed to glide, strong, stable and silent. But Matt still felt on edge, as the guards and the driver's eyes kept darting from side to side, never missing anything.

"Where to first?" Matt asked.

"Prince Najif al ibn Saud's northern residence." Khaled grinned. "He might just be able to fit a few extra guests in."

They were soon outside of the main hub of the city and then entered another small built-up area.

"How far to the prince's residence?" Rachel had donned her dark glasses.

"We're within it now." Khaled pointed to the small city. "All this land is the prince's Riyadh estate."

The fleet of vehicles slowed as they came to a boom gate, and half a dozen men in uniform with automatic weapons fanned out. Matt could see that there were machine guns mounted atop two taller structures, their guns weren't pointed at them, but the men were alert and ready.

Khaled motioned to the desert out in front of the huge walls. "There are motion sensors, thermal signature detectors and a fleet of fast attack helicopters, as well as a small army of ex-Special Forces. We'll be safe here."

He wound down his window as a large bald man approached. Khaled greeted him in Arabic, and it was clear the two knew each other. They shook hands, as the huge guard obviously welcomed him back. Khaled pointed to each of his guests, and then turned and requested their tinted windows be dropped so he could take a look at them. Matt and Rachel complied, and the big guy's eyes expertly passed over them, lingering for a few moments longer on Rachel.

He slapped Khaled on the shoulder, and then waved them on, speaking rapidly into a walkie-talkie as the boom lifted, and the procession moved into the main compound.

"Ho-*oooly* shit." Matt's jaw dropped. It was like another country. Sprinklers fanned the verdant grass with peacock tails of water that sparkled iridescent in the sunshine. There were palm trees, olive trees and orange trees all positioned carefully to create forest-like stands, and rose-covered gazebos were tucked in and around secret spots for private prayer or just relaxing.

The road continued on, and they had to travel another half mile before they even reached the first of the buildings and yet another large gate. This time they were ready for the entourage and the gate lifted for them as they approached. Khaled swung in his seat.

"For you lot, *hmm*..." He rubbed his chin for a moment before snapping his fingers.

"Either Japanese Garden, Tahiti theme, or perhaps an English forest." He grinned. "Tahiti, I think." He swung back around, pointing his driver to one of the offshoot avenues.

Matt raised his brows at Rachel. "Tahiti?"

As they passed by different residence modules surrounding the main complex, Matt now saw what Khaled was referring to – each of the modules was designed around a different theme. One had raked stone beds, weeping willows and peach blossom trees. There was a small stream with a tiny wooden bridge running over it. It would have been right at home somewhere on the outskirts of Tokyo.

The next module was theirs, and entering the grounds, there was lush jungle, big pools of clear, blue water, and huge blooming frangipani and hibiscus trees. Matt could even see a few parrots arguing in among the foliage.

"I don't believe it; your uncle even has parrots in the trees." She turned. "Why don't they fly away?"

Khaled shrugged. "To where? There is hundreds of miles of sandy desert all around us." He showed her a line of perfect teeth. "Some pretty birds grow to love their cage, yes?"

She groaned, and Khaled pointed at another peacock roaming the grounds. "My uncle believes in authenticity. He has travelled many times to rainforests, to Japan and many other places in the world. If some part of the world takes his fancy, he will try and reproduce it here, so he can enjoy it over and over again."

"It's magnificent," Matt said. He wiped his brow, the outside heat now closing in on him.

"I hope you, Agent Bromilow, and Mrs. van Helling, will enjoy it here." He turned to watch one of his huge bodyguards open the door so Greta could lift the old woman from the SUV and lower her into her wheelchair.

"Will we get to meet the prince?" Rachel asked.

"Of course, at dinner tonight, 8 pm, a car will come for you. If you need anything at all, there are multilingual servants on hand."

Matt nudged Rachel. "We got servants."

Khaled waved over his shoulder and slid back into the car. Matt watched him go as he slowly unbuttoned his now-sticking shirt. "Did you see the swimming pool?"

Rachel looked over her shoulder to where Eleanor and Greta were just disappearing into their part of the mansion.

"So, my choice is, I can either go and make small talk with an angry old lady, who probably thinks I'm a waste of space, or I can go for a cool swim in a Tahiti-style swimming pool." She turned, tapping her chin. "Golly; what to do, what to do?"

Matt waited, grinning.

Rachel started to unbutton her shirt.

*

Matt and Rachel swam, and then fucked, and then swam some more. Matt could have happily spent a week here, weeks even, doing nothing but eating, swimming and having great sex with the limber FBI agent.

By 6.30 in the evening, Matt had stepped out of his shower, and walked into his bedroom to find racks of clothing waiting for him. There were lightweight suits, sports jackets and half a dozen pairs of shoes – all in his size.

He guessed his chinos, T-shirt and deck shoes just weren't going to cut it when he met the prince. He turned the collar back on one of the suits.

"Holy crap, Zegna." He whistled. Khaled was right about anything they wanted or needed would be made available to them. He was paid quite well as a Harvard Professor, but that never extended to buying Italian suits.

He pulled a crisp white shirt from a hanger and slid it on. Cool, brand new, and it felt great. He grabbed a blue single-breasted jacket and slipped it on. The fit was so good he decided he looked sharper than he had in years – and that was before he even put pants on.

"I am so keeping this outfit," he whispered to his reflection.

He dressed quickly – socks then shoes so highly polished they reflected the overhead lights. He stood and practiced buttoning and unbuttoning the jacket, tried one hand in the pocket or not, and then checked left side and right side view. He swept his longish hair back and nodded.

"Oh yeah."

Matt looked at his watch – 7.45 pm – Khaled was picking them up at eight, and he decided to wait out front in among the lush tropical gardens. He grabbed his folder of information, and then stepped out of his apartment.

It was still warm and light, but the sun was nearing the horizon. It would be twilight for a while – he expected sundown to be right on 8 pm. He sat down on a wooden bench just under a palm frond and leaned back, throwing both arms out wide on the bench back.

I've had worse field trips, he mused.

He breathed in the warm, flower-perfumed air and let his mind wander. It was hard to reconcile the lush paradise setting with the knowledge that only a few miles away was the start of the desert – hundreds of miles of sandy or rocky dryness where temperatures could rise to well above hundred degrees, day in day out.

"Where's our taxi?"

His head snapped around. Rachel stood on the step, smiling and wearing a long, body-hugging black dress and killer heels. She slowly turned.

"You like?"

"Yeah, I like a lot." Matt felt his heart jump.

"They even had a makeup artist come in to see me." She nodded, her lips turned up in a small smile. "I think I could get used to this life."

Matt was still admiring her shape. "It'd spoil you, Agent Bromilow."

"Oh, I think I'd be able to suffer it with good humor." Rachel came and sat beside him.

Matt checked his watch. "Still five minutes to go." He turned to watch a couple of small peach-faced parrots bickering in a tree beside them.

"Do you know much about Prince Najif?" Rachel asked.

"I did a little research, but don't know that much, really." He shrugged. "Worth billions, part of the Saudi royal family, and fourth in line for the throne. The guy has a degree in engineering, studied in America, and is apparently ruthless in business. He's quite the local hero."

"Yeah, from our security perspective, we have a strong relationship with the Saudis. They are a supporter of US policy, but paradoxically also fund many of the schools that turn out to be breeding grounds for anti-west extremists." Her smile faded. "Best left up to the politicians to worry about."

At exactly one minute to 8 pm, two long, black cars glided up to the front of their building. As if by magic, Greta appeared, pushing Eleanor van Helling's wheelchair.

"Where do you think she was hiding?" Rachel whispered.

Matt leaned closer to her. "I think she's in her stealth chair tonight."

Matt noticed that both women wore evening dresses to their ankles. Eleanor was heavily made up and looked like a sun-dried, over-dressed child. But the outfit Greta wore did nothing to hide the woman's muscular shoulders. He also saw that both women wore shaylas, a longish headscarf that went over the head and swept over the shoulders.

"Oh oh." Matt turned to Rachel. "Do you think you should be wearing one of those?"

"Yeah right. And maybe next time they're in Texas, I'll ask them to wear a ten-gallon hat." She folded her arms.

Matt laughed, stood, and held out his hand to her. "Let's go, our carriage awaits."

A driver got out and held the door. Matt and Rachel climbed in and slid across on the leather seats of the second car. The limousine was new, and there was a set of crystal decanters in holders waiting for them.

"Brandy?" Matt poured himself one.

"Really?" She curled her lip. "You're gonna drink that?"

"Sure, why not?" He sniffed the tumbler's contents. "Single malt, and I'm betting, very fine."

"We're going to meet a prince of Saudi Arabia, a kingdom that's one of the biggest theocratic patriachical, conservative societies on Earth. I'm pushing it by not covering my hair."

She nodded to his glass. "But you, sir, are asking for trouble meeting him with booze on your breath."

"I really want this." Matt looked at the glass and made his hand tremble theatrically. "Is this where it's my turn to mention that ten-gallon hat thing?"

She looked at him deadpan.

"Okay, okay." He replaced the glass on the tray. "Definitely on the way home then."

"Foot patrols." Rachel pointed to several groups of armed men with large dogs weaving through the small stands of trees. There were also camera poles everywhere that probably had thermal and infrared vision. She grunted in approval. "I guess nothing's going to be creeping up on us here."

They soon turned into a long, wide road that had a Californian feel with palm trees down its center, and at the end was a huge mansion with roman columns rising three stories in the air.

"More security." She pointed. On top of the building there were anti-aircraft batteries peeking out from underneath sandy colored camouflage netting.

Once again the boat-sized car sailed to a stop and the door was pulled open. This time Khaled was waiting for them on the steps, leaning forward to talk to the diminutive Eleanor van Helling. When Matt and Rachel pulled up he waved and nodded appreciatively as they departed their car.

He clapped his hands together. "You both look magnificent."

"I think it's your taste in clothing that's magnificent." Matt opened the jacket. "Fits perfectly."

Khaled bobbed his head. "Needs a bit of tailoring for you, but the size was right." He clasped his hands together, but still made no move to lead them in. He looked quickly at Rachel's hair, his smile dropping a little. "Just a few quick protocol things that I also mentioned to Mrs. van Helling: the prince is a traditionalist. Ms. Bromilow, as a single woman, you must not expect him to shake your hand. It's best if neither of you make any attempt to lay your hands on him at all." He shrugged. "His guards may intervene if they think you are trying to... *invade his space.*"

"Right." A muscle in Rachel's jaw twitched.

"Fine with me," Matt said.

"Good, then this way." Khaled bowed and then took them through.

They all passed through a metal detector, Matt was patted down by a huge man wearing gloves, and Rachel, Greta and Eleanor by a scarf-wearing woman, who expertly ran her hands up and down Rachel's lithe figure, and then quickly peeked in her clutch bag.

Greta had to help Eleanor to her feet so the wheelchair could be x-rayed, and Matt noticed that none of the security stages applied to Khaled, who passed by untouched.

They walked down a hallway with paintings of past royalty on the walls, many holding curved sabers or sitting on thrones, and then entered one of the many drawing rooms. Matt was pleasantly surprised, as he expected floor-to-ceiling gleaming metals and polished marble that displayed great wealth but no taste. Instead, it was a room with islands of plants, Chippendale furniture and magnificent 18th century antiques that blended perfectly with their surroundings. Against one wall, a line of waiters stood ready with small, interesting things on plates.

There were dozens of other people in the room, many wearing the red and white checked keffiyeh headdress and Thawb robes. Matt noticed there were no women at all. Khaled nodded to a few, but made no move to introduce them.

"Stag night?" Rachel said, casting her eye around the room. "Jesus." She whispered as the men stared hard at her.

"Who are they?" Matt asked.

Khaled shrugged dismissively. "Some lesser relatives, administrators or people needing approval from the prince for capital transfers, weddings, business ventures, or the like. Nothing related to what we are interested in."

The huge double doors at the end of the room opened and a group of men came through. At their center was a small, bearded old man. He was nearly eclipsed by a huge figure beside him who was stuffed into a black suit. The giant kept his arm jutted to the side, near the old man, and just as Matt wondered why, the old man teetered for a moment, and then quickly reached out to grasp the arm beside him. The big guy obviously doubled as bodyguard and walking frame.

"The prince," Khaled whispered.

The prince wore a white headdress with the black rope of an agel around his crown. His robes were a blinding white, and though the skin of his face had the gray hue of age now, it would have been coffee dark when he was younger. A large nose completed the image of a true prince of a desert kingdom.

He stood atop the step, nodding to individuals who bowed, some deeply. The prince's eyes moved to Khaled, then Matt, and finally Rachel. He ignored Greta completely, but looked to Eleanor van Helling and nodded briefly.

Prince Najif came down the steps and walked slowly toward them, an arm held up, with some of his robe draped over it. He stopped about a dozen feet from them, and Khaled bowed deeply, speaking an honorific in Arabic.

Prince Najif held out his hand and Khaled kissed its back, and then straightened. Khaled then half-turned to stand by the prince. He first motioned toward Matt.

"Professor Matthew Kearns of Harvard University." He then moved along to each of them. "Eleanor van Helling of the New York van Hellings. Agent Rachel Bromilow, FBI."

The prince spoke softly to Eleanor, and Matt was surprised to hear the old woman reply in perfect Arabic. The prince offered her a small smile, but didn't spare even half a glance for Rachel. He stepped closer to Matt.

"I understand you are a professor of languages and ancient writing." His dark eyes were steady.

Matt felt the eyes of the room on him and he nodded. "It has been my passion and career for many years now." He bowed slightly.

"You've come a long way to see my map. Or at least the portion of it that isn't locked away in a dusty, old museum vault." He grinned. "What value is there in beauty or knowledge if it isn't shared?"

Matt bowed again. "Sharing it is a gift. It is both an honor and a pleasure, sir."

"There is a price." He shook a finger at Matt.

"A price?"

"You will join me at dinner, and sit at my side. And you will tell me everything you have learned about the prophet Noah's wellspring of life."

"My pleasure, Your Highness." Matt beamed.

The prince turned away to speak to more of his guests, and Matt turned to Rachel and raised his eyebrows.

"Oh please." Rachel looked pained. "You did everything but kiss his ring."

He grinned. "I'm hoping to be adopted."

They then followed the crowd into a large banquet hall with an enormous table that was curved like a horseshoe. The guests sat around its outside with the prince at the center so everyone could see him. Waiter after waiter brought silver cloches to the table, whipping the lids away to reveal mouthwatering roasts of different birds, mutton, beef and then plates of vegetables and fruit. There were also pitchers of water, juice, teas and coffee, and some sort of warm honey drink that Matt had never tasted before, but was delicious.

Matt was just to the right of the prince. Khaled was immediately to the prince's left, and fanning out to each side of the royal after Khaled and Matt were the other junior members of his family, some business men, and then Rachel and Eleanor right at the end, both of whom wore stormy expressions. Greta had obviously been asked to eat somewhere else – no servants allowed, Matt guessed.

Matt tried to catch Rachel's eye, but she seemed intent on looking carefully at all the faces at the table. The waiters offered their trays to the prince first, and he pointed at one or the other, selecting choice portions from many. Once done, everyone else tucked in.

In no time, Matt's plate was piled high with everything from duck to slow-roasted mutton and some sort of seasoned bread, plus an enormous side plate of tropical fruits. He noticed the old man's plate was near empty, and he picked at small portions of meat and fruit, popping them into his mouth, chewing joylessly and wheezing as he ate. He wiped his lips, and then leaned toward Matt.

"Is it real, Professor? This wellspring of life?"

Matt turned to the man, and up close he could see the white of his eyes carried a tinge of yellow – *liver problems*, he guessed. It confirmed to him why a frail old man, one who was wealthy beyond Croesus, would be interested in the idea of being able to claw back an extra few years. His eyes slid to Eleanor van Helling, who was staring directly back at him. He nodded to her, but she never changed, her gaze remaining snake-like in its intensity.

Matt suddenly had a horrible thought – was she trying to read their lips? *Impossible*, he hoped. *But...* He turned back to the prince, and lifted one hand up beside his mouth to shield it.

"I've learned that there are things in this world that defy logical explanation, Prince Najif. I've seen beauty and horrors beyond heaven and hell, and I've come to believe that with all myths and legends there is a hard kernel of truth buried within their center." He shrugged. "So, my answer is, at this point I don't know for sure, but my mind is open and the clues are exciting."

"But you suspect." The prince played with his food a little more, rubbing the flat bread between his fingers and letting its crumbs fall back to his plate.

Matt shrugged. "The wellspring was purported to be the last remnants of the floodwater that the Ark rested in. I *suspect* that there will be something there, but whether or not it has anything to do with extending life or health is another matter. However, some other group certainly believes there is something there as we have been dogged by assassins along our journey." Matt leaned forward on his elbows. "This group of people are eradicating clues as fast as we can find them. Sometimes before we even get to them. I'd have to say they're a step ahead of us most of the time."

The prince grunted. "They won't trouble you here." His head turned briefly to Khaled. "My nephew tells me there were – *strange things* living in the bodies. That you believe may play a part in extending life."

Matt was glad that Rachel was sitting many seats away, as he guessed that Khaled had already shared all the information they had told him about the chemical analysis and their suspicions about the tiny organisms they had found in the body of the priest.

"We are not sure about the link, but we think they may have something to do with…"

"*Immortality*." The prince sat back, smiling.

"I don't know if it was that. Best if we don't get ahead of ourselves."

"But I do." The prince chortled and turned to Khaled. "And he wonders why there are some who would kill to hide this secret? Its value is beyond calculation." He reached out and placed a hand on Matt's forearm. "My nephew will accompany you on your immortality quest, and for protection you will also take some of my most trusted people with you."

Khaled smiled. "Ex-Special Forces commandos – all former Airborne Brigade."

Matt knew of them, the Saudi equivalent of SEALS.

"That's very kind of you, but…"

The prince held up a finger, and then leaned closer to Khaled for a rapid whispered conversation. The younger man listened and then nodded. The prince turned back. "Khaled will also organize some scientific specialists to support you. Anything you need, you will now have."

"Thanks, but…" Matt held up a hand, desperate to regain control. He knew Rachel would go crazy if she thought the Saudi was overwhelming them.

The prince knocked once on the table. "Then it's settled."

Matt sighed and slumped back in his chair. All that was left was to try and explain it to Rachel – *fuck that* – he'd leave it to Khaled.

From then on, Prince Najif largely ignored him. Perhaps having got what he wanted, information and placing more of his men on their mission, he was satisfied.

Dinner marched on – a pianist performed perfect Bach pieces that were followed by a well-rounded belly dancer that elicited a lot of admiration from the men around the table. Matt watched intently for a while, and then glanced at Rachel who looked bored. He just shrugged and smiled, hopefully imparting a *when in Rome* sort of vibe, but her expression told him she was having none of it.

By the end of the night, Khaled helped the prince to his feet, and then the huge bodyguard took over to guide the old man from the room. The other guests then also got to their feet and began to break into smaller groups. Khaled and Matt then rejoined Rachel and Eleanor.

Khaled walked them toward the door. "It's late, and I think we'd all benefit from some sleep. Shall I call on you tomorrow? Say 9 am? We can plan our next steps."

Matt looked at his wristwatch. It was just on 11 pm. "Works for me. I can get a few laps in before breakfast."

Khaled gave them both a small bow. "Thank you for being so understanding. The ways of the kingdom are still old fashioned and your patience is very much appreciated." He flashed his most dashing smile.

Rachel sighed. "Yeah, it's fine; everyone was charming, in a men's club kind of way."

Khaled nodded once and then turned toward his long black car. The driver immediately jumped out and came around to open his door.

"Until tomorrow." He allowed the driver to close the door on him.

Matt watched him go, and then felt something land on the forearm of his jacket and cling there.

He jumped. "Jesus." He looked down, ready to vigorously brush the offending thing off. But instead of some sharp-legged beetle, he saw a bony hand. Greta had soundlessly pushed Eleanor out from the shadows.

"Damned Arabs," she hissed in the direction of the disappearing limousine.

Matt winced and quickly looked around, hoping that they weren't in earshot of any of the locals.

The old woman wasn't finished. "If it wasn't for their oil, we wouldn't give a shit if they all blew themselves up or not."

"*Um*, did you have a good night, Mrs. van Helling?" Matt patted her hand and then carefully levered it from his arm.

"No, the person I was sat next to spoke English like a bad New York cab driver – incomprehensible!" She looked up at him, suspicion in her eyes. "What did he say – the prince?"

Matt shrugged. "He just asked a lot of questions. He was interested in finding out a little more about the source of the wellspring, and whether it was true or not." He shrugged. "Things we just don't know yet."

"I'll goddamn *bet* he was interested. Once we've seen the map, we should just all leave. I don't trust him."

Matt smiled and held a hand up to their driver, who nodded and came around to open the door for them. "Khaled's okay though, and we need his help." He shrugged. "Besides, we trust him."

"*You* trust him," Rachel said.

Eleanor grunted. "About time you said something agreeable." She looked toward her car.

"Greta."

The big woman immediately eased Eleanor down a ramp toward the waiting car.

"What a horrible old witch," Rachel whispered.

Matt smiled. "I dunno; I kinda got the feeling you two sort of clicked there for a moment."

"Not in a million years," Rachel replied with conviction.

The driver was a large man and quickly came around and bent beside the wheelchair as if preparing to lift the old woman into the back seat. Greta placed a hand on his shoulder, firmly, and levered him back a step. She then eased Eleanor into the car.

Greta followed and before she closed the door, she looked back at Matt and Rachel. The woman's expression was cold and hard, and it made Matt feel a tingle of unease run up his spine.

"Jesus, that's one scary woman."g

"And here I was thinking you two sorta clicked there." She nudged him. "Come on, it's late and I'm tired."

They slid into the car, and it soundlessly drove them back to their accommodation. Upon entering the foyer, Rachel turned and pinned Matt to the wall with a hard kiss.

"Hey, I thought you were tired."

She grinned, kneading him to hardness.

"Helps me sleep."

He grinned in the dark. "Always glad to help."

*

He floated on his back in the shimmering bath-warm pool. It was just gone 5 am and there was still a chill in the morning air. The sky was still a fathomless black, but the dry atmosphere promised another hot and cloudless day.

The stars had been chased away by the approaching sunrise, and like the old saying went, the night was always darkest before the dawn.

He wondered what it must be like to live like this day in and day out. Having so much wealth that nothing was beyond reach or forbidden to you. He spat a stream of water into the air.

Nothing was forbidden except something that could never be bought, he mused. And that was life, or simply, more of it. He had the feeling that both Eleanor van Helling and the prince both believed strongly in the mythical wellspring and were prepared to use their wealth and influence to find it.

He came upright in the water. And what then? Perhaps they would sip from some golden goblet and magically become younger? He'd seen a lot of strange things, but even that stretched his beliefs.

He breaststroked for a while and then turned on his back again in the oasis-style pool. This thing, if real, this pool, spring or fountain, would be the best kept secret on Earth. You were either allowed to know, or you were killed.

But who was allowed to know? And how did Clarence become part of the secret group, and then why did he leave?

Matt let himself float as he stared up at the blackness. It made him think of the glass window they'd seen in Fort Severn. Could that have been what the starless dark referred to, some sort of predawn image?

He closed his eyes, and using just his hands glided slowly through the warm water. Inside his eyelids, there was the darkness, but cluttered now by his imagination. He tried to assemble all the stained glass window's images in his mind's eye – the massive Ark, the images of great cliffs or a mountain range. Animals of many varieties, as well as thick forests with lush trees and ferns – perhaps this was the depiction of the Garden of Eden. The darkness, striped by the beams of light – the glory of god's radiance, he wondered.

He felt the tingle of fear as he remembered the huge creature smashing in at them. It had been in the glass as well. It was one of the Nephilim, he was sure of it, a guardian, but guarding what or whom? He concentrated, trying to tease out the small details locked away in his memory. In the glass, the thing had been pointing at a group of figures kneeling before a pile of stones. He tried to focus, but it all scrambled into confusion and he let it melt away.

Matt floated in the warm pool and it began to seep into his imagination. He saw again the magnificent sapphire-blue pond, the beautiful naked woman, who smiled at him with a mixture of confidence, seductiveness and something else – recognition.

It almost made sense, but as he tried to focus on it and draw out more meaning, it escaped him. Like chasing a dollar bill down the street on a windy day. The moment you went to grab at it, another gust would lift it to dance away from your fingertips.

His imagination wove in his memories. Some were of good times, like swimming in warm nighttime surf, or lush lagoons with shimmering waterfalls he had visited on exotic holidays. Others were much darker and were of haunted places that were full of shadows, with ink-black water below, and no light above, and rocky caves of dripping moss and secret, stealthy noises.

Matt's eyes flicked open. *That's it* – where he had seen the image before – vast bodies of water that existed in the darkness of a lightless cave.

"Could it be?" he whispered. "Underground?" His head collided with the side of the pool. "*Ouch.*" He came upright and then lifted himself from the pool. On the far horizon there was a blush of blue as dawn approached.

"Okay, Noah, is that what were you trying to tell us?" Matt grabbed his towel from a pool chair, sat down on it and rubbed his face.

Rachel stepped out in a one-piece swimming costume. The thin material hugged her body in all the right places. She skipped lightly down the steps and headed to the pool. She hadn't seen him yet, and she started to do stretches.

"Morning, Beautiful."

She flinched. "Jesus." She threw her towel at him. "You nearly gave me a heart attack, Professor."

"I see, party is over, back to Professor, is it?"

She grinned. "We're not dating."

"Not yet." He smiled up at her. "Hey, heads up."

A pair of large guards dressed in black, combat-style uniforms came around the corner. Both had huge German shepherd dogs on leashes that had furious eyes and straining necks.

Rachel quickly threw the towel around herself. They nodded to Matt and let their eyes linger on Rachel.

"Hey, pooch." Matt reached out to scratch one of the enormous dogs on the head as it went past.

"*La!*"

Matt recognized the Arabic word for "No" too late. The dog spun and sunk its teeth into his hand.

"*Fuck!*" The dog hung on, making a furious noise.

The guard yelled a command, and the dog released Matt, but still stood with its neck craned and gun-barrel eyes on him. It wanted another taste by the look of it.

"*Son of a...*" Matt gripped his wrist and looked down at the deep puncture wounds in his hand.

The guard apologized profusely, and by his pallid complexion, Matt guessed he would probably lose his job for allowing one of the dogs to bite a guest of the prince.

"Ofar has never, *ever* done this before." He shook his head. "I am so sorry. I will call a doctor."

Matt flexed his fingers, and then wrapped his towel around his hand. "It's okay; I guess I scared him. And don't worry, it's already stopped bleeding." The pain was excruciating, but he smiled anyway. "Just scratched me really."

Matt knew that wasn't true as his hand throbbed mercilessly and the towel began to redden even more. "You can continue your rounds, no harm done, and no one needs to know."

The man nodded, almost bowing, and dragged the dog away. Ofar looked back over his furred shoulder and licked his lips.

"Never work with animals and children. Haven't you ever heard that before?" Rachel said, and came to kneel beside him and unwrap his hand to check it.

"Did you see the look that dog gave me? He wanted more fingers." He sighed, flexing his throbbing hand.

"Come on, let's get some iodine on that before you turn into a werewolf." She turned back to the compound.

Matt followed her, feeling his hand tingle strangely beneath the towel.

*

The sand shifted and then slid away from the figures as they gently surfaced. One after the other they rose up until they numbered over 100 strong.

Their black clothing was set aside for desert fatigues and beneath their skullcap full-face helmets the emblem of the crossed keys was seared onto their foreheads. Their clothing was nothing like standard military attire in that it had other features designed for covert infiltration – cooling lines ran throughout the framework like spider veins that protected the wearer from the savage heat of the desert, but also masked them from any thermal readers in the area. Above the cooling lines was a Kevlar mesh that could withstand a direct hit from anything up to an assault rifle round, and also survive close proximity fragmentation blasts. It was a combination suit of armor and cloak of invisibility for the modern warrior – or assassin.

Two men at the front made hand signals and the group flattened, melding into the soft sand again, but this time they began to worm forward, like slow stroking swimmers through shallow water. It had taken them hours to reach the wall of Prince Najif's estate, but the pace meant none of them had registered on the motion sensors they knew were feeling for them.

Their destination was close now, and their objective was clear – destroy the seekers of the wellspring.

*

Matt and Rachel stood out front and at exactly 9 am, a limousine pulled up and Khaled stepped out. He had rolls of stiff paper under his arm and he waited and watched as another man exited the car with a wooden case that he held out flat in front of himself.

Just inside their module, Greta and Eleanor waited as Khaled bounded up the steps and grinned widely.

"A magnificent day." He waved a hand, theatrically.

"You got it?" Rachel asked.

"Of course." He shook Matt's hand and bowed to Rachel. "I said I'd bring the missing piece of the *Tabula Peutingeriana*, and we keep our word here."

He led them into their building, bowed to Eleanor, and then headed to one of the large side drawing rooms. He clicked his fingers and pointed to a large central oak table. The man carrying the wooden case went to it and lay down his load, bowed to Khaled, and then left.

Khaled immediately began spreading his rolled papers out flat. He pointed at one. "Lake Chad."

The first image was of the current size of the lake. Khaled flattened it with his hands. "Not a friendly area – the lake borders Niger, Nigeria, Cameroon, and of course Chad. It's shared by all, and it's still shrinking." He traced the outline with a finger. "About 520 square miles and averages five feet deep."

He flipped another sheet over on top of the first. It was made of a clear material that showed a much larger lake overlaying the current one. "Lake Chad about 5000 years ago. It had a surface of about 100,000 square miles and an area greater than that of your Lake Superior. Its depth averaged 400 feet and dropped down to 600 in some areas."

"*Whoa.*" Matt traced it with his fingers. They'd talked about it, but seeing it graphically represented was astounding – the early lake was enormous, and he could just imagine the surrounding wetlands teeming with life, and nothing like the dry desert now circling the shrunken body of water.

"And now..." Khaled flipped it again. "... we see what the lake looked like 35,000 years ago, and perhaps what it might have become during the biblical flood."

"Ho-*ooly* shit." Matt shook his head. The map showed an area that was nearly all water.

"Yes, impressive, isn't it? Satellite photographs reveal striations that show that Lake Chad covered an area of over 400,000 square miles. It would have taken a year to sail across and it connected to the Niger River and the Atlantic."

Rachel blew air slowly through her lips. "If a flood did that, it would really have seemed to cover their entire world."

"Yes, and if it happened quickly, then if you were without a boat, you were as good as dead. You couldn't climb a tree, and even most mountains were covered." Khaled straightened. "And Noah had boats."

Matt traced the rim of the prehistoric lake. "So big, so much coastline, and so many places he could have ended up."

"How long was he onboard?" Rachel asked.

"After the 40 days of rain? According to Genesis 7:24, 'the waters prevailed upon the earth a hundred and fifty days'. So he may have drifted anywhere." Khaled ran a hand over the prehistoric mega-lake. He looked into Matt's eyes from under lowered brows. "And that's why we need a place to start our search." Khaled's eyes twinkled.

"Well then; let's see what you've got." Matt nodded eagerly to the still-closed wooden box.

Khaled slid the box closer and clipped open the seals. "Give thanks to the prince. This is a rare honor that has been refused for too many people to count."

He lifted the lid and Matt crowded closer. Resting inside in a padded slot was a scroll on wooden rollers.

Khaled then reached into his pocket and pulled free a pair of cotton gloves, which he quickly pulled on. Once done he carefully lifted the scroll free.

"One minute." Matt raced back to his room to retrieve his laptop computer, which he flipped open, and carried back to the group. He called up the images of the map image embedded in the stained glass.

When he returned he saw that Khaled had spread a damask cloth on the table and had carefully unrolled the scroll. The intricate colors were faded, but the designs, contours and markings were all still strong.

"Oh wow." Matt carefully slid his laptop onto the edge of the table. "The missing segment." He leaned over the map tracing its ancient lines. "It's magnificent."

Eleanor had Greta wheel her closer, and she gripped the table with one bony hand. Her fingers caught the edge of the scroll.

"Please, no touching," Khaled said gently.

Eleanor clicked her tongue in disdain.

"He's right." Matt straightened. "Even our exhalations will be slightly acidic so we need to be quick."

"Yes, yes." Eleanor's lip curled. "So? What does it tell us?" Her eyes drilled into Matt's.

"Let's see." Matt switched to his computer, and slowly shrunk down the image of the map from the glass so its size corresponded to that of the *Tabula Peutingeriana*. Then he stood back, his gaze going from one to the other.

"We're looking for a piece of coastline to match our stained-glass map that looks a little like a fishhook, and with a small island in the curl. Maybe like..." He let his eyes run down the *Tabula Peutingeriana's* coastal contours. "Ha, maybe, this..."

Khaled leaned closer, his eyes going from one image to the other. "Mukawwar Island in Sudan." His lips lifted on one side. "If this is it, then no wonder we couldn't find it. The starting point is the Red Sea."

Matt nodded. "We suspected the map we found in the glass from the old church ended in Chad, but miles from where the lake is at today." He turned and grinned at Khaled.

"But of course, it would have had to be somewhere that was inundated during the great flood."

Matt pointed along the contours. "To the north, the Tibesti Mountains are the highest mountains in the Sahara and rise to over 10,000 feet. Also they're volcanic and riddled with caves that many have been found to contain cave art from as far back as 12,000 years ago, and was still being added to about 5000 years ago – the period we're interested in."

Matt closed his eyes for a moment, trying to remember information about the area. The details slowly leaked back. "Straight after the flood, the land would have been immensely fertile, but then climate change conspired to kill it for good. The mega flood was the last of the great waters. It got dryer and all the people left – they went north to the Middle East; forced to leave their lands and move to the Nile Valley or other areas with more water."

"They left everything behind?" Rachel shook her head. "Would they leave the Ark?"

"If it is the true Ark, then maybe it was too big to move." Khaled took a picture of the ancient map. "Professor, I'm sending you the images."

"Great." Matt looked up at Rachel. "The Ark was supposed to have been mainly made from reeds and gopher wood. I think even a few hundred years after the flood the ship would have been decaying. They probably left it behind."

"Never," Eleanor said. "Something that valuable and that holy? Unconscionable. It would never have been left to rot."

"Or they hid it," Rachel said.

"It wouldn't matter; it was made of organic material, and they didn't have any preservation techniques back then. I'm afraid the Ark is long gone," Matt said.

"It matters not. The real question is: exactly what exists there now that could hold the secret to eternal life?"

"There's no such thing as eternal life." Matt felt slightly sorry for her. "Eleanor, sure, there could be something that seems to be extending life, but from what we understand, it might only be some sort of parasitic or symbiotic temporary side effect. We're not even sure if the, *uh*, infected people are in pain because of the affliction."

"Like my Clarence, you mean?" she shot back.

"I don't know." Matt sighed, and looked back at the map as his computer pinged. "Got the pictures. Gonna line them up now." *Saved*, he thought, and leaned into his screen.

Matt edged the image from the *Tabula Peutingeriana* up against the map from the stained glass. He made the stained glass image transparent, adjusted its size, and then slid it across on top of the old map.

"Bingo! Ladies and gentlemen, we have our starting point." He fist pumped once, and then went back to his screen. "Looks like it starts at the coast of the Red Sea at Mukawwar Island, and the marked trail travels across what is today Sudan, enters Chad, and then ends…"

"And then ends here." Rachel smiled lopsidedly. "Somewhere in Chad's jungle, something was hidden."

"It's no jungle anymore. There's nothing there," Matt said.

"There is, or was. It was the Garden of Eden of course." Khaled had one eyebrow raised. "Five thousand years ago it was *Akebu-Lan*, in the kingdom of Bor-Nu."

Matt grinned. "The Fountain of Youth in the Garden of Eden?" He grinned. "Makes perfect sense to me." He straightened. "So what now?"

"That's obvious, Matthew." Eleanor's eyes blazed. "We go there."

Chapter 12

The first explosion shook the building and made dust rain down on their heads. The second made the lights go out.

"What?" Khaled snatched up the maps, shook off the debris and quickly rolled them up. Explosions were occurring all over the compound, and sporadic gunfire could be heard coming from the western side, the walled side that was closest to nothing but hundreds of miles of featureless desert. "*Impossible.*"

Rachel dragged Matt to his feet. Beside them, Greta had flung herself over Eleanor, making herself both a comforter and shield.

Rachel saw Khaled quickly stuff the precious maps back in their box, and she grabbed at his arm.

"What the hell is going on?"

He didn't look up. "An attack – assault rifles, grenades, and by the sound if it, larger ordinance, probably RPGs."

"No shit?" Rachel literally growled at the Arab. "I know *what* it is, but from who?"

Matt shook dust from his hair. "Right now, doesn't matter; seems our fortified oasis has been breached. We need to leave."

"We head to the prince's residence; he has a bomb shelter – we can wait it out." Khaled pulled a phone from his pocket and turned away. He spoke quickly in Arabic.

Matt turned to Rachel, and she immediately knew what he was thinking. "Yeah, I know, it might be the Borgia."

Matt nodded. "And if it is, they're here for us – we won't make it halfway there."

Khaled grunted as he listened for another moment and then turned. "We are under attack by an unknown force. There are a significant number of them, and they have exceptional firepower. The roads leading to the prince's compound have also been destroyed, cutting off any help outside from arriving soon. The prince's forces are engaging them now, and he has invited us to join him in his..."

"No," Rachel said. "We can't stay. Think about it; if these guys have the intel to attack this fortified compound and breach it so easily, evading your lookouts, thermal and motion sensor security defenses, then my gut tells me they know all about the prince's personal panic room. We go in, we're not coming out."

Khaled just stared.

"She's right," Matt added. "They cut the roads so they'd have plenty of time alone with us. We seal ourselves up in a steel box, and we're right where they want us." Matt gripped the Saudi's upper arm. "You need to get us out of here."

Khaled shut his eyes for a second, and then nodded. "Yes, I see it now."

He jammed the phone back to his ear, and pointed to them. "I'm calling in a helicopter – grab what you can."

Eleanor peered out from under Greta's arm. "I'll just need to..."

Khaled rounded on her first, but spoke to Greta. "You need to get moving, or you'll both be staying." He raised thick eyebrows. "I'm sure the prince will accommodate you."

He looked to Matt and Rachel. "Two minutes out front." He headed for the door, maps beneath his arm.

Rachel pushed Matt, jolting him into action. "Let's go, go, go – just grab what's closest." She looked over her shoulder at Eleanor, and for just a moment, she hoped the old women had decided to stay behind. Unfortunately, Greta was already speeding back to their room, the wheels of Eleanor's chair flicking debris into the air.

In a few minutes Matt and Rachel met at the front door, small bags under their arms.

"Guess I'll come back for that Zegna suit later." Matt grinned nervously.

Rachel looked at her wristwatch. "If that chopper doesn't arrive soon, they can bury you in it."

"Thank you." Matt went to push though the doors, but Rachel grabbed his shoulder.

"Wait." She peered around a column and seeing no one, waved him on. "Come on."

As soon as they exited through the glass doors the muffled sounds became frighteningly real. It was like a war zone – the yelling, flames, smoke, explosions and rattling gunfire. Rachel saw the bodies strewn over the lawn, and she crouched and ran to some bushes, Matt was beside her immediately.

She checked her watch again. "He's late."

"Then we wait," Matt said. "It's not like we have other options."

"Down and quiet." Rachel uselessly checked her hip. "No gun, so we'll have to throw stones."

"*Matthew?*" Eleanor's voice floated down from the front of the building.

"Oh, Jesus Christ." Matt lifted his head. "*Shush,*" he whispered harshly back to her.

"Leave her," Rachel shot back.

"Can't do that." He began to stand.

"Sure we can." Rachel grabbed him and dragged him back down. "Least for now."

Six of Prince Najif's bodyguards jogged across the lawn, speaking rapidly in Arabic into microphones looped over their ears and along their jawlines. Rachel had the urge to yell to them as one of them suddenly threw his head back as if he saw something interesting up in their air, just before he fell backwards like a felled tree. She had seen it before – the bullet to the face punching the head back on his neck.

The other five guards raised their automatic weapons and one dropped to his knee as two of the strangest looking beings Rachel had seen in her life sprinted forward firing as they came.

"What the hell?" she breathed, as she watched the strange robot-like men take hit after hit in the chest and head, and whatever armor they wore protected them from most strikes. But not all; she saw plumes of blood spray out behind them, but determination kept them coming until they had emptied their own magazines into all the Saudi guards. Only then did both of the attackers seem to wind down to death, kneeling and lowering their chins onto deep chests.

"*What* the fuck are those guys?" Matt snarled, his eyes wide.

"I'm betting our fanatical friends from the church," Rachel whispered, laying a hand on his shoulder and pulling him back down.

The night-black helicopter came in low and fast, and before it even touched down, two men leapt free.

"Black Hawk," Rachel said and stood. "Good, armored, we'll need it."

Khaled spotted them and pointed to the chopper. He then sprinted off in search of Eleanor. Finding them quickly, he and the other man ran to collect them, but before they got there Greta had the small woman from her chair and was sprinting hard to the open door of the large, muscular helicopter.

She yelled back over her shoulder to grab the chair as she went. In another few seconds, they were all on board and Khaled pulled a set of headphones on and ordered them to take off. Almost immediately, the dull *thunk* of bullet strikes peppered the undercarriage.

"Hang on," Khaled yelled.

The helicopter banked hard to the east, and then accelerated. Rachel looked down and saw a bright flare from the ground that was followed by a wobbling tail of fire. The pilot tilted the helicopter almost 90 degrees in the air.

"RPG," Khaled said.

Rachel nodded, but had already known what it was. RPGs were fast and deadly, but dumb. The real threat came from something a little smarter, something like a guided surface to air...

"Missile...!" Khaled's roar jolted Rachel into clinging on even tighter and leaning forward with her head down. She saw Greta wrap her arms around Eleanor, hugging the small old woman to her large frame.

The helicopter first accelerated, and then she heard small popping explosions from the rear of its undercarriage, and looking back she saw the spray of hot stars trailing behind, just before they banked hard.

Thank god, she thought. They had countermeasures to deploy – the pyrotechnic flares burned hotter than their engines and were irresistible to most heat-seeking ordinance. The missile exploded in the air behind them, and in another few seconds, they were out of range,

Rachel sat back, letting out a breath she didn't even know she was holding. She also realised she had a throbbing headache – most probably from her surging blood pressure. Beside her, Matt pushed long hair off his face, and grinned.

"Hellava day."

Rachel exhaled through pressed lips. "And it ain't over yet." She looked down and back; behind them Prince Najif's estate was a cauldron of fire.

Chapter 13

30,000 feet over the Red Sea

Khaled had told them that the prince was safe, and as soon as their chopper was out of range, the attackers had simply melted away. It was obvious now that they were the only targets.

Matt had the bandage on his hand peeled back and was looking at the skin where the dog had bitten him only hours ago. His heart beat faster as he stared – there were some indentations in the flesh, but the wounds had fully healed.

What the hell is happening? he wondered. He stared hard at the flesh as if trying to see beneath the skin to the muscle, blood vessels and bones below. He had a sinking feeling he already knew.

"Hey." Rachel approached down the aisle and he quickly pulled the bandage back up and covered the hand.

"What's up?" He turned.

She sat and then looked over her shoulder to where Greta and Eleanor sat talking. The old woman had her eyes closed but from time to time she nodded.

"Matt, really, how the hell is she ever going to keep up on this trip?"

Matt glanced back over his shoulder and then shook his head. "Maybe Greta will carry her the whole way."

"Or maybe one of them." Rachel's teeth showed as she then glanced at the six burly men who Khaled had brought with him; obviously some of the prince's Special Forces bodyguards.

"So now we have these guys with us." She had her hands on her hips. "I knew I should have asked Wybrow for more backup." She sighed. "You leave a vacuum and some asshole fills it."

"That's a nice image." He grinned. "Look at the upside…" Matt leaned closer to her. "… where we're going isn't exactly the safest spot on Earth. So having a team of hardheads with us can only be a good thing. Besides, you do remember Najif's estate, right?"

She turned to him. "I'm not debating that. All I'm saying is, I wish they were *our* hardheads."

He chuckled. "I hear you."

Rachel settled back into her seat. "How long?"

Matt checked his watch. "Another six hours before we arrive at N'Djamena International Airport." He eased back. "You know much about Chad?"

"*Nada*. But I hear it's very nice?" She pulled in a cheek and snuggled lower in her seat.

"Some would say it's a melting pot of different ethnicities, cultures and religions. Others would just call it a boiling crucible of violence."

"Right then, so not that nice, *huh*?" She smiled. "Give me the thumbnail sketch."

"An old country in an old continent." He crossed his hands on his stomach. "People have been living in the Chadian Basin for many thousands of years, and it was once one of the crossroads of civilizations. One of the earliest empires was the legendary Sao that had existed there since 3000 BCE. They were an ancient race only known from their artifacts. The Sao fell to the Kanem Empire, about 2000 years ago, who in turn fell to Islam and the Safwaya rule around 1000 AD."

He turned to smile to her. "Who then fell to the Bulala, invaders from the area around Lake Fitri to the east." The desert reclaimed much of the empires then, and the peoples scattered across the land. It wasn't until the French arrived around 1900 that they took to stopping the tribal warfare and secured full control of the colony and incorporated it as part of French Equatorial Africa." Matt bobbed his head. "The French granted self-rule to Chad after World War II, and then that's when the despots and tyrants took over."

"Bloody history." She grimaced.

"It gets better, or rather worse." He sighed. "Just in 2013, security forces in Chad foiled a coup against President Idriss Deby. You want to be a ruler in Chad, you've got to have eyes in the back of your head."

A muscle in Rachel's jaw twitched. "Now I really wish I did ask for more backup."

He sighed. "I guess we work with what we've got."

"Yep, and we'll soon find out if these stuffed suits of Khaled's know what they're doing." Rachel raised her eyebrows at him.

Matt glanced quickly back at the bulky men packed into the rear seats. "They look pretty tough to me. I wouldn't want to pick a fight with any of them."

Rachel reached across to stroke his cheek with the back of her hand. "You, dear, are here for your brains."

Matt laughed and turned back again. He saw that a pair of the group, seated at the very back, seemed more normal looking, even nerdy. "Well, most of them look tough." One of them lifted a hand to wave, and Matt nodded back. "I think a few of Khaled's team are the specialists he mentioned; *excellent.*"

"Then at least he's done something right." Rachel eased back and turned to the window.

Matt sighed. "Wake me when we get there." He closed his eyes.

He turned his mind to the ancient Roman map of the country, and also the stained glass representations of some sort of destination. The problem was that given the scale ratio, the map end-point was somewhere, *nowhere*, out in the desert.

Matt tried to get comfortable. He wanted to sleep, but didn't feel tired. The strange thing was he needed less and less sleep, but was feeling more and more invigorated. In fact, his entire body, inside and out, tingled with a weird energy. He licked his lips, feeling thirsty, *sort of*, but not desiring water. It was something else he craved but couldn't think what.

Matt opened his eyes a slit, and peeked under the bandage on his hand. There was nothing now – no weeping wound, scabbing or even a scar. Impossible, as the bite had been bone deep and only happened half a day ago. He took off the bandage, rolled it up and stuffed it into his pocket. He flexed his fingers. He had a sinking feeling in his gut.

And then there was the bomb blast – that was something else he had walked away from. In the haze following it, he had fragmentary memories, like torn pieces of a photograph with many bits missing. There was a man, tall, broad and bearded, who had talked softly to him. *Welcome, Brother Matthew.* Did he really say that, or was it just a load of damaged neurons in his brain misfiring after the explosion?

What's happening to me? he wondered.

Infected, his brain whispered back.

Impossible, he thought.

You know it's true, his mind sneered.

Don't think about it, he demanded of himself. He wriggled in his seat, trying to relax and began the waking dream of the beautiful, tall woman rising from the sparkling blue water. She made his heart leap in his chest, but also calmed him.

"Professor Kearns?"

Matt jolted forward. "*What?*"

"Doctor Joshua Gideon." The man adjusted a pair of wire spectacles and then sat on one of the seats facing Rachel and Matt, and stuck out a hand for Matt to shake.

Rachel opened her eyes and he shot the hand back out toward her. "And Agent Bromilow, I presume. I'm from the parasitological department of Tel Aviv University." He smiled and shrugged, "You might say I'm on loan."

She frowned. "Really? How are you guys even working together?

He bobbed his head. "Relations are good right now – we're both allies of the US, who share a concern about the Middle East. We cooperate on numerous things. And more importantly, Prince Najif has a lot of connections." He grinned. "I think I was summoned and on my way before your dinner with the prince was even finished."

"Pardon me, Joshua." Another older man excused himself and squeezed himself and his large stomach into the last vacant seat over from Joshua. "Abdul Ebadi, archaeology." He shook hands and sat back. "I specialize in ancient religious artifacts and history. I also cross majored in geology."

"Perfect; that'll come in handy." Matt turned to Rachel. "See? This is more like it."

"You can never have too many eggheads," she said. "But, Mr. Ebadi, I think my little friend here has got your field covered." She nudged Matt.

"Maybe," he said. "But my knowledge is primarily focused on religious studies. I even worked on the Babylonian tablets."

"No way?" Matt moved to the edge of his seat. "From the Mesopotamian excavations?"

"Yes, indeed; and they're possibly the world's oldest clay tablets that contain a flood story." He smiled at Rachel. "They were discovered by the British Museum archives curator, Irving Finkel, and they specifically mention an Ark and the flood."

Matt grinned, and looked briefly at Rachel. "Babylonian, and dated around 1750 BCE. Maybe the oldest telling of the biblical tale *any*where, *any* time."

Ebadi nodded. "You might say I specialize in *Ark-eology* as well as archaeology." He chuckled and held up a hand flat.

Matt high-fived it. Rachel exhaled through pressed lips and looked back out her window.

Matt turned to Joshua. "And I'm betting you're here because you obviously heard about the biological samples we discovered."

"I am, and I must say I'm beyond intrigued. The information that was forwarded from the FBI laboratories was extremely useful."

"What?" Rachel sat bolt upright. "What information, and forwarded by who?"

"Hey, thought you were dozing?" Matt leaned away from the bristling woman.

"We got a briefing pack on the stained glass images as well as the parasites." Joshua seemed to search his memory for moment. "Ah, from Assistant Director Vynow or Wynow? He was pretty high up?"

"*Wybrow*. Just *perfect* – out of the fucking loop once again." Rachel got to her feet and paced up toward the front of the plane.

Professor Ebadi frowned, probably at Rachel's burst of profanities, but just momentarily tightened his lips and then turned back to Matt. "This is a dream fieldwork opportunity."

"Let's hope it stays that way. Pretty hostile territory we're entering." Matt said.

Rachel had paced back. "Pretty hostile where we just came from," she added with a tight smile.

Matt sighed. "Yeah, there are hostile forces at work; been several attempts on our lives."

"We heard," Joshua said. "I think that's why we brought them." He thumbed over his shoulder to Khaled's commandos.

Rachel flopped into her seat, her face like thunder. Matt grinned. "And I brought her."

She scowled, but Matt ignored her. "So what did you make of the organism? It's weird to say the least."

Joshua raised his eyebrows. "Sure is, weird and unique. We mammals, and in fact *all* animals, have been hosts to all sorts of intrusive creatures for millions of years. Did you know that they uncovered a T-Rex skull with trichomonas boreholes in it? Parasites have been around longer than we have."

"But in human beings, have you ever seen anything like this?" Matt asked.

"Not exactly." Joshua bobbed his head. 'No, never. We normally deal with two types of parasites. There's the ecto-parasites, like fleas, scabies, nits and the like that infest the external realm of our bodies, and then there's the endo-armies, that live in our organs, blood and cells."

"The harmful ones, right?" Rachel said without turning.

"Sometimes. The dumber they are, the more harmful they are. The smarter ones can actually alter their environments; alter us, to be better, healthier and stronger – the healthier we are, the healthier their homes are. And of course the really exceptional ones are the symbiotes, that are beneficial to us – we give them a home and food, and they look after us."

"Sounds like what the worms were doing to the human body – extending life and health." Rachel said, turning to face them.

"I'm going to ask a dumb question." Matt faced Ebadi. "Have you ever heard of something like this in your religious studies? Anywhere? This seems somehow to be inexplicably linked to the biblical flood."

"There's always been an association of worms with biblical plagues," Ebadi said. "There's the taking down to the worms referring to the degradation of mankind in just about every holy book, but there's nothing I know of that offers some sort of divine immortality." The man seemed to think for a moment. "I would have thought that would have been godlike, and for man to aspire to it, would be seen as blasphemous."

"Matthew…" Eleanor's voice floated up from behind them.

"His master's voice." Rachel smirked.

"Oh boy," Matt muttered before turning in his seat. "Yes, Eleanor?"

"Come back here, dear, and tell me what you're talking about."

Rachel half-turned back to the window. "Go on, dear. Go tell Mommy what you've been doing."

Matt groaned, and leaned toward Joshua and Ebadi lowering his voice. "She's not really my mother." He stood up. "Excuse me." He headed down to the rear of the plane where Greta and Eleanor waited.

"Ladies." Matt sat facing both the women. "How's your flight been so far?"

The old woman pursed her lips, her eyes half-lidded. "Long, uncomfortable and very down market." She half-turned to the large men just back from her. "And overly crowded."

"We're nearly there now. But we did warn you that it wasn't going to be very pleasant." Matt smiled patiently.

"That was supposed to be when we arrived, not when we were traveling." Her eyes slid to Khaled and her lips pursed momentarily.

"Please sit down." Eleanor smiled sweetly. "You haven't yet told me what the specialists are talking to you about? They look more like the bookish types; scientists like you. Are they?"

Matt nodded. "Religious expert and a biologist; Prince Najif has managed to assemble quite a good team, plus security.

We were just talking about the evidence as we now know it – nothing you aren't aware of, so no new revelations yet."

"Matthew…" her voice became softer. "Thank you for helping me; you're the only one I trust." She eased herself closer and put a hand over his.

"I'll do what I can." Matt patted her hand that was little more than wrinkles over gristle. He looked to Greta and smiled. But the large woman never flinched, and in her eyes he saw something unpleasant. Matt slapped his hands down on his knees. "Well, if I find out any more I'll let you know. Like I said, only a few more hours now, and probably not long until we start to cross into Chad."

"Goodie." Eleanor eased back into her seat, and Greta pulled a blanket around her shoulders making her look even more like a tiny animal snuggling back into its nest.

Matt walked back to his seat and sat down. Joshua and Ebadi had left, maybe frozen out by Rachel. Her eyes were on him.

"Well?" She asked.

He shrugged. "She's impatient, uncomfortable and bored."

'Welcome to the club." Rachel snorted. "And how are you holding up?" She looked at him from under lowered brows. "I've never known anyone to have such bad luck, or is it good luck, in my life."

"Don't worry about me; I'm a survivor, and I'm lucky. Right about now, I'm just looking forward to what we might find." He swallowed and looked away from her eyes.

Rachel grunted and settled back in her seat. "Well, just make sure you save some of that luck for where we're going. I hear we might need it."

"Me too." Matt settled back, closed his eyes, but still couldn't sleep.

Chapter 14

N'Djamena International Airport, Republic of Chad

Khaled's plane taxied into the airport, stopping several hundred feet from the main doors. Security was little more than six feet of wire fencing running around the perimeter of the runways and airport building. Men, some in uniforms, some not, seemed to wander around and over the runways.

Khaled joined Matt and Rachel. "We will be met by a local official. We should not need to enter the main airport building, but..." He shrugged. "... things tend to change quickly here. Be ready to move on my word." He straightened.

Matt got to his feet with Rachel, and Joshua and Ebadi stuck close by, probably preferring Matt's company to that of Khaled's Saudi commandos, or worse, spending time with Mrs. Eleanor van Helling and her intimidating companion.

The door was pushed open and Matt heard a greeting in Arabic. Khaled responded and was first down, smiling broadly. The waiting official had a shaved head, and was the color of dark coffee. He wore a blue suit that was dust-brown from the knees to his shoes.

Khaled shook his hand vigorously, as the Saudi's security team came down the steps and fanned out, their eyes moving from the low buildings to the trucks, and then lingering on the stragglers moving across the airfield. Matt bet they were armed, but doubted there'd be any sort of screening when he saw Khaled hand over their passports for stamping, plus a thick envelope which vanished into a breast pocket as if it were something unpleasant.

Matt and Rachel came down next, and to her credit, Eleanor managed to be carefully led down the steep steps, which took a while, but proved she was mobile when she really wanted to be.

"*Oh god.*" Rachel winced.

The heat was as bad as Saudi Arabia, but here there was very little sense of the healthy clean air from the Saudi capital. Instead, what *was* in the Chad air were bugs of a frightening size and number.

Matt turned to Ebadi. "Now this feels like a biblical plague."

"It'll be better when we're away from the city." Ebadi grinned. "I hope."

Khaled came back with their passports. "All done. And now…" he pointed to a small plane waiting on the tarmac."

"We're not staying?" Rachel grimaced. "It's so nice here."

"No." Khaled spoke quickly to one of his security team, who nodded and went to a carryall bag and removed a small, black handgun in a black holster. He handed it to Khaled.

The Saudi Arabian checked it, and then handed it to Rachel. "I assume you didn't bring a weapon?"

"You know I didn't." She took the gun, half-pulling it from the holster. "Nice – Glock 17 – reliable, lightweight, and a 17-round mag. This'll do just fine." She tucked it down the back of her pants. "Expecting trouble?"

"Here, you must always expect trouble. The wide desert country has marauding bandits, terrorists and opportunists, but they are spread far and wide. Worse to stay in the city, where you can get your throat cut just for taking a wrong turn."

"So where to?" Joshua asked.

"Salal," Khaled said. He looked up at the sun and pointed north-east. "About 250 miles that way – take us a few hours to get there by small plane. It's the closest settlement to where our map seems to point."

"Or ends," Rachel said.

"I know the area," Ebadi said. "Dry, *very* dry. The terrain of this country is dominated by the low-lying Chad Basin."

"And that basin was once the bottom of an inland sea," Matt said. "And why we're here. How far is it from Lake Chad now?"

"To the water's edge, around 300 miles, less in the rainy season when the lakes double in size. But the important thing is where Salal is now, only a few thousand years ago it was all under water."

"Good a place to start then," Joshua said.

Khaled had his security team transport their gear and Mrs. van Helling to the smaller plane.

"Gonna be cramped," Matt said to Rachel who watched with compressed lips.

"It already is," she said softly.

"Well, we're not here on holiday and look at the upside; at least you're packing heat again." Matt grinned.

Khaled led them to a twin prop plane that was roughly the same size as the jet, but from a vastly different era. Its nose and wing shoulders were bug splattered, and oil stains streaked its sides.

"That's our ride?" Rachel groaned.

Khaled grinned. "Commander Aero-680. Built in 1968 and still running – *just*. Not many around now, and I'm betting this one is held together with twine and black magic."

This time their flight was noisy, cramped, and if there was once air conditioning, it was either turned off to conserve fuel or had stopped working decades before.

Matt spent his time looking down on a dry, featureless landscape. Chad was one of the larger African countries and more than three times the size of California. Thankfully, their trip was short and in no time they were dropping fast toward a long, flat, dusty track – *the airport*, Matt assumed. The pilot then lined the Aero-680 up, and they came down hard, bouncing, slewing to the left, and then overcompensating to the right. Matt thought he heard laughter coming from the cockpit.

Matt would have pulled his belt a little tighter, but there wasn't one so he just sat back in his chair and clamped his teeth. The plane finally straightened and slowed. Matt ducked to look from the window, and saw a couple of goats scampering away from the plane as careened down the dirt runway.

He dragged out his backpack. His shirt hung slack against his chest, already soaked in perspiration. He felt a weird sensation in his gut and put a hand on his stomach. It was a strange coiling and twisting, not so unpleasant, more like a bad case of butterflies except a dozen times worse. He licked his lips again, parched, and drew forth his canteen and sipped. It quenched his thirst but didn't satisfy him.

The door was pushed open, and a cloud of dust and several bush flies entered in a rush. Things the size of his thumb belted around the cabin. Matt hunched his shoulders; he knew there were large biting bush flies, locusts, praying mantis as long as his hand, and also a delightful thing called a flying scorpion. It didn't really fly, but instead had a flattened body that allowed it to be picked up by the wind so it could glide to attack. Thankfully it wasn't deadly, but had a sting that would bring more than a few tears to your eyes.

He turned his collar up, pulled his hat down, and headed for the door behind Rachel. He brushed a huge fly from her shoulder and it took exception to his attack and flew straight at his face. Matt clamped his mouth shut, and it bounced harmlessly from his cheek to zoom lazily away, searching for something else of interest in the rear of the plane – Eleanor van Helling, he bet. There was one thing that excited insects out in the bush, and one thing he remembered Oscar Ojibwe warning them never to wear: perfume. And the old woman was drenched in it.

Three covered army jeeps bumbled out from a low, squat building and roared to a stop close by. Khaled waved and jogged toward them. A tall man the color of mahogany stepped out of the lead jeep. He wore an iron-gray uniform and black beret, and mirror glasses with a cigarette dangling casually from his lips. He sauntered toward them.

The man flicked the smoke away, saluted, and then reached out to shake Khaled's hand. Straight after, just like in the airport, the Saudi handed the man a thick envelope that the officer opened and peered inside. Satisfied, he slid it into his shirt, and clicked his fingers for the other drivers to step out and load luggage.

Khaled gathered the group together. "Captain Abdulla Okembu has given us these drivers who will take us out to the geographic point we wish to go to." He grinned. "He said there's nothing out there, but sand, dust and giant bush flies. They think we're all crazy." He grinned. "I think he's right."

Joshua turned to the group. "Has everyone taken their medications?"

"I'm practically rattling," Matt said.

"They make me sick," Eleanor added.

Joshua scrutinised her for a moment. "Mrs. van Helling, what will make you sick is avoiding your anti parasitics and getting bitten by something like a local deer fly. They carry a particularly nasty creature called the Loa Loa filariasis, also affectionately known as the African eye worm." He held his hand up, inching his finger along in the air. "As a nymph it makes its way to the tissue of your eye. Once there, it feeds and grows, and when it's large enough to be observed moving just below the surface of the eyeball, usually the only way to get it out is through total removal of the eye."

"Goddamn hellhole," she muttered.

"Sorry you came?" Rachel's mouth curved into a smile.

Eleanor's lip curled. "Don't try and tell me you're happy to be here, girly. At least I've been to places like this before. I'll wager the farthest you've been is Central Park."

"*Boom.*" Matt grinned at Rachel who turned gritted teeth on him.

The joys of a family field trip, Matt thought, and looked over his shoulder at Eleanor. *Tough old buzzard*, he thought.

Khaled chatted briefly with his commandos. They all seemed to know Khaled well, and they shared a few jokes before he separated them all into three groups: himself, Matt, Rachel and one security team member named Saeeb. The next jeep would hold Eleanor, Greta, Ebadi and a second security team member named Rizwan. And the final jeep would just hold Joshua, Zahil and Yasha, the last two security guys, as well as most of their luggage.

Matt headed to the lead jeep, and jumped in next to the driver. Khaled slid into the back and Rachel beside him, and the blocky commando, Saeeb, sat in a sort of rumble seat at the rear.

Captain Okembu stood with folded arms watching them load up. Even though the man wore mirrored sunglasses, Matt felt his eyes on them, scrutinizing their every move. Matt turned to the driver and greeted the man in Arabic. The driver gave him an insolent nod and turned back to the windshield.

Oh well, he thought. *We're not here to make friends*. He turned in his seat. "How long?"

Khaled shrugged. "Just a few hours; but better to ask him, he knows the terrain better than I do."

Matt looked at the man again and sucked in a breath. "Okay, how long until we are at our destination?"

The driver looked at him, his eyes still half-lidded, and the whites of his eyes yellow from being in proximity to an open fire one too many times. There were also tribal scars on his temples, and Matt bet there were more hidden under his cap.

He fished a crumpled packet of cigarettes from his pocket, stuck one in his mouth, and then lit it with a plastic lighter. He blew thick smoke at the dashboard, and then casually looked at an enormous fake Rolex on his wrist. "Two hours, maybe little more."

"Thank you, very helpful," Matt responded in Arabic.

The driver scrutinised him for a few moments, taking in the long, sandy hair and blue eyes. "You speak Arabic well, but you are not an Arab."

"I'm a teacher – of languages," Matt said.

The driver blew more smoke and turned his yellow eyes on Matt again. "You should not go there." He spat out some tobacco. "Why does a teacher need to drive out into the middle of our country during the dry season? What do you think is out there that requires a language teacher?"

Matt turned back to the windscreen. "Maybe nothing but a legend."

The man grunted. "Then this is the country for that."

"My name is Professor Matthew Kearns. What do they call you?" Matt kept watching him.

The man's lips pursed for a second as he decided whether to reveal his name or not. He shrugged. "Mohammed Asalem."

"Nice to meet you, Mohammed." Matt examined the shining dark face. "I have a question for you; what do *you* think is out there?"

He smirked and then blew more smoke. "Bones. Nothing but bones, dust and death until the end of the world."

"I see." Matt twisted in his seat to check on the other vehicles. Everyone and everything was loaded up except for Captain Okembu. The tall man slowly scanned the horizon, and then seemed to make a decision – he climbed in next to Joshua. Okembu then banged a hand on the side of the jeep and the three engines started in unison.

Matt turned back to Mohammed. "If there's nothing but bones, then why has your captain decided to come with us?"

Mohammed looked over his shoulder and then his eyes briefly flicked to Matt. "Maybe he thinks you know something." He then put the jeep in gear and stamped on the accelerator. The vehicle lurched forward, throwing them all back into their seats.

Matt was glad he was in the lead vehicle as behind there was a huge plume of dust being kicked up. Beside the dirt track that doubled as a road, there were skinny children with feet so dusty they looked to be wearing long, pale socks. Matt waved and the children stared back at him as if he were an alien from outer space. *Don't think they get a lot of visitors,* he guessed.

A dog that was all ribs belted out to chase them for a few hundred feet, yapping and looking like it wanted to try and take a bite out of one of the tires. Matt leaned out of the open window.

"Give it up, buddy. You wouldn't know what to do with it even if you caught it."

Rachel laughed as the dog peeled away, its thin chest heaving as it was rapidly left behind.

From time to time their driver would flick on the windscreen wipers to dislodge the remains of a bug that had taken a kamikaze run at them and come off second best. The blobs of green, orange and ochre stuck like syrup, and more often than not, the shattered remains of the insect glued to the wipers and smeared into greasy stripes.

Once off the road and beyond the borders of shanty shacks, the three jeeps were able to drive in a V-formation and Matt settled into the cracked vinyl of his seat. Even though the terrain was flat, it still made for a spine-jarring race across the plain.

In another hour Matt felt his lips beginning to scale from the dry air. He felt by now they were in the middle of nowhere in the back of beyond in the vast dusty deserts of Chad. In the distance a pale pink range of mountains begin to appear out of the shimmering heat – not high at only about 2000 feet, but steep, sheer faces of craggy rock that looked more like rows of teeth. The hulk of a tank sat rusting to one side, and a bird, probably some type of vulture, perched on its bent gun barrel watching them from one gimlet eye. Matt wondered whether it would follow them, hoping at least one of their soft, pale bodies would be thrown by the wayside.

He turned in his seat, leaning one arm on the backrest. Rachel looked pained, and Khaled was studying a computer tablet, trying to hold it steady in the bucking jeep. He noticed Matt watching him and turned the tablet around. He tapped it and showed a GPS feed with a dot as their destination and an orange line moving toward it – *them*.

He pointed to a numbered bar. "Another fifty miles, give or take."

Matt nodded and turned back. Conversations in the roaring jeep had to be shouted, and neither of them had the energy or interest right now.

Matt lazily watched the small, dry shrubs and spikes of exposed rock or termite mounds pass by. It was unchanging and almost hypnotic, and if it weren't for the occasional drift of loose sand or pothole, he would have dozed regardless of the jerking of the open vehicle.

In just over an hour, Mohammed started to slow the jeep. Matt took off his sunglasses and wiped his face with a sleeve, before sitting forward. There were piles of jagged rock, like stalactites one would expect to see rising from a cave floor, but standing like sentinels in a landscape that was dusty, dry and seemingly devoid of life.

Mohammed looked in the rearview and then slowed. "The Captain wants to stop, so, we stop."

Khaled got out and stood by the jeep, field glasses to his eyes and slowly scanning a shimmering horizon.

"Anything?" Rachel asked, hands on hips.

"There's a clay pan basin, and according to my GPS, we will hit the dead center of our mysterious destination within a few miles." He lowered the glasses. "Out there."

Matt had both hands up over his eyes as he looked at the landscape – the basin looked slightly sunken, but hellishly hot and dry. The fact was, if their cars broke down or the drivers decided to simply leave them behind, they'd probably all die long before they made it even halfway back.

In the distance there was still a line of mountains that looked blisteringly scorched by millions of years of brutal sunshine.

Abdul Ebadi joined them by the car. "This place is old. Geologically, there are only a few places on Earth like this that are not subject to earthquakes due to being so far from fault lines. Usually because they're in the center of large, old continents like Africa and Australia." He sipped from his bottle. "The downside is they're usually damned hot and dry."

Rachel came and leaned an elbow on Matt's shoulder. "Just think of it as one long beach."

"Yeah, except without the surf at the end." He grinned, and rubbed the small of her back without anyone seeing. She winked at him and dropped her arm.

Khaled was called apart by Captain Okembu who spoke softly to him for a moment or two. Khaled responded and it resulted in Okembu raising his voice and furiously shaking his head. Khaled in turn threw up his hands and paced away, stopping and staring out into the basin.

Okembu folded his arms for a moment, waiting. But then he whistled and shouted instructions to his drivers who had been sharing cigarettes. They flicked their cigarettes away and headed back to the jeeps where they began to unload the luggage.

Khaled spun. "Okay, okay."

Okembu and Khaled talked a little more, and then the Chad captain sauntered back to the rear jeep.

Khaled joined them, sighing.

"Trouble?" Rachel asked.

"Captain Okembu decided this was the time to tell me that this area is taboo for his men." Khaled snorted.

"Taboo? That's a good thing – usually means some myth or legend originated from here."

"I doubt it. More than likely he knew we were close so decided this was the best time to hold out for more money." He almost snarled. "It worked."

"How much more?" Ebadi asked.

"Ten thousand for him, and another thousand for each of the drivers."

Ebadi whistled. "An expensive extra few miles."

"Not if you have to walk back," Matt observed.

"Well then, let us see what we see," Khaled said. "Before the price goes up again."

They loaded back into the aging jeeps and Khaled banged its metal side. Mohammed took off again across the plain. Sand drifts made the going slow, and a wind had kicked up that buffeted the open jeep and sucked the moisture from Matt's nose and eyes. He was glad he was wearing sunglasses, not just to keep down the blinding glare, but also to act as shield against the hard particles that plinked on their lenses.

Khaled tapped the driver's seat back. "*Slow.*"

Mohammed eased back and they ground along at about 10 miles per hour. Matt could see nothing but miles of sand, the remains of an occasional shrub that had long since returned to its maker, and the constant line of the jagged, pink mountains a few miles to their north.

"*Stop.*" The jeep eased to a halt, Khaled lowered his tablet and looked around. "We're here."

The dust settled, and they all sat in silence, staring out at the dead landscape.

"Nothing," Rachel whispered.

Khaled was the first out, then Matt, Rachel and Saeeb. In another few seconds the entire group was out crowding around the lead jeep, and only Eleanor remained in her vehicle. Greta had been sent forward to listen.

"Well, this is it," Khaled said. "This is where your map has brought us, Professor."

Matt breathed in and out slowly through his nose feeling like it was being singed to hairlessness by the oven-hot winds.

"Spread out, look around," he said. "Look for something, anything, that could give us an indication of..." Matt stopped. He didn't even know himself exactly what they were looking for. "Some sort of human interaction."

"Give us a clue – like what?" Rachel asked.

Matt hiked his shoulders. "I don't know. I guess you might know it when you see it."

"Ri-*iiight.*" Rachel jammed her hands in her pockets and meandered off. She kicked a stone chip 20 feet out onto a sand drift. "Anyone spot a big wooden boat, call the professor." She grinned back over her shoulder.

"Thank you, ma'am." Matt touched the brim of his cap.

The group spread out, ambling off in different directions. Captain Okembu and his drivers slouched against the jeeps, smoking and laughing. Matt could guess at what – here were a bunch of westerners and a few Arabs wandering in a sandy desert with nothing but scorpions, big bugs and a few hardy reptiles for company. He could almost laugh himself.

Matt stopped and lifted his cap to wipe sweat from his brow. Down this low, the heat was near unbearable. And there wasn't even high ground he could use to survey the area and the mountains were too far off to be of use.

He set off again, shuffling along, pausing to stop at rocks or indentations in the sand and grit. From time to time he'd look up and see members of his group now spread in all directions.

The figure of Rachel was several hundred yards away and shimmering in the heat. He watched her as she meandered out, and then turned to wander back, kicking small stones as she came.

Something the size of his thumb landed on his neck, stuck, and began to dig in. "Fuck off." He brushed it away, and it relaunched itself to zum away, probably looking for another dripping body to feed off.

"Rock," Joshua said, lifting a flat stone the size of a hubcap and tossing it aside.

Matt snorted, and sat down on a stone – nothing but sand, rocks and big damned bugs, he thought miserably.

He sipped from his canteen, the water now the temperture of blood. *Myths and legends always have a kernel of truth*, he always said. He sipped again, swirled the warm liquid around in his mouth and spat onto the sand. *Except for the times they don't.*

Chapter 15

"Another rock." Rachel chuckled as she flipped a slab of stone over.

Matt groaned to his feet. "Come on guys; we just flew halfway around the world to be here." *Take it fucking seriously*, he thought. He stepped up on the rock he had sat on. It was about the size of a small manhole cover. He kicked at it, noticing how smooth it was. Water smoothed, he bet.

He was about to step off, when an eye trained for decades to pick out the most indistinct markings made by human hands stopped him.

"Hey."

He crouched beside it and used a hand to wipe the sand from its surface. The stone was about three inches thick, and rounded at the edges. There were definite markings on the sides. They weren't in a language he could recognize, but instead just trailing away at the edges.

Matt stared. Hundreds or thousands of years ago there might have been a settlement here. He knew that stones were used to sharpen iron and bronze blades for centuries. But something about these didn't strike him as being random cuts.

He cleared more sand from all the outer edges – the markings were only on one third of the stone, and just at its sides. He gritted his teeth and flipped it over. There was nothing on its underside, and he flipped it back.

"Hey, wait a minute." Abdul Ebadi had been watching him and now jogged over. He crouched by Matt. "Hold that stone up again."

Matt did as he was asked, and Ebadi grabbed it, holding it in place. He ran his fingers over the smooth edges, stopping to trace the odd markings at its sides.

"I've seen something like this before – there were ancient stone pillars found on a mountaintop in South Korea. They were called *jangseung* and were used as message boards... or to give warnings." He looked around. "Good, there's more."

Ebadi dragged another smaller one closer." "You see, when they were first discovered on the mountain, they were all in pieces."

"Like this one?" Matt asked.

"Not sure this is like that. But putting the *jangseung* puzzle back together was quite simple, as long as the archeologists followed the patterns on their outer edges."

"The stones are both the puzzle and the key." Matt rubbed his hands together.

"Exactly." Ebadi grinned and stood quickly. "Everyone, over here... *it's the stones*!"

The group jogged back to Matt and Ebadi. Even the drivers and Captain Okembu walked slowly toward them, obviously not wanting to betray their cool.

Ebadi pointed. "These stones probably formed some sort of structure. I believe they're like a message totem, but the message is on the outside and can only be read in its entirety. We need to try and rebuild it, to see if the message is still there."

Khaled looked around, kicking at a stone the size of a hubcap. "So we just gather the stones? Bring them to you? Some are pretty big."

"*No*, just locate them first. We need to rebuild the totem exactly where it once stood in case they have astral or geological markers – their position will be a critical part of the message." Ebadi stood and brushed off his hands and made a shape in the air as he talked. "I believe it will form some sort of tapering column when reconstructed. The biggest will be on the bottom, so try and find a large flat base. The largest one we find will dictate where we try and reassemble it."

The group formed a ring and started to move outwards. When they found a piece they'd mark its position and move on.

"*Yo*, big sucker here." Rachel tried to get her fingertips under the huge stone. "Too big to even budge."

Matt joined her and knelt to brush the stone down. It was about six feet around.

"Excellent, this might be the base." He rubbed at its edges, feeling the lines and swirls. Even with his vast language skills, the squiggles meant nothing to him.

"Another one, big." Joshua held up a hand.

Ebadi went from Rachel's stone to Joshua's, looking back from one to the other. "Rachel's is biggest, so we'll start from there."

"What happens if we find another bigger one?" Khaled asked.

Ebadi spread his arms wide. "Then we start over." He walked around Joshua's stone. "Step one; we need to get this stone over on top of that one. We'll need several of us to carry it, and..." he turned to Captain Okembu, "... and can you lend a hand here, Captain?"

Okembu took a dry twig from his mouth he had been chewing. "My men can help, but you must pay them.

You hired them as drivers, not laborers." He grinned, his white teeth showing.

Khaled snorted. "And they have proved to be the most capable drivers in Chad, and the most expensive." He planted his legs. "A hundred dollars a piece."

Okembu didn't flinch. "One thousand, and another thousand for the supervisor, me."

Khaled snorted. "250, last offer."

"750." Okembu stood straighter.

Khaled flicked his hand. "Forget it; go and wait in your cars."

Okembu stared for a few seconds, his grin fading. He turned on his heel and clicked his fingers. He and his three men sauntered back to their jeeps.

Matt watched them for a moment. "Please tell me that you didn't pay all their driving fee up front."

"Not a chance." Khaled turned away from watching the men. "Only a small advance, and the bulk when we make it back. We Arabs know a thing or two about negotiation." Khaled waved in his security men. Saeeb, Rizwan and Zahil lent a hand and Yasha stayed on watch.

"Good." Matt turned to the older archaeology professor. "Professor Ebadi, you supervise. We'll carry the stones, but you'll have to tell us where to lay them."

Joshua also lent a hand. His second-largest flat stone was extremely heavy, and together the group grunted and strained to lift it. But even together they only managed to get it about a foot off the ground.

"Damn, we're going to have to drag it," Joshua said.

"Not ideal," Ebadi said. "It would be best if we didn't disturb the surrounding earth with drag furrows."

"Try again." Greta came over and wedged herself in beside two of Khaled's security men. She gripped the stone, waiting.

"Okay then." Matt smiled. "On three, two, one... *lift.*"

Greta strained and Matt saw her forearms flex. The woman's fingers were large and blunt, and this time the stone lifted.

Matt had heard of strong women before. In Nebraska there was Becca Swanson, an American powerlifter and wrestler, who could dead lift 680 pounds and squat 850. He bet that Greta would have given her a run for her money.

This time they managed to carry the large flat stone the 50 feet to hold it over Rachel's tabletop-sized piece.

"Easy." Ebadi crab walked around them. "Okay, turn about 20 degrees, east. Slow, easy, and... *now*, lay it down, there, gently."

Together they eased it down into place. Ebadi walked around it, nodding. "Good, that will do." He looked up. "Now to find the rest, and we must find them all to complete the message."

"I'm guessing we're looking for the next largest," Rachel said.

"You got it," Matt said. "All tapering toward the top."

They were lucky; the remaining stones were all found spread over a cone-shaped area, stretching out to the west. Some were in pieces and had to be reassembled, but luckily the fragments were close by.

The reassembling work took time and care, and often the stones had to be turned, refitted and then re-turned to ensure all the symbols lined up. At least the work got easier as the stones got smaller toward the top.

After several hours sweat-filled, draining, but rewarding labor, Matt stepped back to admire their work.

"*Ta-da.*"

Joshua stretched his back and then removed his hat to wipe his brow. "Well, we've sure got something. I'm not sure what though."

It was a tapering column of dark stone, six feet around at the base, just over that again in height and with a fist-sized flat stone on top. It might have held a capping stone at one time, but that was now long gone.

"I expected a crucifix, or something a little more – biblical," Rachel said. "This look's more like cave art."

"This was erected thousands of years before a holy man was supposed to have ever been nailed to a cross," Ebadi said. "And long before the Christian religion was even born."

Matt stepped back, narrowing his eyes. "I've seen this before." He turned to Rachel. "We both have; remember the stained glass held an image of a pile of stones?"

Rachel gave him a blank look, and then slowly shook her head.

"It was there. I thought at the time it might have been a statue that people were kneeling before." He turned back to the stones. "But now I think it was more likely to have been this."

Ebadi walked around it. "Definitely a marker or signpost. But the symbolism or writing is unknown to me. I can't read it."

"Let me have a look." Matt squinted and stepped in closer. He ran a hand down along the stones. It fit together almost perfectly, and a few thousand years ago, it might have been as smooth as polished marble.

He walked around the tapering stone column. Khaled spoke softly as he passed. "It looks like the inscriptions we saw on the sarcophagus in the mountain."

"That's because they are – Chaldaic." Matt squatted, his eyes narrowing as he concentrated on the ancient language. There were areas that had been totally worn away, and he tried to mentally fill in the gaps with what would logically be inserted there.

"So that's Chaldaic; I'd only ever heard about it. Spoken by Adam and Eve," Ebadi said reverently. "And Noah. Read it if you can Matt; out loud please."

"Just like the stained glass, it refers to the first house of Noach – Noah." Matt ran his hand down along the stone's edges. "Here lies *Akebu-Lan*." He turned to them, grinning. "The real Garden of Eden."

Ebadi grinned back. "It was here. *It was really here*." He turned around, looking out at the dry desolation of the Chadian desert. "Once."

"Yes and no – here, but not here." Matt read some more. "The wording infers it was a secret place even then. Noah's *hidden* place. Perhaps somewhere that just he and his family knew about." He looked again at the ancient writing. "It uses the Chaldaic word for gate or doorway... or at least some sort of entrance-way." Matt stood back. "It's not here, but somewhere close. There's a clue." He put a hand up to shield his eyes, turning about. "Five thousand steps between where the servant of mankind rises and falls." Matt rubbed his head. "Who the hell is the servant of mankind?"

"*Shemesh*," Ebadi said softly. "The sun was referred to as *Shemesh*, the one who serves, or..." he smiled. "... the *servant* of mankind."

Matt pointed one arm east. "Where the sun rises." Then his other arm west. "And where the sun falls." He lowered them. "So that means we have a choice – north or south."

"North," Khaled said. "I would estimate that range of mountains is about 5000 steps." He lifted his field glasses, scanning slowly. "And you said it referred to a doorway, or gate. Well, I can see there are plenty of caves along its base. Maybe inside one of those."

Captain Okembu had sidled up behind them and now loitered and listened. Khaled turned to him. "Captain, do you know those caves?"

His eyes narrowed. "You should not go there; they are haram now, *taboo*." He shrugged, and his lips turned down. "Nothing there anyway, they've all been explored, and are now smuggler's caves, sometimes camel herders will use them as shelter. Nothing."

"Don't worry, you'll be safe with us," Rachel said.

The Chad captain bristled at the woman's words.

"Well, we're here, so let's satisfy our curiosity. Five thousand paces, or five minutes by jeep." Khaled lifted his chin to Okembu who in turn shrugged, and then waved a hand and whistled. The three jeeps immediately started up and rolled toward them.

Okembu turned back to them. "Only a few hours until the sun will be going down soon. We will not make it back to town. Maybe we will need to stay here."

"Then let's get moving." Matt waved Rachel into the first jeep with Khaled and Saeeb.

Mohammed waited. "Where to?"

Matt peered along the distant pink mountains. "For now, directly to the mountains, and hopefully something will become clear when we get closer."

Mohammed stamped on the accelerator and the jeep's wheels spun in the sand momentarily, before jumping forward and pressing the group back into their seats. The three vehicles increased speed the closer they got to the mountains. The ground under their wheels was becoming more hard-packed as it turned from sand drifts to clay pan.

Matt tried to imagine what it would have been like all those millennia ago – lush forests with the flora perhaps climbing the sides of the mountains as well, the noise of birds in the trees and herds of animals on the fertile plans. And then before that, perhaps this entire was area under deep, blue water, an inland sea, also teeming with water life. Matt hung from the jeep window and looked along the edifice. Caves pocked the prehistoric-looking mountain faces, some at ground level and some higher up. There were too many to choose from. He laid a hand on Mohammed's forearm.

"Slow down."

The driver threw an arm out the window and held a hand up flat in the air. He eased down, and the following vehicles did the same. The convoy then bundled along at just a few miles per hour.

Matt held out a hand to Khaled. "Lend me your field glasses."

Khaled handed him the powerful lenses, and Matt lifted them to his eyes. He scanned the caves – some were little more than shallow dens, and some large openings that vanished into endless voids.

He exhaled. "Too many."

They were now only several hundred feet from the sheer wall, and Matt called a halt.

"We need to look closer – nose to wall, I'm afraid."

The vehicles all lined up, and the group got out. Rachel walked forward, and stood with her hands on her hips. "What are we looking for?"

Matt scanned the sheer cliff face. "Chaldaic script would be great. But anything that looks like it might be related. Hell, just see if we can see any indication that one of the caves is the one we seek."

"Let's split up," Khaled said. "Three teams; we'll cover more ground."

"Good idea," Matt said. "We'll take this big cave right here. Remember, we're looking for writing, symbols, even evidence of ancient habitation. And yell if you find anything before exploring it. That'll save us other saps a lot of wasted energy exploring wrong caves."

"Professor Kearns."

Matt turned at the voice. Greta marched toward him, and smiled with thin-lipped formality. "When we find the correct cave, we'll bring in Mrs. van Helling, yes?"

Matt shrugged. "Yeah sure, why not? But we can only take her so far. I don't think it'd be a good idea to try and wedge the old girl into some tiny cave."

"The *old girl* will manage." She craned torwards him. "That's why I'm here." The ice in Greta's words made Matt gulp. She marched back to her own group. Matt shook his head. "Jesus."

He then looked again along the line of multiple cave mouths. *One more thing*, he thought. "And mark the entrances of the caves you've already searched – an "X" will do." He turned and noticed the three drivers watching Captain Okembu as he stood on the hood of one of the jeeps, field glasses to his eyes, slowly scanning the desert.

"What's he doing?" Matt asked Khaled.

"I think keeping watch for pirates, terrorists, bandits, you name it. Around here strangers might mean an opportunity for fast cash or goods."

"Oh boy," Matt said.

"Don't worry; between Okembu and his men, and my commandos, we've got plenty of firepower." Khaled turned back to the caves. "But best we get our work done, and not stay longer than we need to."

"I hear that." Matt waved the groups to cliff face.

They split up the closest 20 caves between them. Khaled, Matt, Rachel and Saeeb went into one of the first, the largest, about ten feet high and double that in width. It opened out just inside and was at least dry and cool.

Matt took off his cap, and pushed long, wet hair off his face. "That's better. If nothing else, this will be where we camp tonight."

"As long as the owners of that old camp fire don't return." Khaled pointed at the remains of a fire pit.

Rachel knelt beside it and lifted a piece of the charcoal. She sniffed it. "Hasn't been used for weeks or maybe months."

Matt fished out a small powerful Mag light and flicked it on. Rachel and Khaled did the same. The Saudi turned to his security man.

"Stay here, brother, and keep a lookout." He went to turn away but paused. "And keep an eye on what our drivers are up to. I don't trust them or the captain."

The blocky man nodded and waited just inside the cave mouth where he could watch his team and also keep an eye on the desert plain.

They edged around the walls. Rachel found the first writing, but it proved to be little more than local graffiti, a rude joke written in Arabic probably by one of the recent occupiers of the cave.

Further in there were faded images on the walls that depicted long-legged birds, antelope and something that might have even been a bear. Matt rested his hands on his hips. "This is more like it – some of the cave art in this area dates back 10,000 to 12,000 years. This place was a forest then."

They spent another 20 minutes examining the interior, but at the absolute rear there was a blank wall.

"It ends here," Rachel said and shone her light up at the ceiling. "And there hasn't been a cave-in to close any further passages off."

"Yeah, this one is a no-go," Matt said. "Let's keep moving while we've got some daylight outside." He led them to their next cave.

After several more hours, the groups convened in the light of a setting sun, looking dispirited. Joshua rolled his shoulders and winced. "You know what crossed my mind after finding nothing in that last cave?"

Everyone waited.

"That we might have put the totem pole up facing the wrong way." He grimaced.

Khaled laughed, but then turned to Matt, then Ebadi. "Please tell me this is *not* a possibility."

Matt felt his stomach sink. "Well, it might…"

"*No*," Ebadi said emphatically. "In archaeology we need to reconstruct artifacts and structures many times. And in some cases we will only have parts, or only fragments of the initial structure to work with." He looked to where the sun was rapidly approaching the horizon. "The great thing about sunshine is it is so powerful, and it always rises and sets in the same area. After hundreds or, even better, thousands of years, you will get greater bleaching on the side of an object that faces the sun." He turned square on to Khaled. "The totem was reconstructed correctly."

"Good," Rachel said. "So now what?"

"Ah, well, these mountains run for hundreds of miles, so I'm betting there are many more caves to check. "Matt rubbed the back of his neck. "We could be here weeks."

"Years," Ebadi said softly. "But this is where the totem pointed." He placed hands on his large hips, and stared at the ground. "What did we miss?"

"Yeah, I've got to agree. This feels like the right place," Matt said.

"Maybe right place, but wrong time," Rachel added.

Matt nodded, letting his mind work. He walked backwards, looking up at the sheer mountain face. This particular one only rose about 3000 feet, but it was like a giant tooth rising from the desert floor.

"Right place, wrong time," he repeated. "The *wrong time*." He began to laugh.

"What is it?" Ebadi asked, walking to his side.

"The wrong time – that's it." Matt grinned and spun to Rachel. "You're brilliant."

"You're welcome," Rachel said, raising her chin. "And I'm brilliant because...?"

He turned to Khaled. "Remember what you said when we first met? That if what we seek is in the past – then that's where we must look."

Khaled tilted his head. "I remember – for the map."

Matt clapped his hands once loudly. "Then that's what we should be doing here. We're looking for clues based on today's landscape. But when Noah was supposedly here, what was happening? What was it like?" Matt held his arms wide.

"He wasn't here at all." Ebadi slapped his large thigh. "He wasn't here because he was riding an Ark... high on an inland sea."

Matt pointed at Ebadi's chest. "Damned right; this whole area would have been under water, perhaps under hundreds of feet of water." He craned his neck and began to back up. "If there are going to be any clues, they'd be up there." He pointed.

Khaled already had his field glasses to his eyes. "Yes, about 250, 260 feet up, there's a cave; a big one."

Matt felt his heart leap in his chest, but tried to remain calm. "Then, ladies and gentlemen, *that's* where we need to be."

Chapter 16

"They have commandos with them, and the vehicles are guarded." Aetius stayed low to the ground.

"Right." Drusus scanned the cliff wall, and then the figures assembling before it. He handed the miniaturised scope lens back to Aetius. "Three Chad National Army soldiers are guarding their jeeps. First, let's stop them getting away. Once they're on the wall, they have nowhere to go. No mistakes this time; *He* loses patience with us."

He turned and made a few quick hand signals, and immediately several of the men started to slither along a low ridge to get closer to the jeeps.

Chapter 17

"I can do it," Joshua said, craning his neck and pushing his glasses back on his nose. "I do wall climbing for exercise and I've scaled cliff faces before – sometimes you need to get up or down into the weirdest nooks and crannies to search out the most elusive of bugs."

"We didn't exactly bring climbing gear – we've got old rope, a single flare gun, and luckily, plenty of flashlights. But no pitons, carabiners, or even helmets," Rachel said. "Long way to fall."

"So your advice is, don't fall." He turned to wink at her before turning back to stare upwards, probably working through his possible route. He pushed his spectacles up his nose. "It's quite a sheer face, but it has plenty of handholds and lots of places for me to tie off. It can be done, and 250 feet is not a long way."

"Should we wait until morning?" Ebadi asked. The sun was now a huge orange ball heading toward the horizon, and the shadows were lengthening. "We've only got a few hours at best."

"Won't take me long to secure guide ropes," Joshua said. "And if it is a cave, then it'll be dark inside whether it's night or day, right?"

"Then we all go," Khaled said. Each of the group members agreed, and even Ebadi sighed, but nodded.

They piled all the rope they had from the jeeps at Joshua's feet. He squatted over it, checking its strength. "This will do. I'll tie off at the first junction." He pointed. "That jutting rock. Then move to the next, leaving the ropes as a ladder. Once we have a few of Khaled's men up there, they can help pull the rest of us further up."

Rachel nodded. "Might work."

Matt turned to Greta who had finally brought the old woman from the jeep. "Not everyone needs to climb up. It might be all for nothing."

"This is it," Eleanor said without looking at him. "We're coming."

The old woman's cold blue eyes were like flint chips, and he saw that Greta's jaw was also set. The big woman reached forward to smooth Eleanor's thin hair down. But if her body was failing, her eyes were electric in their intensity.

Matt sighed. *At least she wouldn't be hard to pull up,* he thought.

Khaled organised them into climbing pairs. He pointed to two of his men. "Saeeb, Rizwan, you two will scale next. One to assist the climbers, the other to act as a lookout. Then, Professor Kearns and Agent Bromilow. After that, Professor Ebadi, and myself. Once we ascertain it is safe, then Mrs. van Helling, and... her nurse can ascend."

Greta's eyes narrowed, but she stayed silent. Khaled pointed to his second-to-last man.

"Zahil, you will help the women climb." He then moved to his final commando. "And Yasha, my brother, you will secure our base." He looked across to Captain Okembu who loitered at the jeeps, but pushed off to walk toward them. Khaled lowered his voice. "Make sure our ride home doesn't decide to leave without us."

Khaled then spoke softly in Arabic to the commando, but Matt understood every word. "We need the jeeps, not the men. If they try and leave, you know what to do."

The commando nodded, and his eyes slid to the three drivers.

Captain Okembu took the twig from his mouth, and looked up at the cave, and then to Matt. "So, Professor, you are going up?"

Matt nodded. "Yup."

"Policewoman is going up? Mr. Khaled and old, rich lady? Then I will too. You will need my protection." He grinned. "No charge."

"No, I think you should stay down here," Khaled said. "Your job is to organize our ride."

"My job is to keep you all alive." His grin widened. "But it is also to safeguard the property of the Chadian government."

Matt groaned. "Seriously? Now, you're getting all patriotic?" *This was going to get expensive*, he thought.

"I assure you, any artifacts we find will be handed over. You have my word." Khaled held his ground, and his four commandos all became a little more alert. Matt could feel the tension rising.

Captain Okembu looked long and hard at each of them. "Yes, you can kill me, or perhaps try. And you will need to kill all of us. But when, or if, you get back to N'Djamena Airport, you will have an interesting time explaining what happened to us." He smirked. "Our prisons are not very pleasant for those who enjoy western luxuries." His eyes slid to Rachel and then Eleanor van Helling.

Khaled glared. "And you'll still be bones."

Matt sighed. "Let him come. *Sheesh*, this is getting way too complicated."

"Wise choice, Professor. That's why I like you." Okembu turned to Joshua. "Better get moving, spectacle man, before the light is gone for good, yes?"

"Spectacle man?" Joshua snorted and began to loop the coils of rope over each of his shoulders and another few loops around his waist. His sucked in a breath and reached up for the first handhold.

"Wait." Khaled walked to the man, and quickly checked the ropes he had looped around him. He looked deeply into the young man's face. "I can see fear. Be calm." He stood back a step. "Good luck, Doctor Gideon."

Joshua nodded and shook his hand. "Thanks." He turned back to the rock face, bounced for a moment on his toes, before leaping and grabbing a small ridge. He levered himself up from the ground.

"And, he's off," Rachel said softly.

"Holy shit." Matt had a whole new level of respect for the skinny, young doctor of parasitology as he climbed deftly, moving like a crab across a tidal rock, never once looking back, ever looking upwards or across to his next handhold. In a few minutes he was a good 80 feet up and onto an outcrop with a jagged rock jutting up like a huge dagger. He wedged himself in behind it, threw a loop of rope around the outcrop, tied it off and then dropped it down.

"Okay, next," Matt said.

Both of Khaled's commandos climbed quickly, looking like they had experience. They were much heavier and less agile than Joshua, and dragged themselves up using raw muscle power alone. By the time they reached the rock outcrop, Joshua was already 50 feet further along on his way to his next island of rest.

"Let's do this." Matt nodded to Rachel, and then wiped his sweating hands on his pants. He grabbed the rope and tugged on it a few times.

Rachel snorted. "Matt, if it can hold that pair of beefcakes, then a lightweight like you should be safe."

"Haven't you heard that muscle weighs more than fat? I'm heavier than I look." He drew in a breath, looking up to the first rest spot.

"If you fall, try not to hit me on the way down." She nudged him in the back. "Get going, Hercules."

He pulled himself up. Matt had climbed before and knew to use his legs as much as his arms and shoulders. The toughest bit of the climb was the abrasion on his hands – the rope wasn't the soft, elasticized type favored by modern climbers but instead an old-style rope that had probably been sitting in the back of the jeep for years. Thankfully, it wasn't long before one of Khaled's two men held out a hand to pull him up the final few feet into the alcove.

"Good view, Professor?" Saeeb asked.

Matt noticed it was the commando from his jeep. The man had largely been silent and invisible.

"It's Matt."

"Saeeb." The man shook his hand briefly. The other, taller man leaned around him to thrust his own hand out. "Rizwan."

Matt turned to look out over the scene. Saeeb was right; it was a magnificent view of the African plain that stretched for miles. In the distance there were a few little dancing dust devils swirling over and around the dry earth, boulder, or stunted shrub.

Matt looked up to where Joshua was scaling high above them. "So, which one of you two gets to go next?"

Rizwan raised a hand, and then turned to start his second climb along the next rope line that Joshua had strung for them.

"I got this one." Matt reached down and grabbed Rachel's arm and hauled her up. She came into his arms.

"Easier than it looks," she said, puffing for a moment.

"Yeah right; we're not even halfway yet." Matt looked up. "But we're doing better than I expected." He looked up and across to where Joshua was approaching his third rest stop. Rizwan was already perched at the second.

"The human fly is nearly there. Let's get across to the second stop before it gets overcrowded here." He looked back over the edge. Ebadi was closing in on where they stood and Khaled was now on the rope. Standing in line was Greta. She had Eleanor lashed to her shoulders like some sort of grotesque backpack. Behind her, the last two of Khaled's men, Yasha and Zahil, waited their turn while Captain Okembu stood smoking a thick cigarette.

Greta reached up, took hold of the rope, and started to haul herself up, hand over hand. She shrugged off any help from the commando.

Matt blew air through his lips. "That is one tough woman."

"Get going." Rachel gave him a push.

Matt started up. In another half an hour he and Rachel were on the next ledge, and now all of them were strung along the face of the cliff wall. He checked his hands; the rough rope had scoured much of the skin off his palms and they stung like fire. He blew on them.

He looked up to see that Joshua had now made it to the cave, tied off his last rope for them to use, and then turned back to give them an enthusiastic thumbs up.

Matt waved back. "Come on. I've got a good feeling about this."

He felt strangely impatient and could feel the buzz of excitement in his stomach. Professional curiosity coupled with something else – an odd feeling of coming home. He took hold of the rope and gripped it tight for a few seconds before pulling one of his hands back to look at it.

"What's up?" Rachel asked, trying to see over his shoulder.

"*Uh*, friction burn." He gripped the rope again. The thing was, his abraded palms weren't abraded anymore. *Must have just been rubbed and flushed with blood*, he knew he was just bullshitting himself now. *Concentrate on the rope*, he thought, focusing; the last thing he wanted to do was make a mistake when he was so close. He started up the second-to-last leg.

By the time he hauled Rachel up to the third rest stop, they were sweating and puffing hard. He had to lean back and catch his breath and was glad there was only about 50 more feet to go.

"Least it'll be easy going down," Rachel said, her own back against the wall. She pulled her small canteen from a leg pouch pocket and took a swig.

Matt looked down at all the bodies strung out over the wall. "That'll be my workout for the day." He rolled his shoulders.

"Hey, what's that?" Rachel frowned as there came several odd popping sounds.

The sounds came again and seemed to echo and bounce around from somewhere out on the desert floor.

"I don't know." He squinted.

The next sound was from a ricochet and stone chips flicked over them.

"Oh shit; gunfire," Rachel said. "*Get down.*"

"I think we've just been found." Matt hunkered down. "Bandits."

"Don't think so." Rachel listened to the gunfire for a second or two more. "That sounds like an HK416 Assault Rifle – a bit high tech for your average desert bandit."

"Doesn't matter, a bullet is a bullet," Matt replied.

"Yeah, it does. Your average bandits can't shoot for shit." Rachel peered around a column of stone. "But these guys..."

More pops, and more shards of stone flying through the air. There came a grunt and yell from below, and Matt leaned out over the edge. One of Khaled's security men tumbled back from the rope and fell like a bag of meat to impact hard on the ground. He didn't move again.

"I think that was Yasha," Matt breathed.

Rachel grabbed him and jerked him back. "... these guys know what they're doing. Got to be the Borgia. Stay the fuck down."

"Ah, shit. How did they find us?" Matt groaned. "For once in my life, I wish it was just Selekan rebels or bandits."

Rachel pulled the handgun Khaled had given her and edged forward. The popping continued. "We've got handguns, and they sound like HK416s and M4 Carbines. We're sitting ducks up here."

"Where the hell are Okembu's men?" Matt carefully lifted his head, and immediately spotted three bodies lying on the sand. "Oh, shit, no."

Saeeb, the first of Khaled's commandos, had made it to Joshua's cave, and he immediately threw himself flat and began to return fire.

"Save your ammunition, buddy," Rachel whispered.

Ebadi and Rizwan were closing in on them, and still at the second rest stop, Khaled waited his turn. Just below them, Greta with Eleanor, Zahil and Captain Okembu clambered along the rope, moving fast.

Matt guessed everyone had the same idea – they had no option but to keep moving.

Something popped and wobbled from the desert floor. It rose to about 50 feet, then it ignited before shooting directly toward them.

"Fucking RPG!" Rachel grabbed Matt and pulled him down flat.

The rocket-propelled grenade quickly accelerated to 600 feet per second, before striking the cliff wall a hundred feet from them. Huge chunks of stone were blasted away, dropping to the desert floor with a shuddering thump.

There came another, and another. The next impacted about ten feet above Professor Ebadi and Rizwan. They hugged the cliff wall and tried to merge with the stone. But even though the impact had been above them, a sheet of rock about ten feet square exploded loose and came down like a massive guillotine, wiping both men from the wall as if they were flies on a windowpane. It was impossible to tell if either of them screamed.

Matt cringed as the rock and human debris crashed into the ground hundreds of feet below and then was followed by an echo that thumped out across the desert.

"Those sons of bitches," Rachel hissed. "We stay here, we're all dead." She dragged on his arm.

"What about the others?" Matt pointed back down the rock face.

"We can stand here and fret about it, or we can climb higher and try to give them some cover as they climb." Rachel peeked over the edge.

Matt felt like crap leaving the others behind, but knew there was no other serious option. "But..."

"But nothing, *get moving*." She gave him a shove toward the rope.

Matt turned back to see that Khaled was climbing rapidly up to their position. High above them in the cave Joshua was yelling for them to climb, and Saeeb was trying to pick his targets down below – it was now or never.

Matt edged out, hanging onto the guide rope. For the first time he was conscious of the height, the breeze and growing darkness. The back of his neck prickled as if waiting for the bite of a bullet, or worse, the slamming impact of a red-hot fragmentation RPG.

Rachel was only three feet behind him. "*Keep – going – don't – freeze.*" She hissed the words, breathing heavily herself now.

Bullets pinged off the rock nearby, but for the most part their attackers were targeting those lower down whom they had a better chance of hitting.

"Don't look down, we're nearly there," Rachel said.

"*Reach up.*"

Matt looked up, to see the scientist leaning out with hand outstretched. His face was streaked with dirt and perspiration, and behind his specs his eyes stood out in a flushed face.

Matt grabbed his hand, pulled and then rolled into the cave to lie on his back, puffing hard. Joshua immediately rolled back and grabbed Rachel, who came up fast over the ledge and rolled for cover. After a few seconds, she was up and beside Saeeb, pointing her gun down at the desert floor.

Matt wiped his brow. The moon was rising and just before he joined Rachel, he saw the moonlight glint on something sticking from the cave edge. He squinted. It was an old metal piton – a climbing spike hammered into the wall. There was more gunfire and Matt rolled over and crawled up beside Rachel.

Khaled wasn't far behind. He had skipped the rest stop on Matt and Rachel's last perch and kept going toward them. Further back, the rest of the group was pinned down.

In another few minutes Khaled launched himself over the cave edge and rolled beside them. The Saudi wiped his sweating face, and leaned back out, cupping his mouth.

"*Zahil, get ready.*"

The man made a fist and nodded, and Khaled turned to Saeeb. "We need to give the rest cover, or they'll be stuck until they're picked off. Ms. Bromilow, do you have ammunition left?"

She nodded. "Okay for now; six still in the mag, and a spare clip."

"Fully loaded, and three spare clips," Saeeb said.

"Good, we'll try and keep these guys' heads down – on my word." Khaled rolled back.

"Hold it, *uh*, question." Joshua held up a hand. "But shouldn't we be going the other way? Once we're all up here, we're still trapped."

"I counted 20 rifles," Saeeb said. "They've got us outnumbered and outgunned. Climbing down would mean getting shot."

"Maybe not; they might just take us hostage, negotiate a sale back to our homes." Joshua raised his eyebrows.

"Not these guys," Matt said. "And just ask our three dead drivers how their negotiation sessions went."

"We've got to get our people higher." Saeeb looked through a small Special Forces scope. "We can't defend our base when it's so strung out." He lowered the scope. "I don't think any of them have sniper rifles, praise Allah – they have range, but no real targeting."

"No real targeting, but lots of luck and just as much ammunition. Eventually they'll hit us by accident." Matt ducked again as another bullet smacked into the cliff wall beside them, making his point.

Khaled leaned over and yelled to his remaining commando who was pinned down with Greta, Eleanor and Captain Okembu.

The man gave him a thumbs-up – he was ready and waiting on their signal. Khaled, Rachel and Saeeb lay flat with guns extended. The Saudi sighted his targets.

"Ready?"

"Say the word," Rachel breathed.

"Yes," Saeeb said, his eyes rock steady.

"Three, two, one… *climb*!" Khaled yelled and began to fire at the desert floor. Rachel and Saeeb did the same, and his commando on the last outcrop began to push Greta and the clinging Eleanor toward the rope.

While the large woman readied herself, Okembu pushed past them, took the rope and began to climb. The commando made a snatch for him, but the Chadian army captain moved too quickly.

The commando yelled something, but then went back to getting Greta out on the rope, and then he followed.

Matt knew that the handguns would have little accuracy at that distance, but all the flying lead should be enough to keep cautious heads down.

The group climbed, Okembu coming fast, Greta slower, with the commando backed up behind them.

"We need to pick our targets. They're going to be a while," Rachel said.

Matt pulled Rachel's field glasses from her pocket and scanned the desert. "It's working; a few of them have been hit." He blew air through his lips. "But I think there's more than 20." As he spoke the three jeeps roared away.

"There go our jeeps," Joshua said.

"They're retreating?" Matt said after the disappearing vehicles.

"No, they'll be back," Khaled said. "I think they'll be getting reinforcements and supplies. I believe they're going to wait us out. I would."

"Well, that's just great. No one's climbing down anytime soon," Joshua whined.

"You can climb down anytime you wish. Maybe you can check on Yasha or Doctor Ebadi for us." Khaled turned to glare. Joshua dropped his gaze.

"Yeah, I think that's their plan," Rachel said. "A siege."

About 50 feet further down and along the rope, Captain Okembu paused, resting momentarily, and Greta caught up to him. Amazingly, the large woman, simply reached around the Chad Army captain, and then kept on climbing.

"Wow." Matt couldn't believe how powerful the woman was as she moved hand over hand along the rope. Okembu started up again, now only just in front of the trailing commando.

The two groups were halfway across the rope when the next round of RPGs impacted against the wall. One too low, the next too high and the third RPG obliterating the perch they had just left, and also the rock the rope had been tied around. The remaining climbers swung free like a giant pendulum with the two women and two men hanging on tight.

Zahil, Khaled's commando, was closest to the blast and also right at the very end of the rope so caught the greatest g-force in the swing. He crashed hard into the cliff wall several times in his high-speed arc. He seemed to have damaged one of his arms and he slipped a dozen feet down the rough rope.

"Zahil is hurt." Saeeb had the scope to his eye again.

Even without scopes they could see the blood over his face and shoulder. Being that close to the explosion would have meant flying rock debris would have been like frag shrapnel. The two men, plus Greta with Eleanor on her back, hung on tight as the rope sawed back and forth across the sharp edge of their ledge. The fibers of the old rope immediately began to pop and fray.

"It's not gonna hold," Rachel said, and cupped her mouth. "Climb, hurry!"

Both Greta and Captain Okembu slowly hauled themselves up the now vertical rope. The strain must have been unbelievable on already fatigued muscles. Khaled's last commando just hung there, and Matt was glad he couldn't see his face, as he knew there might have been pain, maybe fear, or maybe just a calm sense of inevitability.

"We'll have to go and get him," Matt said.

"No," Joshua said." The rope can barely hold them all as is." He grabbed at the rope. "We can at least pull them in."

But even this proved unworkable, as the weight on the rope made getting their hands underneath it impossible and leaning over the edge invited gunfire.

The rope stretched and complained against the ledge, and fibers pinged free to roll back from the main bunch.

"Jesus, we gotta try and wedge something underneath it to stop it cutting." Matt took off his shirt and tried to jam it underneath the rope, when another RPG exploded on the cliff face out to the side of them.

"Shit!" He rolled away as debris rained down on the group.

"They're getting better," Khaled said and scrambled back to the edge. "Climb, brother!"

"Finding their range," Rachel said evenly. "The next one will be right down our throats." She threw herself back out at the edge.

"Goddamn get moving!"

Greta was close now, followed by Okembu, but it wasn't their climbing that would determine their fate, but the rope – more fibers pinged away, and it was now only half of what it was before.

"It's gonna break." Saeeb grabbed onto it.

"It's not going to hold them!" Joshua yelled.

Okembu stared up at them for a moment, and with one hand dug down at his waist to remove a long-bladed knife. He looked down momentarily and saw that Zahil was staring back up at him. In the growing darkness Matt thought he made out the tiniest of nods from the commando.

Captain Okembu looked back up at the group on the ledge, and his eyes met with Matt's for a split second, before his arm and the blade swept down, cutting the rope below them.

The stricken commando fell into space. He didn't flail his arms and didn't say a word. He had already known what was coming.

"Bastard!" Khaled aimed down at Captain Okembu and fired, but Rachel knocked his gun up.

"Forget it. He did what he had to do to save the women," she said fiercely.

Khaled's eyes blazed. "No, this coward saved himself."

"Sure did. But what were his options? Wait until the rope snapped and they all died? Or maybe wait until the next RPG blew them all off the wall?" She met his furious gaze.

Khaled showed gritted teeth, and then glared back down at the Chadian captain. "I still curse him and all his ancestors."

"Let's try and pull them in, before we all get to meet our ancestors," Matt said.

"I can get my hand under the rope now." Joshua had wormed his fingers under the fibers.

They all grabbed on and hauled, dragging the rope and the swinging climbers up and then over the ledge.

Greta knelt for a moment to untie her belt and let Eleanor gently come free. She then held a bottle of water to her lips and let the woman sip. Matt was touched by how gentle the large woman could be.

Okembu got to his feet, his eyes steady and challenging. His hand rested on the butt of his gun. "I had no choice." He looked along each of their faces, stopping at Khaled's.

The Saudi also got to his feet, with the hulking Saeeb behind him. The man looked more hostile than anyone Matt had ever seen in his life, and he bet murder was on his mind.

"*I had – no – choice.*" Okembu's fingers slowly moved down on the gun.

"We know," Rachel said, stepping between Khaled and Saeeb.

The next RPG blast was so close it blew them all flat.

"Into the cave!" Joshua yelled.

They rushed into the mysterious cave and Matt looked over his shoulder to see two screaming smoke trails darting toward them.

"Incoming!" he yelled the word and then dived inside the mouth of the cavern and scrambled forward on knees and elbows.

The first RPG impacted above them, the second just inside the mouth of their cave. It felt like an earthquake as tonnes of rock came down in a waterfall of stone. Boulders as big as refrigerators thumped into the cave mouth, and a wall of dust billowed up just as they were plunged into a stygian darkness.

*

Drusus held up a hand. "It's over."

Aetius stood and cradled his rifle. "Should we follow them? We can reopen the cave with shaped charges."

"No, we wait." Drusus narrowed his eyes as he stared up at the collapsed cave high up on the sheer mountain wall. "It's not us they need to fear now."

*

A rock the size of his fist cracked across Matt's forehead and he saw stars. He rolled into a ball to protect himself from more blows, and lay there, waiting for the trembling and bouncing stones to finish their mad dance inside the cave. It was several minutes before the first flashlight went on.

"Is everyone okay?" Rachel sat up, moving her light around. "*Sound off.*"

There was silence as more lights came on. "*Matt, Khaled?*" She yelled now.

"*Cough* – here." From the Saudi.

"Matt?"

Matt wiped his eyes and mouth. "Yeah, yeah, I'm okay." He felt his forehead for the expected gash or at least huge egg, but there was nothing. Oddly, there was a sensation of movement under the skin, but it quickly went away. *Lucky*, he told himself as he picked his shirt up from the cave floor, and put it back on.

"Greta, Eleanor?"

The voice was faint. "Yes, my dear; we're both alive."

Captain Okembu and Saeeb both answered at once.

"Joshua, where are you?" Rachel waited.

Several lights panned around, searching for the parasitologist.

"Shit, where the hell is he?" Rachel got to her feet.

There was a groan and the sound of rocks sliding. She whipped the light to the source. The man was down with some of the debris covering his legs. Rachel was first to him and set to pushing off some of the larger stones.

Matt and Saeeb helped him to sit up. His legs and back were scratched and there was blood seeping through his torn clothing. In the glare of the lights his face was chalk-white from either the dust or the pain. He put his fingertips to his scalp, and they came away red.

"*That fucking hurt.*" He breathed deeply and then coughed, holding his chest. "I think I might have a broken rib or two." He grimaced.

Rachel sat back. "Well, the good news is, if you can feel pain, you're alive. So there's that." Rachel patted his shoulder. "And the bad news... what do we do now?"

Matt turned his light to the rear of the cave. "Joshua, what was back there?"

The scientist groaned and sat up. "I don't know. I only went in a few feet. But didn't have a chance to explore before we were attacked. It keeps going, I think."

"Might be another way out," Okembu said.

"Out is unlikely. We're over 250 feet up, and still a few thousand more up to the peak." Joshua rubbed dust from his hair and looked miserable. "More than likely it'll dead-end or lead to another portal on the cliff face. Bottom line, we're fucked."

"No, but you'll be fucked with that lay down and die attitude, mister." Rachel got to her feet.

"Hey! Remember why we came." Matt dusted himself down. "This might be the cave that leads to the Garden of Eden."

"And the wellspring," Eleanor added quietly.

Matt turned to the group. "People have been here before. Just before we came in I saw a metal piton hammered into the wall. It was old, but it tells me that someone had been here within the last century."

"Clarence, I bet," Eleanor said reverently.

"Might have been." Matt shone his light toward the back of the cave, and the beam stood out starkly in the still-drifting dust clouds. "We need to see what we've got to deal with."

"I agree, especially while we still have working flashlights." Khaled stood. "Is everyone okay to walk?"

They all got to their feet, giving Khaled his answer. Greta stood and lifted Eleanor van Helling into place. Only Joshua needed help standing. The scientist gripped his ribcage.

"I think we should stay here." Captain Okembu stood rod straight in the darkness. "People will come looking for me. Maybe we can dig our way out."

The next explosion was muffled, but still rained dust and debris down on their heads. Eleanor squeaked, and everyone froze, waiting.

"Jesus," Matt said and turned to the collapsed entrance. "Give it a rest, you bastards, we're already buried." He shone his light toward Okembu. "I'm thinking digging our way out that way might not be a good idea."

Dust still swirled inside the cave. And Matt lifted the front of his T-shirt to cover his mouth and nose. "Besides, if anyone does come, all they'll find is a few dead bodies, the jeeps gone and no sign of us. No reason to think we're stuck in a cave, hundreds of feet up a mountain side."

Okembu cursed under his breath.

Khaled shone his beam toward the back of the cave. "It goes on for quite some way, but the dust is hanging in the air – there is not a breath of air movement. Could mean a sealed environment."

"And maybe not," Matt said. "I've been in caves before, and you only need to drop down into a new chamber to find air circulation. There's nothing to keep us here, so…"

"A waste of time." Okembu stared up at the dark ceiling, and then slammed a fist down onto his thigh. "Why did I come with you fools? You wasted my time, and now it looks like you have condemned me to death."

"You chose to be here, my friend." Khaled's face was grim. "You chose to climb. You chose to accompany your men, and you chose to extract even more money from us." Khaled's mouth curled into a small smile. "In fact, you made every single decision all by your greedy self. So I am happy you are now in here."

"Cool it," Rachel said. "We haven't wasted our time – *yet.*" She pointed at one of the cave walls. "Matt, look."

Matt squinted, and then walked closer to where she was pointing. He grinned, slapped the rock and then turned back to the group.

"The mark of Noah."

*

"*That* says Noah?" Rachel looked at the few scratched scars on the wall. She could have quite easily assumed they were a few odd chisel marks in the stone. She reached up to trace them with a fingertip. "It could be characters, I guess."

"It is; it's the oldest form of his name. It also means 'rest, comfort'." Matt turned, looking at the cave's wall and ceiling. "Perhaps when the water was high, this might have been one of the places they took their rest and comfort in."

Joshua's light wobbled as he brought it closer. "Well, if we're going to be trapped, at least we might be trapped in the right place."

"This is what you came for?" Okembu asked.

"No, this is just a signpost." Matt moved his light to the interior. "We need to go deeper."

"These mountains are not a good place. They have many caves, some very deep." Okembu's eyes shone white in the darkness.

"I know, you told us, taboo, right?" Matt said softly, and then sighed. "But the Captain's right; we need to watch our step. Anyone wanders off in here and they might find they'll be the next artifact uncovered in another thousand years."

"So we follow the yellow brick road," Rachel said.

"Yellow brick road?" Okembu frowned.

"Forget it." Rachel shone her light back into the darkness and headed off.

The group stayed close together. Matt, Rachel and Khaled led them out. Greta and Eleanor were next, then came Okembu, and finally Saeeb helped Joshua hobble along at the rear.

Rachel's senses were on high alert. There were eight of them remaining – only an hour before, there had been 15 including Okembu's drivers. Nearly half their number had been killed in the blink of an eye.

She felt a pang of loss for the affable Professor Abdul Ebadi. The man was enormously enthusiastic, and though he had at least died doing what he loved, he might have just missed out on something that could have been classed as the absolute peak of his life's work.

Rachel's eyes shifted over her shoulder to the tall and sullen Chad Army captain. The guy looked angry all the time now. Three of his men had been killed and he hadn't even mentioned them – out here, life was cheap or worthless, she guessed.

"I can smell something," Okembu said, sniffing.

"Rock dust, minerals, maybe even some of the residue from the explosives," Joshua said.

"Fool, I know more about those things than you lambs who live in western cities. What I smell is earth, fresh earth, and not cave or desert dust. "

Rachel sniffed. She could smell nothing but ancient dryness. But maybe that was due the floating particles that tickled her nose and got deep into the nasal passages, making her want to hock it out.

"Any more signs?" she whispered to Matt, not knowing why she felt the need to hush her voice.

"Nothing," Matt said. "*Yet*, but the passage goes on, and luckily it's not narrowing."

They continued on, the cave bending to the left, and then angling down slightly. Rachel felt the perspiration trickling down her back, even though it must have been 20 degrees cooler in the cave. Thankfully, the gentle breath of a breeze dried the sweat on her forehead and gave some relief.

Breeze?

"Hey," she said. "Anyone else feel that?"

"Yes, and for a few minutes now," Khaled said. "It's coming from up ahead."

They increased their pace until Matt's sudden scream jolted some and made the rest cringe. Saeeb's gun was immediately up.

"He's fallen." Khaled held them back from the circular pit in the center of the cave.

"*Matt!*" Rachel dived forward, allowing herself to slide to the edge. She shone her light down into the void. Matt lay about a dozen feet down on a flat ledge, he was pushing himself up to sit, and holding his head.

"Don't move!" she yelled.

Beyond him, there was nothing but darkness. It was sheer luck he had fallen where he had, because if he'd missed the ledge, he would have disappeared into nothingness.

"I'm okay." He looked up at them, his face white and squinting at all the lights beaming down on him. He put a hand over his eyes and then turned to look around.

"This is it." He faced them again. "This is where we need to be." He pointed. "Look..."

*

Matt sat still for a few moments to let his dizziness subside. He inhaled, smelling the odors on the breeze. Okembu had been right – it did now smell like fresh earth, and there was something else: dampness, obvious after the dryness of the cave.

He hated caves, and darkness and pressing walls of jagged stone. He'd been in them before, and it never ended well. But for some reason in here, it felt... right. In fact, it felt better than right, it felt like, home. He shook his flashlight and it immediately came back to life. Shining it around he saw there were smooth stones beneath him. He got up to crouch; what he had landed on was no natural outcrop of rock, but instead a platform of interlocking stones.

He grinned and rubbed at the stone. *I don't believe it*, he thought, and looked up to the group. "Steps!" He turned back to follow them with his light. They led from the ledge he was on to then curve around the outside of the circular pit. It reminded him of the inside of one of the large smoke stacks he had seen on a trip to London once. Inside the huge funnel structure, there were maintenance steps winding up and corkscrewing all the way up to the light – except here, they spiraled down into the darkness.

Matt crept to the edge and shone his light down further. He couldn't see the bottom, but the steps continued ever onward into the gloom.

"Hey!" Matt yelled and waited for the echo to finish.

"What is it?" Rachel yelled down to him.

He turned and put a finger to his lips. "Shush – I'm checking something."

"Hey!" Matt yelled again, and listened, this time holding his breath and counting.

There was no echo. That usually meant the cave was so large that the reverberation return simply got lost, as the sound waves travelled too far and dissipated. Matt went to kneel back from the edge, when from the depths there was a blink of yellow light that drew his head back around. *What the?* He leaned forward, bringing his light around to where he had seen the glow. Had he seen two lights or one? He kept motionless, just staring for several moments.

"What are you doing?" Rachel's impatient voice made him jump.

"Nothing, I thought…" He knelt back again. "It's nothing." He panned his light around once more. About five feet up the mark of Noah was etched into the wall.

"This is it."

"What have you got?" Rachel yelled back.

"Big cave, but there's a way down. And I can feel a breeze coming up." He got to one knee. "Can you make it down to here?" He shone his light on the cave wall. He could see there probably had been steps once, but they looked to have broken off long ago. To get down it'd mean a jump.

There was a hurried conversation above.

"Yes, we think so. We'll lower each other down," Khaled said.

There was more discussion, followed by scraping and scuffing of boots on rock, and then Khaled was eased down. Saeeb stretched out, lowering him while he held onto his leather belt.

At the end of the belt and with his arms fully extended, Khaled only had about four feet left to go. Normally this would not have presented a problem, but as the ledge Matt was standing on was narrow, and over its edge a seeming bottomless void, the Saudi needed to drop and stick.

"Ready when you are," Matt said softly, standing back but hands ready to catch him.

Khaled let go, and landed lightly, bending his knees and grabbing the rock wall. Matt put an arm around him, but he was fine.

"No problem." Matt patted his shoulder, and then looked up. "Next."

It was Joshua's turn then, straining and sweating as his ribs undoubtedly screamed as he extended his arms. He landed with a grunt and an expression of unadulterated pain. Both Matt and Khaled grabbed at him, as he wobbled for a second or two.

"We got you." Matt held on for a few seconds more. "You okay?"

"Not really, but I'm down." Joshua held his side and moved out of the way. His face looked drawn and he glanced around nervously.

Some skittering against rock and Matt looked up to see Rachel's legs easing down.

"Stand back."

She landed like a cat, and immediately straightened. Next came Greta who refused to let Eleanor drop by herself so still had the tiny bird-like woman strapped to her back. Greta had no trouble hanging on, but the extra weight on her back when she dropped caused her to thrust her arms wide for a second, until both Matt and Khaled grabbed her.

"We've got you," Khaled said.

The woman lurched forward and hugged the stone. Her eyes were squeezed shut. Matt had his arm around her and felt the small body of Eleanor van Helling on her back. She squirmed slightly, and he had the strange sensation of a baby moving in a mother's belly. Matt recoiled and looking across at Khaled he saw that he too had moved back from the big woman.

From behind him there came the sound of rocks falling into the pit – *had they dislodged them?* he wondered.

Captain Okembu came next and seemed to be moving too fast.

"Take it easy; it's a long way down if you miss," Matt said.

Okembu snorted and let go. He landed lightly, not needing their hands on him as his long arms allowed him to come nearly all the way to the ledge. The last to come was Saeeb, and Matt knew the guy was going to be a problem.

He was big and solid, probably coming in at about 220 pounds. And even though he looked fit and agile, the problem was there was no one to lower him. He'd have to lower himself, somehow, meaning his drop would be closer to seven feet as opposed to their four.

"Stand back." The man pushed his legs over the edge and began to lower himself. He found a few handholds and tried to climb down a few extra inches to save him some drop space.

He looked down, readying himself. "Give me room."

Khaled and Matt both took a step back. Khaled stood with hands propped. "Ready, brother."

The commando let go. He came down hard, and immediately needed to take a step back to get his balance. Saeeb put one of his boots right on the edge – it crumbled under his weight – and his arms swung widely.

More chunks of stone broke off the ledge and fell back into the darkness. Matt saw them soundlessly fall, and also down deep the blink of yellow light again – two of them, close together.

"Saeeb!" Khaled leapt for his man.

Matt threw an arm around him, and Khaled gripped his collar. They managed to lever him back before gravity and

Saeeb's significant weight ripped him free. The commando stood back on the edge, his balance restored. He leaned forward with his hands on his knees and breathing hard.

"Thank you." Saeeb looked briefly back over his shoulder. "Long way down." He grinned at Matt.

Matt went to grin back, but the words caught in his throat. Something enormous loomed up behind the commando. Two yellow, pupilless eyes the size of softballs blinked open, and Matt had the impression of hulking shoulders and skin that looked like it was made of broken rock or splintered wood that was all knots and sharp edges.

Ogrish features were twisted as it took them all in. Matt felt light-headed with fear and he backed up, pushing Rachel behind him. Khaled fumbled for his gun.

Saeeb spun then, but before the large commando could even draw a weapon, hands that looked like ancient tree bark wrapped around him, covering most of his upper body, and lifted him off his feet. He grunted in pain, once, and then the thing vanished back into the abyss, taking the man with him.

Khaled was frozen, his mouth open and his eyes wide and staring into the darkness. Matt tried to swallow but couldn't. Rachel gripped his back and peered over his shoulder.

"Was that another one of those... *things?*" she hissed into his ear.

Matt gulped. "Yes. I think it was another of the Nephilim."

"Nephilim." Khaled turned to him. "Just like in the mountaintop." His teeth were bared.

Captain Okembu had a long knife that looked like a machete drawn and held up and ready. He looked out and over the edge. "A demon." He whispered and made some sort of sign in the air. "Gone now." He looked back to Matt, his eyes suspicious. "You have seen this thing before?"

Matt nodded. "It attacked us, or something like it. I think it was a fallen angel, a protector of holy places."

"An angel?" Okembu snarled. "Did you not see that abomination? That was no angel, Professor man."

"No, not now, but they were once according to legend. Before they fell from grace." Matt shook his head. "I don't know. This was Ebadi's field."

"Well, he is not here." Okembu took a step toward Matt, the long blade still in his hand. "But we are here and so is that *thing*."

Khaled stepped closer. "We also encountered one of these things. It was in the cave of Shem, Noah's son."

"Did you kill it?" Okembu asked.

"We tried," Khaled said. "But I'm not sure we even hurt it."

There was the softest of thumps from deep down in the pit. Okembu bared his teeth and looked momentarily back up at the rim of the pit.

"There's no going back," Rachel said. "We're all in this together whether we like it or not."

Greta was standing with her back to the wall. Eleanor rose up from behind her shoulder. "Matthew, might it come back?"

Matt looked from her down into the pit. "Probably. But the last time I managed to see it off. We need to be vigilant, and maybe a little quieter. Less squabbling will help."

"It came from down there," Rachel said following his gaze. "And we're about to follow it."

"We have no choice, dear," Eleanor said. "Like you said, there are no other options."

"No, we do have a choice. We go back." The voice was tiny, and they turned to see Joshua, sitting on the groud, with his hands up over his head. "If we go down, we die."

Rachel went and crouched beside him. "Hey there, you're okay now."

He started to shudder, and at first they thought he was sobbing, until he lifted his head. His eyes were wet, but he threw his head back and laughed long and loud. "Why wouldn't I be okay?"

"Keep it down." Matt looked over his shoulder into the pit.

"Yep, everything is just fine and dandy. We're all having a great time." Joshua laughed some more. He dropped his hands, his voice shrill. "I deal with the microscopic, not with things that look like monsters made from petrified wood." He tugged on his own hair. "Lead on, Professor Kearns, straight to hell."

Matt grimaced and put his finger to his lips.

Rachel stood. "Fine, be an asshole."

"It's okay, Joshua. We're all scared," Matt said, still trying to wave the man to quietness.

After another moment, Captain Okembu growled deep in his chest, and pointed his blade. "Listen, spectacle man, if your noise brings the beast back, I will make sure it is you it takes next."

Joshua put his hands over his face and quietened, but still shook. Okembu stared for another moment, but then turned to Matt and rubbed his chin.

"So, this thing was a guard?" He nodded, sheathing his sword. "One thing I know, Professor; you only have guards for something you value."

Matt turned to look into the tall Chadian captain's eyes. "Or maybe something a god wanted protected."

*

"I can smell fresh air coming up," Joshua said. The young scientist seemed somewhat composed but his eyes were overly bright and he glanced around skittishly, unable to keep still.

Matt sniffed. "I can smell earth and water and something else. But whether that's the outside air is another matter."

"Well, I've got everything crossed," Rachel said.

Matt went to Khaled, who was leaning back against the wall, his eyes closed.

"Are you okay?"

After a moment the Saudi nodded. "Those men, Saeeb, Yasha, Rizwan and Zahil; they were more than bodyguards. I've known them all my life. They were my friends."

"I'm sorry for Saeeb, and for all of them." Matt waited.

After a moment, Khaled nodded and straightened. "What happens is God's will."

Matt gripped the man's shoulder for a moment and then turned back to the group. "We go down slowly, and we only use every second flashlight – not sure how long we'll be in here, so saving batteries means saving light." He looked at each of their faces, but there were no questions. "Okay, let's go." He led them down.

They took the steps one at a time. Following Saeeb's descent into the void, no one needed to be told to take it easy or stay back from the edge. One slip, and they knew they'd be joining the commando.

Though they each watched where they placed their feet, they couldn't help peering over the edge, searching for movement or a glimpse of the pale yellow glow. They knew the thing was down there, somewhere, perhaps watching and waiting for them.

After a while, Khaled leaned out and shone his light downwards. "Still can't see the bottom. We've been traveling for hours, and by my estimates, we should be well below ground level."

"I agree. If this place was sealed, it'd make a great home if the land outside was near totally submerged for months."

"That long?" Rachel asked.

"Well, according to the Bible, it says that after it rained for 40 days and 40 nights, and the highest mountains were covered by a depth of 15 cubits – that's about 22 feet.

Then the world was water. Or at least Noah's world was water. The new ocean prevailed on the Earth for another 150 days, and supposedly, everything that wasn't aboard the Ark died."

"150 days – 5 months – wow," Rachel said.

"Longer than that," Matt said as he walked. "40 days of rain, 150 of flood, then more months just waiting for the first land to appear. They might have been stuck up on these mountains, or inside them, for years."

"They went into the earth – into these caves." Joshua snorted softly. "A perfect sealed breeding ground for all sorts of multi-celled organisms looking to hitch a ride on a passing human."

"Nice." Rachel grimaced.

"Guess we might find out soon." Matt eased over a missing step. "Gap here – watch it."

They descended for another hour, and the air became noticeably cooler.

"Heart of the mountain," Khaled said.

"Heart? Much lower; more like the asshole now, yes?" Okembu grinned and shone his light into the Saudi's face.

"Very poetic." Khaled glared back into the light.

"I can see the cave floor." Matt leaned out. "Another 50 feet below us." He also saw the debris and crumpled and torn body of the security guard. He quickly flicked his light away.

In another moment, they came off the circling stone steps onto the smooth floor. Looking up, there was nothing but a tunnel of impenetrable darkness above them. The group joined him, flicking lights around the base of the giant column.

Khaled went to stand over Saeeb's body, his hands across his mid section and his eyes closed. He spoke a funeral prayer, the *Salat al-Janazah,* for the man, finishing by holding his palms upwards and raising his eyes.

He returned and nodded to Matt, but Matt could see the sagging expression on the man's features. He had been deeply wounded by the loss of his friends.

"Multiple caves, multiple choices," Rachel said.

Okembu pulled a small plastic cigarette lighter from his pocket and flicked it on. The tiny orange flame bent away from one direction.

"See how easy it is?" He pointed. "That one."

"Works for me," Matt said. "You want to lead us in?"

Okembu seemed to think about it for a moment or two. "No, this is your job." He gave Matt a small bow.

"I guess it is." Matt turned his light toward the new cave and headed in. Rachel and Khaled crowded in behind him, followed by Joshua, Greta, Eleanor and then Okembu.

It quickly became apparent that this was a natural opening in the stone; as there was no new stone being added or even any signs of it being worked by tools. It narrowed to about two feet in width, and then opened back out after another 50 feet. The smell of damp was growing stronger, and Matt caught sight of a glint of moisture on the floor and walls. After another few minutes mosses started to appear, and then came the humidity.

"How far down are we?" Rachel asked.

"At a guess, I'd say a few hundred feet below ground level. If there was any biblical flood water, then this is where it would have finally drained."

"I know this region," Okembu said softly. "There are no streams, pools, marshes, or even a single oasis. If there is water in here, then it has never made it to the surface."

"Doesn't bode well for a way back out then." Joshua's voice still had a brittle edge to it.

The passage narrowed even more so they began to travel in a single file.

"Stop." Matt came to a halt so quickly Rachel bumped into his back. Her feet skidded, crunching debris beneath her.

"What is it?" Rachel held her light over his shoulder.

Matt squinted. "I think I saw something moving in there."

"Moving? As in alive, moving?" she panned her light around.

"It's too narrow for our yellow-eyed giants." Khaled pointed his flashlight in another direction. "I can see nothing. Maybe it was…" he trailed off perhaps not wanting to blame it on Matt's imagination.

"Fear and the dark plays tricks on some men." Calling from the back of the group, Okembu had no such timidity.

Matt held his hand out, moving aside something that looked like hanging vines or roots, as he half-turned to the group. "I'm telling you; I saw something move, and I don't think it was a shadow, my imagination, or the damn breeze."

As he pushed at the long vine things to ease them aside, they stuck. He turned back frowning.

"Wha…?"

The tendrils, some as thick as a pencils, seemed to coil and move, winding up and around his wrist and fingers.

"Hey, these things."

They tightened. Matt jerked his hand back, but the hanging vines were enormously strong, elastic and adhesive like they had suckers on them.

"*Ow*! They're getting tight – *little help here, guys*." He tugged but more of the vines coiled around his hand.

Khaled grabbed Matt's shoulders and held on, as Rachel went to grab at the vines over his shoulder.

"Don't touch them!" Matt yelled.

Matt felt his entire hand begin to throb, as the circulation was cut off at the wrist. The vines had circled many of his individual fingers, and they tightened making them first turn red, and then a deep, angry purple.

"Je-*eesus* Chr-*iiist*." There was an audible snap as one of his fingers broke.

Matt yanked at it, pulling with all his weight and strength but it was like fighting against rubberized leather. The coils moved along his forearm, and then his entire arm began to be drawn upwards.

He howled as a second finger snapped and the tendrils tried to reel him toward the tunnel roof. He looked up and saw that the vines disappeared into a large crack above him. Inside he thought he saw something large and fleshy there, like a soft mouth opening and closing as if smacking its lips in anticipation of the treat to come.

The pain made tears well up in his eyes and he screamed again, from the agony and frustration and then braced his legs. He felt more of the crunching underfoot and quickly glanced down to see that the ground was littered with the bones of small animals.

Whatever this thing was, this was where it did its fishing. It yanked again, and more tendrils lifted toward him.

"Get this fucking thing off me!"

There was chaos as bodies tried to shove past him, or around him to help, while also trying to avoid the coiling tendrils. More dropped down, and they seemed to writhe and jiggle in excitement. Matt felt one tickle his ear and felt panic rise in his gut at the thought of them circling his neck and pulling his whole body up so his head disappeared into the red, fleshy maw now just visible in that *fucking* crack in the rock.

"Get it off. Don't let it...!" He knew he was panicking as he thrashed, but his fight or flight instinct had taken control of him now.

There was a thud on his back that wrenched his arm nearly from its socket and caused another of his fingers to snap. The agony was now like a fire all the way up his arm.

The thump and crush came again as Captain Okembu jumped across the top of the crowd, holding aloft his machete blade. He couldn't get a full swing happening, but he managed enough force to hack through several of the vine things hanging down. He severed more on the back swing, yelling a battle cry as he worked.

Sticky liquid splashed down on them, and above it all, there came an inhuman squeal and momentarily the vines seemed to make a concerted effort to drag Matt away from the group. He began to lift off his feet, but Captain Okembu slashed again and again, cutting away more of the writhing vines. He stopped and looked up, and then jammed the long blade up into the crevice – this time the squeal became ear-piercing and was accompanied by mad thrashing as the vines pulled back into the roof and in another instant had vanished.

Matt fell back to the ground, striking his head, hard, and everything went black – the dark cave, the thing in the roof, and the shouting of his companions all vanished. Instead there was nothing but a luminous pool of water, and rising from it, the goddess. It was her again, and this time, she raised a hand, beckoning.

Matt felt his hear race in his chest and never in his life had he felt such raw attraction. An animal lust welled up inside him as the woman approached. Thick blonde hair fell to her shoulders and it seemed to sparkle with highlights of gold, red and silver. She smiled a perfect smile in features that could have been Nordic with high cheekbones, taut jawline and a sharp, pointed nose. But it was her eyes that held him. They glowed with a sapphire intensity that was impossible to look away from.

He smiled back, and she held out a hand. Matt did the same, their fingertips slid past each other and then she took his hand and pulled him closer. The goddess held his hand in hers and angled her head and parted her lips, ready to kiss him. Matt couldn't resist, and his own mouth began to open, desiring those plump lips against his own more than anything else in the world.

Just as they were inches apart, Matt looked down at the parted lips, but inside there was no tongue, but instead a thousand soft, tiny worms welling up from her throat. He gagged and went to pull back but she held on. She still had his hand and her strength was unbelievable. He tugged, but couldn't break her grip, and her hand got tighter and tighter on his, the pain becoming unbearable. His eyes flicked open.

"*Fu-gggggghhh!*"

The word hissed out through his gritted teeth like steam. He looked up at Okembu who stood over him in the dark cave, knife still ready and facing the roof where the thing had dropped down to ambush him.

"Captain, where...?" Matt looked around, grimacing. "Thank you."

Okembu, looking down, nodded. "Professor man, exactly what was that? There is no plant like that in these deserts that I have ever seen."

Joshua was crouching nearby and picked up a piece of the severed tendril. "I don't think it's a plant at all." He sniffed it. "*Phew* – yep, that's not sap leaking from it, it's blood, and it was covered in hairs. Shine that light over here."

Khaled moved his light closer and Matt cautiously leaned across. Joshua squeezed the tendril.

"It's got a sort of exoskeleton, like an insect, but leathery. More like, a spider I guess."

"*Shit*, that thing is a spider?" Matt got to his feet with Rachel grabbing him under the arm.

"This is getting a habit." She held him up.

He grinned brokenly. "This is why I love fieldwork."

"Maybe this thing *once* was a spider. But you live in a lightless cave, you adapt to hunting any way you can." Joshua reached down to pick up a length of tendril that was a good three feet long and as thick as a garden hose – it was spiked with hair. "And I can tell you one thing, for this creature to have adapted like this, it's been here a *long, long* time."

Khaled grimaced. "That thing was big. To sustain that bulk, it must get a lot of food."

Matt pointed at the ground. "All the skeletons on the ground – I should have known. This is its killing field. Fed on bats and anything else that wandered along this cave corridor."

"Yeah, mostly." Joshua picked up a larger shard of bone. It was the remains of a jaw of some sort of simian. "If it only fed on bats, it would have steered clear of something the size of you. I think it's also proficient at trapping bigger game than that." He looked up at the ceiling. Blood still dropped from the edges.

"We should move away from here," Joshua said, looking jumpy again, his eyes showing all their whites.

"Gets my vote," Matt said cradling his hand.

"Hey, look here." Khaled bent over to pick an object up from the cave floor. "*Gold.*" He rubbed at it, and then flicked it open. "*Ha!* An old cigarette lighter." He spun the striking wheel but got no response.

"Looks like we aren't the first people through here." Khaled looked around. "And either this means they made it past the spider-trap." He turned to the group. "Or he was just about to walk into it."

Khaled squinted at the lighter. "There's something written on it – C.V.H."

"Let me see that." Eleanor held out a hand, and Khaled handed it to her. "Well, give me some light here, young man," she demanded.

Khaled held his flashlight over her shoulder onto the object. The old woman's lips curled up at the corners. "C.V.H. – *Clarence van Helling*." She pressed it to her lips momentarily and ground her eyes shut. "He was here."

"And we know he made it out... *eventually*," Khaled said. He turned his light down the dark cave tunnel. "So, this might be the right way after all."

"Then let's keep going," Rachel said. "You okay?"

"Yeah, yeah, let's just get away from here." Matt straightened but knocked his hand, and yelped. He chanced a look at it. The fingers were bent at odd angles, were now multi-hued and looked as horrifyingly painful as they felt. Luckily the skin wasn't broken and no compound fractures had burst through the skin.

"Wait." Khaled held out his hand taking Matt's in his own. "If we don't get those bones into alignment, they may cut off the flow of blood. You'll get gangrene. We need to straighten them." He looked into Matt's eyes. "Do you know what that means?"

"Something extremely painful, I'm sure." Matt tried to pull his hand back but Khaled held on. He felt perspiration break out on his top lip. He looked down at his damaged hand, and at the fingers that bent every which way. He knew Khaled was right.

"Close your eyes," Khaled said softly.

"*Ah*, Jesus." Matt did as he was told and felt the Saudi take one of his broken fingers in his hand.

"Think of something nice," he said. "On the count of three."

Matt took himself to a beach, to blue shimmering waves, endless sunshine, and...

Khaled began. "One..."

There was a sudden yank accompanied by a crunching noise that was immediately drowned out by a scream – *his own.*

"What happened to *two, three, go?*" Sweat had broken out all over his face, and he looked down at the finger. It was now straight, but purple-black and obscenely fat around the knuckle.

"Well, there's two to go," Rachel said, placing a hand on his shoulder.

Matt sucked in a huge breath and looked away. "Go for it."

Two more yanks, and two more fingers, still broken, but at least all poking in the right direction now. Rachel wrapped the hand in her handkerchief, and helped him put it into his open shirtfront to act as a sling.

"We can try to splint it, when we're away from here," Khaled said.

"Thanks." Matt was content to just let it throb away close to his chest. He was also glad the fingers weren't ripped free, or worse; his head pulled up into the thing's lair inside the crack.

"Let's move," he said between compressed lips.

Captain Okembu wiped the sticky, black fluid from his blade and resheathed it on a belt. He checked a large fake-looking Rolex on his wrist. "Dawn is only an hour away."

"In here, that means nothing," Joshua said.

Khaled led them out. The going was slower, as they now needed to check every nook and cranny before they stepped over it, ducked under, or squeezed past it. The slight breeze grew stronger, and thankfully cooler, and soon the cave had opened out into a wider passage.

Underfoot the ground squelched, and here and there small, pale plants rose from the sodden ground.

"Thank all the prophets, there's something up ahead," Khaled said. "And I can hear, I'm not sure, but it sounds like, rustling."

"Like wind in the trees," Rachel added.

They stepped under a low archway, and then stopped. Even though it was stygian dark inside, Matt tilted his head, concentrating; he had the impression of vast size.

Rachel took off her backpack and fished inside. She pulled free a flare gun, which she quickly broke open and checked.

"This is a one and only, so hope it works." She snapped it closed, pointed the gun up and forward, and then fired.

The red flare shot into the air above them, before igniting at about 150 feet up and that far in. It floated down slowly on its tiny parachute, its miniature red sun illuminating the vista before them.

Matt felt his mouth drop open, and Khaled turned, a huge grin splitting his face.

"*Akebu-Lan* – the Garden of Eden."

Chapter 18

The group spread out along the small ledge. The sight that met their eyes was beyond anything they could have imagined.

It was a jungle, enormous, stretching as far as they could see within the glow of the flare. As the ball of light fell, it illuminated the tops of ferns, huge trees, and towering palms, with even the glint of a small stream cutting through it. Matt knew that shallow caves could support shade-loving ferns and, deeper in, liverworts, mosses and lichens, but this was a growth that would rival the jungles of the Amazon or Congo basin.

"It's hollow," Khaled breathed.

"Oh my god." Rachel's mouth was also hanging in an open smile, and the red blush from the flare was reflected back like dots of blood in her pupils. The flare slowly died, and the massive cavern returned to blackness.

Matt held up a hand flat. "Even in the dark, I can sense it – the life." He closed his eyes and inhaled. "There's our answer to the smell of dampness, the fresh air and earth."

"I wish Prince Najif could see this." Khaled smiled dreamily. "I know it is exactly as he hoped."

"How?" Rachel whispered. "How did it get in here? How does it even survive in here?"

Okembu started to look for a way down, but Matt stopped him.

"Wait; we're not ready yet."

"Maybe you aren't." The Chadian soldier snatched his arm away, and then looked at his watch. "I am hungry and thirsty, and I think there will be game here... for all of us." He held up his large watch to Matt's face. "Nearly 6 am, and that is my breakfast time, Professor."

"Look." Joshua pointed.

Out on the floor of the cavern, still partially obscured by the trees, a soft, blue glow had begun to emanate.

"Did we just make that happen?" Matt asked.

"There's more," Rachel said as columns of light began to drop down from above. "Somebody is turning on the lights for us." She flicked off her flashlight.

Matt laughed. "This is so cool. Remember the image in the stained glass – what we thought was the radiance of God?" There were beams of golden light falling from high up to one side of the cavern ceiling. "This is what it meant."

He grinned and pointed. "You asked about how it survives, the forest." He pointed to the huge columns of light. "There's your answer – the cave is punctured, letting in some light." He held out a hand. "And the ground is warm, maybe from some sort of hot spring beneath us. The vents in the ceiling allow light to enter, but the cavern traps the moisture – it's like a giant greenhouse in here."

"It's enormous," Joshua said. "I can't even see where it ends."

The multiple beams of light grew stronger as the sun rose outside the skin of the cave. The golden columns illuminated a lush forest of palms, ferns, and towering trees that could have been banyan, and a broader tree type below them.

"Acacia." Captain Okembu snorted. "Nearly 50 years ago the last acacia died in the Sahara desert. There was much weeping by environment people. And yet here, there are too many to count. Hiding perhaps."

"Eight to ten thousand years ago, the whole area was covered in forest. This is probably the last remnant," Matt said. He turned to Okembu. "This is probably what your country looked like 5000 years ago."

"Beautiful," the tall Chadian whispered.

"Trapped in its own specimen jar," Joshua said. He looked around slowly. "It's warm, damp, twilight-lit and heavily forested – perfect for parasites. We need to be careful."

"Well, that certainly breaks the magic moment," Rachel jibed.

Joshua spun. "I'm being serious." His voice was high. "And I meant it... *be careful.*"

Matt showed his bandaged hand. "Yeah, now he tells us to be careful?"

"The light over there is different." Khaled pointed out toward the center of the huge space, where the soft glow seemed to emanate. But there it looked like it rose up from the ground instead of filtering down.

"It's blue," Joshua said. "Could be some form of bioluminescence. Some organisms are able to activate a protein called *luciferase* that produces a natural blue light."

"We should check it out," said Matt.

"Pretty dense forest – more a jungle," Rachel said. "Given what attacked you in that cave, I'm not happy about all that cover for potential predators." She turned to the group. "And did anyone notice it's not silent in here anymore?"

As one, they turned back to the forest – she was right. They had all been focusing on the visual wonders, but failed to notice that there were now strange bird calls, insects humming, and rustling in among the foliage, and even more movement in the tree canopies.

"Could it have been the light that did it?" Khaled asked.

"Maybe; their own version of a dawn chorus," Matt said.

"This place is a self-contained, fully functioning ecosystem – we should have expected it the moment we saw the plant life." Joshua wrapped his arms around himself. "I don't like it."

Matt saw that the parisitologist had taken to biting his bottom lip, so much so there was blood on his chin. "You okay there?"

"And if I wasn't?" Joshua grinned a little too wide for a moment. "Sure, sure, just a little... overwhelmed."

"I can see a path of some sort." Khaled pointed. "Or a watercourse we can follow."

"Yeah, great, stick to the water." Joshua giggled. "Like no parasites have ever been found in water."

"Will you put a lid on it?" Rachel rounded on him. "Jesus Christ, we're all on edge here. Just keep your shit together, and we'll be fine."

"You keep saying that – *we'll be fine*." Joshua scratched his head. "Thank heavens, because I thought for a moment there that we were trapped in the middle of the Sahara Desert, hundreds of feet underground, after most of our people had been killed, and Professor Kearns was attacked by something that dropped from the ceiling like some sort of spider–jellyfish thing from hell." He put a hand over his mouth to stifle a laugh, but then spoke through his fingers. "We'll be fine, so now let's all walk into a dark jungle."

"See, you sound better already." Rachel walked away from the man.

"The man's a coward and an idiot, but he's right." Eleanor allowed Greta to ease her from her back, so the small, bird-like old woman could stand by herself.

"Gee, thanks, Mom," Joshua sneered.

"We *are* trapped in here," she said. "Maybe we will find everything we seek in that forest. But what good is it if we cannot find our way back out?" She smacked her lips, and Greta immediately gave her a sip from a canteen.

Eleanor pushed her away. "We should split up; a few of us go and explore the pool, and the rest look for a way out."

"Pool? What pool?" Matt turned to her.

"Or whatever that blue glow is." She waved it away. "But I know that you know, Professor, that time is against us now."

"It's not a good idea." Matt felt his slung arm. "We need to stay together. Who knows what else we'll encounter down here." He went to sip his water, but found he had already drained it. "Shit."

"Here." Rachel pulled her canteen from her belt pouch and held it out. She paused, frowning. "Are you okay?" She came closer, holding her light up. She shook her head. "You've got to take it easy, you look like crap."

Matt felt his face. Even with his fingertips he could feel the sunken cheeks and hollowed eyes. He held up his broken hand. "Cut me some slack; I've had a bad day."

Rachel held his chin. "I'm worried, Matthew."

Matt jerked his head back from her tender touch. "I feel fine."

"Leave him be," Eleanor said. The old woman continued to stare at Matt from half-closed eyes for a moment. She turned to Khaled. "We need to find a way out, *now*."

"She's right. Look at Professor Kearns; we're all being worn down. We need to get back home," Khaled said. "We're close to the cave wall, and where the sunlight vents are. Might be a way up to one of them. Wouldn't hurt for a few of us to check them out, save time. Then we can all meet at the blue thing."

"It's been my professional experience that the longer we're exposed to host-feeder environment, the more chance of a parasitic pathogen uptake, and permanent damage to the host," Joshua said, his eyes wide and feverish.

"Parasitic pathogen uptake." Rachel sampled the words in her mouth, before rubbing her neck. "Matt?"

"We don't know if this is even the source of the illness," Matt said. "Or even if it is an illness. I just don't like us splitting up at this time."

"But we do, and time matters, Matthew." Eleanor raised tiny painted eyebrows.

Khaled held up a hand. "I can check for a way out. Meet you at the center; it won't take me more than a few hours."

"I'll go with you," Matt said.

"No." Khaled held up a hand. "You're the only one who can decipher anything that might be relevant and important. You need to go to the interior."

"Where Matt goes, I go." Rachel thrust out her chest.

"Greta will go with you, Khaled," said Eleanor. "And might I also suggest the tall and strong Captain Okembu."

Matt had a horrible thought. "I'm sorry, but I can't carry you Eleanor." He held up his bandaged hand. "I'm walking wounded."

"Oh no, no way." Joshua backed away.

"Shut up, the pair of you." Her wrinkled face creased with disdain. "I wouldn't trust either of you pansies. For your information, I'll walk from here." She straightened, almost coming to Rachel's shoulder.

"Then it's settled," Khaled said. "The captain, Greta and myself will look for an opening to the outside. And successful or not, we will meet you at the interior in..." He checked his watch, "... six hours." He started to turn away, but paused. "And if there's any trouble, fire a shot in the air; we'll do the same."

"Deal," Matt said. "Good luck." He shook the Saudi's hand.

Okembu gave Matt a small salute with a couple of fingers, and then turned away. Greta's eyes lingered on Eleanor for a moment longer, before she followed the two men.

*

Captain Abdulla Mokelemee Okembu was 32 years old and had been in the Chad National Army for a dozen years. Before that he was a boy soldier fighting in one of the many tribal collisions that seemed never-ending out in the desert nothingness of the great plains between Zouar and Bardai.

He had killed many men, and he had come across many people, men and women, who had been killers – some were brutal blunderers that were big enough to crush a man's head with their bare hands. Others used knife, spear or gun, or snuck into windows in the dead of the night to slit throats or throttle the soul from a body.

Okembu could spot them now. All of them, the killers had the same eyes, ones that were dead inside. They were like dark glass, which were windows onto a black soul. He saw that look now.

The group was mostly lambs, but among them hid a wolf. He would need to watch himself, sleep with an eye open, and never turn his back.

He would be patient; if they struck, then he would be ready and strike back harder. Okembu knew how to survive.

*

He watched Khaled's team vanish toward the cave cliff wall, and then Matt faced the thick forest. "Let's follow the stream; it looks like it heads to the interior and to the, *ah*, pool, right, Eleanor?" He turned and raised his eyebrows at the old woman.

She ignored him, and so Matt started down to the forest floor. Rachel grabbed him.

"Seriously, you're going to lead out with that busted wing? Best if you leave this one to me." She stepped in front of him and went to flick her flashlight on, but changed her mind. "Light's not bad now, and I guess it wouldn't hurt to save the batteries."

"I'm not going last," Joshua said quickly.

"Fine, I will," Mat said. "But you go next, and as an added bonus, as you're the only fit man here, you get to give Eleanor assistance, when she needs it."

"I won't," she snapped.

"Team-bonding session is over. Let's go." Rachel stepped down from the rock ledge.

Matt sighed and looked briefly over his shoulder. "And that means I get to bring up the rear – *shit*."

Rachel picked her way down the gentle slope until her feet sank into soft soil. The group followed quickly, with Eleanor refusing Joshua's hand and eventually coming down on all fours like some sort of tiny, well-dressed insect. In no time they were pushing through the dense foliage.

They followed the sound of gurgling water, and soon found a small pool where the water swirled and then drained beneath a large stone.

Matt shone his light in the pond – it was clear and a few small fish darted about in it. Eleanor immediately knelt and dipped a hand into it and lifted it to her lips.

"Don't do that." Joshua lunged, knocking her hand from her mouth. "The water is more than likely the source of the parasite." He implored.

She turned back slowly, her lip curled. "Look to yourself, you young pup." She dipped her hand into the water again and brought the cupped palm to her lips. She closed her eyes and tilted her head back, as if waiting for something.

After a moment she opened her eyes, held up her hand, turned it over and stared hard at it, before turning it over and looking again at its back.

She seemed to deflate. "Nothing."

"What were you expecting?" Matt asked, but already knew. "Rejuvenation?"

"Fuck off." Eleanor rose to her feet, small brown teeth bared.

"*Erk.*" Matt recoiled. *Mad*, he thought. Or perhaps obsessed.

"Come on," Rachel said. "We'll follow the water. Stay on its bank."

They moved slowly, and Matt noticed that none of them needed to be told to be quiet. Even so, they didn't need to be that silent as the forest certainly wasn't silent around them, with all the movement, animal and birdcalls, and water gurgling. The odd thing was, other than the tiny fish they had previously seen, the wildlife seemed content to be vocal but invisible.

The back of Matt's neck prickled, and he couldn't resist looking over his shoulder. He felt sure they were being watched and for the last few minutes he even had the distinct feeling that someone or something was keeping pace with them on the other side of the stream.

Several times he spun, pointing his light into the undergrowth, but each time he saw nothing. Jumpy as all hell, he knew. He grinned, imagining what Rachel would say to him: *grow a pair, will you?* He snorted and hurried on.

Odd, he thought. Now he was aware of the sound of his footsteps, and could only hear them because... the sounds of the forest had silenced.

He spun again; this time there was a round face peering through a bush. The flesh was corpse-pale and the skin oddly moving, rippling like ribbons being wound over each other.

"*Ack!*" Matt jerked back fast and fell onto his ass. The face was quickly pulled away.

"What?" Rachel stopped and turned.

Matt pointed, feeling his heart rate going through the roof. "Something's following us." Matt shone his wobbling light back into the shadowed foliage.

The group each followed his gaze, and then turned slowly, searching the overgrown areas nearest themselves. They all froze, listening and watching.

"I don't see anything." Rachel said. "It's probably just the shadows. We're all tired."

Matt got to his feet. "Bullshit. I know shadows, and they don't have..."

"Kearns, *please*, I'm nervous enough as it is." Joshua's light beam whipped around and into his face.

Matt pointed. "But..."

"You're not in the classroom now, Professor." Eleanor smirked.

"Come on, Matt; stay cool." Rachel's brows were sloping over her eyes in pity. "Do you need to walk up here beside me?"

"Oh, good grief." He turned one last time to the foliage, but there was nothing, now. "Forget it." The sounds of the forest had returned.

Hours passed, and then more. The fatigue was starting to affect all of them. In addition, the angle of the light from the glowing columns from the ceiling was changing as the sun obviously moved across the sky outside. Matt wondered how Khaled was getting on, as even though curiosity was still burning within him, he knew it wouldn't be long until the sun vanished once again, and this time they'd be in the center of a forest in darkness.

"Daylight's burning." Rachel picked up her pace, and together they headed to the glowing place in the center of the forest. The darker it got in the cave, the more light seemed to emanate from up ahead.

They moved quickly, carefully, now in a crouch. Matt saw that Eleanor had one bony hand down the back of Joshua's trousers hanging on tight and allowing the young man to pull her along. He wondered what would happen if she stumbled – would she be pulled forward like a small dog on a lead.

Rachel slowed and then stopped and peered through some foliage. She slowly raised a hand. "Just up ahead." She pushed the fronds aside and squeezed through. Joshua was on her heels dragging the tiny Eleanor with him.

They had to climb the last few dozen feet, as the ground rose before them, and the stream became a small waterfall. Matt slipped and had to grab on tight to stop sliding back down.

Huh? He had needed to use both hands – *both* hands. He unwrapped the severely broken fingers and then flexed the hand into a fist. No pain, no damage, and not even a sign there had ever been trauma. But the hand looked bony, almost skeletal, as if the fat and muscle was somehow missing.

Matt felt his face again, feeling the sharp cheekbones. There was no doubt in his mind; he had somehow been infected, and now the nematodes or whatever they were, were eating him alive.

How? He wondered and dropped his hand again, wiggling the once-broken fingers. *Just like the dog bite*, he thought. But this time it took only a few hours to heal. *Shit*, he thought, and made a fist. He looked up to see Eleanor watching him with a smirk.

He smiled weakly and lowered his hand, but before the woman could speak there came the sound of two quick gunshots from over at the far side of the cave.

"Khaled!" Matt spun.

Chapter 19

Khaled ibn Al Sudairi stopped to wipe his brow. They'd been skirting around the edge of the forest at the cave wall for most of the day. There was a rocky platform several dozen feet over the basin-shaped interior where the lush plants and trees grew out of an obviously fertile enclosure.

So far all of the holes that were allowing the huge columns of light inside the cavern were hundreds of feet above where they stood, with no way to reach them. In addition, the interior walls were steep to begin with, but then towered over them to become a roof, so climbing up was out of the question.

A while back they had crossed a small side tunnel that harbored one of the tentacle things that had made a grab at Professor Kearns. Khaled kept his gun trained on it, as he waved Okembu and Greta past. But it seemed that the creature became triggered by movement and didn't present them with any trouble as long as they moved slowly and stayed out of its reach. Personally, he would have loved to pull the disgusting thing from its lair to kill it, or at least get a good look at the abomination.

Okembu was on edge. A few miles back he had fashioned a small spear and made them wait while he carefully stalked a large, fat parrot sitting on a tree branch. The thing had just sat there, watching him approach. Okembu had lined it up, thrown with unerring deftness to strike its colorful plumed target dead on. But then came the wrongness. The bird seemed to explode. Feathers, flesh, beak and bone all came apart, as if the thing was made of nothing but colored liquid.

"What is this?" Okembu stood with his mouth open, watching as the multicolored liquid soaked into the ground and vanished.

He turned. "Did I hit it? I hit it." He nodded vigorously. "Didn't I hit it? You saw."

Khaled's eyes narrowed. "You hit it."

Okembu went to retrieve his spear, but then changed his mind. "I'll eat when we are out."

Several miles further on lay the lowest of the cave holes that shone in a beam of golden light and was their most promising chance of scaling a way out. Khaled looked at his watch – if it too proved an impossible climb, then they might need to give up on this option and cross into the forest to meet up with Professor Kearns' group and work on a new plan.

"I can't."

Khaled turned. The voice was unrecognizable at first, and he realised he had rarely heard the tall female nurse of Mrs. van Helling speak. She was down on one knee.

"You need more rest?" Khaled asked.

Okembu snorted his derision and looked away.

"I need..." She held out a hand to Captain Okembu.

He looked back at her but his face was without pity. "So, the helper asks for help?"

"Please." Greta beckoned, looking pained.

"No." The tall Chadian officer's expression hardened, and he stepped back.

"Help her up," Khaled said softly.

Okembu half-turned to Khaled. "This woman..."

Greta exploded up at him, staying low. Before Okembu could turn back her hand glinted with a flash of silver that went from behind her back to hammer down and embed itself into the top of the man's foot and into the ground.

Okembu howled and then pulled free his own huge blade. But by then Greta was coming up in front of him. With the knife nailing him to the ground his ability to move was inhibited.

On her rise, Greta snatched one of the Chadian officer's own knives from his belt and jammed it into his neck.

Khaled's mouth dropped open in horror as he saw the 12-inch blade protrude from just below Captain Okembu's opposite ear. The Chad Army man's tongue extended, but no words could or would come. Repulsively, Greta then twisted the blade, opening the wound and allowing the carotid artery to shower the wall of the cave.

Khaled felt an electric shock of disbelief run through him. "*Wha...?*"

The tall woman ripped the blade free, allowing Okembu's body to fall like a tree trunk, but not down to the forest floor, as it was nailed to the ground by the blade.

She then spun and began to advance on Khaled. Her face was calm as if she was just ordering hot tea in her local café, and her brawny forearm was now covered in glistening blood to the elbow. He saw that her huge knuckles stood out like barnacles on a wharf as she adjusted her grip on the long, bloody blade.

Khaled held up a hand. "*Stop!*"

She didn't and closed the distance between them in three great strides and slashed at his chest. He had jerked himself back, but the razor-sharp blade still opened his shirt and sliced the flesh beneath.

Khaled then threw himself down, sweeping his leg around to strike at Greta's legs and managed to knock the woman off her feet. She fell hard, but didn't stay there. Instead snatching up a fist-sized rock in her free hand and coming back immediately.

Khaled reached for his gun as he backpedaled. He tugged it free and brought it around, only to have the rock smash into his wrist and the shots he fired ended up hopelessly off target. He went to adjust his stance, and his next step back was on only half the ledge they were both standing on. His arms pinwheeled as he lost his balance, and the huge woman shot out a hand to grip his gun arm.

Khaled knew her blade would be coming up again, and this time his torso was fully exposed. He used her weight to jerk his head forward to head butt the woman, once, and twice, feeling the satisfying crunch of bone each time. He waited for her to fall, cry out, or even blink, but instead she tore the gun from his hand, and flung it aside.

Greta still held him and he looked momentarily over his shoulder at the drop behind him. When he turned back the huge woman had her face close to his, and the eyes he stared into were the deadest things he had ever seen in his life. There was blood on her teeth and she grinned like a death's head.

Greta pointed the blade at his left eye, and began to bring it forward – he made his choice, and propelled himself backwards, falling the 15 to 20 feet down to the dark rocks and earth below.

He hoped for a soft landing – he didn't get one. The cliff edge was rock all the way to the bottom, and he struck the jagged surface hard, bouncing several times, before finally coming to rest at the mouth of a small cave.

He dragged himself in as Greta followed him down. But when she arrived the huge woman paused and didn't enter. Khaled waited, but instead of coming in to finish him off, the woman began to carefully back away, a knowing smile on her gargoyle-like features.

It was then that Khaled felt the feather-light touch of the first sticky tendril.

Chapter 20

"That's the sign," Matt said. "They're in trouble – we need to help."

"No," Eleanor snapped. "We should continue on. It would be hours until we caught up with them. They are strong and competent, and will have overcome whatever problem assails them."

"Or have been overcome by it," Rachel said, flatly.

Eleanor shrugged bony shoulders. "Either way."

Matt scoffed. "I would hope if we fired an alarm shot, they'd have a different attitude."

"Oh *pishaw*, Professor. Stop being such a Nervous Nelly; we're almost there. I say we continue on." Eleanor turned to Joshua. "Doctor Gideon, what do you say?"

Joshua looked at Matt's miraculously repaired hand. "I say we see what lies ahead – it's only a little more climbing now – we've already done the hard part. It'll take us too long to be of any help to the others anyway."

"No, that's not right. I'm going to see what happened." Matt held his ground.

Eleanor smacked dry lips. "Young man, I'm too old to trek all the way over there now. We should stay together, but if you must go, then you must." Her lips compressed for a moment. "So go."

Matt looked at Rachel, who winced and shrugged. "Matt, give it 10 more minutes. That might mean we need to head over there anyway."

Eleanor stared at him, and her eyes moved down his arm to his hand. Then back up at his face. Her expression was calculating. "Professor, how have you been feeling lately? You seem a little... *drawn.*"

"Fine, I'm just fine." He straightened. "Hey, you think I'm delirious or something?"

"No, Professor." The old woman smiled thinly. "But I'm thirsty, hungry, tired, and I goddamn ache all over. And that's not just because I'm old. I bet your girlfriend there feels the same." She smirked. "And yet, you seem to have boundless energy, while looking a little hollow, to say the least. Why do you think that is?"

"*Huh?*" Matt touched his chest. "I don't know what you're getting at." But he knew exactly what she meant. He did feel fine, in fact, better than fine.

"The bomb blast, Matthew," Eleanor said. "You shouldn't even have survived. You were sitting right next to an FBI agent who was obliterated."

His forehead puckered. "The scabbard; it was supposed to..."

"You know that's rubbish. You barely had a scratch." Eleanor said. "The broken bones, the burns, the dog bite – not even a single scar."

"Oh god, it's true," Joshua said, pushing toward him. He grabbed Matt's head and lifted his flashlight to look into his eyes.

"Get the fuck off me." Matt pushed him away. "What's the matter with you people?"

"The parasites; somehow you're infected." Joshua pointed. "But it's eating you."

"Oh piss off. How? Where?" Matt looked at his hand, turning it over. "That doesn't make sense."

Rachel's gun was suddenly in her hand, but held loosely at her side. "When Samuel died, you were there. When Oscar died at the church, you were there. And you led us here, and now more of us are dying, except you, who feels fine."

"Hey, hey." Matt held his hands up. "This is insane." He started to back up. "What's got into you?"

Rachel's eyes were implacable as her gun came up. "Please, stay where you are. We need to work this out."

He looked along their faces – Rachel's held nothing but resolve, Joshua's was twisted in fear, and Eleanor's had a smirk of satisfaction. He pointed at the old woman.

"She knows something – look at her."

"I know a rat, Professor." Eleanor slowly shook her head. "We know who's been keeping secrets. And I think we now know who's been leading us into all these traps." She half-turned to Rachel. "You need to stop him. He's been working against us ever since we got here."

"You sonofabitch," Joshua said, his eyes round.

"Have you all gone mad?" Matt backed up some more. *This is all going bad now*, Matt thought. He started to ease back again. "I didn't do anything."

"Matt, please, I'm warning you, please, *stop*." Rachel tracked him, the muzzle of her gun a pitiless dark eye following his every move.

"Kill him," Eleanor said, the thin, gray skin over her face making it look like a leather-covered skull. But she wasn't looking at Rachel or Matt, but just past him.

The snap of a twig behind him made him flinch and turn just as Greta's blade came down hard and fast and aimed to bury itself between his shoulder blades. Instead, he jerked fast and it caught the meat of his shoulder, cutting long and deep.

The pain was excruciating, and Matt went down, rolled into the brush, and scrambled to throw himself off the small rock platform they were on. Matt landed hard on rock, but heard shouts and more worryingly there was someone bullocking after him through the foliage – by the sound of the weight, he suspected Greta.

Matt gripped his shoulder and ran, keeping low. In seconds, his entire upper body was slick with blood. There were no paths to follow in the twilight-lit forest, but he managed to worm and squeeze his way through bushes and vines that tried to hang on to every inch of his body. The receding sound of pursuit told him that whoever was after him was having more trouble with the dense jungle-like growth than he was with his new and improved skinny body.

He looked at the hand that was covering the wound in his shoulder – it dripped thick, arterial blood. *Shit, shit, shit.* He gripped his shoulder, and turned, grimacing, and wanting to shout: *you're all fucking insane.* He settled for whispering: "Idiots."

He always suspected that Eleanor was a bit weird, and Joshua had seemed a little out there for a while now. But Rachel was his friend. More than his friend. Or so he had thought. *She's scared, that's all.* He would be too. Matt looked up at the darkening holes in the ceiling. Already it was like early evening. Soon, it would be dark, and the thought of being trapped in this forest with the monstrous Greta creeping about with a huge knife scared the shit out of him. And then there was that weird crawling face.

Matt shuddered. Behind him the light from the center of the forest was a little like a blue sunrise. *So close*, he thought.

He had two options. Creep back and hope for a reconciliation. Which might have been possible until Greta turned up. Or he could look for support elsewhere –

find Khaled. He hoped the Saudi and Captain Okembu were alive, but they'd been with Greta, and now he had his doubts.

People around me seem to die, Rachel had inferred. He sighed. *True*, he thought. *But somehow I don't think I'm the threat down here.*

He'd try to track as far as he could without using his light – it'd be a beacon for anyone trying to find him. He looked again at the blue glow, hoping that would be the group's focus for now.

Matt stayed low and started to push through the underbrush, headed toward where he had last heard Khaled's gunfire.

*

Khaled lay in the mouth of the cave. The slash at his chest had congealed, thankfully. But his head throbbed, and he thought his ankle might also be sprained. None of that worried him now.

The Saudi lay still, watching more of the tendrils drop from the ceiling. They gently felt along his entire body, tapping, caressing, but not gripping, yet. Perhaps whatever the thing was it preferred live prey, and a corpse was of little interest.

He tried to calm his breathing, and also tried not to look at where the thing was pushing more of itself from the ceiling. He had read somewhere that starfish actually push their stomachs outside their gut so they can start digesting food that was too big to take inside their bodies.

His shuddered; it was growing darker, but he could still see that the thing was emerging above him like a pulsating, red sack. A single round eye popped open, looked at its surroundings, and then examined him. Another eye opened beside it, then another and another. *Like a spider*, Joshua had said. They had eight eyes, didn't they?

Khaled could have let his sanity slip, but instead he looked away and tried to think of a plan to extricate himself from under this monstrous thing.

He eased in a huge breath, feeling the sharp jabs of pain. He'd been hurt before – he'd fallen from a horse, had trained in unarmed combat, and been knocked down many times, and he'd survived numerous assassination attempts on him and his family, by bomb, gun, knife and poison. Sometimes it was one's will alone that made some men survive and some fall.

Khaled tensed his muscles and using his good foot and both hands, began to ease himself backwards. He slid about an inch, then another, and felt the brittle bones of other animals crackle beneath him.

One of the tendrils alighted on his chest and tapped for a moment before resting on the sticky blood. Khaled was revolted as the thing felt spiny against his skin, and probably had rough hairs on the long boneless arm. It reeled back up to disappear into the sack – *tasting me?* he guessed.

Forgive me my prince, he thought. *I have failed you.*

The tendril came back and began to move higher, stopping again, this time on the center of his chest. *Did it perhaps detect the faint heartbeat there*, he wondered.

It did, found him alive, and attacked.

The thin questing tendrils were withdrawn and the thick attack tendrils dropped down and began to encircle his limbs. He cried out, and in fear and frustration tried to scramble free, but in doing so was immediately enmeshed.

The power of the thing was phenomenal, and as the coils tightened, the pain was unbearable.

"*Khaled!*"

Never had his name sounded so sweet.

"Professor..." He eased his head around. "*Quickly.*"

*

Matt poked his head inside the cave and recoiled. He immediately saw the Saudi's predicament. He had a knife but it was a lot smaller than Okembu's, and if he attacked with that, he was more than likely to find himself trapped along with Khaled.

"Professor." Khaled's voice was strained as his throat was being compressed. He turned his face to the ceiling, and it was then Matt saw the repulsive red bag starting to descend toward the stricken man. There were multiple eyes, most fixed on its potential meal, but a few also watching Matt. It was beginning to drip with either saliva or gastric juices, and Matt felt his body start to tremble as he remembered a similar horror trying to pull him into the ceiling of a cave – it wanted to drag him into that abomination.

Matt had an urge to simply turn and run – he did. Matt sprinted to the forest, grabbed the biggest, meanest branch he could find and then turned back to the small cave. He didn't want to pause, or stop, or even think at all about what he needed to do, as that would allow the freezing fear to creep over him. He simply charged into the cave, yelling a war cry, and smacked the branch over and over into the hanging bag, the coils, and the alien eyes.

There was a squeal, and a splash of inky blood, and Khaled was momentarily loose. Matt grabbed his shoulders and roughly pulled him free. Matt didn't stop until he was 20 feet from the cave, and then he collapsed. The two men lay together, both breathing hard.

Matt felt his racing heartbeat slow to a gallop. He turned. "So, how's your day been?"

Khaled began to laugh, but it broke down into a painful cough. He held his neck, as he turned to Matt. "This, my friend, is one of the times in my life that I regret my religion does not allow me to drink."

Matt sat up, and pulled the Saudi Arab up with him. "What happened? No, forget that, I've already run into Greta. Where's Captain Okembu?"

"Greta, yes, she attacked us; killed Captain Okembu before we even knew what she was up to. Then tried to do the same to me. I fell into the grabber's cave, and I think she assumed that the creature would do the work for her – and it would have if you hadn't found me." He squeezed his eyes shut and ran both hands up through sweat-slicked hair. He looked up. "And you?"

Matt seemed to think for a moment. "She, Greta, came out of nowhere and attacked. I got the feeling she was under orders – Eleanor's."

"And the others?" Khaled asked.

"I don't know." He looked away. "They seem to be all working together. I ran, left them." He sighed. He was worried about Rachel now.

Khaled stared. "And, did you find it? The wellspring?"

Matt felt the strength of his gaze and looked into the man's dark eyes. "No, but we were close to something. The others are probably there by now."

Khaled reached forward to rub his ankle.

"How is it?" Matt asked. "Can you walk?"

Khaled nodded. "Not broken, I think, but badly sprained. It will hurt like the devil, but I will walk on it." He turned and grinned. "And if we come face to face with Greta, I'll damn well run on it."

Matt tilted his head back to laugh, and then stood. He held out a hand. Khaled gripped it and got unsteadily to his feet, hopped for a moment, as he tested it. Satisfied, he put more weight on it, but still had a hand on Matt's shoulder.

"What now?" he asked.

Matt looked back to the glow from the center of the jungle. "We do what we set out to do – get some answers."

*

"*Let him go!*" Rachel tensed her shoulders.

The tall woman froze, but kept facing the jungle where Matt had disappeared.

"Greta." Eleanor smiled through her words. "Leave him now, that's a good girl."

"You stabbed him." Joshua seemed in shock. "He'll bleed to death."

"You know that's not true. You know he'll be fine… better than fine, and in no time at all." Eleanor's eyes slid to the scientist. "You want that too, don't you?"

Joshua turned to her and stared for several seconds, before his head stared to bob. "Maybe."

"What the hell is wrong with you people?" Rachel suddenly didn't recognize the group. "He was our friend."

Greta turned from the rapidly darkening wall of the forest to face Rachel. She squared her shoulders, straightening and towering over the FBI woman.

Rachel turned side-on and held her gun loosely in her hand. She stared at the woman from under lowered brows. She'd been in standoffs before – the first few moments were key to working out the power dynamics.

Greta's eyes were like glass, empty windows to a vacant soul. Her formidable jaw was set. Rachel held the woman's gaze.

"Who the fuck said you could attack anyone? And where are Khaled and Captain Okembu?" Rachel continued to grip the gun, hard.

"Greta knows to protect me," Eleanor said evenly. "She probably thought I was being attacked."

"By Professor Kearns?" Rachel's eyes went from Eleanor back to Greta. "And where's the rest of your team?"

"They got separated, of course," Eleanor's tone was amused.

"And?" Rachel kept her eyes on Greta, liking both the women less by the second. "Did you find a way out?"

"No," Greta said, placing the large knife back in its scabbard. She went to kneel by Eleanor.

"Hey, I'm still talking to you." Rachel raised the gun. "I haven't finished with you yet."

"Don't antagonize her, Agent Bromilow. I think you might end up biting off more than you can chew." Eleanor grinned.

Rachel shook her head, as she examined the hulking woman. "Who the fuck is she? *What* the fuck is she?"

Eleanor stroked Greta's short and wiry gray hair. "I already told you; I adopted her in East Germany in the sixties." She smiled down at the adoring woman. "She was one of their test subjects for their performance-enhancing drugs regime – State Plan 14.25 they called it. She could have been a champion hammer thrower, weightlifter, or anything she wanted. But they rejected her, just because she had a few psychological... *imbalances.*"

She turned to Rachel. "Where they saw a potential monster, I saw a potential friend."

"She needs to answer some questions, right now." Rachel's teeth were bared.

"You're not the authority here, Agent Bromilow," Eleanor said with a note of boredom in her voice. "Besides, you're not going to shoot anyone." She whispered to Greta, and then climbed once again onto the woman's back like some sort of baby simian. "Now, I suggest we push on, and see what it is just above this rise."

"I'm ready," Joshua said, turning away.

"What?" Rachel let her arms drop to her sides. "Are you shitting me, Joshua? Khaled and Okembu are missing. And this, woman, comes back to us and immediately stabs Professor Kearns. And you're okay with that?"

"I have no reason to doubt her." He shrugged. "And you know there was something weird about Kearns. I didn't trust him, and I saw that you didn't either."

"That doesn't mean we should abandon him," Rachel said firmly. She chanced a look at the foliage, wondering how far away Matt could be.

"Well, you won't find him blundering off into the jungle," said Eleanor. "If he's got any brains, he'll find his own way to the pool and meet us there. He wants to see it as much as we do."

"Rachel could feel the muscles in her jaw begin to twitch, and she went to raise the gun again.

"Oh, put it away, dear." Eleanor's eyes twinkled as she motioned up the hill. "If you want to wander off and get killed by yourself, be my guest. Doctor, shall we?"

Greta still eyed her with cold amusement. Rachel had been an agent for over eight years and had seen some fucked up stuff in her life. But right now, she'd take any of that over having this woman behind her. She held out an arm.

"After you."

Eleanor faked a smile. "Joshua, you get to take the lead, dear boy. You've got a promotion."

Joshua snorted, and turned to clamber up the steep incline.

Greta gave Rachel one more glance before climbing as well. Greta gripped a hanging branch and pulled both herself and Eleanor up onto some rocks.

They were about 20 feet from a higher ledge with the glow emanating from its top. For now, it was still hidden behind a dense stand of thick tees, but would only take them a few minutes to reach.

Joshua almost ran up the slope before stopping and turning. "In here."

He only waited a second or two more, before spinning and pushing through the trees. Greta, with Eleanor van Helling still clinging to her back, barged in after him, and Rachel followed, easing herself in.

The trees had grown up to form a canopy over the top of a glowing sapphire-colored pool of water. Rachel stopped and stared – it was the most beautiful thing she had ever seen. The pool was a long oval shape about a hundred feet in length and so clear it was hard to tell if it was inches or dozens of feet deep. The ghost of a mist lifted from its surface and Rachel could feel its warmth against her cheeks.

She took a few more steps closer and stood by a chest-high pile of rocks that was one of many that were stacked or tumbled every dozen feet or so.

Joshua pointed. "More writing." There was a dark obelisk at one end of the pool with more of the Chaldaic script on its face. "I can't read it." He gave them a lopsided grin. "Where's Matt Kearns when you need him, *huh*?"

He reached up to grab at a tree branch, examining the leaves. "These are different to the others in the forest. And their roots are actually feeding from the water."

"Of course they are." Eleanor cackled. "Do either of you even know what type of wood Noah built his Ark from?"

Joshua shook his head slowly. "Nope, can't say I ever gave it too much thought. No wait, actually, *zero* thought."

"Idiot." She grinned as she looked at the trees surrounding the pool.

"Gopher," Rachel said softly. "Matt told us."

"The old woman's eyes moved to Rachel standing slightly apart from them. "Yes, gopher wood."

Eleanor's eyes narrowed. "In Genesis 6:14, it says that Noah was to build the Ark from gopher wood. But it's a word for a type of wood not known around the time of the Bible or even in biblical Hebrew. However, there is an expression in ancient Babylonian of "gushure is erini", which translates to cedar-beams."

Rachel frowned. "You suddenly seem to know a lot about the Ark, Mrs. van Helling."

"There're no cedar forests growing in Africa, and hasn't been for thousands of years." She laughed hoarsely. "But there are stories of it growing in great forests after the flood. The African Cedar – *Juniperus procera* – was a tall tree with berry-like cones that were blue-black, like giant fruits." She looked up at the trees. "Just like these."

"I see. And these are the last remnants of those ancient cedar forests. The seeds perhaps washed down here in the floods." Joshua followed her gaze.

"No, something far more fantastic than that." She whispered in Greta's ear, and the big woman helped Eleanor slide from her back.

"The Ark was cedar. It came to rest, here." She looked up at the ceiling. "If we could see the roof, I think we might find it was man-made, constructed over this vast cavern."

"Just like the monastery Khaled told us about." Rachel looked up, but saw nothing but a starless black.

"As the Ark settled in its secret place around 4500 years ago, and the waters drained away, the last of the holy flood lay in its belly. Its mighty cedar beams took root – they lived again." She grinned, her eyes wide and fixed on the water. "You want to know what happened to the Ark?" She waved a hand over the pool. "Here it is."

Rachel turned, looking again at the shape of the pond and the surrounding wall of trees. If you squinted, you could see that the pond was long and hull shaped and the stand of trees could even be imagined as the ribbing of the gunwale of a large ship.

"*This* is the Ark?" Joshua scoffed.

"This entire *place* is the Ark. Its lifegiving force exploded into all this." The old woman closed her eyes, hugging herself. "*And when God's wrathful waters receded, the last of them shall be a well of tears he has wept for the dead. And in its depths, there will be no more death.*"

Eleanor opened her eyes. "Do you know what that is from?" She giggled softly. "My dear sweet, stupid Clarence; he sent me that translation 75 years ago just before he disappeared. The only worthwhile thing he ever did." Her face grew hard. "He was supposed to send for me."

Joshua crossed to the pool edge and knelt. He quickly searched pouches and pockets until he found an empty vial and equipment. He uncapped the vial, scooped some of the water and lifted it. In his other hand he held a magnifying glass to his eye.

"Yes." He nodded and grinned. "Yes, they're there, I can see them, almost invisible. They look like glass fibers, but they're there."

"Good." Eleanor turned to her big companion. "Help me now one last time, my faithful Greta."

The huge woman picked her up like an infant and walked with her to the edge of the water.

Rachel felt disgust. "This is what you've always wanted, isn't it? From the time you first started using us, you've wanted this. Isn't that right, Eleanor?"

"Of course." Eleanor's wrinkled face was flushed.

Rachel backed up. "It didn't matter who got killed, who got hurt. We were all expendable pawns."

"Yes again, dear." Eleanor ignored her now, as Greta started to carefully peel the old woman out of her clothing. Joshua turned away, but Rachel watched as the emaciated frame of the near-skeletal woman was revealed. She wore no bra as her breasts had long ago dried and flattened to little more than flaps against her chest. Greta finished by pulling down her underwear.

Greta then took the tiny woman under the arms, lifted and lowered her into the pool, easing her down like she was laying her in a warm bath. Eleanor squeezed her eyes shut and sunk down, mouth open, until her head disappeared below the brilliant blue water.

Rachel and Joshua watched as the water seemed to fizz and bubble around her. For some reason she was reminded of those images of the piranha-filled rivers in the Amazon when some animal wanders into a school of the hungry fish.

Eleanor surfaced and gulped in a huge breath. Joshua stared, mesmerized, and Rachel frowned and stepped a little closer – *did the woman's hair seemed thicker, and the flesh more plump?* Rachel wondered.

She nodded and Greta eased her back under. The water frothed and bubbled furiously now, and after another minute she came back to the surface, coughed and spat, and then hauled herself up onto the rocky edge. She sat with her eyes closed, breathing in and out deeply, and perhaps waiting for her heartbeat to slow.

Rachel stared with her mouth agape, and after a moment covered it with a hand.

"Holy shit." Joshua put both hands to his head. "I don't fucking…" His mouth continued to work but no more words came.

Eleanor sat with her head back, long golden tresses tumbling over her slender shoulders and her eyes still closed. There was a beatific smile on her angular and striking features. After another moment she raised a hand to her face, running her fingertips down over the cheekbone and tight jawline.

She began to giggle. "Why should youth be wasted on the young?" She turned, opening luminous blue eyes. Eleanor got slowly to her feet and turned, arms wide.

Joshua's mouth broke into a wide smile, and Rachel was sure the man stuck his chest out a little. Even Rachel was struck by the woman's sexiness, beauty and raw animal attractiveness.

Rachel hadn't ever used the term goddess before, but now, that's what Eleanor was.

Beside her Greta fell to her knees and clutched hands to her chest before they moved toward Eleanor, not touching but just hovering inches from her flesh. Her eyes were moist and her chin quivered. Never before had Rachel seen such adoration in another human being.

Eleanor reached out and placed a hand atop the woman's head, stroking it as one might a favored pet. She turned to Joshua, her smile widening to show a line of perfect teeth.

"You're right, the pool was infected – what a terrible thing." She smiled as she examined one long, slender arm. "And it all belongs to me now."

Chapter 21

Matt and Khaled crept through the forest, staying low as they approached the soft blue glow.

"I can hear voices," Matt whispered.

Khaled nodded and kept as quiet and low as he could on an ankle that was obviously as painful as hell. Matt got down on his belly and started to squirm forward on his elbows. He heard Khaled grunt as he did the same. Together they came up over the rise and peered through the thick foliage.

Joshua and Rachel stood facing him on one side of a magnificent pool of sapphire-blue water. It made him want to dive in immediately. In fact, it was more than just the multiple abrasions, the heat and dirt that coated him that made him desire the water, but every fiber of his being seemed to be screaming at him to enter it, drink from it, and become one with it.

He knew he'd seen it before, in his dreams. The blue liquid was magnetic, its siren call almost impossible for him to resist. It took all his self-control to tear his eyes away and focus on the people.

The large form of Greta had her back to them and stood motionless, as another figure, still obscured by her broad frame, seemed to be keeping their attention.

"There's the monster," Khaled hissed. "I have a score to settle with that one."

"Yeah, she tried to open me up as well." Matt's eyes narrowed. "So, wait in line."

Greta stepped aside revealing the hidden figure, and Matt couldn't help his breath catching in his chest. It was a naked woman, magnificent in her beauty.

"Oh my god," Matt whispered. "I've seen her before."

"She is a goddess," Khaled breathed.

"Yes, she is." Matt frowned, craning forward. "No, it can't be. I think that's...?"

"Who?" Khaled moved aside more of the fronds in front of him.

"*Eleanor van Helling.*" Matt stared.

"The old hag?" Khaled squinted back at the figure. "Impossible."

"They did it; they found it, the Fountain of Youth." He couldn't help grinning. "It's real; it's damn well real."

"I never really expected it to be true. Neither did the prince." Khaled blinked several times. "And now Eleanor van Helling is restored." His mouth turned down. "But God does not reward the evil with such gifts."

Matt then saw the obelisk at the end of the pool. "Hey, do you still have your field glasses?"

Khaled pulled them from a pouch at his hip and handed them to Matt, who brought them to his eyes. As he expected it was Chaldaic script.

He whispered the words: "*Those who are chosen, must choose. Those who take, have everything taken.*"

"What does that mean?" Khaled looked at him in the darkness.

Matt shook his head. "I'm not sure. Maybe I'm translating it wrong."

"Sounds like a warning." The Saudi turned back to the pool.

"Yes, it does." Matt watched Joshua nod as something was said to him. He held up the small vial in his hand that contained some of the blue glowing liquid. While they watched he brought it to his lips and upended it.

"Looks like he just voted to join the club." Matt said.

*

"Go ahead." Eleanor said. "Besides, there will be no more drinking from the pool now. You may be the last common man I allow, *ever*." She giggled. "I can choose who to bestow this gift upon." She giggled again and clasped her hands together. "We'll be gods among mere mortals."

The huge Greta grunted, and Eleanor eased around, her brows turning down in a pitying expression. "And you of course, my darling, faithful Greta. In time." She turned back to Joshua and nodded.

"Go on, bottoms up."

Joshua held up the vial. "This is madness." He looked at it for a moment or two. "This place; it must be making us hallucinate."

"Don't," Rachel said.

"*Um*, I'm only doing it to record my sensations. Like a test subject of sorts." He looked at the glowing blue vial, smiled dreamily, and then put it to his lips.

Rachel saw his throat work as he downed it in a single swallow, eager to become part of Greta's band of immortals.

He closed his eyes, breathing calmly as a smile began to spread over his face. Rachel's forehead furrowed as she watched all the abrasions, bruises and cuts on his face first lighten, close, and then vanish.

Joshua took off his glasses, blinked, and then began to grin. He dropped the spectacles to the ground. "I feel…"

"*Marvelous*," Eleanor finished for him. She turned to the hulking Greta. "Shoot him in the chest."

Greta lifted the gun without hesitation and fired, hitting Joshua dead center. He was blown backwards into the dirt, sitting there in stunned silence, one hand to the bloom of blood spreading across his ribs. He flopped back, dead.

Greta saw Rachel flinch, and she immediately turned the gun on her.

"Drop your weapon," Eleanor said, evenly. "Now."

Rachel hesitated, wondering if it was possible to draw and fire before the large woman put a hole in her chest – unlikely in the extreme, she knew.

"My dear, if I wanted you dead, you'd be laying at my feet right now. Now drop it, or I'll ask Greta to blow a little hole in your gun arm and then *take* the weapon from you. She never misses. Drop it – last chance."

The muzzle of Greta's gun moved to point at the meat of Rachel's shoulder.

Rachel growled through gritted teeth, and then let her gun fall to the ground. Beside her, Joshua groaned.

"*Huh?*" Her head whipped around – the man had been shot through the heart at close range. The muscular organ was tough, but would have been obliterated – he should be as dead as dead can be. Rachel rushed to crouch beside him.

Joshua sat up, coughed blood and gripped his chest.

"Back away, my dear," Eleanor said lightly. "I want to see something."

Joshua coughed again, but then took a deep juddering breath. "Fucking *ouch*."

Eleanor tittered like a teenager. "I'm not surprised it hurt. After all, you *were* just shot through the heart. How do you feel?"

"Fuck you."

"I bet you'd like to, but I'm well out of your league now, little boy." She smiled and folded her slender arms across her perked breasts. "It was just part of a test, my dear. It seems we'll be very hard to kill. Almost impossible really." She grinned and let her eyes slide to her large servant. "*Almost.*"

"Now, for the second part of our little test," Eleanor said. "Greta, you know what to do."

Greta turned back to the sitting scientist and advanced on him quickly. She gripped his hair with one hand, and with the other, she drew the long silver knife and began to rapidly saw through his neck. Joshua thrashed and blood fountained.

Rachel felt like she was going to faint, and Joshua's scream chilled her blood. Or perhaps it was her own screaming that she heard. In a few seconds, the man gurgled one last time, and then the woman stepped aside to let the headless body fall back on the ground. She held the head up, facing Eleanor.

The woman stared at it, concentrating intently on the still-twitching features. After another few moments the nerves quietened and the dead face grew slack. Eleanor nodded.

"Good, you can dispose of it now, my dear. He's dead – for good, this time."

"Why?" Rachel swallowed the bile in her mouth, and tried not to inhale the hot, coppery smell of fresh blood.

"Yes, I wondered that as well, my dear." Eleanor looked bemused. "When they removed my beloved Clarence's head, it made me wonder *why*. Now we know. It seems we aren't invulnerable after all. Removing the head will finish us for good."

Greta dropped the head next to the body. It thumped to the ground, tongue lolling. The huge woman was devoid of emotion as she stood stock still with her forearms drenched red like a ghastly pair of ballroom gloves.

Rachel wished she still had her gun, as she knew that one word from Eleanor and Greta would be sawing at Rachel's neck in an instant.

Eleanor finally stepped from the pool and began to don her old clothing. She smirked at how tight some of the items were, the top stretching impossibly across her full breasts. She looked up, holding her arms out.

"How do I look?" she turned slowly. Her beatific face an angelic mask hiding the evil within.

"My beautiful mistress," Greta whispered, her eyes glowing with love, lust and worship. She reached out to stroke Eleanor's golden tresses.

Eleanor then faced Rachel. "No words from you, Agent Bromilow? You used to have so much to say."

Rachel looked around, searching for an escape route should she need one. "Why am I still alive?"

Eleanor shrugged. "One of you had to stay alive to help me get home; it just turned out to be you, *hmm*?"

"And then you..." She bit off her words. There was no way the woman would let her live and trust her to keep the precious secret. As soon as they were out of danger, she'd have the giantess remove her head.

"Yes?" Eleanor asked.

Rachel smiled. "I was going to say: *and you look great.*"

Eleanor nodded and went to turn away but then froze. Greta came to stand slightly in front of her, squaring her shoulders. In one hand was Rachel's gun and in the other the bloody blade she had just used on Joshua.

Rachel followed their gaze, and saw a tall, bearded man standing near the obelisk at the end of the pool. She had no idea how long he had been there watching them, but if he had seen what Greta had done, then the word *savages* might be on his mind.

He held up a hand, the palm toward them in a universal gesture of greeting. Eleanor smiled in return and half-turned to Greta.

"This pool belongs to us. He must be one of them, so we'll need to take his head."

Matt and Khaled had watched with horror as Greta had decapitated Joshua. It had happened so fast and unexpectedly that neither man could have done anything other than rush into the path of either Greta's gun or knife.

But it was the brutality and ferociousness that had shocked Matt and Khaled so greatly. The large woman never hesitated for a moment.

"She truly *is* a monster," Khaled breathed.

"Yes, and obviously trained to do Eleanor's bidding. It's no wonder she keeps her so close." Matt tore his eyes away, and then was jolted by the strange new figure. "Hey, look." Matt motioned to the far end of the glowing blue pool. "There's someone there."

"Who the hell is that?" Khaled asked.

Matt watched as Eleanor carefully took the gun from Greta, and kept it behind her back. The huge woman stood stone still, the long blade still dripping with Joshua's blood down at her side.

The bearded figure looked at each of the three women, and then up at the obelisk. He laid a hand on one of the chest-high stacks of rock and started to speak, and Matt strained to hear. The man started with Hebrew, and then switched to German, then Russian, before changing smoothly to English. As a language expert, Matt marveled at the fluency of each of the tongues he used, as each one was without the hint of an accent.

"Why have you come?" His voice was stentorian, powerful and commanding.

Eleanor bowed slightly. "We only came to... seek knowledge. I am Eleanor van Helling, of the New York van Hellings. My husband was here; Clarence van Helling. Perhaps you met him?" She waited a moment until it was clear the man was not going to respond. "And whom am I addressing, sir?"

The man looked her up and down. "I see you came to seek more than knowledge. You would take, and you would kill for your own personal gain." His expression dropped. "Your soul is as black as the pit of hell itself."

Eleanor snorted. "No need to be rude." She smiled. "And you are?"

He held his arms wide. "I am just a servant. A keeper of the last of God's great secrets." His voice lowered. "And a defender against those who would seek to steal it, destroy it, or debase it."

Eleanor lifted one long arm, looking at the silken flesh. "Steal it? No, it was a gift, and one I gratefully accept."

"Join us." The man lifted an arm and beckoned over their heads. Rachel turned, following his gaze. She looked along the wall of trees where Matt and Khaled were concealed.

"Oh, shit." Matt got down.

The man looked almost cheerful. "Come, please, Khaled ibn Al Sudairi and Professor Matthew James Kearns, come out. You have nothing to fear from me."

"What?" Rachel stared now.

"Well, do we go down, or run and hide?" Matt asked.

"We've run enough," Khaled said and got to his feet. "Be ready. Greta is the real danger, and she can't kill us both at once."

"We jump her?" Matt also got to his feet.

"If we have to." Khaled then Matt came out of the foliage.

Eleanor threw her head back and laughed. "You're both harder to kill than a pair of roaches."

Rachel embraced Matt, shaking her head. "Thank god you're alive. I'm so sorry, I should have trusted you." She then put a hand on Khaled's shoulder, and leaned closer. "She's already ordered Greta to kill Joshua."

"We know," Khaled said.

"Welcome, Matthew." The tall, bearded man smiled benevolently. "*You*, I've been expecting for some time."

"Noah," Matt said, not being able to keep the awe from his voice.

"Yes." The bearded man smiled.

"Kearns, he's infected, isn't he?" Eleanor asked, her lip curled.

"Infected? No, he was chosen." He turned a fierce gaze on Eleanor. "You were not."

Eleanor sneered. "You don't know who I am." She smiled cruelly. "I agree this is one secret that should be kept. And as long as I benefit I promise to keep it for you. Although I may share it with a few of the better people I have in mind."

Noah's eyes were hawk-like in their intensity. "I know who you are, Eleanor van Helling, and what you are capable of." His eyes slid to the tall Greta, who seemed like an attack dog barely held back on its leash. He smiled sadly. "And I know you have ordered this pitiful being to kill many times on your behalf."

His eyes then blazed with a dark fire. "Yes, I know who you are, and I know *what* you are. You are dust, you are nothing at all, and you will fall." He looked up at the obelisk again, pointing to the ancient script. "*Those who are chosen, must choose. Those who take, have everything taken.*"

Eleanor smiled thinly. "Oh, I think you'll find me a little harder to deal with." She lifted the gun from behind her back.

"Really, you?" Noah held his arms wide. "Alexander of Macedonia, King Xerses of Persia, Caligula, Napoleon, Adolf Hitler, Stalin, Mao Zedong – great people of history have sought out this secret, and some have even found it. But all of them are dust now."

He reached down and scooped up some of the water in his palm. He looked down into it. "When the great waters finally receded, we found that there were more things that survived than my sons, their wives and the few animals." He smiled. "Sometimes the tiniest of us are the most powerful."

He looked up at them from under lowered brows. "Like sin, be careful that what you desire most doesn't end up consuming you." He brought the liquid to his lips and drank. "Once you have partaken of the water, you must continue to take it." His eyes went momentarily to Matt, and he nodded.

"Lecture's over." Eleanor lifted her gun and fired twice.

Whether or not the bullets struck was unknown, as Noah vanished into the thick foliage like smoke.

Khaled crouched, and then lay flat. Matt pulled Rachel down as Eleanor fired into the foliage.

"Stop it, you fool," Matt yelled and climbed on top of Rachel, who batted him away.

"Get off me," Rachel said, who probably thought she was better able to protect them then he was.

Eleanor turned toward Matt, pointing, her teeth bared. "Greta, cut his head off – there's not room for two of us." She then turned back to keep her eyes on the foliage trying to find Noah.

Greta faced Matt, her jaw set. Khaled went after Eleanor, but she snapped the gun around and fired, forcing Khaled to dive into the bushes.

Matt slowly got to his feet and watched as the huge woman's brawny forearm bulged as she regripped the long blade. Beside him, Rachel also got to her feet, pushed Matt behind her and then got into a combat stance, knees bent, and up on her toes.

Greta came in fast, and Rachel kicked out with a lunge kick to the woman's mid-section. But with the rushing mass of the larger woman, it only succeeded in forcing Rachel back and off balance.

Rachel straightened and came again, this time using a looping right cross to the woman's chin. Greta put her head down quickly, taking Rachel's fist to her forehead. Matt heard bones crunch, and Rachel grunted in pain.

Greta then swung an arm with a bicep like a Christmas ham that caught Rachel across the temple and batted her away like she weighed nothing. The FBI agent flew back into the bushes, collided with a tree trunk and lay still.

Greta then pulled out her knife again, and turned to face Matt. *Obviously saving the blade for me,* he thought, relieved that she didn't use it on Rachel. He held his hands out before him, and stepped back.

"Just wait a minute, Greta." He kept backpeddling, hands still waving in front of him. He glanced quickly over his shoulder at the foliage, contemplating another dash into its green cover.

There was sudden rush of movement, as Khaled charged from the brush and brought a thick branch down across the huge woman's neck and shoulders. There was a grunt and Greta went to her knees.

"*Yes!*" Matt gritted his teeth, fist balled.

Khaled yelled and swung again, this time the branch splintering against the back of Greta's head. The iron-gray curls masked her face, but slowly she lifted her head. Khaled shifted the branch in his hands. The Saudi's eyes blazed, his fury unbound as he took his revenge on the murderous woman.

Matt watched as Khaled raised the remains of the club high above his head. It was then he saw Greta's face, the mouth twisted in a smirk.

"*Look ou...*"

Matt had barely yelled the words, when Khaled's club swung down with all his might, but faster than he could have possibly anticipated; Greta shot an arm up and caught it in her fist. Her other hand moved in a blur, sinking the long silver blade deep into the Saudi's chest.

Khaled looked shocked for a moment, his eyes wide and surprised.

"No-*ooo!*" Matt howled in anguish. Greta grinned, and then rapidly pulled the blade free to immediately sink it in again. Khaled's face went slack, and he fell back like a small tree. He was dead before he hit the ground.

Matt faced her, his fists balled. "You bitch." He knew he was no fighter, but never before in his life had he wanted to kill someone so badly.

Greta grinned. Blood had splashed her face, running into her mouth and also coating her teeth. Combined with her dead eyes, she was a vision straight from hell as she came quickly at Matt.

"Shit." Matt quickly picked up the remains of Khaled's branch and held it two-handed out in front of him like a gate – he'd seen the lack of effect it had on her before, so knew he needed to out-think her rather than out-fight her.

Matt then caught sight of his own arms – they were stick-like, with barely any meat left on the bones. His clothing sagged and nearly fell from his body he was so thin. *It was the worms,* he knew that for sure now, and knew that they'd continue to consume him until he was a living skeleton, only animated by the revolting parasitic life inside him.

Behind them Eleanor looked exasperated. "Just cut his fucking head off." She screamed, the brutal words at odds with her angelic face.

Greta squared her shoulders.

"You can't kill me, you know." He held the log before him.

Greta looked from Matt to Joshua's head, and then back and into his eyes. Her mouth twisted in a familiar smirk; he got the message – *of course she could.*

The big woman adjusted her grip on the knife, and then began to advance. Matt held the log up and tried to picture her next steps and how he would respond – he bet she would come fast, giving him two options: block-swing-fight or throw-turn-run.

Fuck it, he knew he'd have to stay. Rachel was as good as dead if he left.

"*Ha!*" He feinted with the log, but all Greta did was lower her brow and start to accelerate. Matt backpeddled, but caught an ankle and fell back, slamming against one of the chest-high stacks of rock.

It moved.

He sat on the ground and watched it all through Greta's changing expressions – confusion, switched to recognition, and then her broad, cruel features twisted into something he had never seen on her face – fear.

Matt chanced a look over his shoulder and saw the hulking mass rise up. The pile of rocks unfolded, reassembled itself into the massive creature he had seen at the church and that had snatched Saeeb into the pit. Massive yellow orbs blinked open.

It was a Nephilim, a Fallen One, the giants sent to be sentinels until the end of time. One tree trunk thick leg thumped down in front of Matt, and it reached forward a hand that closed over one half of Greta's torso. Unbelievably, she fought on, stabbing down with her knife, but whatever the creature was made off, the blade could not hope to penetrate the skin.

Greta began to be lifted from her feet, and the creature stared with its huge dispassionate yellow eyes into her face for a second or two, before its hand closed. Matt grimaced and narrowed his eyes as he heard bones and cartilage compress and snap like bundles of twigs. Greta's scream turned into a wet gurgle, and her body flopped sideways over the compressed frame. The Nephilim dropped her, but then stamped down hard on her head.

"Greta!" Eleanor's scream was barely heard as the giant turned to Matt. He held up a hand to ward it off, and its huge yellow pupilless eyes stared deep into him.

Words, in Chaldaic, floated over them. Noah had reappeared, and the creature turned to the man, and then instead of attacking Matt, it stepped over him, bent and then folded itself back down until it looked once again like nothing more than a pile of dark rock.

Eleanor's scream had turned into a furious howl, and she held Rachel's gun in two hands as she closed in on Noah. She began to fire, teeth bared and luminous blue eyes blazing.

Bullets smacked into his chest, and he opened his arms wide.

"Those who take, have everything taken."

She continued to fire until the gun clicked on an empty chamber. Noah lowered his brow, his lips moving. Matt heard the Chaldaic words again, tumbling over each other. They were ancient words, forceful and commanding, and spoken in their native form in the way they were meant to be.

Matt concentrated on understanding him; he was calling, no, *commanding*, but not Eleanor, he was calling to something else. He now repeated one line over and over: *back to the water*.

Eleanor's beautiful features were a mask of strain. Sweat broke out on her brow, glistening like tiny diamonds, and her body started to tremble. After another few seconds one of her legs began to move, then the other. She ground her teeth, looking like she was trying to stop them. Eventually she began to turn and walk robotically toward the glowing pool.

Noah continued to chant in Chaldaic, his words deep and hypnotic: *back to the water, back to the water, back to the water*.

Eleanor came to the pool's edge and crushed her eyes shut. A small noise escaped from between her clamped teeth as she fought against her own body. It made no difference; she stepped in.

"*Those who take, have everything taken,*" Noah said softly. His face was furrowed by a look of deep sadness.

Matt stared, trying to make sense of what he was seeing. In the water now, Eleanor seemed to shrink. Her magnificent high cheekbones became softer, plumper, and her jawline receded. Her eyes seemed to grow bigger in a round face. Whereas seconds before she had been tall and long of limb, now she had shrunk in her clothing, smaller and smaller.

Eleanor began to cry, holding up her hands, wailing at each of the tiny fingers. She looked no more than eight years old, then six, then four, and on until she was nothing but a tiny bald baby, floating on the pile of clothing, and then that too disappeared.

Matt could imagine the magic of the first cell division of life working in reverse, until perhaps there was nothing but a glistening egg and a single sperm. And then even the clothing dissolved, as the water hissed and boiled around the small floating island for another moment.

Matt got slowly to his feet. He had to use a hand to hold his trousers up, as there was no meat on his bones anymore.

Noah continued to watch the pool as it settled back to blue crystal tranquility. "I have a story to tell you, Professor Matthew Kearns. And then I have a request." He went and dipped his hand in, cupping some of the liquid.

"This is so unreal." Matt went and crouched by Rachel, brushing dirt from her forehead. She moaned.

"You know it's real." Noah turned and crossed to Matt. "Here, drink."

Matt recoiled, but every fiber of his being knew he had to do it. He leaned forward, not able to control his own limbs, and his large head felt heavy on his thin neck. He sipped the water and almost immediately felt an explosion in his stomach that went to his chest and then head. Like magic his skin inflated, turning a healthy pink hue.

Matt sat back, blinking, feeling better than he had ever before in his life. He stared at the holy man.

"I'm sure I've seen you before."

"Perhaps." Noah lifted Greta's body and dragged it to the water, tossing it in. He did the same with Khaled and Joshua. The luminescent pool fizzed and bubbled around the corpses for a moment, before it cleared.

"What the *hell* is in there?" Matt felt his chest, fearing the worst. "It's in me too now, isn't it?"

"Not from hell, Matthew," Noah sighed, crossed to him and sat down on the ground.

Matt cradled Rachel who moaned again. A huge purple egg lumped her forehead. He lifted her head, but she still didn't open her eyes.

"She'll be fine," Noah said. He looked back to the pool, once again magnificently clear, luminescent blue and inviting.

"This is all that remains of my once mighty Ark. Its keel, its powerful beams, and all its saved creatures." He waved an arm around. "This is where we came." He looked up. "This is where we sought shelter after the great waters receded. The last of God's great flood, pooled in the base of the Ark."

"But there were others," Matt said. "The priest in Canada, Father Xavier, and all those other names that he went under – it was the same man wasn't it? *He* was here?"

"Yes, of course, and you're right, hundreds of names in hundreds of places before that. " He sighed again. "But as you suspected, all the same man." He looked up at Matt, his eyes sad. "And not *just* a priest, it was my second son, Japheth."

"Murdered," Matt said. "By Clarence van Helling."

Noah turned, looking a little bewildered. "I don't know why. I sent Clarence and one other, with a message for my son. Something went wrong."

"Very wrong. They cut his head off, destroyed everything." Matt said, and then paused. "One other?"

Noah nodded "George Bass, an explorer who went missing in 1803, and was brought to us here. I sent him to accompany Clarence." He nodded. "They took some of the water with them – enough to make it back across the water to Japheth, deliver the message, and then return."

"And instead, Clarence killed him and destroyed everything." Matt couldn't understand it, and clearly Noah didn't either.

Noah's mouth lifted in a crooked smile. "Japheth never wanted to stay here. Even as a boy he was strong headed and rebellious." He looked up. "And one who often walked among you, unnoticed."

Matt thought about the idea of these immortals walking among them; it unsettled him. "And on the mountain top in Turkey – another son, Shem?"

"Yes." Noah's eyes seemed to lose more light. "Shem. Not as strong as Japheth. After so long, he grew weary, and decided on the eternal sleep. I always hoped he would one day regain his spirit, but..." He looked at Matt. "All gone now – my sons, their wives, my descendents spread far and wide, and not knowing who they really are." He drew in a deep breath and exhaled slowly. "There is only my loving wife, Emzara, and me left of the riders in the Ark. I knew it would happen one day." A line appeared between his brows. "That is why I try and gather good and strong souls like you to help me."

"But who killed..." Matt studied the still youthful-looking face of a man supposed to be 4500 years old. "... Clarence, and the two families in Canada? And where is George Bass?"

Noah's eye's narrowed. "Mr Bass is missing. But he must return soon if the water stored in the church is destroyed. If not, he may be consumed."

Matt shuddered. Noah seemed to think for a moment or two. "Poor Clarence." He looked up. "But I thought it was the police who killed him. That is why your FBI became involved."

"No." Matt said. "The Borgia." Matt's eyes narrowed. "They do your bidding, don't they?"

Noah shook his head, frowning deeply. "The Borgia, the Bruttians, the Meshans, and many other groups that remain hidden. But they would never do this. Ever. And yes, they follow orders, mine, and once Shem's and Japheths, to keep us safe here."

"But they could do it, if you or someone ordered them to?" Matt's voice took on an edge. They're killers. They even attacked us at Prince Najif's compound."

Noah straightened. "If they were so ordered, but that order would never be given. In fact their age-old role was coming to an end and the reason I called Japheth back."

He clasped his large hands together. "Since we first found we had been given the gift of immortality, we decided to keep it secret. We had already seen such evil over the ages, and imagined a world where the likes of Caligula, Genghis Khan or Adolf Hitler lived for a thousand years. We knew there would be nothing left of the goodness of man."

"I don't think we're all bad." Matt leaned his forearms on his knees. "Conversely, imagine a world where people like Abraham Lincoln, Gandhi or Martin Luther King lived forever. I'm not necessarily a supporter of the concept of living forever, but think of the good that would come of that."

"Yes, this is what I came to believe as well." Noah reached out a hand and gripped Matt's shoulder. "I too think good would win out, and the others here finally agreed."

"What? You wanted everyone to be immortal?" Matt gaped.

"Yes, for as long as they wanted it." Noah said. "Like you said, think of the good things mankind could accomplish – short-term thinking would be eradicated, wars would be futile, good works would never have to end."

Matt frowned as his mind worked. "But if you lived forever, you would have seen everything, done everything; boredom would drive you insane."

Noah opened his arms wide. "Then you could visit the stars."

Matt shook his head. "Crime and punishment would be meaningless. If good works could live forever, then like you just suggested, so too could the wrong ones. It might create an everlasting hell on Earth."

Noah smiled. "The gift could be withheld from those that debase it. Or taken from them – remember, we are immortal, not invulnerable."

"I know." Matt pulled in a cheek. "But then who decides who is worthy, and who is not – you?"

"All I'm saying is we would still need laws, Matthew." Noah's smiled broadened. "Your wisdom is exactly how I imagined it." Noah gripped Matt's forearm and shook it. "This is exactly why I need you. I've been following you, looking over you for years. You know evil, Matthew. You have fought it before in many of its forms. You have courage, intelligence and honor. You have what we need, to show all of them what we can achieve."

"So you infected me to recruit me?" Matt lifted his hand to look at the fingers. He flexed them – the ones that were broken only hours before, now all strong. "In New York – I survived the bomb attack. I remember someone... *after*. Was it you?"

"It's why you survived the attack... *all* the attacks. I chose to have you saved. It's why you have been dreaming of this place, seeing what I see. The waters now connect you with here, and with me. It is a gift, Matthew."

"And if I don't keep drinking the water from the fountain, then the worms will consume me." Matt sat down, and held his head for a moment. "This is no gift; it's an addiction, *no*, a curse – an *immortality curse*. And now I'm doomed to remain here as well?"

"Would it be so bad?" Noah waved an arm out at the lush growth surrounding them. A colored bird alighted in the foliage of a tree, to cock its head and peer at them from one eye for a moment, before squawking its displeasure, and then flitting away.

"This is my home, my paradise, and my Garden of Eden. The world outside is tearing itself down and decaying from within. It needs to be steered in the right direction. You can help, or sit back and watch it destroy itself, and everything you love with it."

"I'd be trapped." Matt shook his head.

Noah sighed. "No you wouldn't; a small sip of the water will sustain you for weeks. Many have left here already. Some return, some do not; it's their choice. Think of it; a world without pain, disease, infirmity."

Matt nodded as he continued to examine his hand. Only moments ago it looked like parchment stretched over bone, now it was young again. Would that be so bad? He wondered.

"A world without pain, disease, infirmity or death, and even a restorer of vitality. I guess the knowledge you could gather would be immense." He looked up. "The old become new, the crippled could walk again."

Noah's smile faded a little. "It has its limits, Matthew. George Bass lost a hand in an accident aboard his ship before he drank from the pool. It never grew back."

"Oh well." Matt smiled sadly, but then his brow furrowed as he remembered something. His head snapped up. "*Lost a hand* – was it his left one?"

"Why, yes." Noah tilted his chin.

Matt's mind spun. "But, the body in the church; it was missing its left hand. Then it must have been George Bass."

"What?" Noah's eyes blazed. "That means..."

Matt was grabbed by the hair and dragged backwards.

"It means I'm still in time to stop you." The voice was deep and commanding.

Matt looked straight up into the darkest eyes he had ever seen – but eyes he recognised from the old photograph in the church at Fort Severn.

"Japheth." Matt gasped.

Matt's neck was laid bare, and a long blade appeared in the man's other hand. He faced Noah, who was now on his feet.

"So, my son, you came back after all." Noah started to walk slowly forward. "You followed him?"

"You left me no choice." Japheth responded.

Matt strained in a grip that was impossible to break. He looked up. "It was you all along; who tried to kill me with the grenade, and have been commanding the Borgia."

Japheth looked down. "And we would have succeeded until the Nephilim detected the life givers in your body." His jaws clenched momentarily. "You were the last piece he needed – the communicator who could talk to the world, in their own tongues. You were to be Noah's voice – his pawn."

Matt struggled, his eyes going from the blade back up to the dark eyed face. "You killed Clarence, the family, the child. *You're the murderer.*"

Japheth's eyes were rocks steady. "Unfortunate, but the secret must remain just that." His mouth was a thin line. "At all costs."

Japheth dragged Matt's head back again and he looked to Noah. "I warned you; this gift is too great to spray across the globe. They are not ready, and from what I have witnessed, they may never be ready."

"I think they are. And the world needs a miracle now more than ever." Noah edged closer. "I don't wish to fight with you, my son."

Japheth looked pained. "But you would give me no choice if you continue on this path. Death is renewal. I think even Shem knew that at the end. We cannot allow the human race to stagnate. Children are its legacy, not an enduring population of morally decaying immortals. *Like we are.*"

Noah now just watched the man, and Japheth pointed the blade at him.

"They would be like squabbling children, all wanting to be kings or gods. When you say a world without war, I think you would provoke a war that will end the world. They rush to build up their weapons of fire. It would be regrettable if they destroyed themselves, but it would be intolerable if they succeeded in also wiping out all life on Earth." Japheth bared his teeth. "It is all God's creation, and you would have a hand in ending it." He looked down for a moment, into Matt's eyes before looking back up, slowly. "You may provoke another flood."

Noah looked like he had been slapped, and his eyes widened. He seemed frozen for a few moments. "Every year more people believe in nothing." Noah seemed to sag. "Then perhaps the floods will truly be needed once again."

Off to the side, Rachel groaned and began to stir. Noah raised his eyes, now wet, and lifted a single hand. "I will hear you."

Japheth let Matt go. "This decision is too great to just be yours."

"Or yours." Noah said. "One of our greatest strengths and our greatest weaknesses is a free will." He turned from Japheth to Matt. "Then let Matthew make the decision."

"What?" Matt's brows shot up.

Japheth's eyes narrowed momentarily, but then relaxed. "Agreed."

Noah turned and smiled benignly. "Matthew, we can choose which path to take. I chose you to continue my work with me. But you don't have to choose to part of it."

"*Those who are chosen, must choose*," Matt said and scrabbled over to Rachel to lift and cradle her.

"Yes." Noah straightened. "What do you choose?"

Matt stared at the tall, bearded man. Matt liked the idea of never feeling the ravages of age, illness or injury. But it wouldn't really be him anymore. Where was the thrill of life if the element of danger was removed? It would be like playing a game of chance, where you always knew the outcome.

"I choose to leave."

"Good." Japheth said softly and only then seemed to relax.

Noah sighed and clasped large hands together. "I will be here in a year, in ten years, and in a hundred. You can choose to come back anytime."

"I won't be back," Matt said. "My life is out there."

"Today and tomorrow it might be. But maybe in a thousand tomorrows you may feel differently." The bearded man smiled. "The world is changing. I know you feel it too."

"So, I can leave? But how?" Matt asked.

"I can show you the way out." Noah got to his feet.

"But the worms; they'll consume me – you said so yourself." Matt rubbed both hands up through his hair, pushing it back off his face.

"That won't happen now," Noah said.

Before Matt could reply, Rachel stirred, and he reached down to brush dirty hair from her eyes. Matt looked up. "And she can come with me?"

"Of course."

Matt stared, trying to process all the information, and the warning. "You've been here so long; how come you don't succumb to the symbiotes?"

Noah looked briefly to the pool. "The symbiotes are as much a part of me, as I am of them. There is balance. They stay benign for a long time, but eventually, they need the water, they need to return home."

"You control them?" Matt asked. "I saw what you did to Eleanor."

Noah tilted his head as though listening. "I... *we...* understand each other. You can feel it now too."

"I'm sorry." Matt meant it. "But I don't want it. I choose to be me; normal again."

Noah placed a hand on Matt's shoulder. "If you change your mind."

"I won't," Matt said, trying to sound resolute, but he couldn't help feeling a tiny hint of regret.

Noah looked into his eyes, deeply, and Matt could swear the man was reading his mind. Perhaps he found a seed of doubt there, as the corners of his mouth lifted a fraction.

"As you wish."

Noah began to whisper and immediately Matt felt a wrenching of flesh from his toes to his scalp, and then his stomach exploded as a torrent of blue fluid burst forth from his lips. With only the glow of the sapphire pool it was hard to see, but he knew that the puddle at his feet wriggled with tiny life.

Matt wiped his mouth. He immediately felt tired, and sore all over. He looked up. "That's it?"

Noah just smiled. He reached out a hand and Matt gripped it in his own. He looked up at the fading sunlight beams making their way across the cavern.

"You must go now and make a start before the sun goes down." He continued to hold onto Matt's hand. "We'll meet again, Matthew Kearns. After all, life is long." He grinned. "For some of us, *very* long indeed."

"I don't know how you do it." Matt studied the man. "The ennui must be crushing."

"It is for some. They leave, and succumb, on purpose. History is littered with those who seem to have long life spans. But a life lived long, must be lived sparingly, and in the shadows. People fear what they don't understand. And people drive off, or even kill, what they fear."

"Both a gift and a curse," Matt said.

"Perhaps." Noah pointed to the end of the cavern. "There is a cave that will lead you out. A hidden stone door will pivot." He stood. "Don't worry, nothing will harm you."

"The Borgia might not let me." Matt turned to Japheth.

Japheth shook his head. "The Borgia will not trouble you, now."

"Or ever." Noah looked sternly at his son, until Japheth nodded again.

Rachel groaned, and Matt lifted her to her feet. She was still groggy.

Noah touched her forehead. "She won't remember a thing." He looked to Matt. "And you must never tell anyone of this place or of our meeting."

"I won't," Matt promised. "And I'm sorry, but I won't be coming back."

Noah just smiled.

*

Noah waited until they had left, before turning and nodding to each man and woman that appeared from the forest.

"He chose not to stay," a woman said.

Noah nodded. "A good man always refuses a gift... the first time. But he'll be back." He turned to Japheth. "I told you that there is honor among them."

"Perhaps." His dark eyes stared after Matt and Rachel. "When there are more like him than not, then I'll believe they're ready." His eyes shifted to Noah. "You told him he was purged. That's not possible; you made sure he'll return."

"It *is* possible." Noah's mouth curved into a smile. "Mostly."

Japheth shook his head. "We are no better than them." He half bowed, and then slipped away into the forest.

Noah then turned to the figures gliding from the lush green growth. "Our work is done for now." He looked along each of the faces. "It is time." The shining, smooth skin, the luminous eyes of youth and broad shoulders, now slumped in despair.

"Already?" one asked.

Noah nodded and each but one turned away, stepping into the forest, and vanishing.

The last woman smiled. "He'll return."

"But not yet, Emzara." Noah closed his eyes, and held out his hands flat. "And maybe not soon enough." The birds of the forest grew quiet, so did the hum of insects, and then even the slight breeze receded to nothing. From all around him, there came instead a hissing and popping like water drops in a hot frying pan. Then the tallest of the trees began to tremble.

As if the massive trees were being subjected to extreme heat, they began to melt. Around Noah the huge banyans, cedar and oak began to shrink and drop, then the ferns and bushes beneath them. The birds on the tree limbs simply melted like colored wax to puddle on the ground, and beside Noah, Emzara stared for a moment, her smile drooping to one of sorrow before she too dropped into a fizzing liquid, joining up with the masses of fluid that wriggled with life.

The vibrant colors faded to a milky soup that ran into the cracks and fissures in the rocks. Only Noah and the glowing pool remained. He was a solitary figure in a vast, dark and empty cavern.

Noah waded into the shimmering water and sunk down. The blue light immediately went out, and it too started to drain. For a few seconds there came the final pops and hisses of the receding biological material as it ran away, and then there was nothing but an enormous, silent space.

The Garden of Eden, and its fantastic Fountain of Youth, had hidden itself once again.

Chapter 22

One of their jeeps sat waiting for Matt and Rachel when they came out of the caves. Matt stood in the empty desert, scanning the horizon. It seemed devoid of life, like an alien planet with no animals, birds, bandits or even a breath of wind. Just silence.

Rachel sat quietly for most of the trip, a dazed expression on her face. A few miles back she had turned to him and touched his arm.

"What happened?" She rubbed the lump on her forehead and frowned. "I can't remember... *anything*."

He put his arm around her, and she slumped against him. "There was a cave-in. We survived, but unfortunately no one else did."

"Oh, god no." She looked up at him. "Did we find it, the wellspring?"

He looked out over the vast dry desert. "No, no, there was nothing to find; a dead end. It was all just a myth after all."

He reached across to stroke her forehead and she eased back in the seat and closed her eyes. "Time for us to go home."

END

Author's Notes

Many readers ask me about the background of my novels – is the science real or fiction? Where do I get the situations, equipment, characters or their expertise from, and just how much of any legend has a basis in fact? In the case of the Fountain of Youth, Noah's Ark and the man himself, much is from the Christian Bible and other holy books. To some, they are absolutes. To others, they are just hearsay, legend and allegorical tales.

But as for the Fountain of Youth and longevity, there are still searches going on in remote places today. Perhaps the real breakthroughs in our quest for longer lives or indeed immortality, will not come from some remote jungle, desert or icecap, but instead be made in a pristine laboratory, right around the corner from you any day now.

But before we look at some of my research, I'm including a new section called: "The Cutting Room Floor". These are some of the scenes that didn't make that cut – see what you think:

The Cutting Room Floor

Epilogue

6 months later – Huntington Ingalls Industries, Newport News, Virginia

The tall, bearded man sat in the wood-paneled office of HII, the largest ship-building company in the United States. His immaculate three-piece suit was perfectly tailored and expensive, and his shoes so polished they reflected the overhead lights as tiny halos in the toes.

He declined the offer of coffee, and instead sipped from a sterling silver flask he had with him. He smiled at the room full of beaming executives.

He capped the flask and slipped it into a breast pocket. "I need you to build me a ship – the biggest one you can."

He grinned at the hungry-looking executives. "And money is no object."

The Fountain of Youth

Man, like all creatures on Earth, is tethered to mortality. Having an "end" defines everything we do in life. But many of us would like more of the one thing we can't buy, steal, or bargain for – *life*.

Does something exist that can do it? Many in history have thought so. A mystical wellspring of vitality or Fountain of Youth has been a popular myth dating back thousands of years. In the 3rd century AD, Alexander the Great searched for a fountain of youth, supposedly crossing an otherworldly land covered in eternal night called The Land of Darkness to reach it. And another early formal written references to such a place comes from the 5th century BCE, when the Greek historian Herodotus spoke of a wellspring in the land of the Macrobians. This small and secret body of water gave the people virility, health and an exceptionally long life.

During the Crusades there were many expeditions to the Middle East during the 11th and 12th centuries. And even in Japan, hot springs that can boost strength and restore youth are said to still exist today.

Our quest for immortality has manifested itself in many ways over the millennia, with sacred charms, potions, and divine artifacts, such as the Philosopher's Stone, all said to grant immortality. Maybe in some remote place there is a hidden spring where bubbling forth is an elixir that can grant everlasting life to those who drink it, and the persistence of the myth has not yet dimmed.

That's why there will always be adventure seekers looking for the magical fountain of youth. And who knows, maybe some have already found it but won't tell – would you?

The Elixir of Youth

Is the Elixir of Youth already hiding within us? It is the Mount Everest of scientific and health research, discovering the keys that will help people live longer. Now, scientists may just be one step closer.

A Yale School of Medicine team has identified a hormone, FGF21, produced by the thymus gland that can extend a lifespan by up to 40 per cent. The hormone boosts the immune system and protects against the ravages of age.

When it is functioning normally, the thymus produces new T-cells for the immune system, but as we age, the gland loses the ability to manufacture the vital cells. This loss of T-cells in the body is one cause of increased risk of infections, cancers and cell destruction.

Researchers led by Vishwa Dixit, professor of comparative medicine and immunobiology at Yale, found that increasing the level of FGF21 in old mice protected the thymus from age-related degeneration and increased their system's ability to produce new T-cells.

This is one study on one hormone, and the team is confident it can lead to a future extension of life by up to 40 per cent. Other studies are ongoing. We await their findings with interest, aging eyes and hope.

The Garden of Eden

Whenever we think of the Garden of Eden we usually think of the images of a pair of alabaster-skinned youths, buck-naked save for a fig leaf or two for modesty. There's an apple involved and usually a leering reptile somewhere to complete the picture. This is the biblical "Garden of God", described most notably in the Book of Genesis, and also in the Book of Ezekiel.

However, there are numerous more references to "trees of the garden", "the place of trees", and simply "the garden", in Genesis 13, Ezekiel 31, the Book of Zechariah, and also the Book of Psalms. All are said to reference Eden. The word Eden itself is related to an ancient Aramaic root word meaning, "fruitful, and well-watered".

Another clue is that the ancient name for Africa was "*Akebu-Lan*" (mother of mankind) or "Garden of Eden". The Moors, Nubians, Numidians, Carthaginians, and Ethiopians used this name. The name is an ancient one, many thousands of years old, and would have referred to northern Africa when it was lush and green, rather than its current dry Sub-Saharan manifestation.

Lake Chad now and before

Lake Chad was there before the country – in fact Lake Chad actually gave its name to the country of Chad with the name being a local word meaning "large expanse of water".

Lake Chad today is a pale shadow of its former self, and is just the remnant of a former inland sea that archeo-geologists refer to as Paleolake Mega-Chad.

That part of Africa was much wetter than it is today due to climate cycles and the African rifts that created great watersheds or troughs. The lake was massive, and at its peak, sometime before 5000 BCE, Lake Mega-Chad was the largest of four Saharan paleolakes, and is estimated to have covered an area of nearly 400,000 square miles, larger than the Caspian Sea is today, and its depths reached down to 600 feet.

Sadly, today Lake Chad has a surface area of only 520 square miles, and average depth of just five feet, and a maximum depth anywhere of 30 feet. And for the most part, it is more marshland than lake.

Rock art from around Chad reflects the changing climate and environment. Much of the art there may date to up to 12000 years or more and depicts many animal species that either don't inhabit the area anymore, or are long extinct. Like much of the Sahara at that time, the area was lush and fertile and experienced an influx of wildlife and humans from the Middle East. But around 4000 years ago, dramatic climate shifts forced the inhabitants to leave their lands and move to the Nile Valley or other areas with more water.

The Peutinger Map

The Peutinger Map, or *Tabula Peutingeriana*, is one of the first and largest, fully illustrated roadmaps in existence. It shows the cursus publicus – the road network – of the Roman Empire.

At this point in time it is kept at the Austrian National Library in Vienna. The original map was prepared by Agrippa during the reign of the emperor Augustus (27 BCE–AD 14). The present map is a 13th-century copy, of a 4th or 5th century copy, and covers Europe (without Spain or the British Isles), North Africa, and parts of Asia as the Middle East, Persia and India.

The map was discovered by Conrad Celtes hidden in a library in Worms. The man was unable to publish his find before his death and bequeathed the map in 1508 to Konrad Peutinger, a German 15–16th-century antiquarian, after whom it is named. It was kept in the Peutinger family until 1714, when it was sold. It was next purchased by Prince Eugene of Savoy for 100 ducats, and upon his death in 1737, it was obtained for the Habsburg Imperial Court Library in Vienna, where it is today.

In 1911 a sheet was added to show the missing sections of England and Spain, and then finally in 2007 the map was placed on the UNESCO Memory of the World Register. In recognition of this unique event, it was displayed to the public for just a single day on 26 November 2007. Because of its rarity and fragile condition, it is now not on display, and is unlikely to ever be again.

Nephilim – the fallen angels

The Nephilim were said to be the offspring of angels and young human women before the Great Deluge (according to Genesis 6:4). The name, Nephilim, was also the name of the giants who inhabited the area at the time of the Israelite conquest of Canaan.

The word is a derivative of the Hebrew verbal root n-ph-l "fall", and the general consensus is that it refers to "fallen apostles", or angels that have fallen from "God's light" (his grace).

However, the majority of ancient biblical versions interpret the word to mean "giants". And more fearsomely, the Symmachus translates it to mean "the violent ones", or even as per Aquila's translation, to mean, "the violent ones who fall upon their enemies".

The Nephilim were said to be banished to the Earthly plane to serve God's will and be sentinels and servants, violently, if necessary. They would perform these tasks until the world ends, or until they managed to return to God's light through their good deeds and actions.

Noah

Was Noah real? Many believe so. He was said to have lived between approximately 2490–2415 BCE, when the Sahara experienced a wet period. This is the period of the Old Kingdoms, and a time when the land was split by vast waterways all feeding into a massive inland sea (Chad).

Research is blurred here, but one story refers to Noah as a descendant of the Proto-Saharan ruler named in Genesis 4 and 5, and not a humble or simple man. Instead he was a local ruler, and like most of the local rulers named in Genesis he controlled the major water systems of Lake Chad, the Nile, and the Tigris and Euphrates. The interconnected waterways were their roads, and Noah would have known them like the back of his hand. He would have also been very familiar with boats and likely had a fleet. In addition, proto-Saharan rulers such as Noah kept menageries with male and female specimen animals for breeding purposes.

Noah likely lived in the region of Bor-No (called the Land of Noah) near Lake Chad. This is the only place on Earth that claims to be Noah's homeland.

During Noah's time, the water systems of Lake Chad, the Benue Trough and the Nile were connected and Noah controlled the waterways of the Lake Chad Basin. If Noah did exist, he would have easily been able to construct an Ark, stock it with animals, and keep his family safe from any flood. If the Ark existed, then that's where its remains might just be.

Noah's Ark and the flood

Noah's Ark is the vessel from the Genesis flood (chapters 6–9) through which God saves Noah and his family, and also a portion of the world's animals. The Ark story is repeated in the Quran, and it is also similar to numerous other flood legends from a variety of cultures. The earliest known written flood myth is the Sumerian reference found in the Epic of Ziusudra.

Despite many expeditions, no scientific evidence of the Ark has been found. There are several reasons suggested for this, the most likely being that the Ark never existed. But given the time period (4500 years ago), then as the Ark was made of gopher wood (cedar) and mostly of reeds, there's little hope of finding remains after all this time.

But for dreamers like myself, I tend to think that people are looking in the wrong place. Noah's Ark more likely came to rest on Mount Meru in East Africa, 230 miles from Lake Chad. The old Arabic text of Genesis 8:4 identifies the resting place as "har-meni", which refers to the mountain of Meni or Menes, another name for Mount Meru.

The final resting place of Noah

There are many who claim to have the remains of Noah. Just a few are: the Imam Ali Mosque, Najaf, in Iraq; The Tomb of Noah, Jordan; The Karak Nuh, Lebanon; and also a vault in Cizre, Turkey.

But the one with the most support from scholars is in the southern part of Nakhchivan, Azerbaijan, where there is a mausoleum dated from the 8th century that is regarded as Noah's Mausoleum or the Tomb of the prophet Noah. In the middle of that sunken vault there is a stone column and , according to legend, relics of Noah are buried there beneath it.

Lightning Source UK Ltd.
Milton Keynes UK
UKHW040636041021
391643UK00001B/6